THE LAND OF FROST

THE STEEL CITADEL SERIES
BOOK ONE

WHITNEY WELSH GIBBS

HUMAN
AUTHORED™
AG THE Authors Guild
5400277

For everyone who has made it to death's doorstep just to find their own strength and power.

THOIRMÓR
OLEAÍNCUDD
ROMIODÓG
Bascogar
DÚN
MURCEAN SEA
THE BORDERLANDS
Golden
Wulver Pub
TONNFÓRSCA
GOLORGLEANN
Gairdin
GÁLAMÁISTIR
Bastan
TINEMALLACHT
IRANNDAIR
Thuaidh
Thiar
Thoir
Theas

TRIGGER WARNING

Abuse (off page), Attempted murder, Death, Drugs, Hallucinations, Infertility, Murder, Profanity, Sexually explicit scenes, Violence

PRONUNCIATION GUIDE

Bode Buell
Bow-dee Byoo-uhl

Dedra Blos
Dee-drah Bloss

Drustan Anwyl
Druh-stahn Ann-wil

Eoghan Kael
Oh-wen Kay-ehl

Finn Rhodes
F-in Row-dz

Gálgalesh Devenallt
Gahl-ga-lesh Dev-en-alt

King Cashel
King Cash-ehl

Kruz Lanzo
K-rooz Lahn-zo

Maeve Moran
Mayve More-ann

Nuri Darwish
Ner-ee Dar-wish

Peadair Okenshem
Pea-dar Oak-en-shem

Prince Cai
Prince K-eye

Rian Doherty
Ry-ann Doh-er-tee

River Hayes
Ri-vr Hay-z

Sir Oli Raven
Ser Ah-lee Ray-ven

Sonja
Sohn-ya

Tiernan Damaris
Tear-nan Duh-mare-is

Báscogar Prison
Boss-ko-gar Prison

Bastain
Bass-tain

Caisleán Rialú
Cash-lan Ria-loo

Fáintìrean
Fane-ter-ain

Gairdín
Gar-deen

Murcean Sea
Mer-sea-uhn Sea

For further pronunciations and world building, please see The Steel Citadel Series Glossary located on the final pages of this book.

Moran Family
Line of Succession

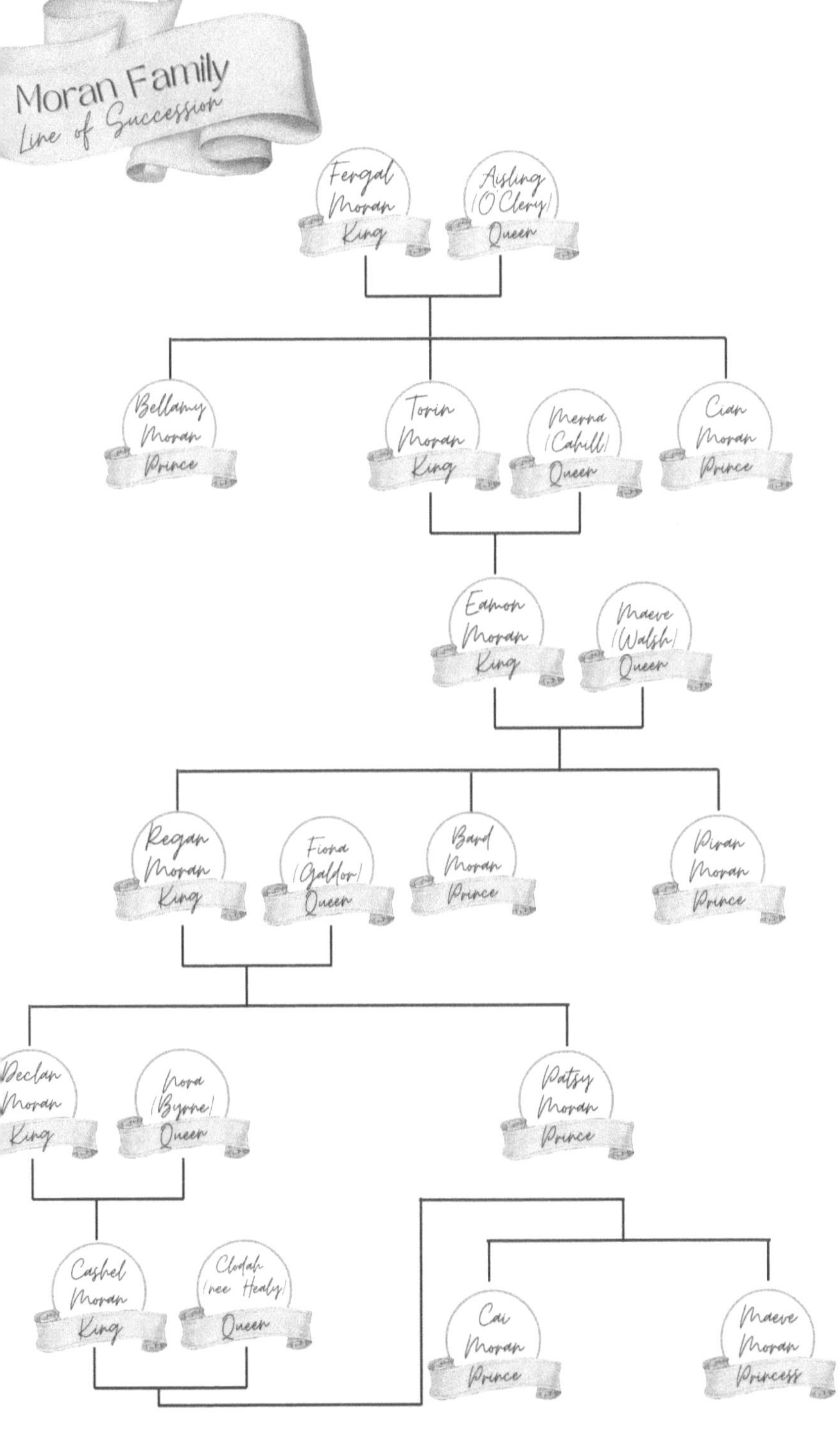

CHAPTER ONE

"Mmm," I moan in protest as I sense his fingers gently glide over my exposed shoulder. I sink deeper into my pillow, burying my face in the soft silk.

"Maeve." A comforting warmth accompanies his breath, and he delicately brushes my ear with his teeth while whispering my name. "Come now. We need to wake up."

"Five more minutes." I do not dare open my eyes as I feel a laugh shake his body. Pressing up against me, he envelops me with his large frame.

"Ah, but if I give you five more minutes, that five will turn into ten, and that ten will be twenty, and pretty soon, we will sleep the day away. I do not think our guests will forgive us for missing our own wedding."

The wedding. How could I forget the wedding? I have been counting down the days for the past six months. My eyes open lazily, and a smile curves the corners of my mouth. I roll over under the blankets to face him and wrap my arms around his neck.

I met Rian Doherty—the son of a wealthy merchant from the western sea territory of Tonnfórsca—on an unseasonably warm summer night five years ago when he arrived as an envoy with his father to meet with mine, King Cashel of Draíocoinnigh. I had been running in the gardens as the sun reached its lowest point in the sky during the White Night— the endless twilight of the summer months, when the sun only kisses the horizon, painting the sky blue and purple— chasing after will-o'-wisps with the cook's young daughter. He came bounding across the grass and frightened me as I took in the powerful physique of his arms and the scowl on his brutish yet handsome face. It was clear he was a sailor, with his salty blond hair and lean build, and I nearly hid behind a nearby tree as he cursed wildly in the forbidden language. When he turned and his eyes met mine, his expression immediately softened to something like remorse— perhaps fear. I watched his countenance curiously, and I realized he was only a young man, barely two or three years older than I—and I was just a girl of fifteen myself.

"I am sorry, Princess," was all he managed. He made to move toward the entrance of the castle, where he had exited just moments before.

"Will you teach me?" I said as I took a step closer, and his brow cocked up on the right side quizzically. "The forbidden language," I continued. "Teach me the forbidden language, and I will convince my father of anything yours asks in return."

And so it was. As months passed and seasons changed, he would return to Caisleán Rialú to meet with my father—and to find me in secret. Five years later, his father had received every trade route he asked for, and I had grown to love Rian Doherty, even enough to accept his marriage proposal.

"Fine, I will get up—but only because we can't keep the entire kingdom waiting for us."

His fingers run through my caramel-brown hair that falls to my waist; light dances through it as though illuminated by shooting stars. He smiles down at me and places his forehead against mine. "I get to call you mine in a few hours."

"I thought you did that last night," I whisper, and a smirk plays on his lips.

"Now, I get to tell the entire kingdom."

"Don't tell them about last night." I kiss his lips softly and then release him from my grip. I roll off the bed and leave him to lie under the soft, midnight blue blankets while I walk from the room.

———

"MAEVE, I NEED YOU TO HIDE!" Rian grabs me by the shoulders and shakes me hard, as if to snap me out of some sort of dream. The room is empty, but I can hear screaming from the halls just beyond the door, which Rian had pushed open when he ran through it just a moment before. There is a gash on his left cheek under his eye, a lump rising on his head near his hairline. He turns me around roughly and pushes me toward the monstrous fireplace at the far end of the room.

"Climb up into the smoke chamber and wait there until dark. Do not come out, no matter what you hear. Once the house is quiet, you run as fast as you can out of Caisleán Rialú, as far away from this city—hell, away from Draíocoinnigh completely—until you get to the border. It doesn't matter which. Watch for border guards. I'm not sure who we can trust, so don't tell them who you are. Just run and hide and don't look back. Do. You. Understand?"

I blink furiously as I try to make sense of his words. "Rian! What is hap–?"

"Maeve, we don't have time for this!" He cuts me off sharply and pushes me further into the cold firebox. "Climb! Stay hidden and *run*! I love you... I'm sorry."

He kisses me so hard, my teeth ache from the pressure of his lips against mine, but it is over long before it is time. He lifts me into the chimney, and I grasp the brick covered in soot, trying to find some sort of hold or traction. I work my way up into the claustrophobic space, and my gold and blue wedding dress, made of heavy lace and far too many skirts, catches and tears as I climb. I pull it—and my waist-length hair—as close to my center as I can and wedge myself against the brick, my feet pressing into one corner and my back into another.

Rian acknowledges me with a nod and disappears from sight, the sound of his footsteps gradually fading as he exits the room.

"There's the Loverboy," a raspy voice I do not recognize sounds from the hall. "Grab him too."

The sound of leather soles sliding across the floor reach my ears, and a scuffle ensues as Rian's voice grows louder in protest. I hear the faint sound of fists against flesh and bone, a muffled response following as Rian grunts in pain. I make to move but remember his words of warning; instead, I drag myself further up into the chimney. They are hurting *my* Rian, and there is nothing I can do. I cover my mouth and begin to sob silently in the darkness as the sounds of the strangers pummeling my beloved echo through the halls.

"Take him to the others while I check the room," a voice calls, and two pairs of heavy footsteps drag Rian off down the hall. The door creaks, slowly opening for the stranger, and I count his strides as he enters. "Hmm," he steps forward as he speaks, "I wonder where his bride might…be."

The room goes so painfully silent, I can perceive my heartbeat reverberating softly off the smoke shelf. I pull my eyes shut and begin to pray to the gods—any of them who will listen—to save me. I hear nothing in response; not that I had expected anything. The gods care little for the people of this world. Slow, heavy footsteps shake the ground near the hearth. Another and another. I look down at the floor.

Shit. The skirts of my dress have slipped from my lap and dangle down below me. I begin to pull them frantically back up and out of view, but a hand dives into the fireplace and catches them firmly in a set of grotesquely large fingers…and pulls.

"Hello, beautiful," says the stranger with dirt-caked skin, a scarred face staring menacingly down at me as I hit the tile floor. "We've been looking for you."

He grabs me, covering my face with a fabric bag before he flings me over his shoulder. I throw out my hands to fight, but it's no use. He has me by at least a hundred pounds; there is no way I'm going to free myself from his grip. The smell of body odor and urine emanate from him, and bile rises in my throat as the stench fills my nostrils. I cry out, beating my fists against the man's back, but he is undeterred as he makes his way through the halls of the castle. Completely blinded by the canvas sack tightly fastened over my head, I attempt to count his steps, but he moves unpredictably, alternating between left and right and left once more, seemingly aiming to disorient me. *I'm getting kidnapped on my wedding day.* The thought makes my heart pound heavily, and my breathing quickens to heaves. I hear the creaking of another door, and my captor takes two steps into a room. He bangs my body against the door frame as he enters, and I groan as my skull knocks against the hard ornamental door casing.

"Found the last one," the man says to someone in the room.

"Are you sure it's her?" another voice says. "No one outside the castle has seen her, other than the lover and his father."

"She's wearing a wedding dress!" The first man sounds exasperated. He fists the ends of my hair and yanks it. "And her hair is shining like glitter bugs. Is that enough proof for you?"

There is silence for a moment, and then the second voice speaks, "Take her out with the others."

The others? That means Rian wasn't the only person captured. This is not a bid for a ransom from the king. No, this is worse—so much worse. We're on the move again, but this time, it is only for a moment. Without warning, my captor stumbles stupidly through another doorway, and the unmistakable chill of outside and the light of the afternoon sun through the sack overwhelm me. The sound of my captor's footsteps change, turning hollow, as though he has gone from walking on stone flooring to wooden planks of some kind. A platform, perhaps. He drops me hard against something, grabbing my hands before I can react and securing them behind me with metal cuffs to a wooden pole.

He walks away, and I listen hard, hearing a low murmur in the distance. I try to count the voices, but I give up in defeat when there are too many of them to count. Their excitement suggests a crowd of some sort eagerly awaits whatever is about to happen. Beside me, I perceive the light stroke of fingers against my bound hands and someone slumping towards my shoulder on my right.

"Maeve?" Rian whispers to my left. My breath catches in my throat, and I try to pull my hands free to reach for him, but the cuffs refuse to budge. "Maeve, why are you here? I told you to hide and then run!"

"I did hide!" I hiss back. "This damn dress is too long." He swears under his breath. "Tell me what's going on!"

"There was some sort of coup against your father. This group of men burst in from the city, took out every guard as if they knew where they were stationed, and then rounded us all up, bringing us here. That's Faebond around your wrists, by the way." He taps at the cuffs.

"Faebond?! So we cannot wield?" I feel the undeniable sting of pain as the cuffs dig into my skin. "Faebond is against the law unless they have been convicted of the four high crimes."

"I know. Look, Maeve, I'm so sorry. I tried to..." He pauses, and I can hear him swallow dryly. "But they found you..." I feel Rian's head coming to rest against my shoulder.

"Don't apologize. Ri, I–" I hesitate for a moment, knowing this will be our last goodbye. "Thank you for everything. I love you."

Rian begins to speak, but as he does, the crowd roars and hollow footsteps thud against the wooden dais beneath us. I feel boots kick my knees as someone presses up against my sides, reaching toward the pole. I yank at my restraints so hard, it feels as though my thumbs might dislocate. The captors do not move to release my bonds, but I recognize the dragging of bodies and the screams of my brother, father, and mother rising up to meet the deafening roar of the crowd. I lean to my left, and Rian is gone. To my right, I find just empty space. I am helpless, alone and blindfolded.

"Citizens of Draíocoinnigh," a booming male voice shouts to the crowd, "I give you your king, your queen, and their heir." The crowd responds with hisses and shrieks. "You have traveled from every corner of this kingdom to meet your ruler, and in a moment, you shall get your chance to show him exactly what you think of him and his reign, what we have been crying out for for years. His blood for his people. Today, we will take what we deserve!"

A struggle breaks out on the platform, and my mother's cries echo through the air as the crowd howls in delight. The low grunts of my brother tell me he is trying to fight off his captors. He would never go down without a fight—for honor, if for nothing else. Then, an abrupt silence steals the air from the space. They've bested him. Our captors, in their astuteness, foresaw his fight, besting him with the aid of the Faebond. The anticipation builds, delighted and sickening as a knife being pulled from a leather sheath sounds.

"For Draío! For Liberty! Iy Donn, d'anam!"

For Donn, your soul. The forbidden language. I fight with all I have. It is utterly useless against the Faebond, but I have to try. This is my only chance—*their* only chance. I need to get to them, I need to do...something! My feet slip against the wood, finding no purchase, only able to lift myself an inch or two above the planks for just a moment before my feet slide out from beneath me. Then, the unmistakable wet slice of blade to skin drains all the color from my face. Once...twice... My ears ring loudly, my stomach souring as I pull once more against the Faebond and sob into the cloth covering my face.

"You want them? Take them!"

Amusement laces the man's words, and something like a stampede overtakes the platform. Fabric tears, and the sound of punching and kicking, pulling and slicing, saps the last of my strength, and I fall back into the tethering pole as warm, sticky liquid flows slowly to my knees and puddles before me, drenching my skirts and skin.

I have no concept of time as the bedlam draws on. Has it been ten minutes? Twenty? An hour? I can't be sure. All I know is, my family fell silent much too long ago, and soon, I would too. Movement begins to slow, and the crowd calms from a booming cry to a dull chatter. The voice of the obvious leader cries out again.

"Now, for the girl!"

Immediately, large hands find my flesh, unlocking my binds and pulling me to my feet. I kick and shake, hoping against hope to break free, but the hands remain firm and walk me forward with ease, as if I am only a minor inconvenience. When we stop, the man pulls the cloth sack from over my head, and I am nearly blinded by the sun, which still sits high in the summer sky. I squint and stare out as the crowd rises in chants and cheers once more. Hundreds of people of every age—male and female—stand on the front lawn of Caisleán Rialú, their faces twisted in anger and hunger for more bloodshed. My hands tremble as I take in the crowd, and then I look down at my knees to find the entire front of my skirts dripping with the deep crimson of my father, mother, brother, and lover. Their bodies are nowhere to be seen—only red streaks of blood left behind from being dragged away by the crowd.

The man beside me, a general from my father's army, the king's crest of midnight blue and gold and five stars on his shoulder, looks down at me and smirks before he speaks again.

"Ladies and gentlemen, behold: your princess!" Boos erupt around us. "Are you not pleased to lay eyes on her? She has remained locked away inside this castle for twenty years, and only those *worthy*—and the help—could glimpse her *beautiful* face." He turns toward me and runs a calloused thumb across my cheek. "Princess, is it true you are the only person in the kingdom to wield the healing magic? That this hair of yours holds the power to keep you from all harm?"

He surveys my bloodied wrists and releases the Faebond. My hands fall to my sides and, instantly, the wounds heal. "Interesting." He looks me over once and then raises his hand, smacking me hard across my cheek with enough force to throw my head to the side. "Not even a mark. Tell me, does it sting?"

He laughs, and the crowd mimics him with enthusiasm. They are enjoying this, savoring the humiliation of it all. "And what of this we have heard? King Cashel and the others finding healing in your blood? I'm told it only takes ingesting a tiny vial, and one is a picture of health. It's not surprising the king has never endured even a minor injury; rumor has it, your brother has enough of it on him to be unbeatable in every battle."

He leans in close and grabs my chin between his thumb and forefinger. I stare daggers back at him, my lips pressed firmly together, and deny him a response or a plea for mercy. "They have kept you like a cow to milk whenever they so desire. They squandered your power for their own means."

The crowd becomes restless, and chants of "kill her" ring off the stone walls. The man lifts his hand, and the crowd silences once again.

"But why should you be the only one of us with such a gift from the gods? You don't even deserve it. You deserve nothing, Princess." He reaches into his pocket and pulls forth a long razor blade extending past his fingertips. "A sacrifice, and then we shall see what *they*," he eyes the crowd, "will do with you."

He lifts the blade to my scalp and drags it across my skin with ease. My hair falls to the wooden boards at my feet in devastatingly long clumps. Over and over, he tugs at my flesh as my tresses fall, and I sense my magic slowly depart from me. My body grows weak with each pass of the blade, and I tremble as hot tears roll down my cheeks.

He ensures not a single strand remains upon my head, and once he finishes, he forcefully throws me to the ground.

"To you brave ones, a tribute! Take her and do with her as you see fit."

With no other comment, he turns and walks back into the castle as the crowds rush in on all sides. I try to pull myself to my feet to run, but there are hands all over me—dragging me, tearing at me, punching me. A fist collides with my jaw, another with my gut. Someone knocks the wind out of me, and as I buckle toward the wooden floor, another person takes the opportunity to grab my arm and yank me off the platform. I hit the ground with a hard thud, and the crowd begins to kick and stomp on me with all the malice they can muster. I lift my hands to cover my face, but someone kicks them away with such force, I cry out in pain. They repeatedly batter me with a relentless barrage of fury until every inch of me aches.

Just kill me, my mind begs. *Just let me die now so this will all end.*

I perceive the ground beneath me going damp, unable to discern if it's from the torrent of blood or tears escaping me, but I imagine it is both as my pain and fear meld together. Then, I see a boot being raised above me, and I watch the black sole hover above my face for a moment that feels like an eternity. This will be the last blow, the last moment of life stamped out much too quickly and with little to show for it. I stare up at it, and a part of me waits in anticipation for what's to come. Then, as though the terrible foot of the gods themselves, it barrels down into me, and the world disappears into darkness.

CHAPTER TWO

"I'm telling you, she's dead. We were too late," a female voice hisses into the darkness.

"She is still breathing. How can she be dead?" a man snaps back.

I think the woman might be right. I might be teetering between life and the house of Donn—the bringer of death. No part of me feels unbroken, and my eyes are puffy and tight, as if they might be partially swollen shut. The pain rushing through me as my awareness ignites past the haze of unconsciousness has me wanting to scream, but there is something in my mouth. There is fabric of some kind tied at the back where my neck meets the base of my skull.

"Whether she's breathing or not, she won't be for long. Look at her! I have never seen someone so shattered in my entire life!" I sense a breeze as a hand waves over me. It hovers but does not touch me. "You are supposed to be such a *great* alchemist, but what you have given her hasn't helped much, has it?"

"Dedra, it takes time! Could you please keep your voice down? If someone overheard you calling me that down here, we would both be in trouble!" The man's breath hits my face.

"Drug peddlers," the woman scoffs. I make an effort to move, and only my fingers wiggle weakly. I wince. The action is almost unbearable, and tears begin to stream from my eyes. "Hey! T, look at her hands! She's moving!" I detect shoes shuffling against stone and become aware of a presence as the woman crouches beside me. "Princess? Can you hear us?"

"Ugh," I groan against the gag in my mouth. Quick hands begin to loosen the tie, and in a moment, I'm free. My mouth feels like sandpaper, and my throat burns with thirst. "W-water?" I croak.

There is a frenzy beside me, and then the coolness of metal against my lips. I part them just enough to let the cold liquid roll into my mouth and down my throat. Gods, everything hurts. I remember the crowd striking my broken body with pummeling blows on the platform where they killed my father, mother, brother, and lover. I hesitate while I assess my ability to move my body. At best, I estimate I could be paralyzed; at worst, I might take my last breath in minutes. I drag my eyelids apart, and to my surprise, they give way; not entirely, but enough that the room begins to come into view.

Two familiar faces stare down at me in a blurry haze. The first is Dedra Blos, the royal seamstress apprentice, with a wiry frame, dark skin, and pale yellow hair reminiscent of the hay bales kept in the royal stables. She can't be more than nineteen, having only come to work in the castle atelier two summers ago. I had only seen her once from the hall as she delivered a dress to my mother last spring. The other is Tiernan Damaris, the potion alchemist for the royal army. He became the army's youngest head alchemist at twenty-two after graduating from the military academy in Gálamái-stir a few years earlier, thanks to my brother Cai's recommendation. His hair is a dark brown, and the bridge of his nose dons a pair of large, framed glasses. His post keeps him at the base in the Capital most of the time now.

The pair stare at me expectantly, as if I'm meant to do anything at all with the fragmented parts that make up my body.

"Where are we?" I ask as I take in the rounded ceiling high above.

"The tunnels under the city. It was as far as we got, given your state." A solemn expression settles upon Dedra's face as she speaks softly, reflecting the seriousness of the circumstances. "We were hoping for you to wake before we attempted to move you any further."

"How long have I been out?" A sharp pain pulses through my lip, and I use my tongue to investigate, finding a gash at the corner with a thin scab forming on top.

"Two days." Tiernan turns over his wrist to inspect his watch. "Nearly three, actually. I gave you what I could to help with your healing, hoping it would at least ease the strain on your body, but I'm not sure how much it will help. You aren't used to healing without the aid of your magic."

"I don't think I can move," I concede. I press my fingers into the stone floor and try to lift myself, causing such searing pain that I gasp and cry out. Tiernan shoves the gag back into my mouth to silence me, and I bite down as waves of fire rush through me.

"Don't. Your body has many fractured bones, including in your face and skull. *We* will move you, but I need to give you something for the pain first, and I didn't want to without your permission."

I let the pain subside enough that I can catch my breath and release my grip around the gag. Tiernan removes the cloth from between my lips.

"Why do you need my permission to take my pain away?"

"It's not exactly—" Tiernan begins, but Dedra cuts in.

"He wants to give you Ama." Dedra throws a nasty look at Tiernan.

My mouth falls open. "Ama? Possessing Ama means in fifty lashes to the back with the scourge. It's said to drive the user mad with hallucinations or, at worst, kill them instantly."

"It is also a powerful pain reliever, the only one that will help us move you to safety. We are all aware of the risks; that's why it is your choice." Tiernan raises his palms in submission.

I become aware of the space around us as I weigh his words against my better judgment. It should not even be a decision. Ama is dangerous and potentially lethal, even in the smallest doses. It is a poison more than a medicine, sold on the black market to addicts and criminals. Yet, the cold stone floor makes my back scream, and my limbs feel bent and crushed to where even the faint breeze passing through brings tears to my eyes. I'll never survive in this place. Even if my body can heal, I might beg for death before it gets far.

"How do you know it will help and not just kill me?" Dedra shakes her head in disbelief and rubs her forehead. Tiernan takes me in and then glances over his shoulder, as if to make sure no one is hiding somewhere in the dark beyond.

"It's my recipe." His voice is low and hurried. "And D, do not start on the 'drug peddler' rant! If not for my *peddling*, we could never buy out this tunnel for three whole days."

"This is the *princess* we are talking about, Tiernan!" Dedra shrieks.

"And her brother was my friend! If for one moment I believed there was anything else that could be done, do you think I would even suggest this?"

Each moment that passes, the pain grows more and more

fierce. My skin is boiling, as if everything inside me is working to mend me and overheating as a result. Sweat drips from my brow; it takes all my energy to inhale and exhale. I cannot stay here. Even if I die, I'll die trying to move from this cold, damp stone.

"Give me the Ama." My voice shakes as I speak. "It's the only way, and I trust you." I look Tiernan over. "I have to."

The faces of the other two blanch at my words, but Tiernan nods his head and begins to dig into his pockets. He pulls a vial about the length of my thumb fingernail out and shakes it, gazing at the contents. He pulls the stopper from the top of the vial and looks down at me.

"No matter how many times you beg me, I will only give this to you this once. Got it?" I nod my head almost imperceptibly, the movement sending knives into my spine. "Whatever you see or feel or hear, you need to pull yourself out again. When we get to where it's safe, I'll give you a tonic that will ease you into a rest to allow your body time to heal. Now, open your mouth."

I obey, and he pours. The foulest taste fills my mouth, and I retch as my body convulses. This was a mistake. The liquid slides down my esophagus and burns like fire doused in oil. I writhe as my insides feel like they are melting. Perhaps I would rather die than spend another second like this. The Ama swirls down into my stomach, pooling inside me, burning me from within. I hear myself scream, but I feel disconnected from the sound; disconnected from anything but the fire inside me...

And then, as quickly as it began, it's over. The fire subsides, and I feel every ache in my body being wiped away. It is an out-of-body experience like none other. I feel like I am floating weightlessly, and all around me is quiet and utterly still. I must be dead; it's the only explanation. I blink twice. The tunnel is still around me, but I feel as far away from it as I would laying in my bedroom back at the castle. Faintly, I can hear Dedra and Tiernan speaking to me, and I nod in agreement to whatever they are saying. Whatever they need, I could not care less. The room begins to shift as they hoist me into the air and set me upright before we start to move. Deeper into the tunnel we travel, following the labyrinth of passageways as the darkness overtakes us, and I am unbothered as I am swept away at their mercy.

"But what if they try to kill you?" My brother Cai stands beside us in his usual midnight blue dress uniform, a sword sheathed across his back and the gold cuffs used to harness his magic in battle secured around his wrists. His brown hair has sun-bleached highlights from the time he spent training in Tinemallacht, and his chocolate eyes glimmer with warmth. He casually pushes his hands into his pockets and easily keeps up with our pace.

"He's your friend. Will he kill me?" I ask teasingly and watch as Cai smirks.

"Probably not on purpose, but accidents happen."

"I'm already half dead anyway," I shrug. "I suppose death might be a mercy." Cai looks down at his shoes but remains silent. "You look better than is to be expected."

"Of course I do. I have never looked bad a day in my life." There's that sense of humor I have always loved. "And what about you?" He points toward me, and I look down in surprise at the radiant gold dress that hugs my figure. It is the one I wore the night before my wedding to the dinner held in Rian's and my honor. I twist to the right and left, watching in delight as the skirt flares around my ankles. "It's not complete, though, is it?" Cai runs his fingers through my hair and lifts the crown of King Fergal, nearly three thousand diamonds and eighty sapphires glistening across the surface. He places it atop my head and looks me up and down. "More than a princess—a queen."

I balance it on my head—surprisingly light for its size—and glide across the floor. Two double doors are cracked open ahead, and light makes a triangular shape across the stone as it peeks through. If I can just make it to the next room, I can show the entire kingdom the beauty and brilliance I am. I try to bound forward, but I stumble, and the light fades as I tip sideways dangerously. I reach for the crown to hold it securely to my head.

"Stop moving!" Dedra's voice echoes angrily against the tunnel walls as she catches herself against the smooth black surface. "She needs to stop twisting!"

"It's the Ama. She doesn't know what she's doing." Tiernan points to a small hatch above us with his free hand and orders Dedra to it. "I'll raise her up to you. Be gentle; she can't afford another injury. Once you reach the top of the ladder, we should be around the bend from the house."

I close my eyes with a sigh and sink my weight into Tiernan's shoulder. He grunts beneath me and continues our ascent toward the street above. When I open them again, I look for Cai once more and spot him behind us, both feet settled onto the stone floor. He looks back at me with a warm smile on his face.

"A queen," he whispers again. Then, in a blink of an eye, his features change dramatically. His eyes turn black, his nose twisted and broken. Matted locks frame his face, and blood pours from a long slice in his neck, covering his shirt in red. "A queen of death."

My mother's screams fill my ears as an angry hoard rushes toward me from the darkness on all sides, catching me by my legs and ankles as they pull me back into the tunnel. I kick and howl as I try desperately to pull myself free, but their hands are as quick as lightning, crushing me under their weight.

"Damnit!" I hear Tiernan curse beside me. "Dedra, we need to get her inside now!"

Throwing all caution to the wind, Tiernan hoists me over his shoulder with a breathless apology and races up the ladder into the cool of the evening air. The street is deserted, and Dedra is already bolting around the far corner of the quiet alleyway. I can see the mob gaining on us, and I cry out in fright once again. Tiernan does not slow his pace, and he spins around the corner, nearly losing his footing as he barrels through an open door along the stone building front. He bounds into a small house toward the sitting room and throws me down onto the sofa. He tears another—much larger—vial from his pocket and yanks the stopper out with his teeth. His other hand is holding my arms down as my body convulses in uncontrollable tremors of terror. He forces the vial to my lips.

"Drink!" he orders as he pours, and this time, the liquid is like ice. I feel paralyzed instantly as my body becomes rigid and frozen. Tiernan takes a few deep breaths. "Sleep," he says, and the cries of the mob begin to cease. My breathing levels out, and the invisible binds that held me in place ease as I sink down into the pillows. I watch the figures of the mob fade away one-by-one as if they were mist, and Cai, with his gruesome face and bloodied neck, is the last to go. He fades away with one last whisper.

"A queen of death."

The room is still for the first time and lasts for only moments as my mind drifts away into a gray abyss.

———

I WAKE five days later in the small sitting room Tiernan carried me into on the night he moved me from the city tunnels. The swelling in my face has disappeared, and the bruises painting nearly every inch of my skin have faded to a sickly brown and green—a promising sign of healing. I can move my arms and legs now, albeit with pain, but the bones feel much more set than they had when I had woken in the tunnel days before. I take in the room, sunken down into the earth with tiny windows near the ceiling, looking over the cobbled stones of the outside pavement. My stomach growls angrily as the smell of stew reaches my nostrils.

Dedra comes into view around the wall separating the sitting room from the kitchen.

"You're awake," she sighs, and her shoulders sag in relief. "Are you starving?"

I nod, and she smiles before disappearing again. I rub my eyes and examine myself from fingers to toes. There are splints and bandages everywhere. I notice cloth slings support both of my arms against my chest while a sticky substance wraps around my legs, bracing them. I have never experienced being bandaged before, and now I might have more bandages than anyone in all of Draío. I look positively mummified; and worst of all, I feel weak. My eyelids are heavy, and I wonder if I close my eyes to blink, I might drift off before they open again.

Dedra enters the room with a tray in her hands. She sets it down on the table in front of me and then moves to prop me up on a large pillow so she can begin to feed me. She lifts a bowl from the tray, and I try to grip the spoon, but she pulls the bowl away from my reach.

"Allow me, Princess."

I oblige, too hungry to protest. She fills the spoon and holds it out to meet my lips. I take it in eagerly, and my eyes roll back into my head in ecstasy as warmth passes over my tongue. I swallow without taking the time to chew and open my mouth for more. Dedra takes her time filling the spoon again, causing me to groan impatiently.

"You need to slow down, or you'll be sick. When you finish eating, I want you to sleep again. You need all the rest you can get." Dedra runs the bottom of the spoon across the side of the bowl before offering me more.

"You've cleaned me up," I say between mouthfuls, and she nods. "Thank you." I inhale the next bite, and she eyes me reproachfully as she dips the spoon back into the bowl. "Where is Tiernan? Is this his house or yours?"

"Mine. Well, it was where I grew up, at least. I've lived in the atelier for the past two years." She examines my expression. "Don't worry, no one else is here. Tiernan will be back after his run tonight, and he will give you whatever you need."

"I'm fine," I say, though I'm not sure she believes me. "I'd just like some rest and maybe a proper bath."

"When Tiernan arrives," she says simply and then nothing else, ending all conversation. She finishes feeding me and then wipes my face before fluffing my pillows and instructing me to sleep. I oblige—less because I care what she thinks I should do and more because my eyes threaten to pull me under at any moment.

When I wake again, Tiernan is sitting beside me in a faded purple armchair. There are deep bags under his eyes, darkened from a lack of sleep, his hair unkempt as his slim figure slouches in the chair with fatigue. He turns to look at me as I adjust myself on the sofa. He smiles weakly at me, rubs his face with his hand, and straightens in his seat.

"Princess." He dips his head respectfully.

"No need for that." I try to sit up, and he rushes over to help me. "Just call me Maeve. What time is it?"

He glances at the worn timepiece on his wrist—it is gold and must have been expensive once, but now, it is battered with age. "Just after one in the morning." The faint glow of the White Night pours through the small windows. "How are you feeling?" he asks as he examines my injuries one by one.

"Like I was half-dead, which I imagine I was—so, to be expected."

"Lift your left arm for me and wiggle your fingers," he directs me softly as he releases my arms from the cloth slings. I do as I'm told, and he nods in approval. "Now the right, please." We work through the motions with each of my appendages, and he bends my legs at my knees a few times, noting my range of motion. "You seem to be healing, which is a good sign."

"I didn't know you were a healer as well." I raise an eyebrow.

"I'm not." He smiles, and I can't help but smile back. "I just do what I can. Can you stand?"

"I haven't tried yet." I look at him nervously, and he nods. He takes my left hand in his right and places his left on my waist gingerly. With a soft tug, he coaxes me to stand with him, and my knees shake beneath me before settling. He looks me up and down once.

"We will keep the Iaslium Gum on for a few more days, and then I think you will be healed enough to walk without it. You had the most damage to your legs and face, but every-thing seems to be coming back together nicely." His hand holds me steady. "I'm not a healer, but alchemy works in tandem with healing. I just wasn't sure anything would work now that your hair is…" He stops as I pull back in surprise. "I'm sorry, I thought you had seen."

"Seen what?" I lift my free hand toward my scalp, but his hand flies from my waist and catches mine. "Tiernan," I warn. "Take me to a mirror."

"Maybe in a few days—" he begins.

"Now."

He sighs in defeat and then adjusts himself so he can bear

my weight as we walk. I sling my arm over his shoulder, and he leads me through a cramped hallway to a small wooden door. He pushes it aside and waves his hand, causing a warm light to fill the washroom as he eases me over the threshold.

Hanging in front of us is a mirror, and I nearly stumble back as I take in the stranger standing where I should be. Sunken cheeks and bruising mark my face. My body is frail, and though once slender, I am now skeletal, as if my body had eaten itself to find the energy needed to heal and keep me alive. Every bit of beauty I once had is now but a shadow, though that is nothing compared to what awaits me as I bring my gaze to the top of my head.

Where my caramel locks had just days before cascaded down to my waist, now lays the barren, pale landscape of flesh. I take a step closer, and Tiernan follows. I lean into my reflection, my brows pulling close together. Peeking from the surface, almost imperceptibly, are red shoots of new hair the color of blood. I lift my hand once more, and this time, Tiernan does not try to intercept it. My fingers meet the prickling surface, like a thousand tiny needles against my skin. I pull my hand away quickly as tears fill my eyes.

"There's no magic left," I sigh, and my shoulders sag.

"We don't know if magic can return once severed, but give it time. It has been less than a fortnight. Perhaps the magic can heal like your body can." He eases his grip, and I place my hands on the cool surface of the sink. "I'll give you a moment," he says and exists the washroom, leaving me alone for the first time.

Rage fills me from my very core. I glower at my reflection and let a scream out into the face of the stranger who has stolen me away. The memory of the platform, the blood filling my skirts—now mercifully discarded and replaced by the loose linen of housemaids' garbs—race through my mind. The face of the general smiling in delight as he raises the blade to my scalp after dragging his dagger across my loved ones' flesh. The crowd's cheers as they try to rip me apart. My hands shake and my knuckles turn white as I claw at the stone basin to keep upright. My hair falling against the gore-stained wood. Rian's pleas for me to hide and find safety. My face turns red, and I swing my hand as hard as I can against the mirror, sending it crashing to the floor. Pain sears up my arm, and I let it rage as it finds its match with my fury.

Tiernan and Dedra throw open the washroom door and spring into the room. Dedra swears loudly as her eyes meet the sharp fragments of glass splayed across the ground. Tiernan picks me up softly, one arm against my back and the other behind my knees. I don't resist as he carries me from the room.

"I want them dead," I whisper. "I want them all dead."

His body is rigid against mine, but he does not hesitate or reprimand me.

"I know." He drops me to the sofa and settles me into the cushions. The back of his hand brushes gently across my forehead before he reaches into his pockets and takes out a cloth he dips into a bowl of cool water on the table. He wipes it against my skin, and the coolness of the cloth sends a shiver through me. He sighs and places it beside the bowl. "Survive this, and I'll tell you how."

CHAPTER THREE

Dearest Maeve,

We will be across the Murcean Sea to Trader's Bay by the time you read this. I have not slept since I last looked into your deep brown eyes and felt your feverish skin against me in the shadows of the night. I cannot stop thinking about you—the way you tasted on my lips, the way you moaned my name as we hid beneath the wisdom tree near the garden wall.

At our next meeting, I would like to teach you about how our Ancient Fathers used the forbidden language to breathe their magic into the Draio foundation stones at the heart of Caisleán Rialú. Perhaps you will one day breathe your own unique magic into one and heal the lands for an eternity.

Yours,
Ri

————

It has been seven weeks since the massacre, and my injuries have healed impressively, according to Tiernan—though I continue to feel weak and drained as my magic eludes me. I have not ventured from our small townhome refuge, and I wonder if Dedra will ever stop fussing over me long enough to let me see the sun again. The house feels cramped, and although I have graduated from the sofa to a shared room with D, I have found the days monotonous and oppressive. Tiernan is the only one of us who is allowed to leave—and even then, only by the veil of night, as there has been a bounty put on all the heads of royal staff and military personnel who did not report to their posts the morning after the coup. When he does go, he ventures out to trade for food and supplies, but most often, he spends his days creating potions and tonics in a small room at the end of the hall.

"Ouch!" I pull back my finger and place it in my mouth as a drop of blood beads up at the end. "D, I don't think sewing is for me."

Dedra's eyebrows pull together tightly as she examines my work. She takes the pale blue cloth from my hands and pulls the stitch I've been working on. A pair of scissors cuts away the thread, and she resets everything to the start again.

"You were worse in the kitchen," she says simply as she hands me the cloth once more. "Without any discernible magic, you are just going to have to learn a trade by hand. Once you have gotten this down, you can work with me as a seamstress wherever we feel is safe. I heard Oleaíncudd has no winter at all."

I crinkle my nose. "You want to leave Draíocoinnigh?"

"Don't you? You aren't exactly popular here presently. I don't foresee any time soon when you will be able to walk the streets freely to sell or trade." Dedra speaks as her own sewing works at a steady pace in front of her. She picks up a cup of tea from the table and lifts it to her lips.

"I'm not sure anyone will recognize me here regardless. I was not very well-known to begin with." I stick my finger again and swear under my breath. "Maybe we could try next week at the village market."

D's expression hardens, and she sets her cup down with a loud clatter against the wood. She crosses her arms against her chest, and her sewing stills.

"I have told you before, I think it is too dangerous. I think all of it is too dangerous. Tiernan's runs three times a week keep me awake with worry every time…and he isn't even my favorite of the two of you."

I slouch in my seat as I continue to struggle with my sewing. "Draío is my home. I do not want to run away."

She has no answer for me besides a shrug of her shoulders, so I change the subject. "You and T seem to be familiar with one another." She also seems to hate him most days, but the nights, when they giggle and whisper with one another in Tiernan's bedroom, have not gone unnoticed. "Did you know one another before…well, before you met me?"

Dedra's cheeks flush slightly, and she refuses to meet my gaze. "Last winter. There was a party at the base for the soldiers who had come back from the border, and a few of the Royal Staff decided they might like to meet the men stationed there."

"And you met Tiernan?" I watch a smile tug at her lips as she tries to keep an even expression.

"I met Tiernan. He was the only half interesting man in the room, and we stayed up all night talking about his work as an alchemist and mine as a seamstress..."

"And you *only* spoke all night? T is quite handsome. I cannot imagine me *only* speaking all night with someone like him."

"Do not be crude! It is unattractive in a lady!" She bats her hand at me, and I stick out my tongue in her direction. "We spoke and then we kissed. He was a gentleman, unlike so many of the others."

I can see on her face that there had been nights when men had not treated her as kindly as Tiernan had—nights when they did not want to say one word at all. She valued his attention just as I had so valued Rian's. He makes her happy despite how they fight, and I wonder to myself if I might ever smile and feel happy like that again.

"Do you love him?" It's a blunt question that earns me a reprimanding glare.

"Concentrate on your sewing," is her only reply.

We keep at our work in silence for the rest of the afternoon. Tiernan finally leaves his room to join us at dinnertime, his pack loaded with goods for his latest run. He sits at the head of the small table beside me and bends over his bowl of rice and fowl meat—a rare treat in our regular menu of leek soup and lentils—as his glasses fog with steam. He only wastes a moment to breathe in the aroma before he begins to shovel his meal into his mouth as if it might be his last. As Dedra's face pales at the sight of his pack, I wonder if it actually might be.

"Where are you headed tonight?" I ask as I push my food around with my fork.

"Borderlands," he says as he chews.

"Borderlands?!" D's eyes are wide. "That's at least a day on foot!"

"I would expect a day and a half. A cold front is moving into the upper region, so it will slow down travel."

"Why are you going to the Borderlands?" Dedra's knuckles clench tightly around the edge of the table as she speaks.

"There's a friendly company there that served under King Cashel. They are willing to pay double. It could be enough for the winter months if all goes well."

My gaze goes back and forth between D and Tiernan, the former looking as though she might be ill. I have never been outside of the capital city of Gairdín, but during my studies as a child, the Borderlands had fascinated me. They are a breakaway territory positioned in the center of the kingdom that does not recognize the king's authority—though they have always been friendly to King Cashel. Travelers often avoid the Borderlands, even though it is the most direct route between Golorgleann and Romiodóg, as it can be perilous.

"Can I come with you?" I ask against my better judgment, and both my companions look to me as though I have asked to slay a dragon with a spoon.

"You would like to come with me? To the Borderlands?" Tiernan studies me carefully. I nod my head slowly but do not speak up for fear of saying something childish and stupid. "It would not be a simple journey for you. You're still healing... Then again, it might do you some good—"

"The answer is no!" Dedra snaps, but Tiernan lifts his hand.

"She needs to get out sometime." He does not remove his gaze from me.

"You must be joking! There is no way she can go. Don't you remember who she *is*?"

"In one week, I am making a run to a village half the

distance away. Join me on that run, and if you can make it, I'll take you to the Borderlands the next time I go."

Dedra shouts at the both of us, but we ignore her as we make our pact for the next week. A smile tugs my lips into a wide grin for the first time since my assault and isolation. D stands from the table and picks up her plate before stomping into the kitchen furiously. Tiernan bats the air with his hand lazily and continues with his meal. My eyes fall to the pack at his feet, and I notice the buckles are bulging with his wares.

"What are you taking to the Borderlands? Ama?" I ask, and Tiernan lifts an eyebrow at me. He might smuggle Ama on the black market, but he is a respected potions alchemist for a reason, and his service to the Royal Military was not any sort of front. In battle, his talents are coveted as much as those of a skilled marksman, if not more. "Sorry," I mumble and adjust my line of sight to my plate. There has to be a good reason he is risking his life to go to the Borderlands, of all places. "Why do they need supplies in the Borderlands?"

"They *always* need supplies in the Borderlands. There are banshees and faeries and shadow lurkers to worry about on good days. On bad days, there are men looking to overtake the land they think is unclaimed."

"And they need *your* supplies for such things?" I reach to open his pack, and he grabs my wrist. I look into his eyes, but his expression gives nothing away, and he doesn't let me go.

"They would be lucky to have my supplies. But they are lethal, so I suggest you keep your hands to yourself." I pull my wrist back towards myself, but his fingers stay firm around it. He turns my arm over, and his eyes trace down to the bend in my elbow. "Cai told me your father's potion master would collect your blood twice a month and keep it in a vault in the castle. Barbaric, if you ask me. If magic does not manifest into a transferable source, it isn't meant for anyone else besides the wielder." His fingertips trace the blue of my veins running down my arms, and my breath catches in my throat. He looks up at me curiously.

"O-once a week," I breathe. "Once a week, Sir Oli Raven would fill his vials for the vault. He feared if the blood stayed separated from me for any longer, it might become toxic to anyone who tried to use it."

Tiernan's expression hardens, and he drops my hand with a softness that does not match his face. "Disgusting. I'm not sure how you survived as long as you did," he says. He finishes the last of his meal and picks up the bowl. He walks to the kitchen sink and cleans it, then returns to the table, where he picks up his pack and slings it over his shoulder. "I'll see you in three days," he says to me before he disappears out of the front door.

I stare at the wooden door for much too long, aching for fresh air, for anywhere but this crowded house in the middle of the city slums. What harm could it do? The townhouse is situated outside the city center, along the northern wall. There are very few shops on this side of town, and the streets are quiet when the sun sets in the evening. Besides, no one would know it was me if I kept to myself. But if I ask Dedra to walk with me, she'll refuse. She's terrified of the city now. I heard her telling Tiernan as much when they hid away together in his room after his last run. She can't know, not if I am ever going to get out of here.

I scan the room and find a pair of canvas flats Dedra had gifted me when I was finally able to walk again. A sand colored cloak hangs on a hook next to the door. I stand from the table and look down the hall. In her frustration, D has retired to our shared room and closed the door. I take a quiet step towards my shoes, as though my footsteps might alert Dedra of my plans. She might board the door shut just to keep me in. When there is no sound, I quickly make my way across the room and pull on the flats, then I race to the door and wrap the cloak around me, throwing the hood over my head. It's now or never; I do not have time to sit around and think about where I will go or what I will do. If I want to breathe again, I need to walk out that door before it's too late. I take one more glance over my shoulder, and then I drag the front door open and slip out into the night.

I have never walked the city of Gairdín, only once passing through in a carriage on the fifteenth anniversary of my father's coronation when I was five years old. My brother had been allowed to leave the castle and even Golorgleann to travel to other territories and to serve in the Draío military, and he often came home with stories of his adventures. I was captivated by the world outside the castle gates and once nearly climbed the garden wall during the annual Parade of Spirits, only to get stuck halfway over and tear my dress—much to my mother's dismay. Being on the cobbled streets of the city now makes my heart race with excitement.

Without care as to where I should go, I begin my walk through the streets at an unhurried pace. The end of the summer season is near, and the White Night has disappeared beneath the horizon. Still, the dim gleam of night provides enough radiance to illuminate my way. I take a left down a darkened alley and hear the chatter of families sitting down to dinner in rooms just beyond the street. I keep to the shadows to avoid being seen in the small windows that glow yellow in the darkness. I turn right aimlessly as the alley opens before me. The streets are deserted and eerie as I pass by closed clothiers and bakeries. I turn twice more—completely losing all sense of direction. I continue ahead without care, knowing the walls of the city will lead me back to Dedra eventually. I reach a dead-end street and decide to change course, back the way I came, and turn right again, winding my way back toward what I think is the center of town. As I do, I spot two men almost invisible in the darkness, leaning against a stone wall at the far end of the alley, and I stop in my tracks.

Guards. I've walked directly into the night patrol, who are looking for… Oh gods, I am in trouble. I take one step back silently and turn, hoping neither has spotted me. My shoes slide across the stone and make a repugnant, gravelly crunch. I freeze, and the men, who had been speaking quietly to themselves, fall silent.

"Well hello," says one man with a subtle accent I recognize from the desert region. He must be a soldier of some kind; men almost always enlist in Tinemallacht. I hear two sets of boots along the pavement, and I close my eyes tightly, praying for them to stop before they reach me. "What are you doing out after curfew?"

My hands begin to shake as the footsteps draw near. I shove them down into my pockets. "I-I wasn't aware of a curfew," I say quietly, and one of the men scoffs. They step in front of me, and I drop my gaze to the ground to hide my face.

"Weren't aware of the curfew? You're wearing city clothes, and everyone in the city was ordered to obey the curfew—even housemaids. Where were you headed?" The man reaches for my hood, but I take a step backwards out of his reach.

"I was just..." I had no idea where I was to begin with. "I was just..."

"Do you have a name?" the other asks, his voice rough and deep.

"I…umm…I…" They both take another step forward and catch the side of my cloak in their fists. They push the hood from my head and expose my now crimson hair close to my scalp.

"She doesn't even know her name," the first man laughs. "Well, I don't need to know anyway. I can see you're a pretty one. Maybe we can help you get to where you are going…for a fee, of course."

I try to pull away, but their grip is too firm. If I yell, I might cause a scene, and maybe someone will recognize me, and that could be worse. I stiffen as they both take a step closer, filling every bit of space between us. The first man lifts his hand and rubs the back of his fingers across my cheek as the other snickers beside him, amused as my heart beats thunderously inside my chest. *You are so stupid. They are going to kill you, and for what? A walk down a handful of filthy, narrow streets?*

"You wandered the wrong way again," a familiar voice snaps in the darkness, and I breathe a sigh of relief as Tiernan reaches between the men, pulling me to him. "It's left, left, right, *not* right, right, left." He turns to the men and nods to acknowledge their presence. "Slaves from Trader's Bay. Haven't been able to make curfew all week with her forgetting where she is every evening." He pushes me firmly behind him. "Thank you gentlemen." He reaches into his pocket and pulls out two gold coins stamped with the image of my father, the king, and places one in each of their hands. "For your troubles." He smiles, and the two men drop the gold into their pockets.

"Make sure she finds her way tomorrow. The price will be double if we see you out after curfew again."

Tiernan raises his hand in understanding before leading me away by the elbow in a hurried stride that almost has me running to keep up. My still-healing legs cry their disapproval at his pace. When we round the next corner, he stops and turns to face me, glaring furiously.

"What are you doing out of the house?!"

"How did you find me?" I ask him, wide-eyed.

"That's not important. What is important is why you

thought going out on your own was not the dumbest thing you could possibly do."

"I'm bored! I never get to leave. I never see anything besides that tiny place. I just...wanted to take a walk."

"Well, your *walk* just cost us a week's worth of food." My shoulders sag, and my eyes fill with tears. He exhales, and his expression softens back to his normal warmth. "Next time, just ask. We can figure out a way to get you outside safely. Now, come on. We have to get you back before the patrol finds us both again."

We make it back to the house without another run in with anyone at all. Tiernan walks me back through the town-house with his grip around my elbow to the shared bedroom, where Dedra lays in bed, a book in her hands. She sits up as we walk in and cocks her eyebrow in question.

"I thought you left on your run already. What's the matter? Why are you back so soon?"

"Change of plans." Tiernan's gaze remains on me as he speaks. "Maeve is going to come with me to the Borderlands. Help her change and fill her pack."

My jaw falls open in excitement. He's going to let me go with him! I am going to get to leave Gairdín! I rush toward the minuscule wardrobe across the room and pull out boots and snug black traveler's clothes that match Tiernan's. D leaps from the bed and stamps her foot on the floor in protest.

"This is insane! She has only walked properly for two weeks! How will she make it to the Borderlands and back?!"

"We will borrow a horse outside the city. I know someone who lives nearby who owes me at least one favor." Tiernan meets me at the wardrobe and hands me a thick traveler's cloak in deep green. I haul it into my arms eagerly. "Are you upset because she is going, or because we haven't asked you to join?" A smirk curves across his lips.

"Don't be ridiculous. The Borderlands are no place for me, and they are no place for Maeve either. You don't have my permission to take her with you, Tiernan."

I step between them and cross my arms against my chest. "The last time I checked, we didn't need your permission. Help me fill my pack."

D's face looks as though I have hit her with a hot iron. She steps back a pace, mouth agape, and I watch as her eyes begin to glisten with tears. She shakes away her hurt and grabs the bag from my hands before walking from the room. Silence falls, and Tiernan watches her leave. Then, he clears his throat and turns away as I begin to strip down to change. I discard my loose linens onto the bed furthest from the door and tug on the traveler's attire. Once I am clothed, I sit on the edge of the mattress to tie my boots. Tiernan dares to look over his shoulder at the sound of the creaking frame and then kneels before me to help with the laces.

"It'll be fine. She is just a bit cautious. I've been to the Borderlands plenty of times." He finishes securing my shoes with a double knot. "We will be back in two days on a horse, and you can get your *fresh air*." He winks as he stands, and I follow him up.

We exit the room and walk down the narrow hallway to meet Dedra by the front door. Wordlessly, she shoves the pack into my hands, now loaded with whatever food she could manage to find and canteens of water. Tiernan holds out a hand in offering, but she only looks at us both with betrayal written all over her face. She pushes past us as she heads back toward the bedroom without a word of goodbye, and we listen until we hear the door slam shut behind her. Tiernan sighs and then nudges me before pulling the front door open once again and leading the way into the night.

———

THERE IS a low fence and barren field of green, dimly illuminated in the evening glow that signifies the end of the summer's endless sunlight. Tiernan takes a step onto the wooden railing and throws his leg over the enclosure. He motions for me to follow, and I am silently thankful I had changed out of my loose pants that would have caught on the rough surface. We descend into the grassy pasture, and Tiernan leads the way toward a dark barn in the distance. The grass reaches to my thighs, and dew dampens my trousers as I tread deeper into the field. There is a house further beyond, rising like a black mass against the dim sky, its windows dark and quiet, the occupants clearly asleep.

When Tiernan reaches the barn, he raises his hands and mutters under his breath. I hear the faint sound of clicking, and the doors swing open of their own accord. He walks inside as though he is familiar with this place, and I hurry forward to keep up, not wanting to be caught breaking and entering like a common thief.

"Does someone you know live here?" I ask as he counts the stalls we pass. The barn smells of hay and horse manure.

"Yes," he replies in fierce concentration. "My brother."

"Your brother?" I repeat as though I am some ridiculous mocking bird. "I didn't know you had a brother..."

"You never asked." He stops in front of a stall and clicks his tongue several times. A gentle but massive beast of a horse with a grey and black speckled body and silver mane hangs its head from the stall, and Tiernan pats it on its nose. "He won't mind us taking her for a couple of days as long as we return her fed and watered." He unlatches the stall door and busies himself with saddling the horse. I lean against the stable wall and watch him work quietly, expertly. Tiernan secures and readies the horse for riding. Then, he holds out his hand to me and bows his head mockingly. "Princess?"

"Stop that." I bat his hand away and step forward. I've

never ridden a horse so big in all my life, only ponies through the castle grounds. I step up and place my boot in the stirrup, which sends a fierce pain like a bolt of lightning shooting through my tender leg, causing me to wince and pull back.

"Don't be ridiculous. Let me help you." Tiernan sighs and grabs me by my waist with surprising ease, hoisting me up onto the mount. He then situates himself behind me in the seat and takes the reins in his hands. "Hold on tightly, and let me know when you need a break from the saddle," he says, and we find our way back out of the barn and on our journey once again.

My chin hits my chest, and I am jolted awake for the tenth time. We have been riding for almost six hours, and the sun is rising upon the horizon, replacing the hazy bluish dawn with a pink and gold glimmer that paints the landscape. I stretch and yawn as my eyes adjust to the light—the country-side a brilliant green spotted with flowers of yellow, purple, and white. Though Gairdín is beautiful, with its botanical gardens and colorful shops, I've never seen something as stunning as the softly rolling hills around us. I take in a deep breath, and the smell of lavender and a freshly cut meadow overpowers my senses. I close my eyes, and a soft smile tugs at my lips.

"What's gotten into you?" Tiernan laughs, and I notice the ever-present weight of his arms at my sides as he grips the reigns lightly.

"Nothing, it's just… It's so beautiful out here." I notice a herd of sheep a few hundred yards away, and they bah to themselves, unworried by our presence.

"Please tell me you've at least seen Golorgleann before." I

shake my head, and he exhales. "When Cai told me you never left the Steel Citadel—that's what everyone outside Caisleán Rialú calls it—I didn't believe he was serious. How far did you go before now?"

"I only left the castle once, when I was five years old, for a tour of the city in a carriage."

"Once? Did that never bother you? I would have gone mad being locked up for years, especially if my brother was allowed to go as he pleased."

"Cai was the heir to the throne. He had reason to see the kingdom. I was never going to be the heir, so it didn't matter if I wanted to leave or not. Besides, I would have left with Rian after our marriage."

"Do you really think they would have let you leave, Maeve?"

I feel his eyes on me, and his pity soaks each of his words. It makes me feel ridiculous and stupid and *weak*. My stomach churns over itself, and I quickly change the subject.

"Why do you call it the Steel Citadel?" I ask, and Tiernan shifts in the saddle.

"Well, because that's what it is. Surely you know the stories." There is an uncomfortable silence, and then he continues. "What did they teach you in your gilded prison? Your great-great-great-grandfather, King Fergal, ordered the metal wielders to forge a steel cage top dipped in dragon's blood to protect it from fire to keep any threats to him and his title out. They say when the top was built, he became so worried about the rest that he issued an order for steel to reinforce the entire structure."

"That is ridiculous," I scoff and turn in my seat. The movement makes me wince, and Tiernan raises an eyebrow. I ignore him. "Any steel around the castle is *not* a cage. It is to honor the steel forgers in Romiodóg. I would know; it is *my* gilded *castle* after all."

"Would you? Have you really had a chance to see it?" The horse stops, and I notice we stopped by a crystal-blue stream. Tiernan dismounts and then helps me down as well. He grabs my pack from the saddle and begins to search through it, pulling out some bread and cheese. "Stretch your legs and eat something, but stay close. Once the horse is ready to continue, we will head out. I want to make this drop by nightfall."

He wanders off toward a lone tree nearby with his breakfast. I groan in annoyance and reach into the pack, pulling out an apple and taking a bite. My body aches from hours in the saddle, and my legs shake as I stand. *Still, it's better than walking for days*, I reason. *You were the one who wanted to come, after all.* I settle down into the grass a few yards downstream and lay on my back, looking up at the sky. It seems different here somehow. The blue is more vibrant than I had ever seen in the city, and the sunlight seems to be refracted as though through a prism, sending beams of color across the sky. Once, in a letter Cai wrote to me while he was stationed in Tinemallacht, he mentioned the sun appeared different everywhere he traveled. Warm in Golorgleann, dim in Gálamáistir, oppressive in Tinemallacht, and nearly imperceptible in Romiodóg. I always found it funny—perhaps just Cai's way with words—until now. I close my eyes as a welcome breeze kisses my skin, and I fall asleep.

———

SOONER THAN I HAD HOPED, I wake with Tiernan standing over me.

"Time to go," he says as he extends his hand to help me to my feet. "We will cross into the Borderlands in a few hours, and then we will head to the Golden Wulver Pub to make the drop. I can find you a place to rest nearby while I meet with my contacts if you want."

I stand and brush off my traveling cloak. "I want to go to the drop." I am not letting him leave me alone in the woods while he has all the fun. Tiernan studies me for a moment before he nods and leads me back to the horse.

"Well, we better prepare you now then," he says as he lifts me back up into the saddle.

CHAPTER FOUR

The Golden Wulver Pub smells of stale ale and sweat. The flicker of the candles is a low light across the shadowed figures of the patrons as I twist my hands in my lap anxiously. As Tiernan instructed, I have slid into a booth in the far corner of the room, my cloak hood pulled over my head. The room is busy with seedy exchanges of every sort, and I thank the gods my dark travel clothes and plain green cloak make me indistinguishable from the other patrons of the pub. Faeries and shadow lurkers sit amongst the hooded masses, and my skin crawls as I feel their eyes wander the room in search of their next meal. I speak to no one and keep my eyes firmly on Tiernan's back as he orders our drinks and dinner at the bar.

According to Tiernan, the drop was expected to be straightforward. His Borderlands contact—known as Nuri—will come to meet us in the pub and transfer gold to Tiernan discreetly before leaving with the pack of contraband we towed with us. We will stay just long enough to finish a meal and then slip out of the pub without so much as a 'hello' to any of the other customers. The final bit of the plan is the most important, as the pub is crawling with danger, and one wrong word or move might mean our lives. Drawing attention to ourselves could be the most dangerous thing we could do…for both our sakes.

Tiernan slips into the booth and pushes a plate of potatoes and roast and a large stein of ale toward me.

"Eat," he says quietly and takes a drink from his own glass as he scans the room. He has been here before, and though he seems at ease, there is a slight stiffness to his movements as he turns his wrist over to check his watch.

"What's the matter?" I whisper. He shushes me and takes another drink while pointing at my plate with his index finger.

The front door creaks loudly, and a large man with wavy, dark brown hair down to his shoulders and powerful arms enters the pub. His body fills the entire doorframe—not at all heavyset, but toned and trimmed for battle. He has a scruffy beard and mustache, and his brown cloak and shirt nearly match his warm copper skin. Tiernan catches his eye, and they exchange an almost imperceptible nod before the man makes his way toward us through the narrow aisles of the pub. When he reaches our table, he cocks his head curiously at me but slides into the booth without further hesitation to avoid onlookers. I tuck myself up against the wall to make room for his overwhelming frame.

"I thought you were coming alone." His voice is gruff and tense.

"She won't be any trouble," Tiernan assures. "How are things?"

The man sits back in the booth and places his hands on the table in front of him. "As to be expected. Not much we can do at the moment except mobilize and try to persuade anyone we can to join us. It's hard to rally anyone since he's gone, but we do what we can." Tiernan nods and takes another casual sip of ale. "We could really use your help here now, Damaris." Tiernan ignores the postulation, so Nuri continues. "We will need another run in the fall if you can make it this far north."

"I'll see what I can do."

Tiernan's expression promises nothing as the man slides a small leather pouch across the table. Tiernan curls his fingers around it casually without so much as lowering his gaze an inch and drops the pouch into his pocket.

"What's this one's story?" Nuri points his thumb toward me, and I drop my head to look at the table.

"For another time. Send a raven when you think it is safe, and I'll be back with more." Tiernan kicks the bag under the table to settle between Nuri's legs. Nuri reaches down and fists the strap as he slides from the booth.

"That good, eh?" Nuri eyes me and smirks. "See you in the fall." He rises and tips his head courteously my way. "Miss."

With no other word between us, Nuri turns and crosses the pub, exiting without any trouble from the others in the room. Tiernan lifts his fork and takes a bite of his meal, and I stare at him in silence. That was too easy. Why had Tiernan been so nervous about bringing me? I think the black market is silly, with men skulking around like boys, as if anyone cares what they do at all. Clearly, it isn't the risk everyone makes it out to be.

Long minutes go by as Tiernan fills his stomach, and I take a few weak sips from my ale. I watch as one or two lingering eyes slide over me, and I pull my hood further down my face. Tiernan finishes his dinner with a soft clatter of his fork.

"Are you ready?" he asks as he points to my half-eaten plate. I open my mouth to answer when a dark woman with blue-black hair and veins protruding across her arms and face stops at the edge of our table.

All the snarky responses I had lined up for Tiernan vanish as I register the shadow lurker standing in front of us. Her hands twitch at her sides, and her eyes shoot back and forth from me to Tiernan. She's starving, desperate for food she cannot find in this place. Blood of humans and beasts is the only thing she craves. I back up further against the far wall, and Tiernan lifts his eyes to meet the woman's gaze.

"Sonja." Tiernan's jaw works tightly. "Lovely to see you."

"I didn't know you were selling tonight."

"I'm not. I'm just having dinner with a friend."

"Nuri…" She's agitated as she speaks. "Be careful, T; he's not the soldier you fought with. He's gotten himself into a mess now that the Leader and his family are gone." She turns her eyes on me, and I watch out of the corner of my own as she scrutinizes me. "This one is interesting. She's not local, so you must have brought her with you…and she smells like…" Sonja sniffs the air, and Tiernan flinches.

"Careful now, Sonja."

"She smells like death," she says, and her eyes widen in surprise. "Death, but not her own. Not as the sick smell of death." She leans in over the wooden surface of the table and sniffs the air again between us. Her long fingers curl around the wood, and she smiles menacingly. "You bask in it."

My head snaps toward her, and something dangerous inside me boils up just below the surface. Tiernan reaches across the table at lightning speed and grabs my arm, holding me in place. I look down, and I see I am white knuckling my knife in my hand. It is raised high into the air, as if I might stab the shadow lurker with it. My mind is blank with rage. I turn my gaze to Tiernan and let the knife drop loudly onto my plate. Tiernan swears under his breath, and Sonja's jaw has fallen open as she stares at me in surprise and horror. Reaching into his pocket, Tiernan pulls out the smallest of vials to hand to Sonja.

"It was good seeing you," he says, not taking his hand from my arm. Sonja looks down at the vial and grins with delight—all fear disappearing from her face.

"Until next time, Tiernan."

She turns on her heels and bounds off through the room. Tiernan lets go of me, but his stare remains unblinking.

"It's time we go now. You've caused a scene," he says and ushers me from the booth.

He places his arm around my shoulder tightly and guides me across the crowded room toward the door. My breathing is heavy, and I feel the eyes of everyone in the pub follow us as we wind between the tables. We make it halfway before a tall man with dark skin and hair that flows like a silver waterfall to the middle of his back pushes a chair out in front of us, standing to block our way. A faerie. There is nothing more dangerous on the entire continent than a faerie— nothing that will kill you faster, and this one seems especially formidable. I divert my eyes to the floor immediately to obscure my face from view.

"You're leaving so soon, Tiernan." His familiarity surprises me, as does Tiernan's answering grip on my shoulder. I nearly cry out as his nails dig into my skin. "That's… unexpected. Rumor has it, you haven't been seen around the Borderlands since the Leader's death. I thought you never tired of trading here to this particular clientele."

"I've been a bit preoccupied." Tiernan's voice is like stone.

"Did you even shed a tear when he fell? You always played the role of the lapdog— no wonder they found a place for you in their ranks. You have never been good at caring for anyone but yourself."

"It has been years, Gálgalesh. How many times do I have to apol–?"

"Dílsgarwch wedi torri do glóiriant," the faerie spits, and his features pull into a taut glare. "Who have you brought with you to meet with the brute Nuri? Your whore…or one to sweeten the deal?" The faerie reaches toward me, and Tiernan and I step back in unison. "Interesting." A broad smile exposes his razor-sharp teeth. "Ah, Tiernan. She must be delicious if you are unwilling to share."

He bends down to meet my eyes and presses in on me underneath the hood of my cloak. His breath is hot against my face, and my stomach turns tensely as I stiffen. Faeries are known to play with their meals, and they particularly enjoy humans. He stops, his eyes falling upon my face in the darkness, and the amusement leaves his lips. He pulls away from me, his stance becoming suddenly rigid and fearful.

"Damaris…"

The faerie's voice is a deadly whisper as his eyes dart around the room. Everyone is watching; they haven't taken their eyes off us since I tried to attack the shadow lurker. He reaches out and grabs us both roughly by the collar, lifting us from our feet. Sweeping across the room in a blur of dark cloaks and shadowed figures, he hauls us to the door and kicks it open.

"Get the hell out of here with your strumpet!" he shouts and thrusts us out of the pub. I stumble, but Tiernan catches me by the elbow before I hit the dirt. "And before you think about setting foot back through that door…" The faerie looks back over his shoulder into the pub and then strides out to meet us, slamming the door behind him. There is not a moment to process or recover what has happened before he springs toward us once more like an animal on the hunt. He catches me by the neck of my cloak and lifts me once again into the air, dragging Tiernan with us as he rounds the corner of the pub into the darkness.

"You brought her here?!" His voice is a barely audible hiss. "Are you insane?! How is she even alive?!" He shakes me as he speaks, and my barely-healed bones feel like they might break.

Tiernan lifts his hands, palms up to the sky as he says, "I told you I've been preoccupied."

"This is not a preoccupation! This is *treason!* At least now it is. This is the Princess of Draíocoinnigh, and by all accounts, she should be *dead*! For all the world knows, she is, and you are parading her through the most dangerous pub on the continent as though she would not be torn apart and sold the second someone surmises her identity. Does she not know who she is? Does she not know what they've done?"

My blood boils again inside me, and rage creeps up my neck and reddens my face. I punch at his arm, and he releases me as he takes a step back in surprise, as though he had forgotten I was not just a rag doll he had picked up carelessly from the floor.

"Of course I know who I am. I know what they have done better than you ever will, and when everyone stops treating me like some sort of helpless fool, I am going to kill them for what they did to me!" My words come out like venom, and the faerie scoffs ridiculously at me. "What is your problem, faerie?!"

"Even if I believed for a moment someone as tiny and helpless as you could triumph over *anyone*, especially the ones who killed the Leader, how would you kill them? You have no training in battle, no strength. From the way I could scoop you up and throw you out of this pub, you have no sense or care when it comes to preserving your own life—just like your friend Damaris, who is a living, breathing farce of a man. They would finish you before you even made it through the gates. Again, I say, do you know who you are, Princess?"

"You're right," Tiernan says, and I groan in disbelief, but he looks at me with determination instead of ridicule.

"You're right, Gálgalesh. It was stupid to bring her here, and maybe she doesn't have any strength or training, but she will."

"Are you going to train her, oh great one?" The faerie laughs.

"No, of course not. I wouldn't know the first thing about killing another in cold blood." Tiernan looks downright devious, and the faerie looks amused as he cocks his head to one side. "You will."

"Excuse me?" I exclaim and push past the faerie's arm.

"Maeve, meet Gálgalesh, the Warden of Báscogar."

I freeze as my blood turns to ice in my veins. I feel the eyes of the faerie, Gálgalesh, against my back, and a shiver runs down my spine. Báscogar, the place of nightmares our mothers warn us about as children... I hear an incredulous laugh bark out behind me.

"Báscogar?" Tiernan's eyes meet mine as my words fall heavy in the surrounding air. "Báscogar is a prison for the worst criminals in the kingdom. You only get sent there if you commit one of the four high crimes: murder, treason, siphoning another's powers, or possession of Faebond. Becoming the Warden of Báscogar is only possible for those who are sent there for life."

Gálgalesh's long fingers fold around my chin and turn my head so he is looking into my eyes. His razor-sharp teeth are ominous triangles in his snarl of a smile.

"Being a faerie is the fifth high crime, Princess." I tug free of his grip, and the amused look of a predator playing with his prey dances across his face. "I can't train her. I would risk too much, and I don't think she has it in her. She's as power-less as a deer. It would have been a mercy for her to die that day; I'm not sure why you didn't let her. If anyone finds out who she is, she will wish she was dead. You are a fool, Tiernan, and she is a casualty to your foolishness."

"If you won't do it for me and you have no faith in her, do it for the Leader. He saved your family from certain death—perhaps it is time you returned the favor."

Swifter than my brain can process, Gálgalesh rounds on Tiernan, gripping him by the throat and pinning him against the stone of the pub. Tiernan does not struggle, but his breathing becomes constricted to a wheeze.

"Do not *ever* speak of that, feallwr." Gálgalesh's voice is a menacing growl, his teeth mere inches from Tiernan's throat. I grab at Gálgalesh's arm, but he pushes me away, and I fall into the dirt.

"So you will not then? Are you a coward or simply ungrateful?" Tiernan rasps in a barely audible voice, and Gálgalesh tightens his grip, snarling in his face. "Well?" Tiernan remains stoney and, after much too long, Gálgalesh sighs and releases Tiernan, who slumps toward the ground and draws in a rattling breath.

"We leave tomorrow at dawn." Gálgalesh turns toward me, and I retreat to the trees behind me. "Try not to die on the journey," he says, and then with one last, frightening smile, he leaves, disappearing back around the corner toward the pub door.

I rush toward Tiernan, who holds out a hand in front of him. He straightens and rubs the side and back of his neck with his hand.

"Why would he do that?" I sigh and examine Tiernan's features for any signs of injury, as he has done so often to me. "He called you feallwr. That means traitor, doesn't it? Back in the pub he said, 'allegiance broken for glory'. What-?" My words rush out of me like a fierce stream, but Tiernan cuts in.

"We all have something we are not proud of, Maeve. Mine is how many people I have hurt to get to where I am now. Gálgalesh has every right to be angry, but I suppose he isn't angry enough if he has agreed to take you with him." Tiernan smirks. They made an arrangement in my name, one I did not ask for. Like hell! There is no way I am going with that murderous faerie to a prison full of criminals! Even I am not that stupid.

"I can't go to Báscogar! He was right; they will kill me!"

"You have to go to Báscogar. I knew it the moment you proclaimed you would kill the bastards who took your family and your magic, and I knew it when I found you caught up by those patrol guards. You're dead if you don't, Maeve, but you stand a chance if you do."

"Is that why you brought me to the Borderlands? To pawn me off to a criminal's camp in Romiodóg?"

"I had a feeling Gálgalesh would be here on a supply run, but I was not sure he would agree to take you unless he saw you were truly alive." There is no apology in Tiernan's voice.

"What about Dedra? It would kill her if I don't come back."

"Dedra knew you would be going once you were healthy. She might have tried to stop it, but she isn't a fool. She knows you need training, and you would never get it in Gairdín. She will survive." I make to protest again, but Tiernan takes my hand in his and pats the backside gingerly. "If I thought there was any other option, I'd find it, Maeve. This is all you've got. I'm sorry." My shoulders sag, and I look down at my feet. He's right; I know he is. Still, it doesn't make it any better to know I am ultimately helpless no matter what happens. Tiernan releases my hand and wraps his arm around my waist. "Come on; we need to find somewhere to sleep tonight."

CHAPTER FIVE

The softness of warm skin against my fingertips jolts me awake, and I find myself pressed against Tiernan's chest in a small canvas tent. I scramble away from his sleeping body, and a small snore escapes him as he dreams. The tent is instantly frigid, and I quickly tuck in close to him again in desperate need of heat. His arms fold around me instinctively, and I press my hands against his chest to free myself. He stirs, and his eyes shoot open in surprise, widening as he registers our proximity. He releases me from his grip and clears his throat.

"Morning," he says, his voice deep with sleep. "Sorry… The tent was the best I could conjure."

I yawn and stretch my arms. Tiernan had used his magic to fashion a semi-comfortable pad to keep us off the ground, but it did little to help the ache in my still-healing bones. "You cried a little last night. Are you all right?" I look away from him. I'd been dreaming about Rian and my family all night and had woken more than a handful of times whenever the dream would begin to replay that horrible day, and their cries would fill the air. I am not all right. I am not sure I will ever be. Tiernan sits in the painstaking silence for a moment or two before continuing. "We better get going; it is almost dawn."

I sit up, and I feel Tiernan's presence next to me as he, too, rises. I look him over, his glasses discarded near where he had laid, atop his shirt and traveling cloak. My cloak is set aside in the opposite corner, but I had opted against trying to warm myself with just our shared body heat. He is surprisingly well-built for an alchemist, though unassumingly so. *D would kill you for staring.* I shake my head and look away. Tiernan reaches for his clothes and pulls his shirt over his head before placing his glasses on the bridge of his nose. I grab my boots from where I kicked them off as I entered the tent hours prior, but Tiernan moves to intercept them.

"Allow me," he says and fixes my right boot to my foot before he ties up the laces and works on the left.

"You're sending me off to Báscogar, and you won't even let me lace my boots," I protest.

"You are going to Báscogar so you can learn to avenge your family—one of which was my best friend," Tiernan speaks as he makes a loop in the lace. "The least I can do is lace your boots."

He finishes and taps the toe before he looks me up and down, examining me for any injuries or weaknesses. Then, he brushes his hand across the short red hair on my head and down my cheek. I grab his hand and grip his fingers tight.

"This is absurd. I'll die before the week is out," I complain, and he shakes his head. "Why did you save me, Tiernan, when you knew there was nothing for me?"

"I made a promise to protect your family—and that includes you. When the coup broke out, Dedra and I were going to flee with the other sympathizers in the Royal Court, but when we saw they had left you for dead, beaten and bloody and barely clinging to life, we just couldn't leave until we got you out. You were so close to death, we thought we might be too late, but you continued to fight, to breathe. So, no, you will *not* die before the week is out, Maeve. You're going to make it, and you're going to come back to Golorgleann and take the Steel Citadel and kill the men who failed to kill you."

I grip his hand tighter. The dark tent grows lighter by the minute as we sit in silence, taking in the weight of the task ahead. I know I cannot *not* do it, but I will be worse off if I never even try. For Tiernan and Dedra, I at least need to give them that. I release his hand and turn away, grabbing my cloak and pulling it around me. Tiernan moves to tie his own boots. When we are both ready to leave, we exit the tent, and Tiernan takes a moment to get rid of our camp, a few hushed murmurs under his breath. He picks up the pack Dedra had fixed me before we left and slings it over my shoulder.

"Take it with you. I can find food on the way for myself, but you might need it for the journey to Romiodóg." He takes his cloak and pulls it around me as well. "The territory is cursed with a near constant winter, and Báscogar sits high in the mountains. It'll be freezing before you reach the camp, but once you do, Gálgalesh will outfit you with warmer clothes to withstand the cold."

"What about you?" I ask as I stare up at him and realize he might be the first person to ever extend such kindness to me in the entirety of my life.

"I'll be fine. Dedra will love having a new cloak to make. Remember, Maeve, you will not die before you come back to us."

I nod, and we head out toward the Golden Wulver Pub to meet Gálgalesh, towing the borrowed mare behind us through the trees.

A fog hangs low around the forested landscape, a dim light coming from the pub windows. A covered wagon sits alone in front of the building, a black horse hitched to it. Tiernan and I approach quietly. The air is still, and the faint sound of rustling leaves comes from nearby. Tiernan grabs my arm, and we pause, listening and watching from a small thicket. Gálgalesh, the faerie, appears from somewhere near the back entrance of the pub with two others dressed in travelers' clothes that match the dirt of the forest floor. Shadow lurkers. Their skin pulls tightly against their bones, exposing their protruding veins, and their lips are bright red with blood, as though they have just eaten. They carry barrels of ale toward the wagon, and when they reach it, they load them up into the back. We watch as Gálgalesh pays the two men and speaks to them in low tones I cannot decipher.

"What do you know about shadow lurkers, Maeve?" Tiernan whispers.

"They are blood drinkers. They feast on the blood of humans and beasts—but they desire humans the most. They can drain an entire body before they are full, and they cannot stand the sunlight, so they prefer the Borderlands or Romiodóg."

"They *will* kill you if they get too near. If they have just eaten, you might be able to escape, but you can never let your guard down around them. Most of them, like Sonja, are addicted to Ama and are unstable at best. If you ever find yourself trapped, your best option is to cast a blinding spell, but be aware that it might only disable them temporarily, so don't hesitate to run. If any find out who you are, they might drain you just for the power they believe you still possess."

My hands become clammy, and I wipe them against my pants. We watch as the two shadow lurkers who had helped Gálgalesh fill his wagon disappear once again, leaving Gálgalesh alone in the clearing.

"Are you ready?" Tiernan mutters, and I nod. He places his arm around me and guides me toward the wagon.

"I thought you might have come to your senses and taken her back to the Capital…or maybe killed her swiftly and saved her from a slow, painful demise." Gálgalesh leans against the wagon with his arms crossed against his chest. "It is a pity you didn't just leave her. How am I going to persuade anyone to look beyond *his* face she carries? And that is only the first of our worries when we arrive. I need gold, Tiernan. It is a three-day trek back to the mountain, and if you would like her to eat, you will have to pay."

Tiernan reaches into his pocket and pulls out the leather pouch his Borderlands contact Nuri had exchanged for the pack full of smuggled goods last night. He tosses it to the faerie, who catches and then empties it into his hand to count its worth. The gold that would get Tiernan and Dedra by through the winter. I open my mouth to protest, but Tiernan lifts his hand to quiet me. After returning the gold to the pouch and pocketing it, Gálgalesh moves toward the front of the wagon where the horse is hitched.

"I don't have all day," he snaps.

Tiernan turns to me and pulls the two cloaks around me tightly. We walk toward the back of the wagon, and Tiernan grips my waist and hoists me into it. I can feel myself trembling, and my hands shake as I grab Tiernan's, desperately trying to hold him to me. If he slips away, I will be gone, and who knows if I will ever make it back? I taste the saltiness of tears against my lips, and—though my body is numb and almost not my own—the tears make me aware I am crying. Tiernan shushes me softly.

"You'll be okay, Maeve. Stay on your guard, listen to everything Gálgalesh teaches you, and come back to us. We won't leave Draío without you."

"Promise me," I demand. "Promise you won't leave without me." Tears stain my cheeks, and my breathing becomes ragged.

"I promise." Tiernan lets go of my hand and wipes my cheek. I hear horse reins snapping through the ghostly silence of the clearing, and the wagon lurches forward. I grab for Tiernan, but he lets go as we pull away from the pub. "You'll be okay, Maeve," he reassures as the dense fog quickly obscures him from view.

I sit back on my heels and sink into the side of the wagon. I let the tears flow freely and wrap the cloaks around my body like a cocoon.

"I don't want to hear you weeping the entire way, or I might just feed you to the wolves," Gálgalesh barks from somewhere up front as he leads the horses away and then falls silent.

I settle into a seat and pull my knees to my chest, bringing my chin to settle upon them. What have I done? If I would have just stayed put, I would not be here right now, and perhaps Tiernan and Dedra wouldn't be on the verge of starvation, all their gold in the hands of a faerie. Now that I am here, I am not sure what I'll do, but I've promised my friend I won't die, so I have to stay alive somehow—even if we both know that is a near impossible task.

———

IT TAKES us a whole day to reach the border into Romiodóg, and another to reach the base of the mountain, where Báscogar sits at the summit. Gálgalesh and I had little conversation over the first two day, save for when he instructed me to exit the wagon to eat or when he would depart at night to stay in the warmth of pub lodging while I was left to sleep on the wooden floor of the cart with our supplies. The Borderlands are a dangerous place, filled with every sort of horror imaginable. During the day, we pass by more than one lost and hungry traveler. To stop would be to risk our own lives, as the intoxicating fumes of the bornus trees and ever present veil of fog threatens to throw us down the wrong path. At night, the sounds of nocturnal predators echo through the silent wood. I do not sleep more than an hour before we reach the base of the mountain.

"Move up front," Gálgalesh demands from somewhere ahead. "The climb is steep, and it would be disappointing to have to clean you up off the wagon floor after a barrel of mead has crushed you."

I make my way up and take a seat beside him on the uncomfortable wood. Snow is falling around us, and the sky is only a slightly lighter gray than night, though it is already mid-morning. The further we move into the northern territories, the more the sun disappears, taking us from the endless twilight of the southern summers to the eternal nights of the cursed northern lands. I shiver and tuck myself into my traveling clothes, but at the same time, I reach a hand out of its warm shelter and catch a snowflake in my palm. I examine it until it melts against my skin and then catch another.

"You act like you have never seen snow before." Gálgalesh sneers and crinkles his nose at me in annoyance as we begin our climb along the rocky terrain.

"It doesn't snow in Gairdín," I concede, and Gálgalesh gives me a sideways look. I ignore him and take in the surrounding landscape. The trees stand barren, and sharp stones cover the ground, appearing capable of easily cutting through flesh. The mountain has one narrow road up or down it, just wide enough for only one set of wagon wheels to traverse. There is no guard at the bottom of the road, but based on what I learned in my childhood lessons, there is an enchantment at the top that prevents the inmates of Báscogar from escaping. If they want to try, they will have to make it down the unforgiving cliffs that surround the prison.

If anyone ever does, they have earned their freedom and can go about the world as they please. "What did you do to earn a life sentence in the prison?"

Gálgalesh looks straight ahead as he guides our mare along. "It's more of a camp." He pulls on the reins to slow us around a sharp curve.

"Fine. But what did you do to earn a life sentence at the *camp*?"

"I've told you already. Being a faerie is enough to be sent to Báscogar for two lifetimes."

"I bet it was murder," I continue indignantly. "Faeries seem to have a taste for it. Vile creatures."

The wagon lurches to an unexpected halt, and I nearly losing my seat. I can feel the tug of gravity pulling us back toward the bottom, and I fear one wrong move might send us tumbling across the razor-sharp stone. Gálgalesh wraps his fingers lightly but terrifyingly around the front of my cloaks and lowers his face to meet mine.

"Then why is it that I haven't killed you?" He squeezes just enough to pull me in closer for a moment as I feel his power around me. Then, he releases me with a snarling growl. "Enough questions. We will reach the summit by dinner, and when we do, you need to make sure whoever you meet, you do not make them privy to your real identity. They will kill you on sight if they find out. I will book you with the guard at the gate and get you a new set of clothes, and then you will be on your own. If you don't die overnight, you will meet me at five in the morning and begin your training. We will meet every day for three hours until you meet your demise or manage to find a way back to the Capital. Then, I will be free of you."

"What do I do for the rest of the day?" I wonder aloud. "If we are only training for three hours..."

"I do not care," Gálgalesh replies flatly as he coaxes the

wagon to move again. "You will have chores to complete, and then you can do as you please, I suppose. I suggest you make yourself scarce if you value this life you have."

"Stop telling me I am going to die! It's rude!" I snap, and he laughs. "Faeries..." I pull my arms against my chest, and we fall silent again.

When we reach the summit in the late afternoon, my eyes are heavy with fatigue. The wagon stops in a snowy clearing, large iron gates sitting at the center of a stone fortress towering over us. The place is gray and ominous, and an icy wind blows across my face as I stumble down from my seat. There is nothing welcoming about Báscogar, from the uneven surface of its exterior walls to the eyes that follow us from the watchtowers. Gálgalesh arrives at my side and catches the fabric of my cloaks in his hand. He half-drags me across the icy ground toward the iron gate. A man stands on the other side with blond hair that falls to his shoulders and a bored expression on his face as he nods to Gálgalesh familiarly.

"What do you have there?" he asks, pointing toward me.

"A new resident," Gálgalesh replies firmly and releases me with a heavy hand, causing me to slide on the ice and grab the gate to keep upright. It burns my palms—charmed to keep prisoners in and visitors out—and I release it quickly with a small yelp. The other two smirk.

"Name?" the man asks as he lifts a pen against the scroll in his hand.

"Alana Moran," Gálgalesh says.

"Moran? Like the–?"

"She was a slave in the Steel Citadel. As you know, slaves take their owner's family name."

I hide my wince as he speaks. From all I had learned, Gálgalesh is correct, though I have never met a slave before. My father banned them in the royal household because he found the act of trapping someone against their will to be repulsive. No one outside the castle walls would know that from his refusal to ban the ownership of slaves in an act of appeasing the merchants of Draíocoinnigh and our trading partners in Oleaíncudd. I remain silent as the conversation continues around me.

"Offense?" The man doesn't care to look up from his scroll.

"She ran away toward the Borderlands. The new laws call desertion from the royal courts treason." Gálgalesh shrugs coolly.

"Magic?" the man inquires, and Gálgalesh raises an eyebrow toward me.

"The king had them siphoned when I came to his household."

"No magic?" The man scoffs incredulously. "Well then, try to stay within the walls of the camp. Magic doesn't work within them, but outside of them, you're as good as dead. Age?"

"Who cares? She will not last another year here anyway. At least the life sentence will be short." Gálgalesh is impatient as he snaps at the guard. "I want my dinner. Get her some suitable clothes and someplace to sleep." He waves his hand in dismissal, and the gates open of their own volition. He turns to me. "Meet me in the center courtyard at five o'clock tomorrow morning." Without another word, he marches off into the gray walls of Báscogar.

The guard sighs and shakes his head and then rolls up his scroll. He looks at me, and I see what looks like pity in his eyes before he gestures for me to follow him as he begins his walk into the compound.

Besides the snow-covered grounds around the place, Báscogar consists of an impressive stonework building, much bigger than Caisleán Rialú's complex. There are four open connecting buildings that make up the walls of the prison, covered stone bridges on the second level of the building from the main house to the surrounding outposts, and rounded archways throughout. The central courtyard boasts a training ground with matching cobbled stone floors. There is no chatter or sound of life as we walk into the camp, and the wind whistles past us. The man motions for me to follow him further inside.

We reach a small wooden door that looks like it leads to a storage closet, and the man pushes it open and guides me through it. He lights a candle, and the low light brings our surroundings into view. The room is filled with apparel of every size, all black in color, similar to the traveling clothes I wear, although they appear to be made of thicker fabric. Hanging against the opposite wall are black cloaks with a brown fur on the shoulders and matching boots. He looks me over and then hands me a set of clothes and instructs me to change. I do so quickly, hating the instant cold against my skin. While I pull on the clothes, he moves toward the cloaks and boots and pulls some out for me.

"Here. Take a second pair when you go to have in the morning, and then you will change out daily after that. Leave your dirty clothes by your door each morning, and someone will return them to your room by the evening. My name is Morgan, by the way."

"Nice to meet you," I say as I lace up my new boots.

"Let's find you a room. Everyone has their own here. It keeps the murders amongst residents down." He laughs as though he has said something funny and leads me out of the wardrobe closet.

We walk through a network of corridors that twist and turn through the interior of the camp. Every person we pass glares at me, and I sink down lower into my boots as I travel deeper into the place. I probably would be crazy to think I would be making friends here. Even more of a reason to learn what I can and get out as quickly as possible.

Soon, Morgan navigates another turn down a narrow hallway, and I notice there are doors on both sides: the boarding hall. We enter at the center of the corridor and walk halfway down the length of the right side before Morgan stops in front of a door with "262" inscribed on its surface.

"Well, Resident 262, this is where I leave y–" Morgan begins, but the door to our right opens as he speaks. Our eyes trail toward the noise, and a man no older than Tiernan —though perhaps slightly younger—steps out into the hall. His skin glows of the deepest tan I have ever seen, though there is no sun to be found in Romiodóg, and his eyes are a swirl of gold and green. His hair is dark, with faint, sun-kissed highlights from many days spent in the oppressive rays of the Tinemallacht sun. He towers above us, a muscular, dominating figure. He looks at Morgan and tilts his chin in greeting, and then his eyes fall on me. He is the most terrifying person I have ever seen, though I cannot stop staring at him. Why can I not stop staring? He freezes for just a moment, his eyes trailing from my short red hair to my new boots, and then he crinkles his nose in a sneer of disgust. Without a word, he slams the door behind him and walks off down the hall.

"And that is your neighbor, Resident 264: Eoghan Kael. I would try to steer clear of him if I were you, particularly if you want to survive." He throws me a glance that says he is not being remotely funny this time. "Well," he clears his throat, "I hope I will see you again. Welcome to Báscogar."

Morgan leaves, and I open the door to room 262 slowly. There is a candle fitted into a holder on the small desk by the door, a box of matches beside it. I light it carefully, and the room glows softly. It is nothing compared to what I was used to back home, not even anything in comparison to the small room I shared with Dedra. There is a single bed against the wall, dressed in common linens and a scratchy gray blanket. Besides the desk and chair, there is a small side table with a single drawer and a wardrobe across from the bed. The walls are bare except for a window in the center of the exterior wall. I walk over to the bed and fall back in exhaustion, wondering what I got myself into and if I will live long enough for any of it to matter. An arctic chill on my face from the cracks in the window reminds me I probably won't.

CHAPTER SIX

Darling Ri,

How long until I will see you again? My body aches for you. I can barely sleep when you are gone. I'm starting to depend on you being near me, and that scares me a little, because I feel more in love with you when you are near. I'm not sure how that can be, since I love you all the time.

To answer your last letter, two guards are stationed inside each exterior door and just down the corridor from the ancient throne room at the lower entrances from the city into the castle. I do not suppose they would question why we wanted to explore the foundation stones within the walls... My brother has taken more than one woman against the cold floors of the basement chambers and snuck them back out into the city *without so much as a raised eyebrow. If you can finish your meeting with my father by midday, we may not meet a single guard on our way, as they are scarce between noon and supper.*

Come visit me as soon as you arrive back on the continent. I'll be waiting.

Tha grá di,

Maeve

————

I lose myself twice on the way to the courtyard to meet Gálgalesh the next morning. I walk barefooted to avoid making any sound and slip on a patch of ice under one of the stone archways. I swear as my knee hits the ground painfully, but I pull myself to my feet and continue on.

Ice is everywhere in this place—in the corridors, the windowsills… There is no heat in this entire fortress, and I find myself shivering both during the day and throughout the night with just my blanket for warmth. I am not used to the cold. Golorgleann is a mild temperature the entire year, and one can only expect a cool breeze or a bit of rain in the fall and winter months. Romiodóg will take some getting used to.

I walk into the dark, empty space of the courtyard, the snow falling around me. Gálgalesh emerges from the shadows of one of the surrounding pillars, and I jump at the sight of him.

"You're late," he barks. "Where are your boots?" I lift them silently so he can see. "Why are they in your hands and not on your feet?"

"I am trying to survive. Boots against stone can attract attention."

"And freezing can't kill you?" He scoffs then turns and walks to the center of the courtyard. "Put those on your feet, you ridiculous woman, and then come stand in front of me."

I balance on one leg as I pull on each sock and boot and lace them tight. Once I finish, I walk slowly toward Gálgalesh, still wary of my proximity to the faerie. His glare presses down upon me, but I force myself to meet his eyes. He sizes me up, disapproval clear across his face.

"You are so frail, I can almost hear the breaks in your bones I am going to make." A smirk displays his triangular teeth. "How do you plan to kill your enemies when you are as weak as the runt of a litter of hounds?"

"Do not taunt me." My voice is a whisper through gritted teeth. I hate him for treating me like I am nothing more than a privileged child. I hate him for saying what my mind has already told me a million times this morning.

"Show me then." He opens his arms wide in welcome. "I am your enemy. Show me how you would kill me. Show me how you would fight."

He takes a step back, opening the space between us. I've never fought anyone before, and I am not sure where I might begin. I survey the courtyard around us, but there is only uneven stone under our feet. I look back at the faerie and see the amusement on his face—the ridicule I had felt my entire life when locked away in the castle like a damsel begging to be free. I want nothing more than to rip that arrogant smile off his face. My hands clench at my sides at the thought of him taunting me with my impending death. He hates me being here, and I hate him for making me feel like such a fool.

His lip ticks up to the right side in a smirk that sends me over the edge with madness, and I lunge. Arms in front of me, clawing at the air, I aim for his face as the desire to tear his mocking eyes from his skull ignites me. In milliseconds, I am just inches from him, flying forward like a crazed animal…and then my legs fly from underneath me, and I fall hard against my back, knocking the breath from my lungs.

Inches from the stone, I hover on a firm bed of air and then drop to the ground below. The back of my head slams against the surface, and I grunt out in pain. There is no way I escape without at least a bruise; and even then, I might be lucky with the fragility of my freshly mended bones. I wheeze as I attempt to draw the air back into my lungs.

"Magic. Doesn't. Work. Inside. Báscogar."

The rattling of my head on impact blurs my vision, and I watch the cloudy outline of Gálgalesh stride forward unhurriedly. He looks down at me with boredom. "I am the Warden of Báscogar. I have no limits—besides, faerie magic answers to no one, not even your kind's foolish spells and enchantments. Get up so I can teach you something."

Though I am not sure I can stand, I move to sit upright, and my body screams in protest. My face knots up in pain, but I push myself upward carefully. I can feel the soft dripping of blood from the back of my skull as it runs warmly down to the nape of my neck. I rub my fingers across it and bring them into view. My stomach churns at the sight of crimson against my skin. Blood, like the blood that stained my knees on that horrible day; the blood that held such power and now flows weakly through me. My hands shake noticeably, and I wipe them against my black pants to remove the red from my fingertips. Gálgalesh pays me no attention as he positions himself two body lengths away.

"You cannot simply lunge at your opponent and think you will control anything that happens next," he begins and lifts his shoulders. He disappears with not so much as a crack of the surrounding air. Faerie magic is silent and terrifying that does not require hand gestures or channeling cuffs to control it, making it illegal to wield in combat of any kind. Magic wielders do not have any conjuring advantage over faeries when it comes to power, and faeries have always refused to fight with man. As a result, authorities have regulated their kind for centuries by using Faebond, the only power-limiting material that affects both faeries and mankind. There is a breath against my ear, and I rotate on the spot. Gálgalesh presses his hand to the middle of my chest, throwing me across the courtyard and into a nearby pillar. The impact makes me crumple toward the ground, but he is there to hold me in his grip, squeezing me until the sound of cracking bone makes me swallow a cry.

"You need to learn to move in the shadows and strike before being seen. You need to be versed in execution more than battle; battle is what your enemy wants. They are good at it. It is what they goad you with. Stealth and lethal precision are the only ways you can win, and that is why Tiernan sent you here."

He releases me, and I collapse to my knees as I grip my sides gingerly. "What do you mean?" The words come painfully.

"I told you—this is more of a camp," he bites out. "It is a prison for the common criminal and those who think they can hold us, but for the Leader, it was a training ground, where he built his personal army of those with talent and a desire to fight but no allegiance to Draíocoinnigh that might tempt them to enlist." I look up at him as I stabilize myself through the pain. "Will you learn the way of the marked, the tested, and the victorious, or will you settle for death—here or outside these walls?"

———

THE REST of the training finds me battered and bruised repeatedly. If I had healed in the weeks spent in Dedra's townhouse, there is no sign of that now. My face is black and blue, my body fractured and split. I cannot counter him once, and by the end, I am sprawled against the stone, begging for mercy. Gálgalesh looks down at me with no pity in his eyes, but he gestures once with his hand, and a vial appears before him. He drops it onto my open palm and walks away from where I lay.

"Drink it and give it a minute. Then, collect your cloak and head to breakfast. You have to clean the toilets upstairs in the guards' quarters before you can rest."

I lift the vial agonizingly and drain it into my mouth. It's a sweet concoction that fills me with warmth and contentment. I close my eyes as I feel whatever it is course pleasantly throughout me, as if light is filling every inch of my body. Healing potion. A traditional alchemist could never perfect the recipe, but I imagine Gálgalesh is not traditional by any stretch of the imagination. The pain subsides, and after a few moments, as the liquid fills me and then settles, I can stand.

"I will send a contraceptive tonic to your room that you will take each day to prevent any accidents while you are here. I do not expect the men to know what to do with a female resident around, but we do not need the further complication of a child as well." Gálgalesh drapes his cloak over his shoulders and pulls his hair out from underneath the neck.

"I do not need it." There was no sense in putting him through the trouble of making a tonic that must be in full supply each day.

"Do not be ridiculous. There are nearly three hundred men in this prison. Do not pretend you will find none of them suitable to satiate you."

Pink rises in my cheeks, and I round on him. "I. Do. Not. Need. It."

He pauses and takes me in as though he can read a lifetime of memories on my face. Perhaps it is the faerie magic or simply the tears lining my eyes that give me away, but his expression softens to something that looks like compassion for the first time. He takes a step forward, and I take one back as I drop my gaze away from him.

"Who?"

One word. That is all he says, but it is all that is necessary.

"Sir Oli Raven, my father's Potion Master. After my first bleed, my father ordered it. The heir is the only one permitted to have children; I suppose it was better to fix the problem with one tonic and a blade than with a tonic every day."

I remember the fire that ignited in my stomach as I drank Sir Oli Raven's tonic that would remove my ability to bear any heirs. I remember the screams that hardly sounded like my own as I writhed on the stone floor, how, the next day, I was found to be mended by my magic. I remember the blade he used to slice me open and the way he cauterized me to make sure there was nothing that could bring the missing pieces of my womanhood back. Even my magic could not create something from nothing.

Gálgalesh's tone, enraged but quiet, is just between us as he asks, "Who else knew?"

"No one. Not even my mother."

Gálgalesh nods once, his shoulders stiff and his mouth a thin line. "Well then, at any rate, I will see you in the morning. Be safe."

I collect my cloak and shake out the snow that has accumulated on top of it, and then I make my way into the interior of the building.

There is no finding my way here. Every corridor looks

the same, and I am too scared to ask anyone to guide me. Instead, I try to follow my senses, sniffing the air for any hints of food wafting through the halls. It all smells like sweat, blood, and dirt. I get lost about a dozen times on my way to breakfast and think about giving up completely, about heading back to my room for a quick nap instead. *You are starving. You need to eat,* my brain reasons. *Plus, you probably won't be able to find your way back to your room at this rate.*

I stop down one of the passageways once I am convinced it is leading me in the wrong direction again, and I lean against the stone wall. My cheek cools against the bite of the rock, and I take in the silence around me. Maybe I'll just stay here. If I don't show up to my chore duties, someone will have to come to find me…won't they? Or perhaps Gálgalesh will be so delighted by the prospect of being rid of me, he will leave me to rot here in this corridor. I don't care. The cool stone makes me close my eyes and sigh in contentment, but before I can get too comfortable, I feel a fist wrap around the back of my cloak. I react in an instant, but the person who has grabbed hold of me is faster. I feel my toes knock against the stone as they begin to drag me forward through the fire-lit hallway.

I cannot see who has hold of me, as their grip near my neckline keeps me positioned to look only at the ground. My feet fail to find their grip as the toes of my boots catch against the uneven pavement and drag helplessly behind me, toes toward the floor. I spread out my arms, trying to catch the wall, but the one holding me pushes them away hard and continues to bound forward with me in tow. *First full day here, and someone is already going to throw you out of the front gates or off one of the towers for the wolves,* I sigh to myself. My captor does not stop, even as they push me through a pair of heavy wooden doors engraved with grotesque images of men taking lives in battle. The arm thrusts me into the room beyond and frees me, dropping me to the floor.

I look up and push my fallen hood from my face. It is then I see my boarding room neighbor—Eoghan Kael—standing over me. His face is stony hatred, and I drag myself across the floor in a panic to flee him and his beautiful yet terrifying gaze. The sound of cutlery clattering against metal plates draws my eyes away from his, and I take in the room.

Hundreds of men, huge and muscular, menacing and lethal, stare back at me in dumbfounded surprise. Some have bald heads and blackened teeth, while others are so devastatingly handsome, I have to fight to look away. Their eyes all radiate hunger, and I become keenly aware that I am the only person in this room who might make it mixed company. I pull my cloak around myself protectively as I curl up over my knees on the floor. Eoghan Kael does not take his eyes from me, and it is a torturous moment before I hear footsteps coming toward me.

"The girl," Gálgalesh bellows so the entire company can hear and turns to face the crowd, "is Alana Moran, and while she is here, she will be under my protection. Do not act as heathens do—though for some, that might be impossible." A few dubious laughs fill the room. Gálgalesh looks down at me, and his eyes narrow angrily. "Leave her and finish eating. I expect you to complete your duties entirely today…all of you."

The men's voices rise in unison as they utter their understanding, and Gálgalesh remains standing in place. I follow his eyes to Eoghan Kael, who gives me one last, long look before turning and walking away.

"Stay away from Kael," Gálgalesh mutters to me under his breath. "Unless you want an especially painful death."

"Right," I sigh as I start to stand. "That should be simple enough, seeing as he's just my neighbor."

Gálgalesh swears under his breath. "Well then, perhaps sleep with one eye open…and get yourself a weapon to keep on your nightstand."

He walks away from me, and I stand in the dining hall feeling as though I am being served up on a platter. I walk toward the line at the far end of the room for food and sense a group of men silently close in on me. I keep my eyes forward as they examine me from head to toe. Brutes, all of them. As if they have not seen a woman in all their lives. They all have mothers, don't they? I'm sure a few even had sisters and wives at some point. I continue in line, taking a spoonful of something gray and slimy and dumping it onto my plate. The food leaves something to be desired, but my body aches with hunger after having not eaten since breakfast the day before. I pick up an apple and twist it in my hand, and a worm sticks out of a brown spot on the side. I set it back down in the bowl. The men continue to stare as I take my tray from the lineup of toast and gray porridge and find an empty table near the far corner. Once I am seated, I lift my spoon to my mouth and take an unappetizing bite.

"Brave," a man says as he slides into the seat opposite me. He has a husky voice, red hair pulled back into a tight bun at the back of his head. His brown eyes are large and round on his face, and he has a softness to his features the rest of the men do not share. "Most take until they have nearly starved to death before they will trust this place enough to eat anything. Kruz Lanzo." He introduces himself to me, and I nod politely. "Don't worry. Usually, if you follow the rules and don't make a fuss, no one will bother you. Just don't bargain with anyone unless you are willing to pay double what you agreed and leave the Fire Cursed alone."

"The what?" I ask.

"Fire Cursed. The ones from Tinemallacht." I look at him and tilt my head in confusion. "I am from Iranndair, and I know the stories. Do you really not know anything about the Tinemallacht Fire Cursed?" My brows pull tightly together, and I shake my head. I know of Tinemallacht, certainly, know of the legends of their warriors and dragons that surf the sand, but nothing of the name. Kruz leans forward, eager to tell his story. "They say the dragons living there laid waste to their land, making it so hot that not even a tree could grow and the rivers turned to sand. Then, when the people of Tinemallacht began to hunt them, the dragons turned on the people and marked them for eternity to wield fire. It is dangerous magic that often burns marked children from the inside out before they learn to control it. The lucky ones who do survive have nasty tempers and kill for sport."

"And how will I know the Fire Cursed from the other bad tempered ones?" I watch the room as I speak, trying to see if I can see fire dance in anyone's eyes. I spot Eoghan Kael seated at a far table, flipping a dagger over between his fingers.

"You'll know. Like your escort earlier—he is the most dangerous of them all."

I look away from where Eoghan sits as my cheeks flush bright and hot. Tinemallacht Fire Cursed. I shouldn't want to get near him or any of them at all, but curiosity rushes through me in a wave of excitement. What would it be like to watch the fire dance across his hands? The lethal magic quelled within these walls that could set me a blaze at his whim just outside the gates?

I shake my head and change the subject, and we finish our breakfast in quiet conversation. Once we finish, we clear our plates, and Kruz walks me to the upstairs guards' quarters. I thank him, and he promises to meet me after to walk me back to my room so I don't get lost on the way.

The guard who greets me has thick black eyebrows that cover nearly all his protruding brow bone and hood his eyes.

He says little to me and simply directs me to the lavatory, handing me a bucket of soapy water, a sponge, and a pair of gloves. *First time for everything,* I think as I stare down at the filthy toilets, the stench overwhelming me. I get to work quickly as I try to keep my breakfast down.

————

IT TAKES me until midday to finish at the guards' station, and as I make to leave—sweaty and smelling of the foulest stench—the guard informs me I will return at the same time tomorrow to collect the bedding and complete the washing. I nod silently and exit the quarters to find Kruz waiting for me with a new set of Báscogar camp clothes in his arms.

"I figured you might want to get cleaned up after your chores." He shrugs his shoulders and smiles timidly.

"I could kiss you." I let out a sigh of relief as we begin our walk through the corridors. "Thank you." He nods, and we fall into a thoughtful silence for a few passing moments before curiosity gets the better of me. "I have a question." He waits for me to continue. "You don't seem like the others here. I expected everyone to be terrifying and horrible, but you're nice to me."

"That sounds more like an observation than a question."

"What could you have done to get sent to Báscogar?" I watch his features tighten a bit as I speak, but he does not reprimand me for my curiosity. He takes a long breath in as we continue our pace, and I can see his mind wander to a memory of something distant. Maybe I don't want to know why he is here or what he has done. In this new world, that I'd be lucky to survive, my inquisitiveness could be the thing that does me in first. "Sorry," I say and look to my feet.

"When I was fifteen, I left Iranndair with a pack of contraband traps designed to catch merrow—the half-fish, half-human people who live in the waters along the coast of Tonnfórsca. They were ravaging the merchant ships and clearing the waters of fish so many of the region's people depended on for food. The King of Draíocoinnigh and the Fish King made a pact that banned setting traps for merrow, but the people of Tonnfórsca were starving and begging for relief. Hunting merrow is common practice along the Iranndair coast, and we had more than enough traps to spare, so my father—a fisherman himself—sent me to their aid. As soon as I entered through the southern border, they caught me and brought me here. That was twenty years ago." I stop walking, and he waits for me patiently. A scowl washes over my expression as my mind races. "What's the matter?"

"No one gets sent to Báscogar unless they have committed one of the four high crimes. Smuggling isn't one of them..."

Kruz sighs, and his shoulders drop slightly. "Where did you say you were from, Alana? Báscogar is a prison for anyone the King of Draíocoinnigh decides is a threat to his rule or life. Foreigners fit that description even if they have done nothing wrong, and being in possession of contraband made me an even bigger 'threat'. That is why you will never meet a foreigner in Draío—if they are smart, at least. The only ones you will meet are here at the camp or slaves from Trader's Bay who have their powers siphoned from them and therefore are of no threat to anyone at all."

My head starts spinning as I absorb all the information I hadn't been taught in my years of schooling. Kruz motions for me to continue walking, and we fall into a silent stroll through the bitter cold halls of the fortress. We make it to my bedroom door without another question—as I wonder if I might not want to know any more answers—and Kruz hands me the pile of clothes.

"At the end of the hall," he points to a solitary door at the dead-end, "there are the toilets and shower rooms. Make sure you are alone before you strip down. There aren't any bathrooms for women here, and even if Gálgalesh has warned us all to leave you alone, the rules might not apply in there." I nod, and he surveys the hall. "I'm down that way in room 217." He points down the opposite direction. "If you need anything, come find me."

I say goodbye to him and then open my door and walk inside. The room is still dark in the blackness of the Romiodóg day. I drop a set of clothes on the bed along with my cloak, kick off my boots, and pick up a towel someone left in the room for me. It is rough and thin but smells clean. There is also a basket of standard toiletries I scoop up eagerly. They are nondescript and smell mossy and masculine, but I do not care. I leave the room and tiptoe down the hall toward the shower room. I push the door open and peek inside. It is lit by an ever-present glowing orb of some enchantment I am sure has been on this place since its creation, and from the door, I can see it is empty, so I shuffle inside. I drop my things onto the counter and start by brushing my teeth at the sink. After days of travel without any of the luxuries of home, I almost feel sick thinking about the dirt that must coat my skin. When my mouth feels clean, I turn on the tap in the nearest shower and pull off my clothes piece-by-piece. I drop them along the bench that sits between the sink and the showers before stepping beneath the stream of steaming water. The ecstasy of the warmth combines with the uncomfortable sting of my cold skin as the water rolls down my body. I close my eyes and let it wash over me, my hands running over my short red hair.

The bar of soap I have been gifted is a rounded cake of yellowish-white. I take it into my hands and begin to scrub every inch of me as though I can ever make myself as presentable as I had once been. I will try my damnedest, though, and showers are a good start. As I glide my soapy hands over my skin, I wonder at the tonic Gálgalesh gave me after our training session—beating, more like it—as I find not one mark or discoloration against my skin. There is no true healing tonic or spell that can take away deep or life-threatening injuries completely... apart from the magic I possessed just a few short weeks ago—and I was said to be the only one to have ever had such magic to wield. Still, Gálgalesh's tonic might come close. I lift my face into the rushing water and revel in the feel of it as I wash away the soap down the drain. I lift the shampoo to my hair and lather it up before washing it away as well. All my life, it has taken nearly an entire team of trusted staff to wash, dry, and style my long hair. Now, it only takes me moments. I'm not sure how I feel about it, both relishing in the convenience and grieving from the loss, the power it gave me. I get lost in the memory of it for a long moment, and it is not until I hear a creak of the door behind me and the presence of someone blocking the exit that I am brought back to the present.

I freeze, the steam of the shower clouding the room from view. Low voices murmur by the door—though I cannot quite make out what they say. I count three, though I can't see so much as an outline of a single body, and I hope that means they haven't been able to discern it is me in the room either. I look around—panic-stricken—for a way out. There is no other door leading from the room, as the showers sit at the dead-end of the hall. *Shit, I am going to be found. Worst of all, I am going to be found naked and defenseless with no way out.* Like hell I am! My eyes dart around the clouded space and find the only bit of hope I have. A lifeline...if I can call it that at all.

Above the shower is a small, rectangular window just out of reach. It could work; though it might be a tight squeeze, I'm fairly certain I could make it through. The only question is what might be on the other side. From my bedroom window, it is at least a twenty-foot drop to the rocks below, maybe more. Either way, I don't have time to sit and debate the merits of staying or leaving. The voices continue as I try to find anything nearby that might get me closer to my escape. A tiny stool that might barely fit both feet sits against the far shower wall. *That could work.* I move quietly, careful of my balance across the slick, wet surface. The conversation is dying down, indicating I have only seconds until whomever is in the room could move in and find me, so I move faster across the shower.

I pick up the stool and position it against the wall under the window, the water I so enjoyed just moments before a barrier to my climb as it rushes into my face. I cannot risk turning it off and alerting the others, so instead, I carry on with my climb toward the window, balancing on my tiptoes and hoping against hope I don't slip in the torrent of water. Bingo! My fingers reach just over top of the ledge. I claw my way up, and my body slides against the shower wall. I close my eyes and pray the sound is drowned out by the water pounding against the shower floor. I level my eyes with the window as I hoist myself up, gripping the edge firmly with one hand while the other pushes the glass free. It falls away in one piece down the side of the fortress wall to the snow and rocks below. Without wasting a moment, I pull myself through the small space onto the tiny window ledge. I bite back a cry of pain as the stiff wind instantly lashes my naked body. *It is freezing out here!* I reach a trembling hand toward a protruding stone to my left and grab it with white-knuckle force.

I take my other hand and thrust it out beyond the ledge toward whatever I can grab, freeing myself from the relative safety of the window and dangling by my slick palms. It is beyond cold. The wind whips violently around me, my bones aching, and I can feel ice beginning to form as the water on my skin freezes in the cold. I realize if I do not keep moving, I might be frozen to the stone in a matter of moments. I dig my feet into the edge, trying to find purchase. Mercifully, my feet find holds in the wall, and I begin the climb for my life toward my bedroom window.

One step at a time, I reach and adjust as I count the seconds before I must move again. My teeth chatter, and my body trembles violently against the bone-chilling air. *I cannot stop*, I think to myself. *If I stop, I'm dead.* I pass by five windows, which—much to my gratitude—are all empty, and I realize I'm just two away and I'll have made it safely. I reach around the seal of the first and peer inside, making sure the coast is clear. The room is empty and dark like the others I passed before it, but I notice an arsenal of weapons against the walls, the Tinemallacht crest of a skull engulfed in flames across a pack sitting in the chair at the desk. Eoghan Kael's room is a display of might and power that could make anyone tremble, and not just from the cold. I swallow hard, and another rush of wind reminds me to keep moving. I step slowly until I cross to my window. I pull against it, pleading silently for it to give way, and I thank the heavens when it does. I throw myself inside with a thud as I hit the floor. Shivering, I stand and pull the window closed. I look down at the bed, where my discarded cloak and remaining set of clothes lay before I pull them on.

"You climbed out of the window?" Kruz forks the supper on his plate, not hiding the laugh in his voice. "Naked?"

"What else was I going to do?!" I lift my arms in the air in defeat. We sit in the far corner of the dining hall at a nearly empty table, only two other men seated at the opposite end. Their eyes search me with interest as they eavesdrop on our conversation, and I keep my gaze ahead, afraid to give them the satisfaction of eye contact. My face is flush and tender to the touch, and I shift in my seat as my clothes brush painfully against my windburned skin.

"And you said the clothes you abandoned in the shower room were outside your door when you left your room this evening? That means whoever you were trying to escape from either saw you or figured out who you were," he says as he brings his fork to his lips and takes a bite of the warm mush served to us this evening. It smells bland and looks as though someone has vomited it onto our plates. The food keeps us alive, but I am quickly learning there isn't much else to desire or expect from the meals at Báscogar.

"I don't think it would be very hard to figure out. I'm smaller than everyone else here. The clothes were probably a dead giveaway."

Kruz shrugs and swallows, his face still amused despite the gruel he has shoveled into his mouth. I push my food around on my plate and scrunch my nose up in disgust. He smiles lightly, and his shoulders bob as he chuckles to himself, clearly picturing my escape once again. My face turns a deeper shade of scarlet, and I shove my fork into the beans and oats.

"Stop it; you're being cruel. We are changing the subject now. Tell me about this place. What do you do here with your day?"

He continues to smirk and shakes his head, then clears his throat. "Well, I imagine we do about the same as what you will be doing. We train—in groups usually, and we try to avoid anyone we think might try to kill us during a sparring session—and we have our duties. Mine is almost always in the weapons storeroom, mending or sharpening blades. Every couple of weeks, we have patrol duties in Fáintìrean."

"Where?" I lift a bite to my mouth before thinking better of it and setting my fork back down.

"Fáintìrean. It is a mountain village about five kilometers west along the ridgeline. The people there are a wild, nasty breed of hunters who lost their magic around two hundred years ago. We trade supplies and protection from the faerie population that camps near the northern border for animal pelts and meat when they have it. Consider yourself lucky if they never assign you to a patrol unit, though I doubt Gálgalesh would risk sending you anyway. We have at least a few casualties a year on patrol."

"How does a group of kinsmen lose their magic? Are their children not born with it either?"

"Magic is precious," Kruz begins, and he lowers his voice

as two rather-large men walk past him at close range. "As you know, it can be siphoned by wielders with siphoning magic, but it is a high crime to do so, and the person who does will end up here—or at the house of Donn. However, siphoning magic doesn't necessarily impact the family line; the drained wielder can still pass the magic gene on." I nod to indicate my understanding, and he continues.

"The only way magic can be lost for generations is if someone makes a bargain in exchange for it. During the reign of King Lorcán, the people of Fáintìrean sought out everlasting life. They had heard the king had found longevity that surpassed any man had ever seen at a faerie camp in Dún. It was a lie, but the villagers did not know that. So they sought out a local faerie tribe within the mountains of Romiodóg and made a bargain for their lives. They gave up their magic as payment, and in exchange, they received the curse of life. About fifty years ago, they went back to the faeries and begged for their magic back after growing tired of their eternal damnation. The faeries instructed them to sacrifice twelve of their youngest and weakest by tying them to the trees bordering Fáintìrean on the longest night of the year. The screaming lasted through the night, and when the morning came, the curse remained, and the faeries had left the bones of the sacrificed as a reminder to the people of Fáintìrean of the cost of immortality. So to this day, they continue, generation to generation, never growing old but in constant fear of the ones who took their power from them."

I feel bile rise in my throat and swallow hard. I clasp my hands together against the cold wood of the table, and Kruz examines my expression as I search for a response that will not make it past my lips. I had known nothing of the horrors of this world before I had left the confines of the castle, nothing of the fear of death or starvation or war. Faeries and shadow lurkers and banshees were nighttime terrors used in stories to keep my brother and me from acting out as children, as distant as the stars that shoot across the sky at night. Those horrors, however, are no longer stories but realities of what I might face if I do not do as I have set out to do.

"Are you all right, Alana?" Kruz asks as one eyebrow rises up against his forehead. I do not respond, and he snaps his fingers in front of my face, causing me to lose my train of thought.

"Sorry?" I shake my head from side to side.

"I asked if you are all right?"

"I'm fine," I lie. "Lost my appetite a bit." I continue as though I had one to begin with. "Did you learn the story from the people of Fáintìrean while on patrol?"

"Me? No. The common language is not spoken by the people of Fáintìrean, and the forbidden language of Draío is not taught in Iranndair. Their story is widely known throughout the territory, though, and many of the residents here can communicate with them." He sighs audibly and taps my plate with his own. "I shouldn't have mentioned it. Like I said, Gálgalesh would never send you on patrol." His tone lightens slightly. "Finish your supper. I want to show you how we spend our evenings."

WE WIND through the labyrinth of corridors along Báscogar's interior. Kruz takes my hand and guides me to a spiraling stone staircase at the east end of the compound. We begin our descent into the belly of the place, and after about three hundred steps, I stop, gasping to catch my breath, and lean against the wall. Kruz stops impatiently next to me and looks down at my pathetic frame slumped over my knees. His lip ticks up as he appraises me and then wordlessly motions for me to follow him once more as he ties back the red tresses that have fallen out of his bun. I sigh to myself and then continue to follow him down, dreading the ascent when we finally make our way back to our rooms later in the evening.

We continue for another two hundred or so stairs before we reach the stone floor at the very bottom. The air is gelid, and I can see my breath in front of me as icy daggers pierce my lungs. I pull my cloak around me and look around. The corridor beyond is forbiddingly dark and echoes with each movement we make. Kruz takes matches from his pocket just like the pack left on the desk in my room and lights a torch on the wall next to him. He pulls it from its cradle and lifts it high in front of us. Beyond us is a long, sloping passageway traveling downward into the darkness. Nothing good could come from traveling with a strange man into the belly of a prison fortress and down a darkened corridor. I know *nothing,* apparently, and even I know that. I raise an eyebrow, and Kruz's brown eyes glimmer in the yellow-orange light.

"Just this way." Kruz begins to lead us again, the torch held out in front of him. The light fades from me as he marches on, and I follow quickly to avoid losing myself in the darkness.

We walk down into the darkness for what feels like an eternity—but is probably only a few minutes—and my windburned face aches with cold as we traverse further into the earth. The air smells musty and stale from the lack of movement. The walls have a damp texture when touched, and the stone feels grainy, giving the impression of dirt being packed into the crevices. In the dim light, I can see movement across the uneven surface: burrow worms. Tiny worms that live in caves and cellars enveloped in darkness as they eat away at anything in their path: dirt, fabric, even the human body if given the opportunity. Back at Caisleán Rialú, the dungeon cells harbor burrow worms, and there are rumors that more than once, a prisoner has been eaten alive after spending countless days leaning against the walls.

I steal my gaze ahead and carry on. We round another sharp corner, and I catch my first glimpse of light peeking through a partially closed door ahead. It lays a ways beyond us still, but the faint din of voices reaches my ears and grows with each step we take closer to it. We reach the door—which I thought must be at the end of the long hall but sits only about halfway down—and Kruz places his hand against the wood as he fixes me with his gaze. A smile plays at the corners of his lips.

"Keep close. It's still not safe for you here."

He waits for my nod then pushes the door open to reveal a blinding light and roaring tumult that nearly makes me stumble back in alarm. I squint and shield my eyes with my hands, trying to bring the room into view with the contrast of the brightness against the oppressive dark of the hall. All around, Báscogar prisoners revel and drink, chat and gamble amongst themselves. The room brims with a crowd, and the close proximity of bodies makes the heat rise around me. Kruz winks, sets down his torch in an awaiting cradle, and snags two pints of ale from the nearby barrel, shoving one into my empty hands before leading me toward the gathering.

"This is supposed to be a prison." I feel myself shouting to be heard over the room.

"It is technically a prison, but even in a prison, you have to occupy yourself somehow—especially if you are faced with a life sentence." He takes a large swallow from his pint and smacks his lips playfully. "This is an area the prisoners have deemed a refuge from the brutality and hell of this place. A bit of normality for us all."

I observe the room. Where each face in the dining hall this morning had seemed foreboding, here, the air feels much lighter. I see men laughing and clapping one another on the back, men arm wrestling and knocking their drinks onto the floor. I have never been much of a fan of ale, as I was raised on wine and spirits, but the promise of at least one creature comfort from the world I knew intoxicates me. I lift my own drink and inhale the strong malty aroma of barley and citrus. Drinking for the fun of it is something I could enjoy here at Báscogar. I close my eyes as the roaring in my ears over-whelms me.

"Lanzo. Moran." My eyes fly open to find Gálgalesh standing mere inches from me. His silver hair falls across his shoulders, and he holds a pint in one hand casually. Beside him, another faerie with morbidly pale skin and ashen blond hair worn in a braid glares down his thin nose at me. He is broader in the shoulders than Gálgalesh, and rather than the common slender physique of most faerie men, this one is muscular and large. My body becomes rigid at the sight of him, as does Kruz's. I feel his hand drop between us, and I watch out of the corner of my eye as his fingers wrap around the handle of the blade at his side.

"Moran, why is your face so ghastly and red?" I lower my eyes but say nothing, and Gálgalesh continues. "This is Peadair. He is the Second Warden of Báscogar. I expect you to treat him with the same respect you have for me...if not more. If I am ever away, Peadair will train you and give you orders."

"Hello." I smile politely as I greet Gálgalesh's companion, and he growls hungrily my way. I take a step from him in shock and catch myself against a high-top table behind me.

"Peadair, behave," Gálgalesh nearly croons. "It would be less than convenient if you had your way with her, and she would be little more than a snack to begin with." Gálgalesh looks me over with boredom. "Tomorrow at five, Moran," he instructs and then places his hand on Peadair's shoulder firmly, as though pulling him away before he disappears into the crowd.

I exhale audibly, and Kruz loosens his grip on the knife at his side.

"Is Peadair always that intense?" I fill my throat with ale and swallow hard.

"Yes, but it's to be expected. How would you feel if your lover was the Warden of the deadliest prison on the continent? I might be on edge as well."

I choke on my drink, coughing and sputtering ridiculously. Kruz pats my back, his enormous eyes engulfing his face. "*That* is Gálgalesh's lover?!"

"Don't act so surprised, Alana. Gálgalesh has never been impressed by the dark and handsome type. He likes his faeries fierce, and Peadair is as fierce as they come." Amusement coats his words, and I feel embarrassed by my reaction, as if I have missed something important once again. "Just do as he says, and he won't pay you much attention."

WE SPEND a considerable portion of the evening drinking and playing cards with a group of Báscogar residents. Their names elude me as the haze of alcohol takes hold of my mind, but their stories are like Kruz's: foreigners caught within the borders of Draíocoinnigh or smugglers deemed "too dangerous" to keep their freedom. I look around the room and wonder at the mixed bag of prisoners within Báscogar—smugglers and foreigners living amongst murderers and revolutionaries. Had they felt as out of place and scared as I do when they first arrived at the gates of the stone fortress?

As the night begins to pull me under, I bid farewell to my new companions and stand from the table. I feel drunk and unsteady, and I giggle as I stumble clumsily toward the door. Kruz makes to stand as well, but I wave him off and trip over my boots into the corridor beyond. I walk in the darkness, both incapable and unwilling to find fire to light my way. I make it around the first bend, and the dim illumination of the room falls away from me. I feel as though I am in the dark belly of some kind of beast. I bob side to side as I continue, humming to myself. I *am* drunk, and I have only been so twice before in my entire life. Once was with my brother Cai on the rooftop of the castle for my seventeenth birthday. We drank and overlooked the city and wondered what it might be like to walk the streets together and celebrate like proper folk. The next time was when Rian had first come to visit me in my rooms. Sneaking him in was risky, because my father and brother were the only men allowed in there. But after a bottle of spirits he had brought back from Oleaíncudd, something inside us had begun to heat, and I could not wait any longer to take him to my bed.

I wipe my eyes against my sleeve as my emotions overwhelm me...and then something moves across the stone behind me.

"All by yourself," a voice hisses through the darkness, causing me to stop dead in my tracks. "Now, who was dumb enough to let you out of their sight?" I feel the heat of someone's presence at my back, and a pair of boney fingers place a firm grip around my shoulder. "I should thank them for handing you over to me." Hot, wet breath against my skin makes every muscle in my body tense. The smell of blood fills my nostrils as the shadow lurker exhales. My heart races in my chest, and I can hear my own breathing reverberate against the stone walls of the hall. Another hand traces up and down my waist. "Don't worry, I'll be gentle," the voice goads, and I whisper a prayer to no god in particular under my breath. I can feel the lips of the shadow lurker graze my neck.

Oh gods, help me! I cannot die here, not like this. I am pleading with everything and nothing inside me, willing myself to find a way out. *Any* way out.

Then, the hands lose their grip on me, and a loud crash of a body smashing into the stone wall echoes through the dark space. The shadow lurker cries out in pain, and the crunching sound of bones breaking fills my ears. *Run*, my mind shouts, and without being sure of the way forward, I barrel into the darkness. My feet pound against the damp floor at lightning speed before colliding with the stone wall at the end of the hall. I stumble backward, swearing, throwing my hands out in front of me and feeling the wall for the next corridor. As soon as I find my way, I begin to race through the darkness again, meeting each wall head-on until I reach the stairs. Up, up, up, I climb toward the faint light directly above.

"Alana!" I hear Kruz shout behind me, closing the gap between us. I whip around, my body trembling from head to toe. "Alana," he pants again as he places his hands on his knees, trying to catch his breath.

"I–I–I…" Words refuse to form sentences. Kruz raises one sweaty arm and places his hand against my thigh.

"I know. I'm so sorry. I wasn't thinking." The pale light from above illuminates his face, and I can see the remorse in his eyes. "You're fine now. I promise, you're fine."

I burst into tears, and he drags me into his embrace.

I want to go home. I want my friends and the ridiculous townhouse that stifles me. I want to feel safe. I was stupid to want anything more; to experience anything else. Kruz's arms embrace me as I sway, heave, and weep until his shirt is soaked through.

CHAPTER EIGHT

My back hits the stone pavement, and I grunt out in pain. Gálgalesh stands over me and yawns, as if he could think of nothing duller to do with his time. I look up at the black sky of Romiodóg for the thirtieth time this morning. I am getting tired of the view, of the pain vibrating down my spine. I lift myself onto my elbows and give my body an assessment, making sure I have not broken any bones this time.

"You're still too loud. I could hear you coming from a mile away," Gálgalesh says, as though I am failing at the most basic task in existence. He has brought several vials of his potions with him again this morning, just in case I nearly kill myself again.

"It is these boots! No one can be quiet in these boots!" I pull myself to my feet and watch as Gálgalesh rolls his light eyes.

"If that's true, I could not best you every time; yet I always do. Does that mean you are deaf, woman, and not simply terrible at stealth maneuvers that might save your life? It is not the boots. Besides, it would be ridiculous to learn without them, since you won't be barefoot to face your enemies."

"Maybe I will!" Defiance washes over me, though I know he's right; he always is. "I'm tired of working on stealth—we have been at this for a month. Can't we try something with daggers or swords? I don't know how to fight yet."

"And you never will if you cannot get close enough to stab anyone. We continue with stealth until you get it right. Perhaps you should be practicing in the evenings instead of spending your time with Lanzo and his Iranndair bunch." There is hatred in his words, akin to what I had heard the night I first met him. Faeries are faithless creatures with arrogant personalities and easily offendable spirits. I am not sure what the Iranndairians have done to warrant his distaste, but I am not surprised by it either. One would be lucky to *not* offend a faerie. "Get some water, and then we will try again."

I bat the air in front of me and walk toward the far corner of the courtyard, where my discarded cloak and canteen lay. It has been four weeks since I arrived at Báscogar, and though Gálgalesh often reminds me I have little to show for it, I have gained muscle and strength through our training sessions, which makes them more bearable by the day. My hair has grown slightly longer, still the same crimson hue, and I have fallen into step at the camp, making friends with the lesser criminals who have extended me protection against the fiercest. I have yet to have another encounter as I did my first full day at the prison, mostly because of my adamant avoidance of crowds and dark corridors, and for that, I am exceedingly thankful.

"Any news from Golorgleann?" The water from my canteen is pleasantly cool against my parched throat, and I sink to the ground as I drink it down.

"Your boyfriend, Tiernan, feallwr, is fine, if that is what you are asking."

"He's not my boyfriend. He's just a friend."

"Is that why he sends a raven twice a week to make sure you are not yet dead? Some friend." I ignore him, and he smirks viciously. "There are rumblings of rising power from the Steel Citadel, but nothing I have yet confirmed and nothing that surprises us. It was only a matter of time once the Leader was gone that the revolutionaries would make their move to the throne."

I take in his words as I slink down against a pillar.

"You call Tiernan a traitor for joining the Royal Court. You seemed to hate him for it, but you speak of my father as though you would have followed him to battle yourself. It seems like so many would have."

Gálgalesh's jaw clenches tightly, and his head whips toward me. Angry color overtakes the features of his face, and I sit up straighter in alarm. "Your father was a spineless fool, a ruthless conqueror who deserved no loyalty from anyone."

"You call him 'Leader'—" I begin, but he cuts me off.

"You know nothing of it, girl." He is furious beyond reason, and though I am aware of the distrust between faeries and the Crown, this is a wound that penetrates deeper than fights between human authority and creatures. "Get up! You've had your water. We start again!"

His words are as sharp as daggers, and I hurry to my feet. We continue for another hour as Gálgalesh bests me again and again. By the end of the session, I am sweaty, my clothes clinging to my skin. Gálgalesh walks to my side casually, as though he has not spent the last three hours throwing me to the ground and beating me black and blue. He looks me over and nods his head. I reach out my hand, expecting him to deposit a vial of healing potion into my palm as he has done after each of our lessons. Instead, he takes the nail of his finger and traces it painfully against my skin. I pull away quickly and glare up at him, my brows pulling together tightly.

"Stop that!" I demand as I rub my palm with my thumb.

"You are fine. Nothing is broken, which is an improvement, so you do not need the potion." His eyes are transfixed on me as I watch his mind whirl and spin. "What magic have you mastered?"

What a stupid question from an all-knowing faerie. He knows I have been drained of my magic. Does he bring it up to taunt me? I stand, annoyed, ready to be rid of him for the day. "You know I don't have my magic anymore. Besides, no one—except you—can wield inside Báscogar."

Annoyance plays across his own face. "Common magic, woman. What common magic did you master before you came to Báscogar?"

"I've never known any common magic. My lessons never included any teachings on common magic because they deemed it unnecessary within the castle walls."

"No common magic at all?" I shake my head, and Gálgalesh's face pales in a way I have never seen, his eyes glistening with something like disbelief, or perhaps even concern. He swears in the forbidden language under his breath. "We will train outside the gates every other day, beginning tomorrow."

"Outside the gates," I repeat to myself quietly and then look back into his uneasy frown. "I don't have magic, Gálgalesh. What is the point of trying to train something I cannot wield?"

"Some magic does not depend on the wielder's individual gift. Meet me tomorrow at five at the west facing entrance."

Without another word, he turns and stalks away, leaving me in the courtyard alone. I stand, muttering to myself, and an icy breeze blows by, causing my sweat drenched body to shiver. Common magic. I had once asked my father to allow me to train in common magic when my brother had bragged about enchanting his pens to write his essays for him and spending the afternoon by the pond, but my father had denied my request. He had not seen the value it would bring to be able to sew or enchant a sink of dirty dishes to wash themselves. He saw common magic as only useful for the poor and the royals who were meant to lead. I was neither, and my individual magic did not depend on the type of training and wielding others did. I could not channel it or transfer it to anything or anyone on command, so I had given up the fight and forgotten about my desire to wield by the time I reached double digits.

I exhale roughly as my teeth chatter, and I collect my things before I leave to find Kruz in the dining hall. I wander through the now-familiar corridors that lie empty as the first risers for breakfast and morning duties have already made their way to their places. I hope there will be something remaining to eat this morning. I had arrived later than expected yesterday and had to make do with a single stale heel of bread.

I turn the corner of an arched passageway leading past the large outdoor training yard, and when I do, I come face to face with none other than Eoghan Kael. Since my first morning at Báscogar, I had heeded everyone's warnings and was fortunate enough to avoid our paths crossing again. Now, he stands over me, his skin damp from an early morning sparring session, his shirt thrown carelessly over his shoulder, exposing his broad chest and impossibly tan skin. There are one or two red, fist-shaped marks upon his torso, but he seems strong and triumphant all the same. I meet his green and gold eyes that pierce into me with such fierce disdain, I fear he might reach out and snap my neck right here in this hall. He is as dangerous as they come and the rational part of my brain begs me to run in the other direction—but something stirs in my lower abdomen as I struggle to unglue my gaze from his unholy, beautiful face.

"You're in my way." His voice is low and smooth, like the purring sound a dragon makes just before it calls upon fire to torch its enemies. I step aside quickly, and he pushes past me without a second glance.

I watch him leave as a shiver runs down my spine, and I don't move until he is out of sight once again. When I finally reach the dining hall, Kruz is waiting for me with a tray in his hand. I collect my own, and we fall into line to collect our meal, the image of those fierce green eyes consuming me still.

———

FINDING I am terrible at all domestic laundering and cleaning, I am reassigned to the inventory building to stock the shelves with supplies and note what we might need to get us through the upcoming winter months. Romiodóg is formidable in every season as a permanent darkness and snow cover batter the lands, but it is said winter is the harshest. With no chance of leaving the summit for at least the harshest months, I am ordered to compile a list of everything we need to restock, then double the quantities needed. It is boring work, and I am accompanied by Boyle Martin, an infamous slayer of nobility from Gálamáistir, who seems to not know how to count. At least I no longer have to smell the toilets in the guards' quarters.

"Did you ever think that maybe you might use your talents elsewhere?" I ask casually as he hands me cans of beans, one at a time.

"What do you mean?" Boyle rubs his chin, and his lips

curl back into his mouth, filling the gummy holes of missing teeth.

"You must have been good at killing, but maybe you could have been a butcher instead, used your talents for the benefit of others. People? Really, Boyle? Did it have to be people?" I keep my eyes on the cans as I tally up each one, and he shrugs his shoulders nonchalantly.

"I was the man slayer, not the cattle slayer."

I sigh exasperatedly. "It is like I said yesterday, Boyle. You do not have to live up to the expectations of others. What does it matter what they call you? Why not try something new?"

"They call me man slayer because I slay noblemen in their beds, and then I sell their toes as good luck charms."

I roll my eyes and fight down the sick rising in my stomach. "You've told me that already, but you never thought perhaps it would be nice to sell a roast every now and then? Perhaps a lucky rabbit's foot instead of a human toe?"

"A human roast?" Boyle drops a can into my hand, and I shake my head.

"Forget I asked."

———

"You've gone quiet again." Kruz kicks my foot from his position on the floor. I lean over the side of his bed and kick him lightly back.

"Sorry, I found this book in the library, and it is the most normal thing I've read since I have been here." I lift the faded, leather-bound tome with yellow pages. It is an old fairytale that somehow found its way into the prison decades ago.

"Good. Read that instead of asking everyone how they ended up here. I'm not sure how you sleep at night after some of the stories they tell you."

"Everyone has a story, Kruz." I smirk as my eyes trace the pages again. "I just think perhaps someone should know them before the men here are forgotten in the walls of this place."

It's a half truth. My main interest lies in determining the number of prisoners who were sent here unjustly by my father and his men and the number of prisoners who have actually committed terrible crimes. It seems to me to be about a fifty-fifty split.

"Everyone but you," Kruz prods, and I stifle a groan. Not this again. Since we met, Kruz has been trying his best to get my life's story out of me, and since the truth is not something I can tell, I have avoided telling him much at all, for fear of spinning a web of lies I might not remember.

"I've told you before. My story isn't interesting."

Kruz pulls himself to sit, his brown eyes weary from the repetition of the scene playing out before us once again. He searches me as if he can find the right button to press, I might open for him. He has no idea that I am as secretive as the night blooming jasmine in the caves of Brón. I could never open for him, no matter how hard he tries. To do so would be to trust him enough to risk him seeing me in the light of day. That is not a trust I can give anyone anymore, so I remain in the darkness that promises only survival and revenge.

"You were a slave for the king in the castle. That in itself is interesting." He pokes me lightly in the side, and I turn another page, hoping my silence will change the subject. "Where did you come from? Where did you call home before becoming a slave?" He is undeterred.

"Where all slaves on the continent come from: Trader's Bay." It is a safe answer, one he would have already guessed. All slaves in Draío come from Trader's Bay.

"And how did you get to our *wonderful* continent of Thoirmór and the kingdom of Draíocoinnigh?"

He is being specific and deliberate with his questions, and his voice is beginning to irritate me.

"Boat, of course."

"How old were you?"

"Seventeen."

"Before someone siphoned it, what was your magic?"

"They siphoned my magic as a child when I was sold into slavery. I hadn't developed my magic enough to name it before it was gone." His questions grate me, but I have prepared for them. I have prepared my answers, memorizing and polishing them as though they are only dull details of a life I once lived. I know my relentless curiosity has led me to probe him about his own existence, surpassing the number of questions he has ever been allowed to pose to me, but I can't give him more. The web of lies is big enough with these few answers as it is, and any more might catch me up. I would rather stay nameless and silent than tangle myself up so much that I forget my own very real life. I turn toward him, pasting a casually playful annoyance across my face to ease the tension. "Are you done yet, oh brilliant detective? As I told you, it is not interesting. Just an enslaved girl who fled and was sent here for desertion."

"I would have deserted too, if the king and his wretched family had held me captive." Kruz's words carry a venom I have not heard from him before, and his expression instantly turns cold and distant, and I pause at the scorn in his words.

"They were not all so bad. I enjoyed my time in the castle..."

"They are a disgusting bunch with no regard for anyone but themselves. I applaud the ones who ended them. They did Draío a service when they sliced their throats. I might have done more than that, given the chance."

"You didn't know them," I whisper. Where did this come from? I can understand Kruz's feelings toward my father, perhaps grandfathers, who had set the rules to trap him here, but hatred for the entire family? That seems unreasonable to me. My mouth feels as dry as the desert now, and I can feel the coarse texture of my tongue against the roof of my mouth.

"I don't have to know them. I have been here for twenty years because of them." Spit flies through the air with Kruz's words. "I will never see my family again because of that *king*, so why shouldn't he and his entire family pay like mine has? You were sold into his home and kept captive there for their pleasure. I don't need to know them to know they were all monsters."

"I didn't mean—" Panic rises within me, and the words 'Iy Donn, d'anam' ring in my ears, along with the slashing of blade against flesh. My hands shake as I recall the roaring of the crowd as the thick, warm blood pooled around me on that wooden platform. Kruz lunges forward and grabs my shoulders, and I stifle a scream of surprise and fear.

"I am glad you fled, Alana. Glad you got the hell out of that castle. We're free now, you and I—free from them at least. That's enough for now. That, and the satisfaction of revenge. I'm sure you feel it too."

My body shakes violently, and Kruz looks down at his hands gripping me so firmly, pain shoots through my arms. My muscles are tight as stone, and he chuckles sheepishly before releasing me. He sits back on his boots and drops his hands into his lap.

"I'm sorry. I didn't mean to get so excited."

I nod, and my eyes glaze over. Slowly, I rise from the bed and pick up the book I had borrowed from the library. "I need to go," I say and walk toward the door. Kruz mumbles another apology, but I am already in the corridor before he finishes his words. I walk unseeing to the far end of the hall, push open the washroom door, and vomit on the floor.

————

IT'S LATE, too late to still be awake. I need to meet Gálgalesh in a few scant hours for our training session, but I just cannot seem to stop these damn tears from rolling down my cheeks. I sob into my pillow as the memories of my family play through my mind again and again. They are indiscriminate moments from past birthdays, dinners, times of quiet we shared, but they make everything hurt. Had my father been the cruel king Kruz had described? I could not say. To me, he was stern but fair almost always. Had my brother deserved to die on his first trip back home in ages? Did my mother? Did Rian? All of them had been there for me. Perhaps I was the reason why they were dead, and this… Well, this was my punishment for it.

My sobs take over, and I gasp and hiccup for breath as the tears coat my face. I feel homesick and helpless, and I want nothing more than to run back to Golorgleann. Back to Tiernan and Dedra. Back to being me, even if it winds up killing me. I'd welcome the sting of death without complaint. I roll over on my side and slide my feet over the edge of my bed. A door creaks in the hall, and my eyes shoot toward my own in the darkness. Two light footsteps against the stone draw near. I pull my lips together and inhale, trying to stifle my tears. There is silence on the other side of the door— someone stands listening. I tremble as I hold in waves of emotion, but with all I have, I do hold them in. Someone has heard my stupid cries and is probably trying to decide if I am worth shutting up. We both stay quiet for a long while, and then the steps recede, and I hear a door close softly.

I lay back down onto the bed and bury my face in the pillow until I fall asleep.

———

I AM STANDING in the snow, hidden within a grove of trees, my eyes pulled shut in concentration. Gálgalesh stands behind me with his hands clasped around my wrists, moving my arms in tight figure eight formations as I murmur a string of nonsense words he has taught me under my breath. I reach toward the void in my mind's eye as instructed, searching for a thread of power I can pull toward myself and tie around me like an anchoring rope. All I see is darkness. Stupid, unending, useless darkness. I squeeze my face into a tight ball, and I feel my arms tug forward against Gálgalesh's hold. Perhaps if I can stretch into the empty space just inches more, I might see a glimmer of something…

I lose my balance and tumble forward, but Gálgalesh keeps his footing while my arms are violently yanked back behind me, causing me to cry out as I feel the tendons tear in my shoulders.

"You aren't actually supposed to move as you search for the magic." Gálgalesh releases me, and I fall face-first into the snow. I sputter and spit as I roll over onto my back.

"I'm reaching toward nothing. I didn't learn common magic; I lost my own magic. I don't think I will ever be able to wield again. It's hopeless."

"Has anyone ever told you whining is a useless waste of breath? You sound like a child, and you are not a child. You are a woman who is wise enough to know how foolish you sound as you play yourself off to be a feeble victim. You make me appear foolish by training you, and I refuse to be made a fool. So answer me this before I change my mind: are you weak, woman? Would I waste my time training someone who is weak and hopeless?"

"No." I raise my chin, and he throws a vial of healing potion toward me.

"That is what I thought." He eyes me again, this time with a hint of satisfaction on his face. "Common magic is practically useless anyway. Be glad there was nothing to greet you in the darkness. Now stand again. I'm going to teach you the magic of the faeries."

CHAPTER NINE

The dark forest lends no hint of life as we stand together in the grove of trees. My wrists are bound with a rough piece of rope in front of me, then around my waist so I cannot raise my arms. Gálgalesh stands before me, concentration set upon his face as his eyes look beyond me into the invisible realm of magic. He does not mutter under his breath like Tiernan had as he enchants the forest around us, but after a few moments, his milky stare becomes focused, and I sense his presence strengthening around me.

"Now that there is no risk of being overheard, let's begin. Faerie magic," he begins in his usual gruff tone, "is the most ancient wielded magic found anywhere in the kingdom or continent. Only that of dragons is as ancient and coveted. It does not wield weakly like your human magic and, therefore, it is not bound to suppressing enchantments or crippled by siphoning. This magic can flatten the Earth with a nod of one's head, but the wielder must control it, because it comes at a significant cost." He takes me in as though assessing my aptitude to follow. "You must weigh each wielding against the price of your own life. Do you understand?"

My mind aches. I have no knowledge of magic wielding. Nobody ever taught me about the powers or intricacies of human magic, and faerie magic seems to be a much more complicated beast. I am not certain I understand anything at all anymore. "No," I sigh and drop my gaze to the snow at my feet.

"You do not understand?" The sage tone of an instructor coats Gálgalesh's voice. "Then ask and receive answers. You might be a fool, but you do not have to remain so."

"Faerie magic can be bestowed rather than simply passed down; how is that so? How can you teach me the magic of the faeries when I cannot lift a twig with common magic? How is faerie magic so powerful, yet Faebond can harm it? Why is wielding faerie magic tied to my life, and why would I wield it if it is?"

Gálgalesh approaches me and frees one of my hands from the binds. He takes me by the wrist, his sharp nails biting against my skin. With his free hand, he unsheathes a dagger at his side then pulls me toward a round stone within the center of the clearing. He brings the dagger to my palm, and I try to pull my hand away, but his grip is unrelenting. I feel the blade cut into my flesh, searing and quick, making a two-inch gash oozing with blood. He works my fingers back and forth, coaxing the warm red liquid to the surface. The blood rolls from my hand onto the stone. Gálgalesh takes a cloth bandage from his cloak pocket and wraps it around the laceration, then binds my wrist once more.

"Faeries pass down faerie magic from generation to generation, just like common magic. It can also be given—at a price—to others who make a blood covenant with a faerie to share their magic with them." He takes the dagger and wipes it clean before he runs it across his own palm. Blood runs from his hand in a golden stream, falling onto the stone. "It is not dependent on one's ability to wield any magic at all.

If a faerie so chose, they could enter into a blood covenant with a squirrel, and that squirrel could then possess their magic; though that would be ridiculous and a waste of time to do so. Faerie magic is the most ancient and powerful magic you will find, but Faebond is as old as faerie magic itself, coming from what we faeries call the poison trees of the faerie kingdom, Dún. Man possesses Faebond because they stole it during the conquest of the continent. Finally, the wielder's life is tied to faerie magic through the bond of blood. If the magic is used to harm innocent lives, the magic will turn on the wielder and take their life as payment. If you do not wish to wield it, that is your decision, but without any magic of your own, you should ask for me to end you here before someone else does. You will not last one day."

He takes a small pouch from his pocket and empties the contents upon the stone. The expression in his eyes is for once patient and more fatherly than annoyed or arrogant, as it so regularly is when speaking to me. "Any more questions, woman?"

I doubt he has time for all the questions racing through my mind. I choose my words carefully, hoping his calm doesn't wear thin too quickly. "Has any faerie ever entered into a blood covenant with a human?" I meet his gaze, and something becomes pained, as though a memory plagues him the moment I speak the question.

"I have once before. I do not begin to know what the others have done."

"And what came of it?" I watch as the stone begins to glow blue in the darkness.

"The wielder died, but not of his own stupidity. Let's hope in the end, you can say the same."

Gálgalesh places his hand on my shoulder and pulls me down to crouch by the stone. He places his hand against the surface and urges me to follow suit. My fingers meet the smooth rock, icy from the late autumn air. Without warning, as our hands meet the stone, there is a surge like lightning through my veins. My hand is glued to the surface, unable to pull free as the current races from my fingertips to my toes and the top of my head, filling me completely with its luxurious warmth and raging power. I hold true as I feel the connection pass through me to Gálgalesh, then back into the stone. It quakes under our hands, and then a still calm replaces the sensation. Gálgalesh stands slowly, and I follow suit.

"Your blood." Gálgalesh examines me curiously as though seeing me for the first time. "I sense it even now." A slow smile exposes his triangular teeth, and his eyes shine sinisterly in the fading blue light of the stone. "Perhaps I was wrong about you after all. Donn should begin to prepare room for all the lives you will send him."

We continue to train, walking through an introduction to faerie magic for the whole of the morning, skipping breakfast and instead eating stale bread from a pack Gálgalesh brought with us into the wood. It is humbling to watch as he effortlessly moves objects at will and downs trees without so much as bending his pinkie. By the time we finish for the day, I feel no more powerful than I had when we arrived that morning, though I can sense the phantom current still singing to my very bones.

"It'll take time, but you will find the thread eventually. We will keep searching until you do," Gálgalesh encourages as he passes me a canteen. I press it to my lips eagerly. "I am disappointed but not surprised your father kept magic from you with the exception of the magic that was advantageous for you to possess. You were no contest to him without power, though I am sure he saw your potential if you could wield."

"Do you think he kept it from me on purpose?" With a reproachful glare from Gálgalesh, I continue, "He did not keep wielding from my brother—and he would have been much more powerful than I ever could have imagined."

"There is a reason they sent your brother out with the enlisted men."

"All the men in the royal line must serve," I snap back, as if fighting for an honor that has lost all value.

"And why is that? Do you have no idea?" I remain silent, and he sighs. "They taught you nothing of use in that castle; you're as stupid as a field mouse. Enlisted men have their magic marked with a tracking enchantment for the rest of their lives. It is to keep any one of them from forming an army to overtake the crown once they know the intricacies of the royal guards and keeps. The men in the royal line are sent to service so they will be kept under thumb and will not try to usurp their fathers or brothers for the throne. Your brother knew this as well as I. *He* was not a fool to the truth."

Memories flood my mind of my brother and my father arguing the night before Cai was sent to the military academy in Gálamáistir. Once he left, his letters were filled with vague remarks of feeling powerless, even though he possessed the strongest magic the battlefield had seen in a century. My mind races to Tiernan, who had hesitated to conjure up a tent for the night in the Borderlands before doing so in such a hurry that the result was hardly shelter at all.

"And faerie magic?" I ask slowly.

"As I said before, it answers to no one—especially not human enchantments."

"That is why it is illegal on the battlefield and in service. They cannot control it, so they do not allow it at all."

"Maybe you are not so foolish after all." Gálgalesh gives me an approving wink as he turns and walks back toward Báscogar.

———

SINCE I HAVE BEEN EXCUSED from my duties for the day, I choose to spend the afternoon exploring the prison. I have been to the library and to the secret hideaway in the belly of the fortress, but besides these few trips into the leisure wings of Báscogar, I have rarely ventured outside the comforts of my room or my duty stations. I walk until I reach the fork in the corridor to the training grounds, and I hear the faint grunts of men just beyond the curve in the passageway. I steal around the corner and through the arched path. It opens to a circular arena with sloping stadium seating of stone on every side. I've never been to the training arena before, and my mouth falls open at the sight of it. At the center, there are around a dozen men sparring in pairs of two. I slide quietly into the stone bench nearest me and take a seat as I scan the faces for anyone familiar. I see none of the men I had become acquainted with. All the men on the floor are large and muscular, and they fight with the type of ferocity that makes me cringe with each punch. These are the brutal fighters and killers who had made this prison legend.

My eyes move from one match to the next, taking in the quiet, lethal ways in which each fighter moves. I watch as one pins his opponent down with his knee against the other's neck. He does not relent as the pinned man thrashes and writhes underneath him. He could easily let the man die there, and I sense that he very well might; but then there is a whistles, and Peadair walks calmly onto the floor, pushing the top man aside without touching him. Faerie magic, like the kind that now courses through my own veins.

I continue to scan the arena as I watch each pair fight to the brink of unconsciousness or death…and then, I see him. Eoghan Kael engages in a match with a man about his size. Both have sun bleached highlights in their hair: Tinemallacht

Fire Cursed. He punches and ducks, easily nailing his opponent and evading the counter blow. One-two, one-two. He hits and dives, swipes and catches his opponent until the other man is on the floor, gasping for air. He rises above the other man with terrifying ease and unsheathes a dagger at his side I had not noticed until now. I count at his waist and down the leg of his pants. He wears about a dozen daggers just where I can see. Peadair lets them spar with weapons? Isn't that dangerous? Are they allowed or even encouraged to kill in the arena? Kael reaches his opponent and slices against the other man's breast—not a fatal wound, but a mark of his victory. The other man taps the stone beneath him and they both retreat, laughing between winded breaths.

I am mesmerized by him. I have never seen anyone move as he does. He is effortlessly sure-footed, his own flesh pristine and unblemished as he dabs the sweat away from his brow with a towel. I feel myself lean forward as I watch him being drawn to him though every inch of me trembles. Fear? Or something else entirely?

"Alana!"

I jump as I hear my pseudonym echo across the stone arena. All heads turn and find me where I sit. Eoghan Kael's eyes darken with loathing as soon as they meet me in the stands. He grabs for his discarded clothes and canteen before storming out of the training arena and down the corridor. Everyone watches as he leaves. Why does he look at me like that, as though he can think of nothing worse than to be in my presence? Kruz falls down onto the seat beside me as I watch the spot where Eoghan Kael had disappeared for a moment longer before resolving that he would not be returning.

"I didn't see you in the dining hall today. You aren't mad at me, are you?" I avoid his gaze and stare out into the training session that quickly resumes as the novelty of my presence wears thin.

"Gálgalesh had me training until the afternoon." It wasn't a lie, though I had wanted to avoid Kruz since his outburst the night before.

"Oh." He drops his eyes to his hands as he wrings them together in his lap. "Well, either way, I'm sorry about what I said. I know you feel a certain way toward your…owners. I had no right to say what I said. I just—"

"It's fine, really," I cut him off and stand, making my way back toward the Báscogar interior as quickly as I can slide through the amphitheater seating. "I have to go now. I'll catch up with you later." I wave casually and disappear before he can follow me out.

I fly through the halls toward the Warden's quarters and halt as I reach the heavy wooden door. It creaks open when I lift my hand to knock, revealing a dark space bathed in low candlelight. There is a small sitting area with a faded green sofa and a desk in the far corner. Further beyond must be a room and a bathing chamber. Gálgalesh sits at the desk with his back to me, bent over a piece of parchment.

"Go away, woman. I am bored of you today," he says without turning to look at me.

"How did you know it was me?" I take a step over the threshold into the room, despite his dismissal.

"My magic flows through you. I can sense it when it is near, of course. Besides, you breathe much too quickly and shallowly, unlike the others here. It is as though no one taught you that your belly should expand and contract as you do. Now, what do you want before I hang you in the cellar by your toes?"

I snicker to myself and shake my head. I am becoming fond of Gálgalesh, despite his surly demeanor and his once-frightening appearance. His threats seemed less terrifying than they had when I first met him, and he seems much more like a grumpy old grandfather than a dangerous creature of death. Still, I know he would not hesitate to torture me, just to remind me of how dangerous he actually is. I take another step into the room, and he turns slowly in his seat to stare me down, one eyebrow raised in question.

"I want to train with the others," I blurt out, stumbling over my words. "And I want to be sent on patrol to Fáintìrean."

Gálgalesh snorts in amusement and rolls his eyes. "They would kill you the moment you set foot in the arena. We have not *trained*; we began working on stealth and you could not master it. Why on earth would you think you would be ready to train with the others?"

"I will never be ready at the rate we are going! Let me at least try!"

"Stop whining," he admonishes. "No, not until you learn something, *anything,* so I will not have to scrape your remains from the stone and tell your dear boyfriend of your demise." He lifts the parchment from the desk and shakes it once. "And as for Fáintìrean—'Fane-terrain' is more dangerous than the training yard for someone like you. Do not be ridiculous. You have unharnessed faerie magic coursing through your veins, and now you feel invincible? Faeries are not immortal. We simply take longer to die than you humans."

"If I show improvement, will you let me train with the others?" I cross my arms in front of my chest, grounding myself stubbornly into place.

"Real improvement, not simply breaking fewer bones as you fall onto the stone."

"Yes, real improvement," I agree. "If I can learn to take on the others here, the people who killed my family would not stand a chance."

Gálgalesh contemplates my bargain for a moment. He taps his long fingers on his chin as he thinks, his lip pursing into a thin line. "Fine. If I see improvement, I will find someone who might not kill you, and you can train with them. A thief or one of the cooks, perhaps."

I nod my head. "And Fáintìrean?"

"Goodbye, woman. Go bother someone else."

Gálgalesh turns from me and continues with his work at the desk. I feel an invisible hand pushing me backward into the corridor, and the door slams shut as I cross the threshold.

CHAPTER TEN

I am walking through the halls of Caisleán Rialú, a long silk dress of midnight blue and gold flowing behind me in my wake. The halls are empty and quiet as the sound of my footsteps echo across the space. The gilded castle shines in the sunlight of a Golorgleann morning, and I bask in the warmth that wraps around me, pulling me into its embrace. I carry on down the corridor, sure of my destination. I pass two guards, and they bow their heads low in respect as I push forward into the expansive throne room covered in floor-to-ceiling windows and colorful murals.

There, I find Tiernan and Dedra waiting for me. They wear matching finery with the crest of the House Moran on their chests. There is a sword strapped to Tiernan's side, though it seems to be too fine for practicality and rather, is a ceremonial addition to his attire. Dedra's dress is a silky chiffon that falls low between her breasts and down her back before flowing freely to the floor.

They bow to me as I approach the throne, and then they part to clear the way. I smile and take a step forward to ascend the small dais that holds the sovereign power with its towering back and ornate arms carved to resemble every creature conquered in the conquest of the continent. Faeries, dragons, kelpies, banshees, merrow, and even human wielders, hold a blank stare of lifelessness and defeat. I turn to sit on its golden seat and run my hands gleefully over the cool surface. It is my throne, and it feels delightful as I perch atop it. Dedra approaches with two guards as she carries the crown of King Fergal in her hands. Its sapphires and diamonds radiate color in the light like a magnificent display of fireworks. She lifts it high between us and sets it down upon my head. Slowly, she backs away, and the two guards raise a heavy mirror toward me as I take myself in.

My now-crimson hair is long and pulled back into loose curls that frame the crown on my head and cascade down my back. My face is flush with health and color, and I seem older perhaps, but not in age so much as experience. Tiernan approaches, and I extend my hand to him as I remain transfixed upon my visage, and he presses his lips to my fingers in deep devotion. Dedra and Tiernan take their seats beside me, and the mirror is removed. I settle down into my throne, my hands crossing in my lap.

"Bring them in," I command, and the doors fly open. Two men are dragged across the floor by their arms, cloth sacks over their heads. They are thrown against the marble and sink down to their knees, their hands bound behind them. "You are aware of what must be done?" I ask, no sympathy in my voice. "For your treason?" The men make no move to stand or to fight. I look at Tiernan and Dedra, their gazes icy and calm. "Very well," I say, almost bored. "Iy Donn, d'anam." For Donn, your soul. The last words spoken before the execution of my family and Rian.

I nod to the guards, and they grab the men by the arms, dragging them back toward the exit.

"Queen of death!" The voice is Gálgalesh's from beneath one of the cloth sacks. My eyes snap toward the center of the room and land on the captives as my brows pull together.

"Stop," I command to the guards, and they freeze halfway across the room. A smile quirks the corners of my mouth. This time, the

pleasure will be mine. I feel the surge of magic rise from within me as I stand from my throne and cross the room.

I wake with a jolt, panting and dripping with sweat despite the arctic chill of the room. I look around in the darkness as I take in my surroundings. I am still in Báscogar, and the eternal darkness of night brings me back to the bleak reality of this place. No throne room, no sunshine, no crown, nothing of what I was about to do before I woke up. I sigh and lean back against my pillow, willing my heart to stop racing in my chest. I turn over and stare at the wall, and soon, I fall back into a dreamless sleep.

CHAPTER ELEVEN

"It's been a week." I lean against the trunk of a weeping tree, and dewdrops fall from the surrounding branches. "And I have only been able to stack stones on top of each other."

Gálgalesh shrugs as he examines the pile of rocks I have managed to heap on top of one another. "It is a start. Not even faerie magic develops quickly, and you have taken to it faster than I expected. You were also able to catch me twice yesterday, which is an improvement to your stealth training."

"Not to mention, once while you were taking a—"

"Nevertheless, as I said, you are improving." I lift my eyes to him, and he gives me a look that reminds me of my tutor from the castle, Seán, who had always encouraged me despite my difficulties with reading. I have always been quick to disappoint myself, feeling as though I am incapable of the simplest tasks. "Would you like to add sparring to your training tomorrow?" I nod, and he sighs as he relents. "I suppose I do not see the harm in it; although, I still stand by what I said on your first day here. Sparring will do you no good. Assassination will be your only advantage against the cowards who now hold the Capital. Nevertheless, I do not wish to see you caught unprepared any time in the future, so I shall teach you what you need to get by."

"Where did you learn to fight?" We reset, and Gálgalesh lays out the stones around the clearing, further apart this time.

"Do not confuse what this is. We are not friends, and we will not speak as such. Concentrate on the magic, woman." He beckons me forward.

He is fooling himself if he believes we are still nothing more than two reluctant participants in a foolish attempt at revenge. We entered into a blood bond, for goodness sake! "An answer for a stone." I cross my arms against my chest. "I stack a stone, you answer a question."

Gálgalesh scowls at me, but I cock my eyebrow in determination, waiting for him to respond. "You truly are the most insufferable human I have ever had the displeasure of meeting." He rolls his eyes as I grin from ear to ear. I could not care less about his insults. "All right, an answer for a stone. Now, move a stone."

I nearly squeal in glee, jumping up and down before Gálgalesh admonishes me sternly. I turn my attention to the stones, concentrating on the inner expanse of my mind, and my gaze becomes unfocused. I search for the humming of the faerie magic that now constantly whispers to me, and I find it somewhere nestled near my fingertips. As if I am lifting my own hand, I beguile the stone nearest me to rise slowly. It feels as though I am controlling a puppet on strings. In my mind's eye, I move my fingers up and down, back and forth, to ease the stone to the left and then even out the movement to the right. I pause at the sound of crackling leaves somewhere behind me, and the stone plummets through the air, only recovering mere inches from the ground. I hear Gálgalesh urge me to bring my focus back to my center. I move the stone further toward the one lying a few yards away as I work to position it to hover over the top and then release. It falls with a hard thud onto the foundation stone. A grin draws wider across my face as I look toward Gálgalesh, and he nods his head in approval.

"Where did you learn to fight?" I ask again.

"In my home kingdom of Dún, the faerie land to the North. I learned as all faeries do, at the age of passage—the year I turned fourteen."

"How old are you now?"

"One answer per stone." He leans back casually with his hands in his pockets, waiting for me to begin again. There is so much ease and control in everything about him, I wonder if he could bring the entire forest under his will without a drop of sweat running down his dark cheek. I roll my shoulders back in resolve and move another stone without losing concentration this time.

"How old are you?" I huff the moment the stone knocks against the other.

Gálgalesh looks genuinely amused. "I am eight hundred and twenty-seven years old."

My mouth falls open, and it is a moment before I catch myself gaping at the faerie teacher in front of me. How can someone bear to live for eight hundred and twenty-seven years? How could anyone survive? I have only made it through twenty, and I feel that might have been enough for me. I turn back to the stones and heave one on top of the pile as quickly as I can, unable to stop the torrent of questions racing through me. A stone for a question. "Is every faerie as old as you are, or are you the grandfather of all faeries?"

Now, his lips pull downward disapprovingly. "That is cruel, woman. I am not even the oldest faerie at Báscogar! Peadair is nine hundred and forty. Although faeries are not immortal, we can live for thousands of years." I make to open my mouth, but he holds up his hand and silences me. "I suppose you were taught nothing of faeries or immortality in that castle of yours. We faeries, though we may live for centuries longer than you humans, are glad not to be immortal, for it is a curse that plagues only those who are foolish enough to seek it out." I had never thought of immortality as anything but a childhood fantasy. In the months since I have left Caisleán Rialú, I have come to learn it is not only obtainable, but a terrible fate I could not even begin to comprehend. "Move another stone."

This time, I barely have to concentrate when I wield the magic. I plop another stone effortlessly on top of the others before turning back to Gálgalesh and allowing my next question to stumble over itself, falling in a hurried mess from my lips. "Do you miss home?"

"Sometimes," he concedes, and I spy a hint of sadness in his expression. How terrible it must be to serve such a long life sentence so far from home. No wonder he talks of death as though it would be a mercy. "Though I have not been on the other side of the summit in nearly three hundred years. I fear I might not recognize it if I ever did return."

"Do you not miss your family?" Gálgalesh gestures toward the stones, and I groan before plucking one up without even turning toward it and placing it on top of the pile.

"The only family I have left is Peadair. The rest died in the war for the continent some five hundred years ago." He swipes his hair off his shoulder lazily, and I wonder if five hundred years would be enough time to stop missing my own family so badly, I weep every time I think about them. "You really are a relentless woman. Move one more stone, and I will teach you a phrase from my people."

I spin on my heels and close my eyes, this time for dramatic effect. The stone feels as light as air, and I bounce it playfully toward the pile before dropping it to balance at the top, right on its end. I open my eyes and look around the clearing. All the stones are stacked more perfect than I managed to do the past week.

"Sihir amaklar abaskli," Gálgalesh whispers into my ear, and I start at the sound. I face him, his eburnean eyes never failing to cause an uneasy chill to rush through me. "Magic masters the willing. Well done, woman. Now, we can begin your real training."

———

GÁLGALESH'S SHOULDER rams into my stomach, forcing the breath from my lungs and toppling me onto the unyielding pavement. He lifts his fist and barrels it toward my face, but I block it with my forearm. I throw my own and catch his jaw, and he pulls back in surprise, giving me enough time to roll free and crouch into a defensive pose. He lunges, and I dive to the side, but he catches my ankle and drags me back. I kick and hit at him, but his grip is much too firm. He pins me with his knee and brings the tip of the wooden practice dagger to my chest.

"Yield," he commands, and I tap the ground beside me. He rolls off me and glides effortlessly to his feet. "It was foolish to yield. Your knee to my groin would have taken me down, and you could have won."

"You told me to yield!" I move gingerly to my knees and massage my neck. There is a tight knot forming on the left side from the number of times we have sparred today.

"Yes, and your enemy will command you to do the same. That does not mean you have to listen." I rise to my feet and find my position once again. "You have improved, though. I am impressed. Have you been practicing with your smuggler friend, Kruz Lanzo?"

"A little," I say with a guarded tone, and Gálgalesh notices the change in my expression.

"Does he not still please you? I thought you liked being fawned over, dear Princess?" I glare at him, and his lips curl in a wicked way, reminding me he is exactly as terrible as legends suggest. "Are you afraid he will never know who you really are?"

"Actually, I am afraid that one day, he *will*," I admit grimly. "And that he might hate me because I cannot control what family I was born into."

"If he sees you only for who you were before, he does not see you." Gálgalesh positions himself in front of me and adopts a predator's stance. "It does not serve you to deprive yourself of allies in this place. It leaves you vulnerable."

"Are you not my ally?" We begin to circle each other, sizing up the weaknesses we might exploit on our next offensive.

"I am the Warden of Báscogar. Though I can advise the others to leave you unharmed, I cannot stand in front of you if they decide to disregard my words. In this place, there are no rules against causing harm to others, and killing is not even prohibited. You need protection I cannot afford to give."

"I can protect myself, thank you very much." I rush forward and catch him behind the knees before he has time to react. I throw all my weight into him as he falls onto his back, and I pull my wooden dagger from my boot. My arm slams into his throat, the faux blade pressed against his jugular vein. "Yield!" I shout, and flecks of spit fly through the air. Gálgalesh appraises me for any advantage he might exploit, but he finds nothing and taps the ground beside him.

When we finish our training, I skip breakfast and head toward the arena for the third time this week. The prisoners from Tinemallacht utilize the training grounds in the morning, and I find myself willing to hide amongst the shadows to watch their sessions. I stand tucked against the stone archway as Eoghan Kael and three other men work through the motions in unison in the center of the arena. With swords in their hands, they move like waves across the sea, crashing down and then rolling their arms back up in a steady stream of progress. Kael must be the leader, since he moves without a bit of hesitation or regard for anyone else's pace. The others follow suit as they go, the weight of the blade never causing their arms to drop. He steps, they step. He inhales, they inhale. He turns, they turn.

I slow my breathing to match their own, and our chests rise and fall in perfect rhythm. I memorize each movement like a secret dance between us, and then I begin to move as well. In the darkness, I follow his steps, again and again, as if entranced. I could have moved with him all day, the world falling away until it was just him and me alone in the arena. Then, I am roused back to my senses by Peadair's whistle.

The four men stop their battle dance and drop their swords at their sides. The metal clangs loudly against the stones beneath their feet. Peadair approaches and speaks to them in low tones I cannot make out. I watch as the men nod in agreement and then break away from one another. They lay their swords against the side of the arena and move back into the center of the space, where they begin exercises led by the Second Warden.

Softly from somewhere in the distant black corridor behind me, I hear the sound of footsteps echoing off the barren wall. I turn and crane my neck, trying to spot the approaching figure in the low light. When no one appears in the darkness, I turn back to the training ground and fall back against the stone archway as Eoghan Kael glares down at me, our bodies mere inches apart.

"What are you doing here?" His voice is a low and dangerous purr.

"I was not told I could not watch a training session." My voice comes out as a trembling whisper.

"You have no reason to watch *this* session—or any training session here. Have you become bored climbing out of bathroom windows? Was that not enough danger for you?"

I nearly stumble back, and I suck in a shaking, gasping breath. He eyes me fiercely from head to toe, and I feel exposed, as though I am up against the stone exterior being lashed by the wind once again. He didn't have to imagine me naked. He must have seen me as I made my escape. "M-m-my clothes… That was you…" He simply folds his arms across his chest, his brows pulled tightly together. "I-I-I train here too." I stumble for words but find all of them are stolen as his gold and green eyes hold me transfixed.

"So you are here to train then?" He reaches forward and catches me behind the elbow, dragging me toward the arena. "Let's train, *Alana*." I press my heels into the stone, but his strength leaves me defenseless, and my boots continue to slide with a loud scrape against the ground. He drags me forward at a brisk pace until we reach the center of the space. The other men and Peadair clear the way, and Eoghan rips my cloak from my shoulders and throws it aside on the ground. "You can spar with me. Show me exactly why someone like *you* is at Báscogar."

I back away but am met by a hard wall of nothing directly behind me. Peadair is using his magic to keep me in the center of the training yard. Had Eoghan known the others would stand by idly to watch, hoping I might be battered or killed for the sake of their own amusement? He begins to circle me, and I move in time, trying to keep away from him. I assess his stance and his movements, but there is no weakness to make use of. He has perfect form and concentration, and his eyes hold me like a wild beast stalking its prey. I keep moving, hoping just to stay out of reach. If he catches me, he'll kill me.

"Always running," he laughs, the sound like a dangerous bark of a wild canine. "Why? Are you scared of us? Are you scared of me?"

I pick up my pace as I feel him close in on me, but my foot catches on an uneven stone, and I stumble sideways. He lunges forward expertly, just in time to pull me down. My head hits the ground, and I groan in pain as I see double. He straddles my body, pinning me underneath his weight. His thighs press into me, the muscles flexing as he leans forward into view. The sight of him brings out every instinct in me to fight, and I throw a punch toward his approaching mass. He dodges my arm and nails me in the side of my face with his fist. I hear the unmistakable crack of fracturing bone, and my jaw instantly swells to double its size. He lands another and another, pain ringing through my teeth as he catches me hard in the mouth.

"Come now—you train, don't you? Fight back. Make me bleed."

I thrash beneath him, trying to find purchase, but he is too fast and too strong. I catch his cheek with just the tip of my finger and cause no damage at all. I want to claw his beautiful eyes out for the mirth dancing through them, and I reach toward him, my fingers curled forward, only to miss him by inches as he leans just out of reach. With an easy swipe, he pins my arms to the ground, and I throw my legs around his waist, thrusting with all I have as I try to topple him. It's no use; he has me right where he wants me.

"You'll have to try harder than that. I'm nearly twice your size." He leans forward, his lips against my ear. "Unless you like the feeling of being pinned beneath me." My heart betrays me as it begins to beat wildly in my chest, my mind racing between the agony and brutality of his fist bearing down on me, heat rising within me as his hips grind against my own. "Oh, you do." His lips move against my skin again. "You are imagining what it would be like if I held you down and fucked you right here in this arena, aren't you?"

He laughs ruthlessly as he brings his gaze back to mine and then frees a hand to punch me again. My vision darkens, blood gushes from my swollen lip, and my senses threaten to leave me. My head rolls to the side, leaving my neck vulnerable, and I draw in a haggard breath—finding it nearly impossible to breathe under his weight.

"You have no idea how easy you make it to kill you." He reaches to his waistband and pulls a silver blade from it. He touches the tip to my chest, directly above my heart. The blade creates a hole in my shirt and punctures my skin, a small trickle of blood beading up around the metal.

"Yield," he whispers. His voice is deadly and dripping with amusement.

"No," I hiss. My jaw is so swollen, I can barely speak.

He presses the blade further into my skin, and I bite back a cry of pain. He can kill me, but I will not yield to him. I cannot give this asshole that satisfaction. His eyes search my face, and his expression becomes frustrated.

"Yield," he says, louder this time.

"Enough." Gálgalesh's voice is an angry calm, and I feel the blade fall from my chest and Eoghan's weight ease from my body.

"Go back to where you came from." Eoghan's voice is a growl between the two of us, his teeth clenched together.

"I have nowhere to go." The words fall heavy from my lips.

"Then show yourself some pity and end it." He stands and stalks away.

Gálgalesh appears above me, and he appraises me without a bit of amusement on his face. "I told you to stay away from

Kael, not to spar with him." He bends down and empties a vial of potion into my mouth. The familiar warmth has me closing my eyes as I swallow it down greedily. "You yield to me, but you do not yield to him."

"You told me not to," I say wryly as the pain subsides.

"You'll be the end of me." He shakes his head and reaches for me. Blood cakes thickly on my skin, but my wounds have begun to heal and disappear. "Stay away from the arena when Peadair is overseeing the Fire Cursed. He has no reason to keep you alive. He won't kill you himself upon my order, but he will not bat an eye if anyone else tries."

"You stood in front of me while Kael tried to kill me. You said you could not do so." I rise to my feet.

"I stood beside you as Kael bested you in a sparring match. There is a difference. Besides, he was asking you to yield; he did not seek to kill you today. I think he just wanted to frighten you." Gálgalesh picks up my cloak with his long fingers. He passes it over to me, and I pull it toward my chest. It feels stifling despite the temperature being so low, I can see my own breath in the air in front of me. "Stay out of trouble, woman. Do not make my sacrifice be in vain," he pleads and nearly pushes me from the training arena into the corridor.

We wander together down the dark, winding passageways toward the food storage, where I will continue my last counts of stock with Boyle Martin. The halls are dreary and lifeless as winter darkens the ever-black skies until they are an inky void, lending no hint of dim, gray light throughout the day at all. It is colder here somehow than it had been when I first arrived more than a month ago, and the firelight of the torches throughout the prison does little besides give the place an ominous orange glow. By now, Golorgleann would be starting to get a brisk chill in the early morning hours, and perhaps frost would accumulate on the windows until the sun melted it away again, nothing like the bitterness of Romiodóg. I wonder how anyone might be able to stand it here for longer than a few months without losing their mind. Down to my very core, every inch of me cries out for the kiss of warmth sunshine brings. My skin, always so lightly brown from my hours hidden away in the gardens, is becoming pale and lifeless, apart from the constant rosy blush in my cheeks and on my nose. I hate this place. The sooner I can master my training, the better. I'm not sure what I will do if I have to be trapped here for years. Maybe that's why these men continue to train, fight, and kill—to keep themselves from losing their minds as they rot away in this dreadful place.

We reach a door along an abandoned corridor, and Gálgalesh bids me farewell. He cracks it open enough that I can see there is a meeting taking place inside around a long wooden table. Warmth of a fire escapes through the opening, and I lean forward to take it in. Some participants have their backs to the entrance, and I cannot place the faces I do see, apart from a casual pass or two in the halls.

"We've heard rumors of a new seat being established," one voice speaks from where I cannot see at the far end of the room.

"What are we to do about it?" a man asks, his voice stoic and low.

"Nothing," snaps another, his back to me. "The Leader did not ask us to take on just anyone. We have always been told *he* would be the one to tell us when to a—"

"They took the Leader's life. Is that not a worthy target for you?" The room erupts into a flurry of shouts and complaints.

"Enough!" the first voice rises again. Gálgalesh closes the door, and the conversation dies down to only incoherent, muffled din.

"I'll see you in the morning. Try to stay out of trouble until then," he says to me as a means of goodbye.

"What is that meeting?" I grab the hand he has rested on the doorknob, and his eyes flash with vexation at the unwelcome touch. "I want to know what is happening back home. I think I have a right to know."

"Do not wield your assumed power around here. You have no right to anything. You are not welcome in this room; do not begin to think of eavesdropping. I can sense the magic you possess, and I will gut you if I find out that you have."

He tugs at my fingers, releasing himself from my grip before slipping into the room and closing the door tightly behind him. I glare at where he stood for a few long moments before turning to leave. He knows more than he has dared to tell me, though why would he trust me with such information? He still believes me to be a foolish princess who knew nothing of the world before coming to this place. He is right about that. I am finding I know less and less each day. Yet, it is clear he had wanted me to hear the conversation taking place in the room, to ask questions; if he had not intended for me to do so, he would have waited for me to leave before opening the door. Why then would he deny me the most uncomplicated answer? *Could it be that it is something he intends for me to learn myself?* My thoughts beckon me dangerously forward, and I turn and race back down the hall.

The thick walls of Báscogar create an impenetrable barrier that hides even the loudest voices, and only muted babbling can be heard through the door. I press my ear to the splintering timber and strain at my hearing. I cannot decipher a single word. I crouch down onto my hands and knees, bringing my concentration to the gap between the door and the floor. A sea of black boots muddles my view, but the voices are clearer down here.

"That wretched man and his son will eradicate this place the moment they get the chance. What of retribution for their crimes?"

"Are you the voice of justice now? A murderer will pass judgment for murder? How thoroughly ironic." Gálgalesh's tone is as harsh and unyielding as it had been the night at the Golden Wulver Pub, the voice of the Warden of Báscogar. "To what end would you wish to kill them? For the thrill of it? To soothe your anger? If we give in to our own anger and hopes of revenge, are we better than them at all? We hold off until we have evidence that hope is not lost, and then, we take action. Not before."

Had my father been aware of a threat to us all and been preparing this group of men to help him oppose it yet failed to act in time? What sign was Gálgalesh waiting for to go after the men who had killed him if he knew who they were and had the forces to do so? Would it not be better to end it now?

"What are you doing?"

I nearly jump clear to the ceiling at the sound of Kruz's voice beside me. I peer over my shoulder at him and then resume my sleuthing at the bottom of the door.

"Shh, I'm trying to listen."

He kneels beside me and tips his ear toward the floor. "To what?"

"There's a meeting taking place in this room, and Gálgalesh would not allow me to join him in attending."

"Gálgalesh is in there? If he would not let you join, I am sure there is good reason. Come on, Alana, let's go." He tugs at my biceps, pulling me halfway to my feet. I jerk away, and his hands fall to his sides. My glare is as sharp as daggers, and I stamp my foot defiantly against the floor. "I'm sorry." He backs away from me. "Let me help. This is a private meeting hall; there must be a service entrance somewhere that might yield a better vantage point for listening or even seeing into the room."

I open my mouth to speak as someone throws the door wide in front of me. The momentarily brilliant glow of the chamber beyond causes me to lift my arms in front of my eyes as a towering figure appears on the threshold, backlit so they appear only as a black mass. The figure bounds forward, slamming the door closed behind it and barreling into me, its hand on my throat. My body collides with the wall, lifting off the ground with my boots dangling beneath me. Gálgalesh's teeth are bared, and he lets out an angry growl that has the hair on my arms standing. His nails dig into the sides of my throat, digging in with such fierceness, I fear he might tear it from my body.

"You never listen!" he snarls, nearly foaming at the mouth with rage. His eyes turn on Kruz. "Leave us!" But Kruz protectively stands his ground.

"Leave!" I croak, silently pleading that I might die without spectators able to watch the life rush from my eyes. Kruz meets my gaze and then backs away slowly. When he has vanished from sight, I stare resolutely into Gálgalesh's wrath. "You. Wanted. Me. To. Know."

"I wanted no such thing! You make excuses for your own meddling because you are a spoiled child who does not know her place. Do you not realize what we risk having you here? Must you put yourself in more danger each day with your stupidity? I thought the training arena would have made you wary of what might happen to you if you do not heed my warnings!" He tightens his hold, and I sag in his grip. "Do you not trust me to train you and give you knowledge when you are ready? Have I not promised to help you against my better judgment, and yet you still find me to be unworthy of your confidence?" He sighs and releases me, his nails coated with my blood as he pulls them free of my neck. "Go, before I decide gutting you is the better option."

CHAPTER TWELVE

I reach the Warden's quarters and lift my hand to knock on the half-open door, but it slams violently shut before I have a chance to lay my freezing fist against the surface. I sigh. Four days have passed since Gálgalesh sent a letter to my room, informing me he had canceled our training sessions until further notice. He has avoided me in the dining halls at each meal, made himself unavailable at every opportunity I have taken to seek him out. He is still furious about my meddling during that secret meeting, and it is all too clear his attempts to shut me out are punishment for my disobedience. Still, with no training, I have become a less-than-average resident in the mountain prison, watching my days pass with little more than chores to do and the occasional sparring session with Kruz and his Iranndairian friends.

I rub my hand softly against the still-tender wounds on my neck and wince at the touch. I am fully aware of my meddling and the validity of his anger. I have no excuse, even if I think I deserve to know what is going on in the Capital. I had not trusted Gálgalesh when he has given me no reason not to. Despite his surly demeanor and denial of our friendship, Gálgalesh trained me, taught me more than I had ever been taught behind the castle walls, and has been more truthful with me than anyone else.

"Gálgalesh!" I shout through the door. "Please speak to me!" His silence is the only response. "Fine," I huff. "If you will not speak to me, I'll just stay out here until you do, or we both starve to death. I can be *very* insufferable, as you have said." I drop down against the wall and kick my feet out into the hall. I could be just as stubborn as him.

The day passes by at a dull and gratingly slow pace. It feels as though I have been suspended in time, minutes ticking away like hours. The corridor is quiet, devoid of life, and no one passes as I lean against the wall, waiting for a response. At lunch time, a handsome man with light brown hair and piercing blue eyes shuffles past me with a plate of gray food. The door swings open for him, leading me to reason it is my only chance to invade Gálgalesh's space and demand his attention. But by the time I jump to my feet, it is sealed shut again. As the man exits the room a few moments later, he passes through the door quickly—blocking my way inside with his body—and turns to me dutifully.

"He says to leave him be."

"I will not. Thank you."

I dig my heels firmly into the floor, and he looks me up and down with hungry eyes before he shakes his head and disappears back the way he came. I lean my head back onto the stone, sinking to a seat, and hum softly to myself an old tune in the forbidden language. The melody is haunting and beautiful, a folklore from centuries past.

"Across the ravine, the wisest are seen selling souls to the faeries of old." I close my eyes as the words fall from my lips. "They beg for their lives, not gold be the price; they are given for the power they hold."

The door creaks open, and Gálgalesh leans against the frame, looking at me with his arms crossed against his chest, curiosity written on his face. "That song. Where did you learn it?"

"When I was eight years old, I was hiding from my brother in the garden during a game of hide and seek." I can feel the sun on my face as the memory comes drifting back to me. "My father appeared alone, pacing among the flowers and mumbling to himself. I crept closer, trying to make out what I could, and I heard him sing the words under his breath. They were so beautiful; I committed them to memory until I learned what they meant."

"Your father?" Gálgalesh's brows furrow, and I nod. "You always have been a meddling little fool, haven't you?" He pushes the door out of the way and turns back toward the room, beckoning me inside.

I enter his quarters, and he motions for me to take a seat on the sofa. I do so obediently and fold my hands upon my lap. "I'm sorry," I breathe into the silence between us. "I should not have tried to pry."

"No, you should not have tried to pry," Gálgalesh repeats from his desk. He looks through a stack of parchment resting on top, pulling something from the middle of the stack. "Your duties in food storage have ended, I am told." He turns to face me once again, his pale eyes as mild as they had been days before during our training, when I had suspected we had finally become allies, before I had ruined everything with my ignorant desire to interfere. "From now on, after breakfast, you will report here and continue your study of faerie magic, beginning with deciphering these writings. As you are versed in the forbidden language, it should not be too hard for you."

I look over the writings. The language is familiar enough but will not be a simple task to complete. Still, he was letting me in more than he ever had. Perhaps he was right. I needed to trust him to train me, to give me knowledge when he deemed it the right time.

"Meet me at five o'clock tomorrow morning for training. For now, take the day and have a little fun." He sits back down at his desk, and the door creaks back and forth, calling me to it.

Fun? In Báscogar? I stand from my seat. What could be fun about Báscogar prison? I walk across the threshold, and the door closes lightly behind me, leaving me alone in the quiet hall. I reach into my pocket and pull out a small metal sphere Gálgalesh had given me at the start of my faerie magic training. It is lighter than the stones he has me move while learning to wield, but it has enough weight to challenge me when practicing on my own. I bounce it in the air with the magic as I walk, never letting it drop to my palm.

Rian would be furious if he knew I had entered a blood bond with a faerie, I think as I wander through the empty passageways of the prison. *He hated faeries—and all other creatures—as much as my father had, had even suggested their extinction on one occasion. What might they think of me now? Training with a faerie, calling him my friend, sharing in his magic?* My heart sinks in my chest. *Would they have hated me too?*

I drop the sphere into my hand and then place it back in my pocket. My mind envelops me in darkness as I think about how I have betrayed everyone I have ever loved, only to bring honor to them in death. Perhaps they would not find it honorable at all. Maybe they would have preferred if I had followed Dedra's suggestion and run away to Oleaíncudd to become a seamstress or even a woman in one of the many brothels the kingdom is known for.

I reach the open corridors that look out over the central courtyard and pass a familiar resident I cannot name, a thief who got caught in Gálamáistir stealing horses from the Royal

Army and selling them back at a steep profit. He smiles up at me and takes me in. He is one of the more handsome prisoners, and although his eyes wander unabashed down my figure, I mind less than I would if he was one of the brutal residents with rotted teeth and sticky hands.

"All right, Alana?" He pauses, and I do the same.

"I suppose." I shrug.

"You seem upset."

"Missing home." A gust of wind whips past us, and I pull my cloak around me.

"Seems like you can use a drink," he offers, and my mind races toward the memory of the last time I had a drink in the belly of prison. I shudder.

"I don't think I will be going back down to the hideaway anytime soon," I say, giving him a weak smile before turning to leave.

"That isn't the only place to have fun in Báscogar." I pause. Fun in Báscogar… "If you know where to look."

He raises his left brow in question. What could it hurt to have a little fun? I nod, and he motions for me to follow him back the way I came.

———

I STAND in the center of a crowd of men cheering and hollering at me, their eyes transfixed. My mind is spinning—curious, as the cold should stave off much of the effects of alcohol on the body. My blood runs warm through my veins. We are in the far courtyard where the praying tree branches out and shields the ground from the falling snow. My cloak, boots, pants, and shirt lay in a pile on the altar at the tree's base, and my skin is bright red from the freezing wind. The gods will surely damn me now, but what do I care? What are further curses to the one already damned to walk this Earth while everyone around her dies? Besides, it has been months since anyone has looked at me the way these men are now. I could order them to do anything in my name, and they would do it. I am the queen—of heathens and murderers and miscreants.

The bottle of liquor in my hand drops slightly, and I shake my head, trying to focus my eyes on my opponent. He has lost his cloak and his shirt but has bested me twice more than I have him. Not surprising—he is twice my size, with lean muscles and a sharp jaw that frames his handsome face, a bruise forming around his right eye where I caught him in the last round. I take a swig from the bottle and then stumble toward a man nearest me, handing it to him. If I do not win this sparring match, I fear what I will be forced to expose; but a wager is a wager, no matter how humiliating.

The man hands his bottle to another, and we line up face-to-face to begin the baiting dance around our makeshift ring. I watch his feet as we circle each other. He's certainly drank more than me, but he still seems stable. His boots grip the stones beneath him, and I swear as my feet slide across the surface. Where? Where is his weakness? My eyes move up his body, taking in every inch of him. His core is engaged, keeping his stance solid, his hands poised in front of his chest to prevent my attack near his face, as he has nearly a foot of height on me... and then I see it. He has nearly a foot on me! The bastard is standing completely upright, leaving his lower body unprotected.

I tease him, drawing him closer by faking a retreat toward the base of the tree. He races forward, hoping to trap me, and that is when I find my opportunity. I crouch low and quickly shove my fist into his groin. He buckles as his breath escapes him and falls to his knees, my own drawing up and making contact, pushing up against his nose. There is blood everywhere—down my leg and the front of his face and chest, as well as on the pavement. He cries out, and I draw the dagger Morgan, the Báscogar guard, had given me a week ago from a strap against my bare thigh. I fist the man's hair and pull his head back to bring my blade to his throat.

"Do you yield?" I ask, my words slurred as I sway dangerously, lightly tapping my blade on the man's neck. He swallows wetly as his own blood chokes him and taps the ground beside him. I let him go and sheath my dagger, nicking my leg in the process.

"Alana, what are you doing?" Kruz pushes through the cheering masses. I bow to my subjects before I retrieve my bottle from the man in the crowd and bring it to my lips. I empty it and throw it back to him before I bound over to Kruz and watch his eyes take me in. The longing on his face is almost pitiful, and I laugh as I throw my arms around his neck. "Why are you–?" he begins, but I plaster my lips against his.

His body stiffens in surprise, but then I feel his lips part, and his tongue begins to search my mouth as his arms wrap around me. We lock into a tight embrace, my hands in his hair as boos fill the air around us, and we pull away, panting only when we are starved for air. A small rumble of a moan escapes Kruz's lips as he looks into my eyes, and I feel heat rising between my thighs. He wants to devour me, and I can't help but become intoxicated by his steely gaze. I haven't felt more willing in months…apart from the day Eoghan Kael pinned me against the ground and I could feel him grind up against me. The heat rises to a fever pitch at the thought, and I shake my head, trying to dispel the image of Eoghan from my mind as I wink up at Kruz.

"This looks like the end, boys," I say to the crowd as Kruz releases me, and I rush over to my clothes on the altar. I tuck my feet into my boots and scoop the rest of my belongings into my arms. Then, I run back to Kruz's outstretched hand, tapping my opponent on the head as I pass. "Thanks for the fun," I say to him, and he raises his hand in acknowledgement.

Kruz entwines my fingers in his own and pulls me out of the corridor, hunger in his eyes and desperation in his step. Why had I kissed him? Had I always wanted to? I did not expect or find it particularly incredible when he responded to my advance, but now, my head is spinning, and I cannot think of anything other than finding out what he might do with me if given the chance.

He pulls me forward until we are in the corridor leading to our rooms. "Mine or yours?" he asks as he eyes roam my much-exposed body.

"Mine," I breathe, and he carries on down the hallway.

We reach the door marked "262", and Kruz grabs me around the waist, pressing me up against the wood. He kisses me greedily, as if he is a starving man being offered a buffet. He pulls me in, and my arms fall drunkenly against his shoulders. His hands glide up and down my hips and back before cupping me from behind so crudely, I laugh against his lips. He remains undeterred, his tongue diving into my mouth. He moans out against my lips, and I wonder if this is the first time he has ever had his arms around a woman. Has he ever gotten this lucky before?

Through the drunken haze of my mind, something whispers uncomfortably, asking me to retreat. *What are you doing? This is Kruz Lanzo!* My mind is more reasonable than I have ever given it credit for. *You don't want Kruz Lanzo! You want—*

Beside me, I feel the uncomfortable sensation of eyes, and a low, almost imperceptible chuckle to my left tells me we are not alone. I open my eyes slowly to see Eoghan Kael leaning against the bit of wall between our two doors, facing Kruz and myself, his arms crossed lightly over his chest, a condescending smirk painted on his face. My hands fall from

Kruz's shoulders, and I dislodge my mouth from his. The room stops spinning as complete awareness of everything around me takes hold.

"If you are going to have your way with her in this state, you could at least have the decency to not do so in the hallway, Lanzo," he purrs in his captivatingly smooth voice. "Though I would expect an upright gentleman like yourself to have some manners and at least wait until she can see straight. She might think she's being bedded by Davies from 194." Kruz's hands fall from me, and he backs away ever so slightly. "I see you haven't gone back to where you came from yet," He turns his gaze to me, taking me in without shame. "Pity." Without another word, he turns from us and heads down the corridor into the shower room.

I hold my gaze in Eoghan's direction long past when he disappears. Kruz clears his throat awkwardly, and I turn my attention quickly back to him, realizing just how exposed I am. I sigh and pick up my clothes from where they have landed on the floor and pull them to my chest.

"I think I better go," Kruz says bashfully, and I nod in agreement. There's disappointment on his face, and I almost feel bad for him, but relief washes over my senses, and I know he can perceive that too. He backs away with one final, sheepish grin and then stalks back toward his room, fading away through the door. I turn and open my own, throwing my clothes onto my bed. What is Eoghan Kael's problem? Why will he not simply leave me alone instead of insisting on being an arrogant asshole?

Anger rages through my now-reeling mind. I dart from the room—still only clad in my boots and underwear—toward the showers. I push the door open furiously and find Eoghan at the sink, his shirt on the counter and a razor in his hand, which he pulls along his jawline. He studies me in the mirror. There is no surprise in his eyes—rather, amusement

—and he lingers on my breasts for a moment before continuing his shave.

"What the hell was that?" My voice sounds shrill to my own ears. Control yourself, he is just a man—a man who makes my knees shake at the sight of his bare chest, but a man all the same.

"I think the words you are looking for are 'thank you'." He taps the blade against the sink and submerges it in water before bringing it to his cheek again.

"Thank you? Why would I thank you?!"

"So what you are saying is, you *wanted* to fuck Kruz Lanzo?" His eyebrow cocks in question.

"No! I mean…I mean, yes… It does not matter whether I wanted to or not. You were out of line when you said what you said!" I feel my blood rising in my face, my cheeks heating dangerously. Eoghan's expression remains calm.

"You knew what you were doing when you put on that show for the entire camp." His voice is like chocolate, velvety and smooth, and I feel something stir inside me with every word. "You desired to be seen and ogled, and you did not care by whom. I imagine Lanzo is a safer bet than any of the others. Did you think he might worship you rather than make you his conquest, since he drools all over your boots day in and day out?" He again washes the blade clean. "What a prize indeed. You reek of alcohol, and you have another man's blood drying all over your leg. I might question his own reasoning for wanting to take you in such a state."

I look down at myself and realize just how unappealing the sight of me must be. Still, he had taken the opportunity to stare, twice. I take a step closer, closing the distance between us as the razor touches his skin, and he drops my gaze. I want his eyes upon me, want him to see me more fully than the others. "So what *you* are saying is that *you* do not want me?"

I let my words come out slow and tantalizingly, and I watch as Eoghan's hand stops halfway to his chin. Our eyes meet in the mirror, and he drops the blade into the sink. He turns toward me, and I back up instinctively, my thighs pressing into the cold stone of the counter. He places a hand on either side of me, and his mouth comes so close to mine, I can feel his breath fall steady and slow over my face. Oh gods, he smells good. My mind wanders to what he might taste like, and my lips part on their own accord. The seconds of silence feel so agonizing, I want to scream.

"Never. I will never want you," he whispers and moves away from me so indifferently, he could have thrown a bucket of icy water over me, and I could not have been more stunned.

I let out a shriek of frustration and slap my hands against the counter. "I hate you!" I shout, much louder than I expected.

"The feeling is mutual, I can assure you." He wipes his face clean coolly, sensually.

"Since the day I arrived. You've hated me since the moment you saw me."

"Yes, since the moment you wasted my time with your very breath, I have hated you, and no matter if you are stripped down to those pieces of fabric you call underwear or naked crawling from a window, no matter if you are dying on the floor and crying out for my help, I will always hate you."

"Why?" My lip quivers, and I bite back the tears threatening to escape.

"Because you are nothing. I owe you nothing, not even my kindness." He picks up his shirt and razor and pushes past me out of the shower room.

CHAPTER THIRTEEN

"**M**aeve..." *Rian kisses down my spine as I lay in the sunlight on a blanket. My dress is a corn silk yellow, and my caramel waves lay over my shoulder in the grass, my chin resting upon my forearms. The sky above is a turquoise blue with clouds of pink and white painting it like brushstrokes on a canvas. The sun rests just above the garden wall, and I can hear the faintest sounds of the street vendors just beyond it. I close my eyes and feel his lips warm and soft against my skin. He brushes his fingertips through my hair as he always does, entranced by the responding display. "Beautiful." There is an awe in his voice as he takes me in. "I've never asked: why does it shine when I touch it?"*

He is speaking about the magic my hair possesses, which glows like the stars when touched by human hands. The magic is a mystery, even to me. I am the only person in the kingdom to possess it, and in all my searching, I have never found a single instance of its occurrence in any of the histories housed in the castle library. I roll over onto my back to face him, his mop of sandy hair falling into his eyes as he stares down at me.

"Because it is magic, and magic does as it pleases." I walk my fingers up the front of his tunic, a lightweight, elegant garb of the

wealthy in sea foam green, the color of his household. I've always detested how he looks in it, much too formal for an afternoon in the sun, his arms covered in fabric and his chest exposed from the deep v cut into the neckline. I detest even more how much he enjoys my father's approving nods when he shows up in such finery, bands of gold upon his wrists to parade the wealth his father so enjoys. It does not suit him, with his brutish features that could at times frighten me more than tantalize .

"I might like to see you with a shorter style. It would suit the sea better," he speaks casually, as if I can imagine it myself. I have never smelled the salty air or felt the mist upon my face. He pushes my hair behind my ear and runs his hand down my cheek.

I shake my head. "I'd be damning myself for vanity. Sir Oli Raven is afraid it might harm the magic if severed."

"A minor inconvenience, then. You can just wear it in a braid, I suppose." He smiles down at me and plucks a strawberry from a small plate. "Though I would not expect someone from such a powerful family to have limitations on their magic." He pops it into his mouth, and I watch his jaw work against the fruit. I rarely spent time with a man before—apart from my brother Cai before he went off to the Military Academy—and I never realized they perceive everything as quantifiable in terms of limitations or strengths.

"All magic has limitations. Cai's magic can cause an attack to rebound or be redirected, but it does not provide him with a shield against physical attacks on the battlefield. He is vulnerable to a blade, and someone who knows what he can do can easily deceive him."

"Interesting. One might think your family is as common as all human wielders," he says casually and runs his fingers down my back. "Does even the king suffer from such ordinary weaknesses?" Rian props his chin up on his hand and listens as I continue.

"Officially, my father's magic is the greatest of all kingdom secrets... Not even his daughter's lover can know of it—especially *not her lover," I tease as I nestle closer to him. Someone could be listening beyond the wall or a guard from his post on the castle grounds.*

"And unofficially?" His eyes reach mine, and I shake my head warily. "Come now, Maeve. Do you not trust me? Do you not remember me swearing myself to you? Why would I ever betray you?" He holds me in his eyes of devastating blue, and I feel myself melt against his will. There is nothing I would not do for him, nothing I would not give.

"My father," I begin with hesitation, "can control others with his mind and make them do his will, but he cannot change a concrete thought or idea once it has set in. A thought firmly planted has a stronger hold than any sort of manipulation magic can conjure. That's why he could never break me of my hatred of greens as a child. Limitations," I finish with a playful smirk, and Rian takes a deep inhale, sizing me up.

"Inconveniences," he says with a shrug of his shoulders and then brings his lips to mine.

———

"How is your studying coming along?" Gálgalesh is at his desk, laboring over a large map of the continent. I lay on the faded sofa, my boots discarded on the floor, my feet kicked up into the air behind me. This is my second pass-through of this batch of writings today, after translating the word for the silencing incantation wrong and causing the entire room to fall under a veil of black so dark and thick, it took Gálgalesh fifteen minutes in the darkness to figure out where I had gone astray and counter the spell.

"I think I might go cross-eyed if I read any more today." I push the parchment aside and lazily reach for a bowl of beans on the small table to my left. I pull it to me and take a hearty bite. The food is still awful and nearly inedible, but I have no choice. "Is there really no limit to faerie magic?" I marvel aloud, my mouth full.

"No, I've already told you—faerie magic is far superior to your human magic in every way." He turns his head and glances at me for a moment before turning back to the map on his desk. "Do not spill on my sofa, or I will have to skin you alive. The smell would be terrible."

"Ha ha," I feign a dramatic laugh and shovel another spoonful into my mouth. I have grown so fond of my time with Gálgalesh, I have to be forced out of his quarters before dinner each night. I love the warmth of the room with a fireplace we don't have in our bare, resident accommodations. I love the scratchy sofa that feels as though it has been made of horse hair but lends more comfort than the rickety wood chairs found anywhere else in the fortress. I love Gálgalesh, constantly denying his own fondness for me yet rarely without a small smile on his face as he eyes me or exchanges stories with me when the silence becomes too great. "You always threaten to flay me or murder me or hang me by my toes, but you never seem to do a single thing you say you will." I rattle my spoon loudly against the bowl.

"That is because I remind myself you will probably die on your own before I have known you much longer, so why shall I waste my energy?" He rolls up the map and shoves it into a satchel hanging across the back of his chair. Then, he turns his attention fully in my direction, his hands on his knees. "Maeve." He rarely calls me by my name. "I will be going away tomorrow before sunrise and will not return for a week. Now that the food supply count is finished, I can complete the final supply run for the winter months before the path down the mountain becomes too treacherous for the horses to maneuver."

A week? I had not spent a day at Báscogar without Gálgalesh's watchful and protective eye, despite what he says about not caring whether I live or die. With him here, I know I am safe from the residents and anyone who might come calling. He is the only one in this dreadful place who has any idea who I am and just how volatile my entire existence is. I do not want to be left alone in this place, especially not after my last encounter with Eoghan Kael. Besides, I would like nothing more than to leave this stupid prison and its gray walls and frozen halls.

"I would like to go with you on the supply run. Perhaps I can be of help—seeing as I completed the supply count myself." I search his eyes, but they are the hollow mask of the Warden of Báscogar.

"I am certain you would enjoy another trip to the Borderlands, if only to try for a glimpse of your dearest feallwr. Unfortunately for you, neither you nor Tiernan will be making it to the Borderlands any time in the foreseeable future. There have been stirrings in the Capital and a new sovereign has sent patrols there. It would be impossible for a treasonous smuggler or a woman assumed to be dead to make it past the checkpoints." He summons his own bowl to himself from the table and inhales the scent, as if it is not repulsive and unwholesome. "You will stay here and train with Peadair. You will have access to my quarters to study at your will, but I do ask you stay out of trouble. Please do not break any more noses; it is not a good look for an old chambermaid to be making the men bleed while traipsing around like a whore."

I lean over the armrest with my chin in my hands. I had awoken the day after my nude sparring match with a searing headache and bruises speckling my body. Gálgalesh had said nothing to hint at his awareness of the incident when I arrived in the courtyard; rather, he simply declared we would begin practicing with long swords in lieu of our wooden safety blades that day. The reverberating clangs of metal against metal made my teeth clench, and more than once, I had to back away to vomit in the corner.

"Is that what you've told them about me? That I was a chambermaid?" A slave, a chambermaid. I really am nothing to them all.

"I told them you used to empty the king's chamber pot. Does that satisfy you?"

"Hardly." I set down my bowl, thoroughly disgusted. "Does the entire kingdom believe we have no plumbing in Caisleán Rialú?"

Gálgalesh rolls his eyes and points at a piece of stale bread left on the lunch tray. I pick it up and toss it to him, and he catches it with his free hand. "It does not matter what the Steel Citadel has or does not have to these men. They are here only because the man who sat on the throne put them here. That is all that matters to them; but if you would like to fight about chamber pots and running water, be my guest."

I stick out my tongue in his direction and then sigh. "I wish you would let me come with you."

"Grumbling is unappealing. You can stay here and train. Why else are you here? Would you like to make this prison your home for the rest of your miserable life?"

"No." I feel like a child being admonished by their father, and he delights in making me feel so small and humbled. Gálgalesh gives a satisfied nod and sinks his jagged teeth into the bread.

A knock on the door turns our attention to the opposite end of the room. The door swings open to reveal a man in thick brown robes over a portly stomach. He is the prison's resident Highdruí, a class of religious leaders bound to a specific deity, charged with seeking safe passage for others to the House of Donn. His name is Druí Whelan, and he is the Highdruí of the god Baílor—the most fearsome god of pain and destruction, the god of Romiodóg. I have little care for the gods of the north, but Baílor commands respect.

His robes sweep across the floor as he enters the room. "The outriders have come back. The report is not positive."

I nod my head toward Gálgalesh, and he returns my gesture of understanding. I roll over and place my feet on the floor before pulling on my boots and standing from the sofa. "Be safe," I whisper as I make my way to the door.

"And you," Gálgalesh replies. His tone is even—perhaps a bit stoney—but I feel a slight compression on my shoulder, and I know it is his last goodbye. I exit the warden's quarters, and the door closes softly behind me.

By now, I can distinguish the slight changes of the darkened sky over Báscogar to make sense of the time, the days passing in various shades of black and charcoal. As I leave the warden's quarters, it seems to be only about four in the afternoon. I have plenty of time before dinner, and I know the halls will soon fill with men shuffling between their duties and training or heading to their rooms for an afternoon nap. I take the stairs toward the southern tower, abandoned at this time of day for the afternoon guard change. I make it to the small hatch door in the floor and push it skyward, revealing the circular room. It is quiet and cold when I pull myself onto the landing and to the stone half-wall that keeps guards from walking off to their deaths. I can see beyond the walls up here, and although the view is a desolate blanket of white, the freedom beyond the oppressive prison fortress brings me back to this place so often, I have memorized the guards' schedules.

I throw my legs over the wall and perch myself on top, my feet dangling just above the slick roof of the prison. My breath catches in my chest as the wind tears across my face and blows my cloak away from my shoulders. I reach for the sides and pull them tightly around me. My eyes scan the terrain; below, in the courtyard, two men are engaged in a brutal fist fight. One man bleeds as the other drives his clenched hand into the man's teeth. I watch as one ivory incisor falls to the ground and the battered man sways. It is nothing new to this place—everyone spars or fights. Since I have been at the prison, two men lost their lives for stealing food from another man's tray or looking too long in someone else's direction. It would be a miracle to get out of here alive. I turn my face away as the brutalized opponent gets his hand caught in a vise grip, a dagger meeting his finger nail to pry it free from his body. No one is coming to break up the fight, and I pray to the gods the killing ends quickly and mercifully.

Beyond the prison gates, the snow is pristine, unblemished by footsteps in the freshly fallen powder. I look out amongst the bare, dark trees as an owl rustles its feathers from above, and something catches my eye. There, amongst the trunks and fallen logs, a small group of shadow figures move quietly together in the darkening night. I count six of them in total, moving toward the razor edge of uneven stone. Are they escaping? Everyone knows this route claims more lives than the prison ever had.

The hatch pushes open with a loud creak, and Kruz and his Iranndairian friend Tomás enter, ready for their weekly duties on guard. "Hey Alana," they greet me, unsurprised by my now-regular visits to their post.

"Hi," I say distractedly as my eyes follow the dark figures. Kruz meets me at the wall and peers out in the direction of my stare.

"What do you see? Someone approaching?" He cranes his neck for a better view.

"Leaving, I think." I point toward the group, falling deeper into the dark. "Just there, near the rocks." Kruz follows my finger out to the tree line, scanning the unending darkness.

His eyes are used to the dark after twenty years in its merciless grip, and he spots them without a word. He backs away, turning from the side of the tower.

"Eh, don't worry about them."

At the far side of the lookout, Tomás prods a fading fire in a tiny iron stove. He looks toward us curiously, but Kruz simply shakes his head and lifts a log from a stack below my seat to add to the smoldering pile of ash.

"Don't you need to sound some sort of alarm? Shouldn't Gálgalesh be alerted to deserters?" I grab at his cloak, pulling him back. He leans back against the low wall next to me and brings his body close to mine. I can feel his warmth and the light weight of his arm against my thigh. From the corner of my eye, I see him looking at me, not the men down below us in the snow.

"Not them." Kruz shakes his head.

"Why?"

"Because they are Fire Cursed, Alana. We don't report the Fire Cursed for leaving the camp."

The cliff side is infamous for its treacherous terrain. Even the Fire Cursed, who are feared above all else at Báscogar, would be absurd to try to navigate it—especially in this darkness. "Why?" I demand again.

"Because the Fire Cursed are not prisoners here."

I freeze, and the blood rushes from my face, causing me to become a sickly white. The Fire Cursed residents of Báscogar prison, the fiercest fighters in the arena on any given day, are not prisoners here. They live beside the worst criminals on the continent, but they weren't sent here as punishment for any crimes. They have chosen to be here. Eoghan Kael has chosen this, as if it is a choice at all. Impossible. Kruz has made an error in his assessment or is simply lazy and does not want to do his job up in this tower.

"What do you mean, they aren't prisoners here? Everyone here is a prisoner!"

You chose to come here too, I think to myself. I cannot deny the stark truth of my own imprisonment in the bleak hellscape that is Báscogar, but what choice did I have? I had no place to go and no options if I stayed in Gairdín; even the life of a seamstress was not a reality for me. Everything had been taken from me, and in return, I had been given only one simple, unending desire: revenge. Still, if I had any other option laid before me—anything at all—I would have chosen it instead of this. What of the men from Tinemallacht? Could they say the same?

"I don't know, Alana. We aren't permitted to ask questions, and Gálgalesh has never offered any explanation. The bastards arrived at the prison four years ago, and they come and go as they please, but they are *not* prisoners. They do not have chores or duties as the others do, and the most you will see of them is in the training arena—if you are lucky. If you see any more of them, they will probably be the last thing you'll ever see."

My hand drops from his cloak, and he leaves me to tend to the fire. I remain transfixed on the spot where the figures had disappeared into the darkness. Why would they spend their time hidden in this mountain fortress training when Tinemallacht is a breeding ground for brutes and fighters? Tinemallacht births legends. Stories and fables are written about the harshness of the place, from its oppressive sun to its ruthless warriors that demand the ground to quake before them. What could be so important here?

"Why does everyone at Báscogar train in the arena?" I lean against the support pillar that holds the roof in place. I listen as Tomás swears at the embers under his breath behind me, and Kruz mutters to him distractedly.

He responds to me, asking, "What do you mean?" I am

surprised by his bored and slightly annoyed tone, clearly indifferent towards our conversation.

"Everyone at Báscogar has assigned duties, and everyone must report to the training arena each day. Why would it be compulsory for prisoners to train? Many here are lethal enough without additional training."

"We train for our duties on patrol in Fáintìrean. If we did not train, most of the men here would be embarrassingly out of shape. They just want to give us something to do, that's all." He blows a breath into his hands and rubs them together for warmth before taking a seat on the floor.

"But what about the Leader? You've been here for twenty years, haven't you? Who is the Leader everyone talks about?"

"The Leader? What are you talking about, Alana?" He looks up at me as if waiting for me to stop talking and join them by the fire. "Gálgalesh is the only leader who has been at Báscogar since I arrived, and we never call him 'the Leader'. He is the Warden of Báscogar, but he is a prisoner just like us."

He lets out a deep, audible breath, making it clear I will find no answers through him. He was not in the room that day of the secret meeting. He's an ordinary prisoner who was sent here for one purpose: to serve an inordinately long sentence for a crime he committed as a child. He did not have a choice. I climb from the wall and sit on the floor next to Kruz, warming myself in front of the fire.

———

IT IS NEARLY midnight by the time I make it back to my room. I had spent the evening in the guard's tower with Kruz and Tomás, playing cards and listening to ghost stories from their home kingdom. My feet are heavy, and I blink back the sleep that threatens to drag me under as I wrestle with the door handle. The hall is still and dark, with only one or two low rumbles of snoring escaping from someone a few doors down. I press the door with my hand, and it gives way to darkness. I fumble for the matchbox on the desk and strike one across the side, creating a faint glow, then light the candle I have positioned near the entrance and step inside, pulling the door shut behind me. I kick off my boots and pull off my clothes. I drag myself below the covers and succumb to the night not a moment after my head reaches my pillow.

———

"MAEVE, I NEED YOU TO HIDE!" Rian grabs me by the shoulders and shakes them hard. I am back in that empty room on my wedding day, weighed down by the heavy skirts of my wedding dress.

"Rian!" I try to pull him to me, but he turns me around and pushes me toward the fireplace, the scene playing out as it had all those months ago. "Rian!" I shout, but he ignores me completely.

"Climb up into the smoke chamber and wait there until dark. Do not come out, no matter what you hear. Once the house is quiet, you run as fast as you can out of Caisleán Rialú, as far away from this city—hell, away from Draíocoinnigh completely—until you get to the border. It doesn't matter which. Watch for border guards. I'm not sure who we can trust, so don't tell them who you are. Just run and hide and don't look back. Do. You. Understand?"

I attempt to pull him toward me, but I struggle to hold on to him, as if he is made of smoke. "Rian, stop! They are going to kill you!"

"Maeve, we don't have time for this!" he continues, as if I am a spectator watching my living nightmare unfold before my eyes again. "Climb! Stay hidden and run! I love you... I'm sorry."

The scene plays out as it had on that day, and I am hoisted into the firebox once more. I cannot breathe; I want to scream. Panic wells up inside me, and tears stream down my face.

Rian vanishes, and I hear his footsteps fade as he exits the room.

"There's the Loverboy," the raspy voice of my soon-to-be captor booms outside of the room. "Grab him too."

Rian is fighting valiantly for his life—the one he will lose in just a short time. He is no match for the ones who take us. No matter his size or strength, they have too many on their side. It's no use.

"Take him to the others while I check the room," says the voice as they drag Rian's limp body away. The door creaks as it opens slowly for the man in the hall. He's coming for me, and it is only a matter of time before he catches me, takes me to that cursed dais bathed in fear and death. "Hmm," he steps forward as he speaks. "I wonder where his bride might... be."

His footsteps make the firebox shake around me, and I pull at my skirts, but they do not budge. He is going to take me again. I am going to have to listen to them die again. They are going to try to kill me again. I could beg them to end it, to take me first, to slit my throat wide until my blood empties onto the platform. I watch the fingers reach into the fireplace, and I am dragged down just as I was before...

"Hello, beautiful," says the stranger, but his face is no longer scarred and caked with dirt. It is the beautiful and terrifying face of Eoghan Kael, and I am seated on the floor of Gálgalesh's office as Eoghan stands over me, his blade raised.

CHAPTER FOURTEEN

I reach the courtyard the next morning, and Peadair is already waiting with his arms crossed over his chest. There is no warmth in his eyes, and I avert my gaze as I shrug my cloak from my shoulders. The night had been long after repeatedly waking in a fit of screams over unending nightmares, each of Eoghan Kael slaughtering me in cold blood. In one dream, he had bedded me, causing my toes to curl and me to scream out in ecstasy before he snapped my neck. Another, he drowned me in a stream after hunting me through the woods. He stood over me as I lay dying in the snowbank, blood falling red against the white snow.

"Stop," Peadair snarls, and I hold my cloak out in front of me, startled by the hunger in his eyes. If I did not know any better, I would think he was a shadow lurker looking for a meal. "Gálgalesh informed me you train outside of the gates."

"Every other day," I reply cautiously, not daring to move. "We practice sparring in the courtyard on the others. We trained in the forest yesterday."

"We will train outside of the gates every day until Gálgalesh's return."

He turns from me and starts toward the front gates with large strides. *Every day? Why would we need to train outside the gates every day?* I pull my cloak back over my shoulders and rush through the courtyard, trying to match his pace. He does not acknowledge me as we march through the prison entrance, does not even look back as he makes his way deep into the surrounding trees. Snow has fallen during the night, and it now reaches just above my knee. I stumble through it as quickly as I can, though I am beginning to lose him in the forest.

"Peadair, please," I beg, but he pays me no mind.

He leads us further into the quiet darkness than I have ever ventured with Gálgalesh. The trees are thicker here, and some possess a bit of evergreen foliage, making even the faint light of morning imperceptible from this place. The air feels expectant and dangerous, as though there is an evil so great, even the Earth would like to hide from it.

"We will be sparring today." A nasty grin ripples across Peadair's lips, and I swallow hard as my stomach rises in my throat. "Let us begin."

———

ON THE THIRD day of training with Peadair, I stumble through the gates of Báscogar with my body broken and mutilated—he has beaten me beyond recognition. My face is swollen and bruised, my body weak and tender. My ribs ache horribly as I breathe in and out, and I cradle my side as best I can as I limp toward the corridors to my room. Had I thought Peadair might have been as kind as Gálgalesh simply because they were lovers? Faeries exhibit an utter lack of mercy, showing no regard for humans other than their desire to devour them. Where Gálgalesh is an anomaly amongst his brethren, Peadair is more common than I could have ever imagined. He possesses a heart as cold as ice and a cruel nature that sends shivers down the spine. He has found every weakness in me and has exposed them all in a savage display of dominance.

I make the gradual procession to my door to fall onto my bed, my breath escaping me as the pain radiates through every bone in my body. If only I had Gálgalesh's tonic, the white-hot agony that overwhelms me might not paralyze me. I reach down and pull off my boot, my sock cutting into my swollen ankle—clearly broken. I discard the cloth onto the floor and wince. My palms are raw and tender from catching myself upon the ragged rocks so prominently featured in the Romiodóg mountains. He had dragged me across the razor-edged surface as I attempted to flee. I pick at the gashes in my skin, prying out small pieces of granite one-by-one. I'll be lucky if they do not become infected by the morning with no water to clean them and no salve or bandages to dress them.

I lay on the bed, and tears begin to roll down my cheeks. *Only four more days, then Gálgalesh will be back, and you will be safe*, I assure myself. *If you live that long*, I answer back, and my heart sinks in my chest. I lay there in the cold, damp room until it all fades to black around me as I succumb to the relentless torment of my injuries.

———

A DELUGE of freezing water pours over me, unceremoniously rousing me back to the present. My body shakes uncontrollably with chill, and I look around wide eyed as Peadair and three other men I do not recognize stand over me. My eyes dart back and forth between them, their expressions hard and angry. I note one man holds two ropes in his hand. A long scar stretches from his eye to his chin, his teeth rotting in his mouth. Another retains the now-empty bucket that had held the water they dumped over me. This man is younger than the first but no less grotesque, missing a large piece of his right ear. Peadair nods wordlessly, and the third man—a faerie upon further examination, slim, with long black hair and clean jawline devoid of any hints of stubble—wrenches my arm from the mattress. I cry out as sharp daggers shoot through my body, but he simply grabs my other arm with the same lack of care and holds my wrists together while the man with the rope ties them tightly in front of me. He pulls them, yanking me from the bed completely, and I stumble forward. He hands over the end of the short rope to Peadair, who grips it tightly between his long fingers. *It is happening again.*

Peadair growls, and his mouth waters as he hauls me toward him, forcing me to limp on my tender, fractured ankle. He turns toward the door without so much as a word to me or the others, but before he can take a step, the youngest of the three co-conspirators speaks up.

"What about her shoes?" he drawls with only a semblance of sympathy hidden in his words—almost too little to notice at all.

My shoes? What about my clothes? I am drenched from head to toe in water. The black shirt and pants—that I had thankfully been too hurt to worry about discarding—are now sticking to my skin. I cannot stop shivering; I would give anything to take up my cloak from where it lays across the floor and roll myself up in it. My feet, though, are indeed bare and aching with cold.

Peadair rolls his eyes but drops the rope enough to give me room to step back to my boots. "Be quick."

I reach down and pull them to me as fast as my shaking hands will allow. I wrench the tongue out of the way and look around for my socks. Where are my socks? Peadair tugs impatiently, and I nearly topple over. Okay, no socks. It is a mercy he is letting me have my boots at all. I step into the boots with my uncovered feet and lace them quickly, missing an eyelet at the top. Peadair's lips curl up to expose his yellow, keen teeth. He is becoming annoyed and tired of waiting. He turns from me once again, and this time, he drags me out of the room with him.

I fall to the solid stone of the floor. There is not enough slack in the line to allow me to keep up with his long strides. My arms pull up over my head, and I roll onto my back, my ribs pounding against the uneven pavement. I try to throw my feet underneath me and catch the ground enough to rise to my feet, but his pace is too quick, and I only turn my broken ankle under me in my boot. My back scrapes painfully against the rough surface as we continue down the halls.

We reach the central courtyard, and the stone fortress gives way to the deepest black sky I have ever seen. It has to be about one in the morning—the darkness lends no hint of moonlight or sun. Peadair carries on, dragging me against the ice that has frozen hard and slick overnight toward the Báscogar gates.

"Help!" I scream out, but no one is there to greet us at the entrance. As we leave the prison walls, I look up at the two guard towers that flank either side of the camp. "Help me!" My cries echo against the stone exterior, but there is no answering movement from the towers, and the fires have died down to nothing. The guards are gone. They've been relieved from their posts, and from the looks of it, they have been gone long enough that they might not be near enough to hear my pleas.

We hit the rising banks of snow, and Peadair continues to drag me through them into the forest and the trees. My head barrels into the snow, choking me as it covers my face. I am going to freeze or suffocate out here. The camp has been cautioned about frostbite setting in within minutes of being exposed to the winter temperatures, which has already caused my skin to burn with the cold. My wet clothes turn to ice as they freeze against my skin. *I am going to die,* I tell myself. *I am going to die, and there is nothing I can do about it.*

After ages of being dragged blindly, Peadair lifts me above the snow, and I cough and spit, expelling it from my mouth. Ice clings to my eyelashes and down my cheeks as soon as tears roll from my eyes. I do not recognize this place at all. He must have dragged me further into the forest than I have ever been. My teeth chatter as my jaw trembles beyond my control.

"Tie her to that tree," Peadair says and hands me off to the other faerie with the black hair.

He takes the rope and guides me roughly toward a nearby willow. My thoughts flash back to the attack on the castle and how they took me and tied me to the post, waiting for execution. I am now taken once again, at the bidding of my captors, who will tie me to a tree and do their worst...

No. I will not go back there. I will not go back to being powerless and waiting to die. Not this time. They could kill me, but I will at least fight with everything I have until they do. Gálgalesh would have wanted me to. He would have expected it. What sort of survivor would I be if I did not fight?

I kick my leg out and catch the right ankle of the faerie. He loses his balance and falls forward, and the resulting surge of pain through my own leg nearly topples me over. He lets go of the rope as he tries to catch himself before his face hits the snow, and I yank it back toward me, out of his reach, and roll away from him. The others watch me as I fall back into the clearing and drop down protectively, my body stiff but my heart pounding with an animalistic instinct to stand my ground.

The men circle me, and I snarl at them, turning with them, my eyes darting between each. I feel the white-hot rage rise inside me that makes me hungry for violence. I'll kill them all if I have to—I would like to see them suffer and pay. If I am not walking out of this clearing, then neither are they. The man with the rotting teeth lunges for my arms, but I jump toward him and clench my jaws around his filthy hand. He screams, and I release him only after I draw blood, causing him to fall back from the circle to cradle his wounds. Peadair's eyes are wide, but he continues to circle as the other faerie rises to join the others. He moves forward, and I swing my arms hard into his side. He hesitates, not out of pain but out of shock, giving me just enough time to steal his dagger where it hangs from his belt. My body is so cold, I feel nothing but the heaviness of my limbs as I fight with everything in me to keep them aloft. I jump back, putting space between us as I yank the weapon from him and grip it tightly. The faerie rights himself and comes for me again, but I heave the blade forward, a war cry escaping me as I plunge it into his chest. He falls back, and I fall with him, my hands glued to the hilt. I pull it from his bleeding torso and drive it down again and again. Over and over, I stab at his heart until his gurgling breath subsides, his face vacant, golden blood running from the sides of his mouth.

Peadair and the young man stop and gape as I pant wildly, my heart pounding in my chest. I push myself to my feet and slash at the air with the soaked dagger. I cannot feel anything but fury inside me now, and I let it take hold. Death for all of them. I want it to be slow so I can savor the looks on their faces as I take the life from them one-by-one. Peadair holds the other man back with his arm, though it is clear the man has no interest in charging forward. Peadair begins to back away from the clearing, taking the other man with him and leaving the dead faerie in the snow. The man with the rotting teeth jumps to his feet as he cradles his wounded hand and races from me. He disappears before the others do. I watch until they are completely out of sight, and then I collapse into the snow.

———

I HAVE TO MOVE. I have to move or I will die. I have spent the last eight hours where they left me in the snow. I have cut my hands free and taken the cloak from the dead faerie's body, but it has done little to extinguish the chill rattling through me. I need to find shelter. I press up against the cold bank, my hands warmed in a pair of stolen, oversized dragon skin gloves—and fall back down as my leg refuses to bear my weight. Damnit, I have to move!

I take off one of the gloves with my teeth and dive my hand into the faerie's pockets. I pull out a matchbook and a few gold coins—the price of my life, I suspect. I tuck them into the cloak pocket and replace the glove before I look around the clearing. There is no way I am walking out of here and by now, with the fresh coat of snow from the last few hours, I have no hope of making my way back to the prison with the footprints left behind. Peadair would have wiped them away even without the help of the weather.

About a hundred yards deeper into the trees, I can make out a rock formation with a sheltered pocket of brown lying underneath a protruding rock. I crane my neck for a better look. If I can get there, I would have just enough room to crawl into the space, and perhaps I could find enough dry leaves and sticks to make a fire. I place my hands on either side of me and heave myself through the snow. My palms— still broken from the jagged rocks that tore into them yesterday—feel as though they are on fire, but I reset and heave again, dragging myself through the forest as I bite down on my lip to bear the torture rattling through my body.

Slowly, I make my way to the rocks. The earth is damp, and the mud clings to me, but the shelter provides a guard against the winter wind. I gather all the sparse foliage left around me, soggy with dew, and I sigh in annoyance as I drop it back down to the dirt. If I cannot start a fire, I will be dead by nightfall. I look around again, desperate for something I know is not there, anything that might save me in this hellish landscape. But Romiodóg is known for taking lives, not saving them. All that trouble, and I am still no better off. I lay my head back against the rock and pull the cloak around my face. If only I had common magic, I could conjure something for heat—

I look down at my hands. Magic. Last week, I deciphered a writing about elemental magic while studying in Gálgalesh's office. I could not make a spark when I tried it, but I am fairly certain I remember the elements of the incantation. I close my eyes and tie myself to the power whispering to me. With concentration and the right intention, faerie magic has no bounds. I search my memory for the wordless stream of symbols I need to make up the spell. I reach toward it in my mind's eye, asking it to release itself to me...

Crack! Flames rise around me, wrapping me in a circle of heat. I hold my breath, hoping I haven't done something wrong and they won't swallow me up, but they do not grow, nor do they burn out. They remain a blanket of warmth, a shield from the falling snow that melts in their wake. I sink down onto the ground, and my stomach growls with hunger, my body never ceasing its war cry—battered to within an inch of its life but not lost.

CHAPTER FIFTEEN

It takes two days before I can bear any weight on my ankle to stand. My lips are chapped and cracked, and I am so hungry, I can hardly think straight. My throat burns, and my tongue sticks dryly in my mouth as my saliva has run dry. I wonder if I should just give in, but then I remind myself I am still alive, just as I was in the tunnel where Tiernan and Dedra kept me safe. They had not risked everything just for me to die at the top of this mountain, at the hands of a murderous faerie. I pull myself to my feet and look toward the clearing where Peadair and those men left me to perish. The black-haired faerie is nowhere to be found, buried under more than a foot of new snow. I smile to myself at the thought of his body being lost forever—just as they had hoped mine would be.

I cannot remember which direction we had come from, and the dark sky gives no hint of stars to guide my way back. I turn slowly on the spot, hoping to find something to be my guide, but nothing looks familiar, and everything looks so plainly similar coated in white. All I can grasp to find my way back is this: Báscogar sits among the cliffs, along a slender portion of the ridgeline. If I follow it in the right direction, I might be able to spot it among the jagged rocks. I spot the razor sharp terrain to the north, not far off. That is where I need to go, whether my body wants to take me there or not. I inhale and take a step, and my ankle protests against my weight. I close my eyes and let the pain abate before continuing, every step a sheer display of will.

I reach the ridge with labored breaths, sweat running from my brow, and look left and right. I cannot seem to make sense of it with no signs of disturbance or life. I'll just have to choose a direction and hope it's the right one. *To the left*, I decide, turning to the west and beginning the labored hike through the snow.

I walk for hours, and still, I find nothing but relentless slopes of white. I'm sure I haven't made it far, as I have had to stop and rest every few minutes. I am so thirsty and hungry, I can't think of anything else. Being stranded in the unyielding winter of Romiodóg means there is no vegetation or berries to consume, and the rivers run solid and unmoving. My only option is to push forward in the hopes of reaching the prison before the darkness swallows me up again. I wipe my arm across my face to keep the moisture from freezing on my skin.

I climb to the top of the next steep incline and peer out into the distance. A half a mile away, I see the orange glow of firelight, tall stacks of smoke pouring from more than a dozen small stone houses. I inhale, and the smell of burning firewood and roasting meat fills my nostrils. Food. They have food. I pull my eyes shut, convinced I am falling victim to hysteria brought on by my starvation, but when I open them again, the image remains. The wind rushes past me, and with it comes voices, faint but cheerful. It is not Báscogar, but there is life and warmth, and perhaps I will not die out here if I can make it there.

I drag my body over the summit and begin my descent down the other side as fast as I can. I stumble, my body faltering, but I push forward still further. *Safety. Just a little further, and you will make it to safety,* I tell myself. Ahead, a dirt road comes into view on my left through the trees. I hadn't seen it the whole time I had been walking, but there it is, leading right into the village; and there, along its path, stands a girl with light brown hair and a heavy white cloak hidden against the fallen snow around her. She looks straight ahead as she heads back toward the stony houses. *I need her to see me; I need her to know I am here.*

"Hey!" I shout, but my voice is just a raspy whisper. "Hello!" I try again with such effort, it feels as though my throat might tear open.

I wave my hands toward her, but she doesn't even look my way. I pick up my pace at nearly a run as I try desperately to get her attention. My body screams at me to stop, but she has almost reached the walls of the small village. If she disappears, I might not make it. I fumble with the matchbox in my pocket and pull it into my hands. I strike a handful of matches against it, and they erupt in light, blazing against the dark sky. Still, it's not enough. They burn out so quickly, and she doesn't even turn. I need more! I am not sure I have the energy to conjure with faerie magic the way I had when I was so desperate for warmth, not when moving at this pace is taking everything I have, but what choice do I have? I look into my mind's eye, trying to find that thread of Gálgalesh's magic, and hurriedly send the combinations of symbols down the line, begging for some spark…and it ignites. Melting the snow in front of me, Fae Fire burns so brightly against the black, it burns my eyes. The light of it catches the woman by surprise, and she turns and stops as her eyes find me…and then the world turns upside down.

I haven't been paying attention to where I am going, and I

catch my foot against the unforgiving ridge line and hurdle down the ridge. My back collides with the jagged stones on the way down, and they tear through the heavy fabric of the cloak and my shirt, as if they are nothing more than chiffon or lace. I tumble over myself, and the rocks slice through my forehead and pierce my shoulder.

"Ahh!" I throw my hands out in front of me, the large gloves slipping off my fingers. I dig in, trying to stop my trajectory down the hill as I grab onto whatever I can reach. I catch myself, the weight of my body pulling roughly, but I cease to fall.

Oh gods, if I wasn't already in excruciating pain, it is unimaginable now. I use every bit of strength I have to hoist my body across the rocks, and they slice into me as if they are shards of glass. I look up to find I have only fallen about fifteen feet from the ridgeline. *I can pull myself back up,* I think, but even the thought of it makes my body tremble. I look down and see nothing but the tips of spiked rocks waiting to tear me to bits. *I have to pull myself up,* I reason, as if imploring my hands and feet to listen.

I reach toward the rocks above me and slice a deep gash into my arm, blood falling freely, but I am able to grab a sharp handhold and pull. The climb is painful and slow, and when I reach the top, I throw myself over the side onto the white ground, covering it in crimson. Somewhere not far off, someone is shouting something as their voice grows nearer. It sounds like the forbidden language, but the blood pounding in my ears is too loud to make sense of it. A second voice—a familiar low and smooth purr—answers the first, and then the sound of crunching snow under boots surrounds me. The girl from the road drops down beside me, her breathing heavy and her cheeks pink against the cold.

"Blood," I recognize the word easily. "She's covered in blood."

Another figure drops down beside me, and I turn my head slowly, agonizingly. *Oh gods, it can't be him*, my mind screams. Eoghan Kael is kneeling beside me in the snow, his eyes looking over me, horror etched across his face. It's an expression I've never witnessed from him before. He has only ever looked at me as though he wants to see me dead. I drag in a labored breath, and my vision narrows around the edges. I keep my eyes on Eoghan's face, the beautiful, terrible face I wanted so badly to see me now taking me in without anger or lust, but with care and fear. This is the last face I'll see before I die—just as in my nightmare, Eoghan Kael is actually going to watch me die right here in the snow. He reaches out and rubs his thumb gently across the wound on my head.

"Princess," he whispers. "Stay with me."

CHAPTER SIXTEEN

Eoghan Kael hoists me gingerly into his arms, one behind my knees and the other at my back, cradling me against his chest. His body is unbelievably warm, as though he has set me in front of a raging fire. I lean into him, and his scent—sandalwood, bergamot, and the warm aroma of cedar embers after the flames have died down—overwhelms my senses. He rises to his feet and takes off through the snow. My sight is fading, and his voice becomes distant as he calls to me.

"Stay with me." My head lulls as I struggle to keep my eyelids from sliding shut. "Damnit, no!" I can feel him pick up his pace, trying to mitigate the jostling of my body as he breaks out into a run. I try to speak, but the only words that escape me come as incoherent mumbles. "Shh!" he demands as he continues forward, the wind whipping his cloak back.

My body lays limp and weak, unable to move my limbs or lift my head. My lips are pale and bloodless, and my head feels like a thick fog has rolled over me, clogging all my senses. Sleep. I only want to sleep. I sink further into Eoghan's arms, as if curling up under the warm embrace of my blankets, safe as I drift away from the pain, away from the bone-chilling wind. He shakes me, keeping me away from the darkness, and I groan in protest. I need to sleep! I am desperate for it! My eyes shutter again, and I hear him growl once more.

"Keep awake! Keep your eyes on me."

The crunching of snow beneath his feet gives way to the sound of boots sliding along muddy gravel, and I feel him change direction, never slowing our pace. The sound of voices and smell of firewood grows, and his foot hits a hard stone step. He kicks his leg forward, and I feel the weight of it collide with something solid that gives way. I peel my eyes open, just enough to see us bound over the threshold of a small, one-room cottage.

"Rhodes." His low voice is a dominant command. "Where's Gálgalesh?"

Finn Rhodes, another Fire Cursed resident of Báscogar Prison with the same dark hair with sun-bleached highlights and tanned skin as Eoghan Kael, rises from a brown leather armchair near the fireplace. I recognize him as one of the men who trains with Eoghan in the arena. "Is that the girl from the camp?"

"Gálgalesh! Where is he?!" Eoghan snaps as he cradles me to him. Finn points in the direction we came.

"He tended to the sick, and then he left before you came back from your patrol. Why is she out he-?"

"The tonic! Do we have any of his healing tonic?" Eoghan's body shakes in distress. In all the times I have encountered him, I have witnessed anger, frustration, malice, and even ridicule, but never this. He has never seemed so shaken before. Finn reaches into his pocket and pulls out a familiar vial, and I can almost taste its sweet liquid on my tongue, but it is only a quarter of the way full. It will not be enough to heal me. Eoghan eyes it with dismay and then shakes his head.

"Give it to her quickly." Finn obeys, and I feel the warmth of the nectar cascade past my lips and down my throat. A morsel of strength builds up within me, enough that I can resist the waves of fatigue rushing over me. Eoghan looks down at my blood drenched face, his eyes searching for a hint of hope. "I'm taking her to Báscogar. Search the woods and see if you can find who left her out here."

Then, he turns, and we are back out in the cold. He picks up his pace once more as he heads out of the village, along the brown gravel road, back toward the woods. The stone houses fall away, and then it's all barren land between the village and the forest. Soon, the trees are just a blur of dark shadows flying past us. I lift my eyes to my surroundings, but the motion makes my stomach churn sickly, and I lay back lamely in his arms. He does not seem to notice, the terrain and the wind seeming to have no effect on him at all.

I am not sure how long we have been running—minutes or hours—but his fingers tighten around me, and I look down to realize they are covered in me, bright red soaking his tan palms and fingers. I must have drenched him in my blood, although the tonic has slowed the constant stream from the many gashes and wounds that mark my skin.

"Princess, can you still hear me?" His voice is soft but dripping with rage, though this time, I know it is not for me.

"C-c-cold." My teeth chatter, and the word sounds throaty and broken. It feels as though his body heats in response. Was he warming me, or was I just imagining it?

"We are almost there," he assures me, and as he does, I see the towering fortress of Báscogar rise before us at the far end of the trees. Báscogar, my prison and now my safe haven.

He clears the tree line and shoots toward the gates. Morgan, the guard I met when I first arrived, is standing on the other side, gaping at the sight of us bursting into the clearing, my body in Eoghan's arms as if he is bringing his kill home after a hunt.

"Alana?!" Morgan calls out. "Kael, is she dead? She hasn't been seen for days; we thought she might have tried to escape."

"And you didn't send anyone to look for her?!" Eoghan barks, keeping his pace. "Open the gates!"

The iron creaks as they swing the gates wide to let us through. We do not stop once we are inside, and Eoghan continues into the winding corridors lit only by the low light of torches hanging from the walls. He takes the staircase up to the next landing and turns down the familiar corridor to the warden's quarters.

"Gálgalesh!" He shouts through the halls, and the responding creaking of the heavy wooden door of Gálgalesh's rooms tells me he is back. Gálgalesh stalks into the hall, his traveler's cloak still in his hands, his eyes on an envelope, white and speckled with dirt.

"Kael, you do not summon me as if I am—" He raises his head, and his eyes find Eoghan racing toward him, me dangling in his arms. He backs into his quarters and clears the way as Eoghan follows him to the couch, where he finally lays me down. "What happened?" The door slams shut behind us, sealing us inside.

"You tell me! Why was she dragging herself through the snow near Fáintìrean?" Eoghan turns on Gálgalesh, his expression like a rabid beast.

"She was in Fáintìrean? What's happened to her? Have the villagers attacked her?" Gálgalesh kneels beside me and runs his icy hand softly across my cheek. He summons two vials of tonic from his desk drawer and hands them to me. I uncork them and swallow their contents without a word. The effects take hold instantly, and I feel the pain draining from me, replaced by a delightful warmth. I close my eyes and relish in the sensation. He hands me another vial, the contents in this one green. When I remove the stopper, the smell is rancid, and I make a face of disgust.

"Drink it, woman. You have lost too much blood. This one will help with that. The others will seal your wounds and bring down the swelling and pain, but no one has ever produced a true healing tonic. With the sort of injuries you bear, it will take time before you are yourself again." Then, he turns his attention back to Eoghan.

"She was seen by one of the women just outside the boundaries, stumbling toward the village. She tripped and tumbled into the Deep but somehow caught herself on the way down and crawled back up by the time I got to her." He takes a step toward Gálgalesh. "Why?"

"I do not know, Kael. I left on my last run a week ago, just hours after you. I do not know how she ended up outside the gates."

"Peadair," I cut in hoarsely, and both men look down at me in surprise. "Peadair and three others took me from my bed and dragged me into the forest. They were going to kill me, but I killed one of them instead, a faerie with long black hair."

"Peadair?" Gálgalesh's face falls, and he searches my face, as though I am lying to him. When he sees only truth in my eyes, he shakes his head in disbelief. "No, Peadair would not do such a thing. I left you in his care and ordered him—"

"You left her, *the Princess of Draíocoinnigh*, with Peadair?! Does he know who she is?!" Eoghan grabs a fistful of Gálgalesh's shirt, and a low snarl rises in his throat.

"Do not be ridiculous!"

"Does. He. Know?" Eoghan's teeth clench, and his lips barely move as he speaks.

"*You* know who I am!" I blurt out as my mind clears and I

jump to my feet. I sway dangerously, still weak and tender, and Eoghan reaches out to steady me, his hand behind my elbow. "How do *you* know who I am?!" I turn, horrified, toward my faerie mentor beside me. He betrayed me and risked my life when I trusted him. "You've told him! Have you told them all!?"

Gálgalesh looks at me as though I smacked him across the face. *Treachery,* his eyes read as though I have broken his faith. Me! As if I haven't just been brutally attacked and betrayed on his watch. I glare back at him, and my hands clench at my sides. I could punch him, and that would not be even half of what he deserves.

"Of course I did not tell Kael; I have not told Peadair! I have not told anyone in these walls or elsewhere about your existence! Kael surmised it the moment he saw you upon your arrival and came straight to me, demanding I send you away."

Eoghan Kael had taken one glance at me and known who I was without a single prior meeting. How many more can say the same? If Kruz found out about me, he would try to kill me just as Peadair had; all of them would.

"I told you this was dangerous, Gálgalesh." Eoghan's tone is deadly.

"I had no choice!"

"Because of Tiernan Damaris? Please! He is a spineless smuggler with no care for anyone but himself. If he cared so much for her, why would he send her here where everyone and everything can kill her? Once I rip Peadair apart, Tiernan will be lucky if I give him a quick death." Eoghan has not loosened his hold on Gálgalesh, his knuckles white.

"Enough, Kael. *I* will deal with Peadair. He has had a taste for Maeve since she arrived and would have taken care of the shadow lurker himself for her had you not done it before he got there." I stiffen at Gálgalesh's words. The shadow lurker on the evening Kruz had taken me to the prison hideaway. I had thought he had been the one to interfere when he chased me down at the staircase, but it was Eoghan Kael. "As for Tiernan Damaris, no one can argue his intentions are almost always misplaced, but what is done is done. Now, we must do what we can to keep the woman alive."

Eoghan's hand falls to his side, his breathing heavy. His eyes roam my face, the blood and filth dry and flaking now. "I'd like to see you try," he laughs lightly as he appraises me. "It'll be a hopeless task, *Warden*."

"Lucky for me then, you will be the one burdened with such duties," Eoghan and I both turn in disbelief, and a wicked expression flickers at the corner of Gálgalesh's lips.

"Excuse me?" I stammer. "Him?" Gálgalesh only nods.

"You're not a prize yourself, Princess," Eoghan reminds me, his words bathed in loathing. "Find another way. I am not here to babysit a damsel with a death wish."

"Then why are you here, Kael? What would the Leader have you do?" Gálgalesh seems to grow several inches as he squares off against Eoghan, who simply mumbles something about it not mattering now. "You will care for Maeve and keep her identity a secret. You will escort her at all times, and you *both* will do well to find a way to not kill each other in the process. If you cannot, you will have to leave. Do you understand?"

My eyes fall to the floor, not wanting to see the ire written all over Eoghan Kael's face. Not only did he hate me, not only had he made it perfectly clear he had wanted nothing to do with me, but he was now ordered to follow me around day and night, as if I needed a minder to simply walk and breathe. Perhaps I did, but not Eoghan Kael. Anyone but Eoghan Kael. He remains deathly silent beside me, refusing to protest, refusing to speak at all. I had brought another person unwillingly into my bid to stay alive and seek revenge, and I was sure now that this time, I would pay for it.

"It is settled then. Help her back to her room and get her cleaned up. I'll send some food for her while she rests and alert the guards of her return." He speaks as though I am not even here anymore—I'm just an object being passed to another man's care. "Kael, thank you," he says, although Eoghan Kael is looking at him like he wants nothing more than to rip his head from his shoulders. He hates me, and it does not matter if I am some nobody slave girl sent to serve a desertion sentence or a princess; he hates me above all else and wants none of this arrangement. That is not to say *I* want anything to do with it either. I'd rather face my fate of death than spend my days with Eoghan Kael. Finally, Gálgalesh turns to me and lifts my chin with his lean, dark fingers. "I am so sorry."

He nods to us both, and Eoghan places his hand on my back to usher me out of the room. I shudder under his touch as a jolt of unexpected electricity rushes through me. *Stop that*, I admonish myself. We reach the corridor, my body still aching from the deep set injuries the tonic could not remedy. I get halfway down the hall before I stop and lean against the wall.

"Can you not walk?" Eoghan stands next to me, waiting for me to move.

"I'm fine; just give me a moment." I shake my head as I take a few breaths against the wall. I'm still starving and thirsty, and my stomach growls loudly as the pain nearly doubles me over. "Do you have a canteen?"

He reaches into his cloak pocket and pulls out a flask, but I shake my head. I need something to quench my searing throat and coat my mouth. "It's water," he says and pushes it into my hands. "I had nothing else on me when I found a running stream on patrol."

I clasp it in my fingers, my hands shaking slightly, and remove the cap. I empty it in one ceaseless gulp, and he watches me with interest. The water is cold, more heavenly than anything I've ever tasted. I let out a sigh of relief and hand him back the empty flask. He pockets it and then waits. I stand there a moment longer before I push off the wall, but as I do so, my ankle gives out, and I stumble sideways. Eoghan catches me up and sweeps his arms around the back of my knees and my waist, pulling me into him and lifting me once again. He starts our walk down the hall.

"I can do it myself." The last thing I want is for Eoghan Kael to carry me around the prison like a child. He gives me no response and continues through the corridors, his heavy footsteps echoing. We walk in silence until we reach room 262, and he pushes it open and walks me to the bed. As promised, there is a tray with two bowls of stew, bread, and a pitcher of fresh water on the desk.

"Thank you. You can leave now," I say, but he simply reaches for a bowl and shoves it into my hands. The smell is intoxicating, though I know that is only the result of my hunger and not a testament to the chef.

"Eat," he commands as he pulls the wooden desk chair to himself and looks around the room. Since the night of my ambush, one of the men on laundry duty has changed the blankets and washed my clothes, placing them at the foot of my mattress. Fresh clothes—what I would not give for fresh clothes. Eoghan whistles softly as his eyes scan my bleak existence of bare walls and gray linens. "You absolutely know how to make a prison feel like a palace, don't you? No wonder Lanzo was so eager to get you inside."

I glower as I take a healthy bite. "I'm sorry my room isn't to your liking. May I remind you we live in a prison? I also didn't have much time to pack my belongings when they dragged me off to my execution."

The smirk falls from his face. His eyes move to his hands, and he clears his throat as a slight shade of pink colors his cheeks. I have embarrassed him. Good; it's time our encounters embarrass someone besides me. He sits in silence, and I can hear my jaw working as I eat before he finally speaks. "When you finish eating, I'll help you get cleaned up, and then I'll leave."

The room falls silent around us, apart from the metallic sound of my spoon against the bowl. When I have finished the first, he hands me the second, pouring me a glass of water I down instantly and he refills. By the time I have had my fill, not a single crumb remains. He bends down and unlaces my boots, pulling them off one by one to reveal bloody nails and blistered heels. He moves the leather monstrosities aside and rubs my ankle gently. I wince at his touch, and he softens his massage. Once he finishes, he hands me a fresh set of clothes, a towel, and my toiletries before he lifts me once again. I don't protest this time, as the fatigue of the endless days in the woods settles in. He exits the room and heads to the showers, where he pushes open the door to the steamy chamber. Two men stand next to the sink and turn to us as we enter, curiosity filling their gaze.

"Out," Eoghan says smoothly, and the men nod once at the command and rush to the door. When we are alone, he asks, "Can you do this on your own or will you be making another daring, yet idiotic, escape?"

I laugh in earnest for the first time in weeks—months, perhaps. "Just watch the door." He sets me down and then bows dramatically before exiting the room. I slowly undress and appraise myself in the mirror. I look like I've survived a war, and perhaps I had. There is no bloodless spot on my face or most of my body, and though the tonic has helped in the ways Gálgalesh promised, I still wince when I lift my arms or touch the red lines across my skin that had been open wounds. I turn on the shower and let the steaming water envelop me as I scrub my body clean. I take my time, savoring the warmth as the stream runs down my shoulders and chest. *He had known. He had known, and he had hated me,* I think to myself. There was no denying the fire in his eyes when he looked at me, had told me I was nothing…and yet, he had saved me. The gods only know why. I turn off the tap and reach for my towel. So normal, but it's a luxury I almost never had again. I pull on my clothes slowly, brush my teeth at the sink, and then collect my things and leave the room.

Eoghan Kael is waiting dutifully for me as I exit, falling into step as I slowly walk back down the hall. I want to collapse on my tiny, scratchy bed and sleep for a week. Maybe I will. Perhaps I will lock myself away in my room and never leave again, forget about my training with Gálgalesh and just make my permanent home among these walls. We reach our doors, and I grab the handle. Eoghan nods once to me and begins to turn his own, and he is halfway over the threshold when I stop him.

"Thank you," I say, and he only shrugs. "But why?" I continue. "Why save me? You said you wouldn't even if I was dying on the floor, crying out for help."

"I said I would still hate you. I never said I wouldn't help you." I stand there staring at his beautiful face in understanding. He hated me, but he was not the brutal killer—the heartless warrior—everyone claimed him to be. His eyes tell a different story completely, and it's one I would give the world to hear. But he hated me. He still hates me. I was going to have to find a way to reckon with that understanding— lest I succumb to the relentless agony of trying to help him see something more in me. "Goodnight," he says and leaves me in the hall.

"Goodnight," I say it to myself as I stare at the vacant

space in front of me, my world becoming more complicated still.

CHAPTER SEVENTEEN

I wake up just before five in the morning and pull on my clothes and shoes. I find a comb in my toiletries kit and run it through my hair—which has now grown ear-length and shaggy. The style is unfamiliar, but I cannot deny it compliments my face nicely, giving me a delicate look so vastly dissimilar to the brutes living around me. I pick up my cloak from my chair and wrap it around my shoulders before wrenching open the door to head to training with Gálgalesh —only to find Eoghan Kael standing directly in front of me.

"You." I take a step back, but some primal part of me heats at the sight of him.

"Me." His voice is a low drone of indifference. He could have been speaking to any dog and sounded more enthusiastic. "Shall we?"

"I know the way," I respond, and I pull the door shut as I push past him down the hall, limping slightly on my still-tender ankle. He keeps two steps behind me and follows, undeterred by my cantankerousness. I have always loathed being followed, regardless of the reason. Perhaps that is because escorts and attendants have composed my whole life, tasked with keeping their eyes on me, as if I might disappear into the abyss if left alone. Every second demanded my attention then, and now...now, I have Eoghan Kael following me every single useless minute of the day, all because I couldn't avoid being attacked like some worthless fool. He will hate me for it, and I will hate him for making feel me as tiny and useless as I truly am.

We pass through the corridors without a sound, apart from our slow, deep respirations. I can feel his eyes on my back the entire way. I turn into the courtyard, and there, in the center, Gálgalesh lazes upon a small stool, a barbed whip in his hand, Peadair standing beside him. I halt, unable to will myself any further, and Eoghan nearly runs into me as he enters the quad behind me. I swallow hard, and Eoghan steps into my side view, assessing the scene.

"What's this?" My head cocks to the side, and Gálgalesh rises to his feet. He walks toward me, and I move away from him, retreating the way I came. I feel the gentle pressure of Eoghan's hand on my back, holding me in place.

"At Báscogar, we have rules barring disobedience. It is an egregious error to knowingly and willingly defy the Warden, and though almost everything is permissible here, such offenses cannot go without punishment." Saliva wells in my mouth as my stomach churns sickly over itself. Gálgalesh continues without so much as batting an eye. "Peadair defied my orders to keep you from harm when I left you in his care. He has insulted me, dishonored his position as Second Warden of Báscogar, and nearly killed you for sport. Under Order Twenty-Five of the Prison bylaws, he must receive ten lashes to the back by the one he has mistreated." His gaze meets my own, his warden's mask is firmly in place. A seething anger consumes him, yet he maintains an eerie calmness. "I hereby condemn Peadair Okenshem to such punishment and order you, Maeve Moran, to administer it now."

Peadair's eyes grow wide, and he turns to Gálgalesh, muttering wildly in Anquonda, the language of the faeries. Gálgalesh has made my identity known—not to endanger me and sell me out in this godsforsaken place, but so Peadair might know the gravity of his attack. He knows as well as I that Peadair will not be telling anyone my secret—not now. Gálgalesh holds up his hand without averting his gaze from me, and Peadair falls silent.

The color washes away from my face, and I sink toward the ground, my hands gripping my knees. Regardless of what Peadair has done to me, I cannot do such a thing to him. I would not do such a thing to anyone. I shake my head violently back and forth. "I will not," I say as the bile rises in my throat.

"You will." Gálgalesh steps forward again, now standing an arm's length from me. "You must."

"I cannot." My head begins to spin out of control, and I have to close my eyes to keep upright. Gálgalesh pulls my right hand roughly from my knee and shoves the whip into it. I let it dangle at my side, the terrifying metal ends rubbing loudly against the stones below. "Gálgalesh, I cannot harm him. I will not. You care for him too greatly. I could never do such a thing."

Gálgalesh snarls furiously, and I lift my head to see his menacing teeth exposed as his lips curl back from them. "*Everyone* has someone who cares greatly for them. This is not about my feelings for Peadair or your connection to me! This is about *retribution*! Do you not understand? Revenge is never kind, and it is often brutal, but sometimes, it is deserved. Sometimes, it is the only choice if you want to break free from the shadows of fear and pain, to live once again. Now, swallow your pride and your virtue and step forward."

I turn my eyes to Eoghan, who nods to me, his mouth a thin line. There is no reconciling this, no discussion that would end with Peadair unmarred and me unsullied. Agonizingly, I stand, my knees shaking beneath me. Gálgalesh and Eoghan move toward the faerie, who has now knelt onto the stool where Gálgalesh once sat. They each take a side of his shirt and yank it over his head, throwing it to the ground before placing a firm grip on either of Peadair's arms. I take another step. Gálgalesh's face is hard as stone, but Eoghan Kael's displays a sadness as our eyes meet, one I feel so profoundly as I raise the whip high.

Crack! The leather bands snap thunderously as they come down upon Peadair's exposed back. He hisses as the metal barbs catch his skin and tear through, golden blood rising to the surface. *Crack!* Another lashing meets his skin, mutilating it again—another and another and another. I close my eyes, but Gálgalesh admonishes me, and I force them open once more. It is as important to him that I witness this as it is for Peadair to bear the consequences. Six, seven, eight, nine... After the tenth beating, I drop the whip from my hands, and the men release Peadair, who collapses to the ground. Immediately, Eoghan is at my side, a hand holding me steady. I hadn't realized my knees had tried to buckle.

"Take her away," Gálgalesh says, his voice hollow, his eyes not daring to look up from the stone pavement. Eoghan wordlessly turns me away from the barbarous scene, and we make it to the archway of the corridor before I empty my stomach over the ground.

———

I RETURN to my room for the rest of the day, refusing to leave for food or otherwise. Instead, I lay in the icy darkness as tears fall from my eyes, landing silently onto my pillow. Apart from the sparring—where I seldom make a mark upon my opponent and never one that would not heal—I have never hurt anyone in the whole of my life. Until that day in the forest; until my life had depended on it. Today, however, I was not in danger. I had left my mark on Peadair to remind him of what he had done to me. *Retribution*, Gálgalesh had said. The very thing I had come here to achieve…and I had nearly crumbled at the thought.

Eoghan does not bother me after he returns me to my room, but I hear the faint sound of knives being pulled wetly against a sharpening stone, and I know he is waiting, listening for me to re-emerge. Twice throughout the day, a man on kitchen duty sets food at my door without a note. An offering of peace from Gálgalesh, perhaps; I wonder what he must be feeling now. How had he been able to bear the horror of watching his lover maimed? Did he have to fight every urge to stop from tearing me limb-from-limb as blood spilled from Peadair's back? I remember how powerless I had felt when Rian was dragged away from me, how badly I wanted to scream out his name and break the people who had broken him as I sat helplessly, listening to him struggle against his captors. Had Peadair's eyes shown fear? Had he begged Gálgalesh to show him mercy? I would have sent me away, back to Gairdín, before letting anyone harm my lover, even if he had deserved it. I would have taken the beating myself. Yet, Gálgalesh stood, his expression blank while he forced Peadair to bear the punishment he earned.

I pull my knees to myself and let the sorrow undo me completely.

———

WE REACH the dining hall the next morning as breakfast is served, queuing up with the others. Gálgalesh arrived late to our training, his eyes ringed in deep circles of black, as though sleep had eluded him the night before. We did not leave the prison gates, instead practicing finding the thread of faerie magic behind the walls. I had practiced many times before in the confines of Gálgalesh's quarters, and although faerie magic could indeed bypass the enchantments placed on the prison, it felt harder to concentrate somehow, as though a mental block had been placed between myself and the Gálgalesh's magic. By the end of our session, I was able to confidently summon Gálgalesh's dagger from his sheath a handful of times and summoned Eoghan Kael's twice—much to his annoyance.

I grab two trays and hand one over to Eoghan, who takes it silently and then falls back, allowing another resident to step in line between us. Of course, he would refuse to be seen with me; why would he want anyone to assume we were friendly when he hated me so? There had been enough of us together for a lifetime when we arrived back at the prison gates. I fill my tray with the same bland porridge and bruised fruit the cooks offer us each day and exit the line as I turn to head toward Kruz, Tomás, and the other Iranndairian men. Eoghan clears his throat behind me, and I stop mid-step.

"I sit over here." He points to an empty table near the corner of the room, clear across the hall from Kruz and the others. The other Fire Cursed must not be back at the prison yet.

"Well then, I suppose you are going to just have to keep your eyes on me from there. I hope you don't need glasses." I do not dare glance at him before I saunter away, and when I reach the table, I set down my tray softly to take up my usual seat directly opposite the red-haired smuggler. I smile weakly at them as their jaws fall open at the sight of me.

"That is definitely not the hello I expected," I say as I lift my spoon and dip it into my breakfast.

"We thought you were dead! No one could find you for days!" Kruz stammers, dropping his own in the process. "Where have you been?"

"Gálgalesh ordered me on a training outing near Fáintìrean," I reply as casually as I can, though I still feel ill from yesterday's encounter.

"Gálgalesh sent *you* to train near Fáintìrean?!" Kruz is gaping so badly now, I have to look away to keep from rolling my eyes.

"With me," Eoghan Kael cuts in. "Move."

He indicates to Kruz and the others, who look up at him with surprise, but then he bares his teeth menacingly, and they move down the table to let him take Kruz's seat across from me. He glowers, annoyance written all over his face, as if I have embarrassed him by dragging him across the room to sit with me. As he drops down to the table, his tray clashes against the wooden surface. Kruz takes him in and then turns his attention to me, as if trying to understand how Eoghan and I have come to be sitting together at this table without his knowledge or approval. Eoghan pays him no attention at all, instead taking a bite from an apple he picks up from his tray. Kruz evens his expression and then continues.

"Kael," he acknowledges him flatly, and Eoghan ignores him outright, as if speaking to Kruz would embarrass him further. Kruz recovers quickly and plays up the most casual tone he can muster. "How are the sparring sessions going with Gálgalesh, Alana? You seemed to be getting better the last time you practiced with Tomás and me."

"All right, I suppose." I keep my eyes down as I feel Eoghan's own upon me as he watches me and red colors my cheeks. Eoghan laughs under his breath, taking another bite.

The others look down at their plates, keeping an ear on the conversation while becoming exceptionally interested in their food.

"What is so funny, Kael?" Kruz sighs. He seems unnaturally perturbed by the other man's presence, and I am reminded of their last encounter in front of my bedroom door.

"Nothing." Eoghan shrugs his shoulders lightly, his eyes still on me. I shake my head and clear my throat.

"I'm too small to spar effectively against anyone here. I know you and Tomás pull your punches with me during practice, or else you'd kill me every time."

"That's not true," Kruz counters as he reaches for my free hand and intertwines his fingers with mine. My hand falls loosely into his, although there is something possessive about the gesture that makes me feel as though I am an unwilling performer in a show. "You just need a little more practice and confidence, but you could give us a run for our money."

"Don't lie to her." Eoghan's voice is dominant, if not a little heated. "She has no use for sparring anyway. She needs to learn how to kill."

"Not everyone here has a need to kill." Kruz's voice rises slightly, and the prisoners at nearby tables stop and look toward us. "Not everyone is *you*."

"You're right." I look up through my eyelashes and meet Eoghan's gaze, making me feel indecently exposed as I pull my hand away from Kruz. "But Alana does. Alana is a killer, whether she wants to be or not." His lip curls up to one side, and the room becomes stifling. "She might be the most terrifying little thing in this whole damn prison."

I jump to my feet, my food still untouched on my tray. "I'm leaving," I announce, and Eoghan rises with unhurried ease. I pick up my tray from the table and stalk over to the receptacle, where I clear its contents and hand it to the man on kitchen duty. My whole body feels as though it is boiling, and I know if I look at Eoghan Kael once more, I might burst into flames. *Why does he do this to me? Why does he make me feel as though I want to punch him and press my lips against his at the same time?* I head for the exit, desperate for the winter air to rush over me as I fight the urge to pull my cloak from my shoulders. I will throw myself into the snowbanks if I have to. I reach the dining hall doors and push my way through, gasping for breath. I stumble onto the gangway and catch myself on a nearby column for support.

Moments later, Eoghan Kael emerges from the double doors. "You can't leave without me, *Alana*. Or perhaps you forgot what Gálgalesh said," he reminds me, as if I could ever forget he is bound to me against both of our wills.

"Just leave me alone, would you?"

"I would love to be absolutely anywhere else," he hisses, as though I had forced his hand myself. "If I did not have to see your face for one more second, I would pay homage to every single god on this continent for the rest of my life. But because you have decided you want to risk all our lives by being here, I have no choice." He is radiating with so much heat, my already scorching body can barely stand to be so close to him. "You are a spoiled, relentless, whining baby. You have no idea how many people will die when you screw everything up for us because you are looking to avenge, what? Your family, your lover…or your pride? All while you sit there playing sweet, innocent damsel for a smuggler who cannot take his eyes off you. It's pathetic, it really is."

Fury clouds my thoughts, and I round on him, my chest heaving as I try to control my rage. "I'd rather leave this place and meet Donn in death than spend another minute with you! You know *nothing* about me! You have no idea what I lost. You cannot comprehend what brought me here!" My lip quivers, and I reach my arm above me, my hand clenched into a fist. I hurl it through the air toward him, and he grabs it just inches from his face. I shove hard, trying to free myself from his grip, but he holds firm. I swing my free fist toward him, but he grabs that one too. "You arrogant, narcissistic, conscripted scum. You are not worth anything to anyone. You live here in this prison and make yourself seem so tough and menacing so *someone* will fear you or care about you at all. *You* are nothing. Now let. Me. Go!" I scream, and he shoves me back, just hard enough to make me stumble but not enough to harm me.

"Fine. *Go*," he says, turning from me and walking in the opposite direction. I watch in silence as he stalks out of sight, my blood rushing loudly in my ears.

Kruz and Tomás exit the dining hall at a run, and Kruz places his hands on my arms tenderly as he reaches me.

"Where's Kael? Did he hurt you? We heard you screaming—are you all right?"

I do not meet his eyes as my gaze remains transfixed onto the darkness. Why had his presence made me so angry? He had no right to assume he understood me or what had brought me here, but I had done the same to him. Had he not been simply doing as ordered, yet I treated him as though he had been the one to take something from me? As though he would ever want anything to do with me? Was he wrong about me, or was I threatened by the fact that he—unlike everyone else in this world—saw me for who I was?

I shrug myself free of Kruz's grip and push him away gently. I raise my hand wordlessly between us as tears roll in waves down my cheeks.

———

THE PRAYING tree is a quiet place without many patrons in the far courtyard. What is the use of praying to the gods for anything besides a quick, merciful death here? I fall to my knees on the cracked stone, roots rising between the surrounding pavement, and I set a small dish of incense upon the altar. I traded the two gold coins I had pocketed from the dead faerie in the forest for them this afternoon. I light them and the smoke circles around me, filling the space with a strong smell of sage.

I do not know any of the prayers offered up to the gods. My father did not allow tributes to be paid to anyone but himself, and I did not think much of offerings or prayers or asking for blessings or mercies much then. I always saw them as a waste of time when nothing could harm me and everything was given freely. Common people always had something to pray about and ask for, but I was not common... until now. I close my eyes as the smoke continues to rise, searching for anything to call forth—a memory, or even just the image of a face to grasp as I hunt deep inside for the pain I have so suppressed.

In the first days after the coup, sadness consumed me, and tears flowed freely both day and night. Each painful movement was a reminder of the suffering and loss I had endured. Now, here at the prison, where has that sadness gone? All I feel now is rage or emptiness, an icy heart to match the bitterness of this place. I miss my brother—his visits from the Tinemallacht military camps so infrequent in the last days. The day he arrived for my wedding, I marveled at how much he'd changed since we had last seen each other. His tanned skin and bleached hair was so like Eoghan Kael's, his once gangly physique trained and trimmed similar to the desert fighters he lived with. I miss my mother doting over me and braiding my hair, her singing echoing down the long halls of Caisleán Rialú. I miss my father and the secrets he kept, the ones I had promised to uncover from childhood but never got a chance. He was a mystery still, a man I had never quite gotten to know. I miss Rian and how he smelled of the sea. I miss his attention, his love, even if I cannot quite capture his voice anymore. His face is fading in my memory as the days pass by. If I do not keep missing him, I might lose him completely.

I lift my eyelashes and whisper the names of Rian, my father, my mother, and my brother Cai as I empty the fragrant ashes from the bowl onto the altar stone. I take my hand to the instantly cooling ash and spread them across the plane, painting the white surface black. Black for mourning; black for death; black for the depths of my soul I still cannot reach. As my fingers pass over the lower left corner, they stumble across two letters carved discreetly into the rock that now rises as the ash settles into the etching.

"CM," I whisper to myself as I trace the letters lightly with my fingertips. Initials, perhaps? Whomever had left their mark on the altar had little regard for the gods as well. Next to the letters, I feel something etched lighter, more reverently. A "G" and a "D" and the word "muinsa"—"trust" in the forbidden language. Trust. No one in the whole of my life has ever trusted me enough for it to matter. If they had, maybe I would not be here right now; maybe they would not be dead. Gálgalesh, however, trusted me. He trusted me with his magic, and when he placed that gruesome whip in my hands, he asked me to trust him. The least I can do is trust his decision of placing me in Eoghan Kael's care—even if Eoghan hates me and drives me insane and makes me burn with some emotion I have yet to understand. I can trust Gálgalesh because he trusted me first; because my life depends on that trust.

I rise to my feet and brush the knees of my black pants clean. I need to find Eoghan Kael. Maybe it is too late.

Perhaps he has already gone to Gálgalesh and refused me, choosing to leave Báscogar rather than to spend his days with the spoiled princess. Would his reason to stay be enough to keep him here? I could only hope.

I exit the far courtyard and follow the halls to the training arena. If Eoghan Kael was anywhere in the prison, it would be there. I bound down the corridor and deftly navigate toward the amphitheater, knowing the way perfectly by now. I round another corner, the curved archway leading into the pit of the training ground, and as I do, I spot him. He's alone, his shirt discarded—unbothered by the cold. He holds a sword in his hands, and he wields it above his head and through the air like a war dance, battling the invisible opponents masterfully as sweats rolls down his body in an outward display of his efforts. I take a silent step forward, leaning against the cool stone flanking the pathway leading to the center of the ring as I am held captivated by him.

He continues to move, his eyes holding an undetectable target in his sights. I cannot fathom how anyone could match his quick, decisively lethal strikes with such grace. It's as though he moves with his breath as he takes complete and steady strokes, never falling out of pace and never losing his concentration. He is so skilled on his own that a partner would be left in the dust. His chest rises and falls, and with it, his blade drives further toward victory. A swipe of his sword brings him to one knee as he hurls it forward for the kill. His dance of death ends with a bow of his head as he inhales and exhales heavily.

I move forward into the clearing, and he turns as the sound of my boots rouses him, his blade piercing the stone beneath him, his knee resting next to it. His brows pull tightly together at the sight of me, and I hesitate for a moment before forcing myself forward. What will he do— stab me? Not Eoghan Kael, not the man who carried me through the snow and the forest to save me. I stop within striking distance and take in his glistening skin and wet hair. He does not move to stand; instead, he begins to speak, annoyance written all over his face and drenching his words.

"What do you want?"

"To ask you for forgiveness," I concede. "I had no right to treat you the way I did."

"And what way was that? Was it when you called me scum or when you tried to hit me like a disobedient dog?" He shakes his head lightly, and sweat falls from his hair.

"B-both, I suppose." I wring my hands in front of me. If he had not truly hated me before, it was clear he loathed me now.

"Don't worry about it, Princess." He pushes himself to stand and trudges toward a small wooden table where his clothes lay, along with a canteen of cool water and a towel. He lifts the cloth to his face and disappears behind it, clearing the sweat from his eyes. Then, he runs it across his arms and chest. "I'll find Gálgalesh and let him know I'll be leaving by the morning. I'm sure he won't send you away. He made a deal with Damaris to take you in." The side of his mouth lifts weakly, as though the irony and humor of it might make me feel less terrible than I do. It does not help. Why would I be able to stay if I am the one unable to deal with our situation? Báscogar has been Eoghan's home for longer than it has been mine. If Gálgalesh makes him leave...

"I'll sit with you," I blurt out.

"Excuse me?" He drops the towel back onto the table and lifts the canteen, taking a long drink as he eyes me over the top of it.

"I'll sit with you in the dining hall. I'll train with you. I'll stay in my room if you ask me to. You do not have to leave on account of me."

My voice is pleading, as though I need him to agree, as if I need him to stay. Eoghan laughs against the lip of his canteen and removes it from his mouth before he twists the cap back on slowly. "What makes you think I would want you to sit with me or train with me or do anything with me at all? What if I want to be free of you? What if I know that if I don't, I might be the end of you?"

"You don't mean that." I try to keep my voice level. "You say those things, but you don't mean them. You would have let me die the other day if you did." His expression remains even. "I'll do whatever you want, but don't leave. Please, don't leave. You were right—what you said about me. I am spoiled and relentless, I whine all the time, but this place is my *only* hope of surviving and maybe living again one day…and I have a feeling you might need this place as much as me. So, please stay."

Eoghan takes me in, and I stand my ground. After a long moment, he sighs and rolls his eyes. He scoops up his belongings and stalks off toward the arena exit. I stare after him in silence. Not one word. He has not said one word to me. He reaches the archway and turns. "Are you coming, then, or are you just going to stand there all day?"

CHAPTER EIGHTEEN

Our first meeting back in Gálgalesh's quarters is the next afternoon. Like clockwork, the snow has begun to fall in heavy droves, the courtyards and the outer perimeter of the prison filled with feet of white powder. The training grounds—much to my surprise—remain unaffected, protected by enchantments. The prisoners do not seem to mind the ever-growing oppression, as though they have come to terms with their own confinement. I, however, felt immediate dread the moment I saw the heaping piles of ice and slush this morning. I'll never get used to this dreadful, inhospitable place. To think, I had always wanted to experience a Romiodóg winter before I arrived here.

I concentrate on the pages in front of me, the words of the forbidden language trailing off the page and onto the next. Defense charms; a replacement for the useless everyday common magic I have been studying for the past several weeks. I suppose Gálgalesh has decided now is the time to leave the introductions behind now that my life depends on it. I concentrate hard on the words and symbols, willing the magic to let me in. Faerie magic, unlike that of humans, has to be drawn out by a request and the right combinations of symbols and utterances, and though Gálgalesh says it will rarely—if ever—deny the wielder who offers the right combination, consequences do exist for evil and wrongdoing. The magic has a mind of its own.

"How are you and Kael enjoying your arrangement?" Gálgalesh holds his weekly correspondence with the Capital in his hand, a pair of reading glasses resting on the bridge of his nose.

"He hates me, but we are both trying to make the best of it." I succeed in creating a small barrier of glowing blue light in front of me, but it dies out almost immediately.

Gálgalesh raises his gaze over his glasses toward me when the magic erupts but then drops it again to the letter. "Do not hold your hands in front of you. It is not a parlor trick. The magic does not need silly hand gestures to be effective." I throw him a hand gesture of my own and stick out my tongue, and he chuckles lightly to himself. "Kael also does not hate you, but I am glad, for both your sakes, that you are trying to get along."

"He *does* hate me. He's said so himself." I place my hands in my lap and try the charm again; this time, I squeeze my face tightly in an effort to make the barrier last. When it erupts, it stays for five seconds longer before falling away weakly.

"Maybe hating you is the easier emotion than what he truly does feel for you."

"What are you saying, Gálgalesh? Does Eoghan Kael *love* me?" I laugh at the absurdity of it and turn to him. He does not look my way, instead picking up a pen and writing on a piece of parchment on his desk.

"Love and hatred are not the only emotions we possess, woman. Do not be ridiculous. Have you thought that perhaps your existence frightens Kael?"

Me, frighten Eoghan Kael? What would I possess that could frighten Eoghan Kael? I am not an opponent who would even make him break a sweat in a sparring match, as we have so clearly seen. I am small, weak, and I have mastered no magic. Hell, even the little magic I do possess is no match for anyone with actual power or talent.

"There is no way Eoghan Kael is frightened of me." I shake my head and rustle the piece of parchment covered in enchantments before trying the same barrier charm one more time.

"Do not be so sure you understand anyone here…or what your existence means to them." Gálgalesh finishes writing and drops the pen. He stands and walks over to the sofa to watch me conjure again. This time, the blue barrier emerges and holds true, though it flickers and shakes like it is threatening to give way. Gálgalesh picks up a small, balled up piece of parchment and throws it at the barrier. It collides with the blue light and falls onto the table. The charm weakens and then falls away into nothing again. "Very good. Take the notes with you and practice tonight. I want to see your progress tomorrow."

I wipe my brow, beads of sweat forming from the effort, and I scoop the pieces of parchment into a pile on the table. Gálgalesh leans against the wall near the sofa and watches me as I lace up my boots. We have not yet spoken about Peadair's attack or the aftermath, but something in his eyes tells me he might be ready to discuss it now. I clear my throat, breaking the silence as I pull my laces taut and loop them around each other.

"How is Peadair?" I ask cautiously. Every word feels like a precarious chess maneuver that could threaten all progress or victory. Gálgalesh is silent for a long moment, and I panic. What line have I crossed by asking about his disgraced lover? Could I salvage the conversation before the silence gives way to Gálgalesh's fury? Would he blame me if the attack had caused harm to their relationship? My mind is racing wildly when Gálgalesh finally speaks.

"His wounds will heal with time, but his pride might not." He summons two glasses and a decanter of brown liquor toward himself, and the glasses fill on their own. "That is the problem with faeries—their pride." He pushes a glass toward me, and I take it between both hands. "I would not hold my breath for his apology if I were you."

"Of course not." I shake my head and look into the glass. "I am so sorry, Gálgalesh."

He lifts his glass to his lips and drinks the contents down before refilling his drink immediately. "Drink," he commands. "What do you have to apologize for? I gave the punishment and made you fulfill it. You did as you were told."

I take a sip of the liquor, and it burns my throat on the way down. I cringe slightly, and the corners of Gálgalesh's lips curl upward. "But it would not have happened at all if I was not here in the first place." Gálgalesh tips his head in thoughtful agreement and then drinks again—this time, only emptying his glass halfway.

"True, but it was Peadair's own stomach that caused him to act. Faeries are dangerous creatures, woman. They are not to be trusted. Above all else, they see humans as delectable treats. Peadair loves the tenderness of female human flesh, especially women from the southern regions. The women of the north have not baked in the sun all their lives, and they lack the delightful flavor the meat gets, as though it has roasted slowly on the fire. I should have known better than to leave you with him. There was no way he could resist when I was not here protecting you."

My face turns sickly green at the talk of human flesh, and I fear I may never desire food again. I take another drink, hoping to burn the thought away. "Why did he not just do it then? The first day we trained together? Why did he bring the others?" If he had wanted me so desperately, I doubt he would want to share.

"Peadair had sworn not to harm you; our promises are binding, but I had not thought to have him swear he would not indulge in you if another killed you. Peadair has lived long enough to be clever. Sometimes, even more clever than me."

"So he paid the others to kill me." I throw back the rest of the warm liquor and set my glass on the table. "Are you still angry with him? I would hate to be the reason you—"

"You are a peculiar human," he cuts in and studies me intently. "I have told you Peadair hired men to torture and kill you so he might tear your flesh from your bones, and you worry you would be the cause of my anger toward him." He shakes his head incredulously. "I certainly do not like being made a fool, but Peadair has been my partner for more than six hundred years, and he will continue to be until my last breath. Love is not a simple thing to break."

Love is not a simple thing to break. I had only known love once, and the thought of being betrayed by him… I am not sure I would ever recover, let alone be able to proclaim to love him still. Perhaps six hundred years of love changes more than a handful do. I never got the chance to find out. I nod and collect my pile of parchment from the table before rising to my feet. Gálgalesh follows me to the door that swings open of its own accord.

"Thank you, Gálgalesh," I say, and his long fingers sweep across my forehead softly; a peace offering. A silent understanding.

———

I LAY on my bed in the darkness, spinning my small dagger between my fingers. It is late, though I still have not been able to sleep. I've sat for hours in the darkness, staring at the blank walls. Since Eoghan Kael became my guardian, Kruz and his Iranndairian friends have been inexplicably busy with their daily duties and nightly posts, leaving me alone every afternoon and night. *Cowards.* I throw the blade up and bounce it dangerously off the defense barrier charm. It races toward my face, and I catch it before it strikes true. Being alone all the time reminds me of how isolating this prison really is, how isolating this existence is now. I would give anything to have someone to really talk to, someone who knows who I am, why I am here. I throw the blade up again, but I fail this time, forcing me to roll away from the knife as it barrels into my pillow. I gasp and then laugh to myself as I pull it from the fabric, bringing a feather along with it.

As I continue my dangerous game of chicken, I hear heavy footsteps reverberate off the stone of the hall, growing louder as they approach. Someone coming back from their watch, perhaps? The resident in 263 has been working doubles after being caught trying to escape last week; perhaps it is late enough for them to be returning after their last shift. The footsteps draw nearer, too determined and even paced for a guard after a double shift. Whoever they are, they are heading this way. They stomp past my door, then stop immediately as they reach the next room, and I hear a muffled knock on 264—Eoghan Kael's prison quarters. I pause, the dagger held loosely in my grip. The door creaks open, and Eoghan's low voice sounds indecipherable through the walls. The visitor's responding voice is hushed and unrecognizable, and they continue back and forth just as a second pair of footsteps begin to echo somewhere down the corridor, drawing nearer at almost a run. I strain my ears as I try to discern the voices, Kael's low purr an irritated mumble now. The second man halts just as the first had, and another excited male voice joins in. This one is louder than the other two, drowning out the rest of the conversation completely. I peer out the window to my left; it has to be nearly midnight, quiet hours already in place. I hear Eoghan's frustration as the others rattle on, and then there is movement—shuffling, as though a fight has commenced.

I sit bolt upright as a hand grabs my doorknob and rattles it violently. Boots squeak against the stone floor, and someone forcefully knocks an arm away, causing the doorknob to momentarily stop before it is grabbed again. This time, someone turns the knob a full rotation to the right and pushes open the door in the darkness. I gasp. You have got to be kidding me!

In an instant, I release the blade from my hand and heave it toward the darkened doorway where the three black figures stand, piled together, wrestling each other in utter chaos. The blade soars through the air with precision, barreling toward the men, but a lightning fast hand reaches forward, grabbing the blade from the air before it hits the mass of bodies. My breath catches in my throat at the speed of the defensive maneuver.

"I told you not to open the door," I hear Eoghan say as he wrestles one man down to the floor. "She almost blinded you, and you would have deserved it, you idiot." The third man laughs as he stands next to Eoghan, observing the fight.

I jump from my bed and pull the thread of faerie magic to me. The room illuminates in a warm light as the candles placed around the small space burst to life. I see Eoghan Kael, clad in black pajama bottoms and a gray sleeveless undershirt, half-standing before me with one knee resting on the floor. Heat rises within me, and I feel my mouth nearly salivate as I take him in. I quite like the way he looks from this angle, looking up at me. My cheeks become an embarrassing shade of pink as I stare. *Stop it*, the last sensible part of my brain commands. I push the thought from my mind and swallow hard before I turn my eyes to the others—two Tinemallacht men, no older than Eoghan. The one on the floor, I recognize as River Hayes, the brawny, Fire Cursed warrior with the crooked smile and trademark tan and sun-bleached hair. He trains with Eoghan in the mornings. The other, who remains standing and smirking next to Eoghan, is Finn Rhodes—the man who was on patrol in Fáintìrean when Kael found me. The two men are dressed in their traditional black shirts and pants, and snow still clings to their cloaks. It seems they have finally made it back from their patrol.

Eoghan rises to his feet and steps forward into the room hesitantly, his cheeks slightly red. He pushes River with his foot admonishingly, and River snorts as he stares up at me from the floor. Eoghan passes me the dagger, and I take it from him, my fingers passing over his warm skin before we both pull away quickly.

"Now I get it," River says from the floor, and my head jerks toward him.

"Get what?" I drop the blade onto my mattress.

"Why he skipped out on patrol to come back here with you." River's smile spreads wide across his face, and he hits Eoghan playfully in the shin. Eoghan sighs grumpily and bats him away.

"I did *not* skip out on patrol. She was dying, I brought her back to Gálgalesh so he—"

"But then you didn't come back to Fáintìrean. Look, we aren't judging you, are we, Finn?" Finn refuses to answer and gives me an apologetic smile. River continues, "Send a raven next time, though, because we waited two extra days to see if you were coming back."

Eoghan, for the first time since I arrived at Báscogar,

looks less like his collected and powerful self. As I look up at him, I see only a twenty-five-year-old man embarrassed by his—apparently very familiar—friends. It feels as though I am seeing him in earnest for the first time. A smile spreads across my lips, and Eoghan shakes his head and clears his throat.

"It's complicated," he says down to River before addressing me. "Alana, this is River Hayes and Finn Rhodes: the only two men in Tinemallacht who were born without an ounce of civility or manners."

River jumps to his feet, reaching his hand toward me, and I take it. "Our mothers tried to teach us, but it was no use."

"At least not in River's case," Finn adds, politely extending his hand in greeting. "Sorry for the intrusion. When Eogh said Gálgalesh had paired you up together, River lost his senses completely."

"I just couldn't understand why Gálgalesh would pair *Eoghan* with the only woman at Báscogar! Seems unfair, really, if you know him."

"How so?" Despite the intrusion, I actually like the way it has humbled Eoghan Kael to near speechlessness.

River shoots a devious look Eoghan's way—who looks as though he might have pummeled him if they were not standing in my bedroom. "Because why should he *always* have the fun?! If you needed an instructor, I'd be more than happy to—"

"I said it's complicated," Eoghan cuts in, rounding on his friends and turning his back to me. Their smiles immediately fall from their faces. Even to them, he is dangerous. "Now, let's leave Alana alone. It's late, and we barged into her room without her permission." He begins to make his way back toward the hall, pushing the other two from the room as well. "Sorry. I'll see you tomorrow." He does not look at me as he speaks, but River leans over his shoulder as they reach the threshold.

"Do you want to come hunting with us tomorrow evening, Alana? Leave this stuffy old prison for a bit and spend some time with someone other than this grump?"

"No, she doesn't." Eoghan does not hesitate to answer as he continues his exit from the room.

"Actually…" Eoghan freezes, listening as I speak. River's expression is brimming with uncontainable joy. "I'd like to go…if you'll have me."

Eoghan lets out an exasperated breath, making it known my presence on their hunting outing is the last thing he wants. Yet he does not say another word, simply moving once again to the dark corridor.

"Perfect!" River beams, and I see a smile play across Finn's lips as well. "See you tomorrow then!"

The door slams shut behind them, and I laugh to myself as I pick up my dagger and lay back on the bed. Tomorrow, I will not be a just a prisoner of Báscogar, looking out on the world from the guard tower above or spending my days in the confines of this intolerably bleak room. Tomorrow, I might actually feel free for the first time since coming here, and whether Eoghan Kael hates me or fears me, I do not care in the slightest.

Dearest Little Sister,

Congratulations on your engagement! I have never been able to lie to you, so I must admit to being the slightest bit surprised by your choice of partner—I never pegged you as the sea-faring merchant type. I would have loved for you to have found someone with a few more calluses on his palms. Nevertheless, love knows no bounds... or at least that is what I have been told. Mother informs me Rian is honest and trustworthy and will care for you, and I plan to see to it that he does, that he takes you to see the continent, as far away from Gairdin as possible.

Tinemallacht is mercilessly hot no matter the season; the winter has brought little relief to our training camp, and some days, I think my blood might boil after hours in the sun. Despite the *weather, I love it here, more than I could ever explain. The work I am doing is worthwhile, and I hope one day to tell you all about it, about those who helped me along the way.*

I love you, Evie. Always remember that.

-Cai

"Alana." Kruz stands at the end of the table where the Tinemallacht residents take their meals and glowers down at me, sat across from Eoghan and Finn, River seated at my side. The men lean back in their chairs, casually assessing the red-haired smuggler as if he is some sort of animal that has walked into their territory. "What are you doing?"

"I'm having supper." I point down to my meal with my fork. "Do you want to sit with us?" The others shift in their seats, and Kruz stiffens.

"I mean, what are you doing with *them*? We haven't seen you in days, and when we do, you're with him." He nods his head toward Eoghan and scrunches his nose in disgust; Eoghan looks amused as he brings his hands to rest behind his head. "Are you just not interested in spending time with us anymore?"

Annoyance boils within me as he looks down at me expectantly. Had I not asked Kruz and the others every day since I had arrived at the prison if they would like to train or spend the evening with me? Had they not turned me down every single time, telling me they were too busy? Hadn't I spent every evening in quiet solitude because of their rejection—all because they would not dare be near Eoghan Kael, the man I was stuck with?

I dig my fork into the meat pie on my plate and shrug my shoulders. "I guess not." My tone is even and bored, though my breathing is heavy, and I take the fork between my teeth and eye him as his mouth falls open.

"Damn," River whispers under his breath. "I think you should leave now, Lanzo, salvage the last bits of your dignity before the lady buries them in the snow along with your manhood."

I glance over at Eoghan, who remains in his casual recline, but a small smirk whispers across his lips. I hardly ever see him smile, and I have to pull my eyes away to keep my own expression even.

Kruz's eyes narrow as anger and humiliation soak his features. "I had hoped for better from you," he speaks to me, refusing to look away from the other men. "Come find me when you're done with whatever it is you and Kael are up to."

Kruz sighs loudly and stalks across the dining hall past Gálgalesh, who cocks an eyebrow toward me in question. I shake my head, and he turns his attention back to the guards seated beside him to resume their conversation. Eoghan, Finn, and River watch Kruz until he disappears through the doors, and then their posture relaxes as they sink back down into their chairs.

"He's always been an irascible bastard, has been since the moment we arrived here. Iranndairians do not trust anyone, but they are Tinemallacht's neighbors to the south, and that means they hate us the most." River picks up a warm piece of bread from his own plate and spreads butter across the top before taking a bite.

"He is probably still angry Eoghan stopped him from

bedding me." I move my fork around in my food, and River and Finn both lean forward in surprise.

"You and Lanzo?" There is judgment in Finn's voice, and his eyes dart to Eoghan, who remains his same casual calm.

"Was not my finest hour," I admit as I remember the blood running down my leg and the ignominy of Eoghan's rejection in the shower room. I look up and catch Eoghan's gaze, and I understand the same moment is replaying in his mind as well. Something in his eyes smolders amorously, and color floods my cheeks.

"Lucky for Eogh, then, right?" River chimes in, but all words have escaped me, and Eoghan clears his throat loudly.

"Enough talk about Lanzo. Let's finish up here and head out before the cold sets in."

THERE IS no telling the difference between day and night now that winter has fully taken hold of Romiodóg. The sky remains the darkest shade of black with no relief. Even the charcoal grays indicating the early and late afternoons have eluded us for days now...which is nothing compared to the cold. Yesterday, they swapped out our black prison attire and cloaks with pairs made with even thicker fabrics. The weight of the new cloak is so heavy, it feels like it's dragging me down as it rests on my shoulders. The snow continues to fall thickly, growing to my waist in the courtyard, even after the guards shovel it away.

We pass through the interior of the prison together as the rest of the residents fall back to their sleeping quarters or evening duties, waiting for the call of lights out. Eoghan walks by my side, the other two surrounding me, creating a barrier as we reach the front gate. The guard on duty tonight is a Tonnfórsca man, around thirty years of age. He nods to us, and the gates fall away, beckoning us outside of their protective walls.

"This way," Eoghan says quietly, leading us toward the familiar woods where Gálgalesh and I began my training. As he leaves the clearing, the snow piles high around us, and my legs—half the length of the others'—sink down into the snow, now up to my hips. I stumble, and Eoghan catches me by the arm. "Hold on."

He rubs his hands together and then holds his palms out in front of him, the faint glow of fire emanating from them. Fire. He actually wields fire. The snow begins to recede in front of us. I feel heat to my side and at my back and wheel around, finding the others doing the same, the snow falling away on all sides. They all wield fire. *The stories are true after all.* It is down to around my calves in just moments thanks to their magic, and once I can step easily through the sleet, Eoghan drops his hands to his sides.

"Clear a path for us, would you?" He turns to the other two men. "Just down by the stream."

"With pleasure." River tips an invisible hat, and the two men bound forward, the snowbanks falling away in their wake.

I take in Eoghan, who gestures me forward patiently. "You're actually fire wielders…"

He laughs lightly as we continue behind River and Finn. "Some stories you've heard have to be true. We can't wield in the prison, of course, but the heat remains almost constantly."

I examine him closely—his cloak is lighter than mine and he is wearing the same clothes I was given in the fall. Of course they would be. For fire wielders, the cold would not bother them the way it does the others. They are probably boiling simply by being clothed. I had not imagined him warming me when he carried me back to Báscogar, his body heat when we fought in the corridor making me want to rip my clothes off, piece by piece...although I suspect *that* specific desire had little to do with the actual temperature.

We walk to a small clearing, where an icy stream flows softly down the next white hill and past the trees. The other two men are waiting for us, amusement and joy written across their expressions. I see no weapons among them besides the daggers strapped to their sides, no snares or traps of any kind. I am not even convinced any animals live in these forests at all—if *those* stories were true.

"Alana," River begins, his lip curled on one side of his crooked smile as he speaks out of the side of his mouth. "We have brought you here to see if you might join our ranks for an evening on the hunt. For glory, not sustenance, and perhaps to teach you a thing or two about Tinemallacht superiority among men."

"You really are so dramatic," Finn cuts in. "It's very simple, Alana. We come to the forest when the winter snow becomes dense for a game of catch and release. Rabbits run rampant near the river, and in the winter months, they are nearly impossible to catch by hand—only the most silent hunter who values stealth over speed or force can do so. So, we spend the evening trying until we either embarrass ourselves too much or freeze, and the winner receives the title of 'Assassin Supreme' until the next winter."

"Oh really?" I lean against a tree at the edge of the clearing and survey the men. "And who holds the title now?"

"I do, of course," Eoghan purrs at my side, his amusement softening his fierce features.

"Of course," I sigh. "I've never hunted before, but I would like to try." It was as good a time as any to practice the one skill that could help me end the person who took my family.

"Let Sir Kael show us how a natural born killer does it."

River throws a handful of snow at Eoghan, who rolls his

eyes and instructs us to move from the clearing. He shrugs his cloak from his shoulders and discards it over a low branch of a nearby tree. He surveys the clearing and eyes his target at the opposite end: a nearly concealed rabbit hole at the foot of a large, bare tree. His movements are slow and steady as he wades through the snow, his boots nearly silent against the icy banks. I lean forward as I watch his killer's dance, so similar to the nimble way he moves in the training arena, as if lethal grace flows from his very breath, as if he was born to make an art-form of death, captivating his victim before they have the chance to even understand the dangers of his presence.

He slinks down near the tree, and Finn nudges me, as if I lost concentration for even a moment. An impossibility. All I can see is Eoghan Kael—he is the only thing that exists. Beautiful and frightening. I have never met anyone like him; not one person can make the world disappear as he does. I am captivated so completely, I almost feel embarrassed by the way he holds me to him without showing the slightest bit of interest in me at all. Except for that look at dinner…the one there and gone in a flash. Perhaps I had concocted it in my mind, that desire I swore I saw at the mention of that day in the shower room…but maybe not. Maybe there is more to Eoghan Kael that I would like to explore.

"He's incredible," I whisper, almost to myself.

"You should see him when he wields." I catch River's smirk out of the corner of my eye.

"Wields fire, you mean?" I had just seen them all do so and, though impressive, it was not unique to him, not like this deadly dance.

"Not just fire. Everyone from Tinemallacht can wield dragon fire, but we all have our own magic as well. Eoghan's is some of the most powerful on the continent."

Powerful. I imagine that is an understatement for Eoghan

Kael's abilities. I cannot begin to comprehend the extent of his intricacies I have not yet witnessed.

He waits patiently, his breath so shallow, it appears he is not breathing at all, and then so softly—as though he has coaxed the rabbit into trusting against its better judgment, it peaks its head out of the hole, gray against the blanket of white. Kael's strike is swift and decisive. The rabbit doesn't even see him coming, and then Eoghan lifts it through the air by its ears and into his arms.

The two men sigh beside me. "There is no one better," River whispers before raising his voice to echo off the trees. "All hail Sir Eoghan Kael of Bastain! Catcher of rabbits and god among men!"

Eoghan laughs heartily and pats the rabbit once before releasing it back into its hole. He trudges from the clearing to my side, where he motions for the other two to stop their whooping and hollering, which only encourages them. He takes a seat casually in the snow and looks up at me as if in question. I sit down beside him carefully and wait for him to move away, but he remains—a mild, pleasant warmth emitting from him.

River and Finn are next to try their hand as they stalk a pair of poor rabbits from their holes and chase them around the clearing. Not once but twice, River falls face first into the banks, spitting snow wildly as he rolls defeatedly onto his back. Where Eoghan is graceful, the other two are clumsy and heavy-handed. The two bound around the clearing, picking up snow and tossing it in one another's faces, more of a fight between the two than any real hunting at all.

I love watching them play, and for a few moments, I forget entirely why I am here, the despondency that has rattled me for weeks and months. Somehow, in watching these men act more like boys than ferocious warriors, I start to feel at home.

They carry on, laughing as they collide and tumble into the freezing stream. I move to get up, but as they begin to splash around, pushing each other down again, I settle back into my seat. Beside me seated in the snow, Eoghan smiles and shakes his head, his shoulders bobbing slightly as he laughs to himself. The two emerge soaking wet but no less deterred.

"How long have you known them?" I ask as I hug my knees into my chest and pull my cloak tightly around me.

"Since we were kids." Eoghan watches the others with interest, his voice lighter than I have ever heard it. "We grew up together back in the desert. Our fathers were friends."

Childhood friends. I know nothing of what that might feel like. Apart from my brother and one or two children of the castle staff, I never had the luxury of friends…until I met Rian. Even then, I am not sure our friendship was the typical kind. I would give anything to run and play with someone my age, someone I could see as my equal—who saw me as their equal.

"What's it like—the desert, I mean?" I rest my chin on my knees and take him in as he turns his attention away from his friends and onto me.

"Hot," he admits with a small laugh. "The sun is almost always overhead, day and night, the exact opposite of this place, but it's home."

I nod in understanding. "I miss home too, though I could not really tell you what Golorgleann is like, apart from the palace grounds. Still, I miss the sunlight, the warm breeze."

"It is a shame you've never seen the continent, though I never enjoyed Gairdín much. The rest of it is a beauty to behold." He leans back on his elbows, the faint laughter of the others feels distant now, as if they have run off somewhere beyond the clearing.

"You have dragons in Tinemallacht," I begin, and he nods. "I would love to see a dragon one day."

"I heard the king was a worse beast than any dragon of ours." He smiles weakly, and when my face falls, he clears his throat. "Do you miss them?" His voice is soft, his expression is softer, sympathetic, even.

"More than I can explain." I will any sort of emotion to stay clear of my eyes. "My brother mostly. My father, of course, but he was always busy and my mother... Well, she had her court to tend to. They loved me though. I have to believe that." I hate myself for sounding as though I need convincing on the subject.

"And what of your lover? The merchant's son. Do you miss him as well?" I am not sure why he continues to speak to me, as if he would care to hear what I have to say, but there's no impatience in his gaze or annoyance in his voice.

"Rian." I give him a weak smile, and he tips his head respectfully as he waits for me to continue. "He is the reason I am here, though admittedly, I do not miss him as I feel someone should miss a lover. I think there must be something broken inside me, because I feel like I should miss him more. I cannot seem to place him, though...as if he's disappearing along with all the reasons I loved him."

"Tell me about him," Eoghan urges. I shake my head, embarrassed by my admission, craning my neck to see if I can spot River and Finn and change the subject. Eoghan sits up straighter, moving into my line of sight. "Don't worry about them. They are off to wield before we go back to the prison. Tell me about your lover, Princess. What was he like?"

"Rich," I laugh, and I watch as Eoghan's posture stiffens. A poor joke for the wrong audience. "Not that his money mattered to me. I was more excited about the adventure. He promised to take me with him across the Murcean Sea to Oleaíncudd one day."

"Ah." Eoghan runs his fingers through his hair softly, causing me to look anywhere but at him as my cheeks warm. "The merchant's life. I wonder what a princess might find captivating at Trader's Bay. I am told no slaves were ever kept in the king's household." I am not sure how he, of all people, would know such a thing when the rest of the continent believes the worst. "Was he powerful?"

"In what ways?" I drop my fingers to the snow and run them over the wet surface.

"What did he wield? He must be a powerful wielder to be a companion to the Life Bringer."

Life Bringer… I had only been called that by one person…

"He was a silencer. He could silence any space to protect important information from being overheard."

Eoghan laughs lightly as he collects snow in his hands, forms a ball, and then watches as it melts away. "Not his common magic. What individual magic did he wield?"

My brows pull together. I had only ever seen Rian wield one type of magic beyond summoning. "Like I said, he was a silencer," I say again. Eoghan looks at me, amused, but as he studies my expression, his changes to confusion. His brows pull together this time.

"You don't know, do you?"

"Don't know what?" I roll my eyes. "You cannot ask me a question and then just decide you do not like the answer and—"

Eoghan throws up his hand, and the forest around us falls deathly still. Not the breeze nor a sound from the rabbit fifteen yards away thumping its legs against the base of a tree can be heard, nothing except for the sound of my racing heart and heavy breath. "Silencing is common magic."

He drops his hand back down to his side, and the forest erupts with life once more. He surveys me for a long moment as my mind races around me. Rian never shared his magic with me. He had been so interested in my own magic and that of my family, but when I pressed him, he lied to me. Had I been taught any magic at all, I could have seen through it in a moment…but he knew that as well. He knew everything about me because there was nothing I kept from him, nothing I would not share. What else had he lied about? What else had I been stupid enough to believe?

Eoghan sits quietly, his eyes never leaving me. Not only does he hate me or fear me, but now, he knows just how worthless I am. Worst of all, as he stares into my eyes with an intensity I can hardly bear, I realize he actually looks sorry for me. Pity… That's almost worse than hatred and fear. I stand and dust the snow from my clothes. "I think I'll go back to the prison now."

Eoghan stands beside me just as the others reemerge from the darkness of the trees. "No." His voice is a command, but it is not unkind. I freeze at the firmness of his tone. Tears well up in my eyes, and if I do not leave now, I think I might break completely. I close my eyes and take a deep breath to still myself. "Let me teach you first."

His expression changes back into the fierce warrior of Báscogar, the graceful predator so skilled at catching his prey. Fire flickers in his eyes, and I swallow hard as his jaw sets and his breathing slows. Then, he takes my arm and leads me into the clearing—into my first hunt.

CHAPTER TWENTY

*"**P**apa, please!" I cry as I skid across the marble floors of the throne room. My mother's screams are distant as the blood rushes loudly in my ears. My cheek is white-hot from the sting of his hand as he bounds across the room toward me. He knows he won't leave a mark, but he has no idea how the pain lingers as he grabs hold of my arm just above my elbow, yanking me to my feet before his palm smacks across my face again.*

I thought it would be nice; I could not wait to tell my parents about Rian and his proposal. After all, my father liked him—so much so that he had been a regular visitor to the castle for four years. I could not have guessed my father would be so angry to find out I have fallen for his charm as well.

"WHORE!" he screams, and I feel spit coat my face as he shakes me violently.

"No, Papa! No, I swear it!" I try to tug my arm free, but he squeezes harder, cutting off the circulation. He'll break my arm just to show he can. He has done it before. It doesn't matter to him if it heals; the memory of it is enough.

"You sneak behind my back and give yourself to this man? This

commoner? Have I not been clear with you?! Do you not know your place?!"

My place. My place behind these walls. To give and give and give and to never leave. To never speak to any of the guards who might eye me with interest. To never join in on the banquets held in the grand hall, or on the revelry with the others, whether it be birthdays or holidays, only permitted to listen behind locked doors. To only play with the staff children who had been made mute by royal decree so they could not speak of my existence outside this prison of a castle. To only speak to the staff who had their tongues removed when they assumed their positions behind the palace walls.

"But I love him, Papa!" I shoot a glance toward Rian, who stands by the dais where my mother weeps in her seat beside my father's throne. He looks unsurprised and unamused, bored, even, and he makes no effort to intervene. He hasn't tried once since we arrived, and when my father stepped forward in rage, he backed away from me.

"Love? You do not know the meaning of the word, you stupid girl! You meet one man with a bit of wealth, and you defy me and throw yourself at his feet! Disgusting." I have never seen him so angry as his nose crinkles and he looks me up and down. "Did you spread your legs for him and let him bed you too?"

I gasp, and his eyes widen. He slams me onto the marble floor, pinning me under his firm grip. He reaches for a dagger hung on his belt—Romiodóg steel with a gold hilt. He brings it to my stomach, which is bare apart from the sheer fabric that runs from the skirt to the opposite shoulder of the midriff top, an outfit brought to me by Rian from his last trip to Trader's Bay. Slowly, he presses the blade to my skin, and I scream as it cuts into my flesh. There is madness in his eyes, and he pulls the blade through me, etching his anger into my skin. W-H-O-R-E. The letters fade as quickly as they appear, but blood coats my stomach, and the stabbing of the knife brings me close to unconsciousness.

When he finishes, he stands, leaving the bloody blade on the white marble. He looks down at me as he pants, and the letters blaze up at him in glaring red against my white skin. Footsteps leisurely approach from the far end of the room, and Rian appears in my line of sight at my father's side. He places his hand lightly on my father's shoulder, and the king tenses at the touch but does not move or shout.

"Your Majesty, perhaps we can come to an agreement."

———

TWO MORE LONG winter weeks pass by after the hunt, and I am still struck by disbelief as to the revelation made during the outing. Rian—*my* Rian, who had asked of me secrets that were never to be told, secrets perhaps not even my brother or mother knew, lied to me. He had so expertly utilized the information I had given him and weaponized it against me because I was a fool. I cannot decide what makes my skin crawl more: that he lied, or that I was now cursing a dead man in his grave. My heart sinks in my chest at the thought that the only genuine connection with another person I had ever possessed was no more than a farce. To what end? Money? Rian had enough of that to build himself a palace if he so desired. Power? I suppose we could see where such power caused him to end up: his body broken and buried in an unmarked grave somewhere in the slums of Gairdín.

Was there no end to the depths anyone might stoop to get ahead? Had Rian loved me at all, or was the merchant's son no better than the harlots that flood the city streets and darkened brothels to make their way?

Gálgalesh has taken to having Eoghan and me train in the arena in the mornings, making clever work of our arrangement, and Eoghan sees to it to best me every time. He has every advantage in size and talent, and he lacks the humility of a man willing to let a woman win. Still, he is a wonderful instructor, calling out maneuvers and walking through counter attacks as we go, regardless of his mood.

"Do not rely on your magic! He will use it against you. Remember, here he might not be able to wield, but out there, you have no advantage against him."

Gálgalesh stands at the edge of the arena, his arms crossed over his chest and his boot propped up against the wall behind him. Eoghan beats down the daggers I have summoned from his belt, breaking my concentration, and lunges toward me, throwing us into a barrel roll. He lands on top of me and pins me beneath his body, his knee resting on my chest.

"Underneath me again, Princess?" He clicks his tongue. "I'm starting to think you're down there by choice."

"I'm starting to think that is what you want." I use my elbow to swipe the side of his knee in hopes of throwing him off balance, but he doesn't budge.

"I've already told you exactly what I want."

He dives forward, his fists holding tightly to my shirt, and pulls me into yet another circumrotatory maneuver that flips me backwards to my feet. He releases his hold and shoves me away, and I counter with my fist, hurling it toward his face. He blocks it with his forearm, and I throw another punch, but he grabs my wrist.

"You're never going to best me that easily," he croons in that low, smooth, sensual voice of his, and he gives me a once over as he pulls my arms close to his chest, showcasing his control.

"I don't know about that." Our bodies are hot against each other, and I can feel his chest heave with each breath. My eyes trail to his lips, and I run my tongue softly against my own. I feel his muscles tighten in response. "I thought maybe I was bringing you to your knees."

I swipe my leg behind his, and he buckles as his knees collide with the stone beneath him. I heave my arm hard into his chest and push him flat onto his back while my free hand takes the dagger from my side and slides it up under his chin.

"Do you yield, Kael?" I whisper, and a faint shadow of a smile tugs at the sides of his mouth.

"Very good, woman." Gálgalesh grabs me under my elbow, and Eoghan releases my arm as I stand. I reach down to offer him my hand, and he rises, dusting off his clothes. "Perhaps you do have at least one advantage over Kael after all." I smirk, and Eoghan murmurs something under his breath as he heads for his canteen. "I think we are finished for today, but I wonder if I could speak with you for a moment."

He indicates toward the far end, and I follow him. I can feel Eoghan's eyes trail behind us, but he remains respectfully out of earshot. When we reach the empty corner, he pulls a piece of parchment from his pocket and unfolds it carefully. It appears weathered at the edges, a footprint on one side, as though someone dropped and stepped on it. Gálgalesh hands it to me, and my heart falls into my stomach. I open it to find my own handwriting on the page—the guards' schedule I had memorized for my trips to the tower.

"Are you wishing to inform me of your plot to escape a prison of which you are not a prisoner?" Gálgalesh's eyes glint with mischief. I crumple the paper up in my fist; there is only one other person in this entire camp who would know of the schedule's existence.

"How did you get this?"

"Curiously, a concerned guard brought it to my attention, stating he had found it lying in the corridor between yours and Kael's rooms. After careful inspection of said mystery parchment, he found it may be part of a devious plan by the Fire Cursed warriors to kidnap and harm our only female resident. Imagine my surprise when I heard such treachery was taking place under my roof."

He is almost laughing outright now, the amusement so evident, I think I could hit him and it might not sour his mood. Of all the ridiculous lies Kruz could come up with, this really had to be the worst. I hand Gálgalesh the ball of parchment, and he throws it in the air and catches it.

"I hope you told the concerned guard the next time he is worried about my kidnapping, he should try knocking himself over the head for a few hours of worry-free sleep."

"Perhaps you might be interested in showing him just how capable you are at handling a would-be kidnapper. I suspect Kael would allow him a round or two during training." He lifts his chin toward Eoghan and then sighs. "Perhaps not…" I turn to see Eoghan standing transfixed by our conversation. "I'd offer to have Lanzo as a snack, but Iranndairians are said to be a bit fatty, and I'm watching what I eat." He turns his gaze back to me. "Enlighten me, woman. Why would you need to know the guards' schedules when you are free to come and go as you please? I would advise against it, but you are not bound to this place. I cannot keep you here if you wish to leave."

I lean back on my heels. Though I have always known I am not a prisoner, I never suspected I might just be able to leave. How could it be that simple? Could I escape like the Tinemallacht men without any repercussions at all?

"I like the view from the rooftop," I finally admit, and Gálgalesh gives me a sideways glance. "The guard towers lend the best view. The walls become so oppressive…and I've always hated walls. Up on the rooftop, I can see for miles. I just…love the view."

Gálgalesh looks at me as though I am sprouting a second head. He pockets the ball of parchment and straightens his cloak. "You are such a curious woman. You would like to see the world, but you never think about stepping foot outside. The rooftop is yours, and so is the open gate, any time you seek it."

Without another word, Gálgalesh pushes past me toward the arena's exit. I make it back to Eoghan as Gálgalesh reaches the stone archway.

"Oh, Kael." He turns back, his face the mask of authority only the Warden of Báscogar can wear. "I almost forgot: next week, you will be making a patrol run to Fáintìrean for a few days. The villagers are still in need of assistance. Take the woman with you as your aid. Show her the *world*."

As he leaves, Eoghan hands me my canteen with the cap already removed. I take it from him eagerly and empty the contents. He picks up his shirt from the wooden table where our cloaks and personal items lay for safe keeping and pulls it over his head.

"What was that about?" His attempt at casual conversation is marred by the bite in his words.

"Oh, nothing, really… Just that Kruz Lanzo fears you might kidnap me and whisk me away from here."

I pull my cloak into my arms and run my hand through my hair. Eoghan scoffs with such ridicule, I suspect he would rather not take me anywhere at all. He throws his cloak over his shoulders, and I wonder why he wears the damned thing at all—it is just useless protection against the cold he hardly feels. I imagine he could run right through the snow, wholly unclothed, and not be more than slightly uncomfortable. Then, I remember what he said to me the night of the hunt. Tinemallacht, the severe, unrelenting desert that darkened his skin and lightened his dark hair—that was home, and he missed it as much as I have ever missed anything in my life. He can bear the heat, and he would welcome it gladly.

"I want to shower before we eat," he says as he motions for us to leave. "Let's stop by our rooms first." He drops his hand to his side where he replaced his daggers in their leather holders. He draws one from its resting place and turns it over in his hand, offering me the hilt. "You earned this today. I bet Gálgalesh you would not best me for at least another month; I suppose I was wrong about you, Life Bringer."

That nickname again. A pang of heartbreak shoots through my chest for just a moment, but I grab hold of the dagger and place it on the opposite thigh than the one I already possess. I give him a weak smile, and he leads me from the arena back through the now-stirring halls.

We make it to the passageway leading to rooms 262 and 264, making casual conversation about this morning's training. He still does not believe I need to spar and reasons another hunting trip might do me more good than bruising each other might ever do. Much to my amazement, in the months I have been at Báscogar Prison—nearly four now in total—my frail, breakable body has become toned and nearly unrecognizable. I no longer require Gálgalesh's tonics at the end of each training session, and my thighs and arms no longer burn from exhaustion halfway through our sparring matches. I feel simultaneously less like myself and more like myself than I ever have in my twenty years of life. Not weak, and certainly no longer the damsel with a death wish Eoghan Kael saw me to be.

As we reach our doors, Eoghan turns to me, completing his final thoughts on my left hook he so easily evaded this morning. As he opens his mouth to speak, the door at the end of the hall creaks open, steam and the sound of the showers filling the halls. In perfect unison, Eoghan and I turn to find Kruz Lanzo, his red hair wet against his black shirt, his boots held lightly in his hand as he exits the shower room into the hall. His eyes narrow at the sight of us, and his shoulders square as he saunters our way. I haven't spoken to him since that evening in the dining hall, and it is clear he has not forgotten my words of dismissal. Eoghan lets out a deep, quiet growl from some primal place in his chest, and his brows pull together. Is he angry over Kruz's attempt to cause Gálgalesh to separate us? Or is it something else that makes his eyes glow with fire like I've never seen before? He turns to me and, just over his shoulder, I see Kruz quickly approaching, doing his worst to appear unbothered by our proximity while craning forward to eavesdrop on what one might think to be a private, intimate conversation. Eoghan's chest rises with an audible inhale, and he takes a step closer to me, filling my view. Kruz's bare, damp footsteps against the stone floor become louder as he closes the gap between us, and Eoghan lifts my chin softly with his thumb. My eyes shoot to his—his stare so intense, it might be possible he has the power to see to my very depths. The need in his eyes makes me feel for the wall behind me for support as my knees quake under me, the sound of the world falling away completely. Even after a morning of sparring, he smells so good, I can hardly stand it. My breath hitches at the softness of his fingers against my skin, and it takes everything in me to not pull him into me further. He lowers his lips so the faintest movement would have them brushing against my own.

"Close your eyes," he whispers almost inaudibly, and I obey as his lips fall upon mine in a kiss.

I no longer remember where I am, who I am—not even my name can slip past the electric current sealing our mouths together. My lips part; I feel Eoghan's fingers brush lightly up my cheek to cup my face in his hands, and I melt against his touch. I have little to compare a kiss like this to, but I would have to admit, it is better than any I have experienced. Eoghan Kael tells a story with his mouth, one of longing and emotion mirroring my own that I have so desperately tried to keep at bay. I am completely at peace, cherishing every passing second or lingering hour. I could remain in this state for all of eternity and feel fulfilled. His lips move against mine soft but possessively, as if I am his to kiss, his to touch, and I am for those seconds or hours he wants me...until he pulls away, and the cold prison air once more replaces his warmth.

"Sorry." He wipes his forefinger and thumb across either side of his lower lip and takes a step away from me, creating a barrier of space between us.

I look down the hall, now empty apart from the two of us, and it's clear Kruz has stalked away from our show, which Eoghan obviously orchestrated just for him. My mind floods with understanding as I take in the stoic response on his face. I am such an idiot. He did not kiss me because he wanted to. He did not feel as though if he were not to touch me, he might never be able to breathe again. No, because he does not care about me—he does not want me at all. It was a show, put on to get back at Kruz Lanzo, who had hurt Eoghan's pride. It had worked, of course—all because I had desperately wanted him to kiss *me*, to touch *me*, to want *me*. Another pawn in a man's game, played like the fool I am.

I turn and leave Eoghan standing alone in the hallway, his stare blank as I close my door behind me.

———

I FIND myself in my usual place upon Gálgalesh's sofa that afternoon, my feet kicked out behind me and my boots resting on the rug. Common faerie magic is coming easier now, with me moving from defensive charms to offensive attacks and tricks to blindside one's opponent.

Eoghan has taken to accompanying me in my daily hours of study, and he and Gálgalesh pour over secret letters and maps at his desk that I am not allowed to see. It is endlessly irksome as they mutter and plan amongst themselves, never bothering to let me in, as if I am not here at all. I hate them for it. I hate that I sit here every day muttering spells to myself as they do something of importance. Men have all the fun, and I am once again the silly woman left to her own silly devices. My temper rises to the surface as I wallow in self-pity—whining, as Gálgalesh, in his endless wisdom, loves to remind me. Gods, I hate this place and these insufferable men and this stuffy old room… Well, actually, I quite like the room. The men, however, I could do without.

I throw up the blue defensive barrier between us; I have become so competent at it that it spreads across the length of the room. I pull my daggers from my thighs and throw them toward the two men. They clank heavily against the barrier and fly back toward me, landing on the table at my side. One for Gálgalesh, who treats me as though I am little more than an incompetent child. One for Eoghan Kael…for being Eoghan Kael. Two for Eoghan Kael. Three. I throw my fourth dagger straight at the back of his head as I drop the barrier. It soars through the air, and without so much as a glance over his shoulder, Eoghan tilts his head to the right, the dagger missing him by an inch and flying into the wall. It sticks, its handle protruding from the mortar between the stones. Gálgalesh turns on his heels, his face bright with outrage, his jaw slack in shock, and I cover my mouth to hide my amusement.

"We do not throw knives at the backs of our allies! What has gotten into you, woman?" I shrug my shoulders and turn to the parchment in front of me. Gálgalesh takes me in and then wheels around to Eoghan, who has not so much as lifted his head from the map on the desk. With an outraged huff, Gálgalesh pulls the dagger from the wall, tossing it onto the table. "I do not care about your quarrels. Do you understand?

Do *not* throw weapons in my quarters again, or I will see to it that the shadow lurker in the basement drinks your veins dry."

I mumble under my breath and slap the parchment in front of me loudly. "Gálgalesh?" He groans at the sound of his name. "I think I would like to stay at Báscogar when Kael leaves on his patrol in Fáintìrean."

Gálgalesh picks up an envelope from a pile next to him and opens it with his long fingernail, pulling out a letter he will once again not allow me to read. "Do not be ridiculous. You will go, and you will *not* murder each other while you are gone. The people of Fáintìrean have enough to worry about without you two causing trouble."

I sit up and cross my legs underneath me. "But why must I go? I will be of no help to Kael, and he does not want me there to begin with!" The scoff that escapes Eoghan is so mocking and laced with ridicule, my cheeks turn crimson with embarrassment. Oh, how I hate him and his arrogance. I'd like nothing more than to get him into the training arena again and bring him to his knees. I reach for one of my daggers on the table, but Gálgalesh is quick to summon them, catching them up in his right hand.

"Enough! You are acting like a child, and I have half a mind to dump you straight out over the ridge line myself! You *will* go to Fáintìrean with Kael, you *will* aid him in what-ever task he requires of you, and you *will* do so with a better attitude, or else you have no place here! You are going because I say you are, and that should suffice. Now, pack up your belongings, both of you. I tire of you today."

I slap my feet heavily onto the floor and pull my boots to me. Eoghan rolls up the map on the desk and hands it over to Gálgalesh who pulls open his desk drawer and locks it away inside. I pile my guides and stand, lifting my cloak from the arm of the chair beside me and over my shoulders. Gálgalesh hands Eoghan my daggers, and instead of pocketing them, he ambles toward me and kneels coolly, shoving each into their sheaths before smacking his hand loudly against my thigh and rising, full of mirth. I cannot even look at him. He finds me amusing, my anger nothing more than something to tease. I turn and stomp away, grabbing the doorknob and yanking it to me. It does not budge, and I roll my eyes as I refuse to take my concentration from the ancient wood. Gálgalesh insists I am not a prisoner, and still, he refuses to let me be.

"Do not forget what I said," Gálgalesh warns, and the doorknob turns hot in my hand. I release it with a wince but nod my head silently in understanding. The door swings open, and I am nearly halfway down the hallway before Eoghan has passed over the threshold.

CHAPTER TWENTY-ONE

*"T*ell *me again about the dragons!"*

I roll myself across the large four-poster bed with golden vines sculpted into the headboard and around the posts. King's gold. All the furniture in Caisleán Rialú features at least a small amount of it, and the vines represent the plentiful fields and gardens of Golorgleann, our capital territory. Cai has returned for his birthday banquet—his twenty-sixth—and he lays across an immaculate blue sofa in front of a large marble fireplace, a book in his hand as I lounge on the much-too-soft bed no one has slept in since he last visited nearly a year ago. He sleeps on the floor most nights now, preferring the hard wood and thin rugs to the luxuries of the castle. His laugh fills the room, and I cannot help but beam at the sound I have so missed the entire time he has been gone.

"What would you like to know about the dragons, Evie?" He is every bit as cool and calm as I remember, much to Father's dismay, and a hopeless bachelor, much to Mother's. Still, to me, all I see is how adventurous and kind he remains after his years of service. He is everything I wish deep down inside to be.

"Are they as terrifying as the legends say? Have you seen them

hiding amongst the dunes? Is it true they are untrusting of royalty?"

"There are worse things to fear in this damned castle than the dragons of Tinemallacht...though they do hide amongst the dunes and can be downright frightening when they breach the surface without warning. And to answer your question, it does not matter if one is royalty or common. Dragons trust no one unless they have reason to. We could learn a thing or two from them, actually."

His golden brown arms lift him to a seat, and he runs his fingers through his hair. He has refused all finery since arriving home, opting instead for his torn Tinemallacht pants and shirt in the reddish-orange of the desert sand. I have never seen anyone dress so casually in the castle. They have never allowed me to even wear my riding clothes outside of the stables. Cai, however, has never had a problem bending or even outright breaking the rules. That is something I have always admired about him.

I wonder if he will ever find his way back to this place, or if home is somewhere else completely now. Tonight at the banquet, they will unveil his new portrait, a ridiculously ostentatious painting portraying him as the perfect heir our parents desire, rather than the man of myth and legend he has become on the battlefield and beyond. They will parade a thousand women in front of him for him to choose from. He will take one for the night, I suppose, but that is all. He has no desire to marry, no desire to sire an heir for the royal line. He dreams only of the warrior he has become and his pledge to keep our kingdom safe.

He said as much two summers ago, when he requested placement on the front lines during the Third War against Iranndair. I remember the shouting, the bruises, black and blue, mutilating his face as he refused vials of my healing magic over and over. It was not until he and his company had been victorious in the Battle of Buaeth that my father had given up on fighting Cai's desire to remain in Tinemallacht full time. He even claimed it was he who had sent him to the battlefield and won us the war.

Cai's short sleeve rolls up his arm, and a blue-black image inked across his skin becomes visible: a skull engulfed in flames. It's the Tinemallacht crest of the desert people, the warriors of legend and nightmare. I push myself down the comforter and onto the floor, crossing the room barefoot on the opulent carpet. I grab hold of his bicep and examine the tattoo etched so brutally there. I can tell it had been hand-tipped without magic, as the lines run smooth but imperfect. It had to have taken hours or days to score the color onto his flesh—to mark him not as a prince of Draíocoinnigh, but as an equal. My thumb passes featherlight over the image.

"Dualdanas, Urrir, Ghlóiriant—Duty, Honor, Glory." His voice is filled with pride. "One day, Evie, I'll take you from this damn castle and show you the people and places that matter."

"Really?" I am transfixed on him, on what he's become. It is as though I am seeing him fully for the first time. He nods and smiles up at me. He is so much like the brother I grew up respecting and trying to imitate, but at the same time, he is nothing like him at all.

"The Life Bringer." He catches the end of my braid between his thumb and forefinger, creating a soft glow of light. "You might be able to save us all...to save Draíocoinnigh."

"Does Draíocoinnigh need saving?" My hands trace the contours of the skull up to the tips of the flames.

"More than we could ever know."

WE PACK UP EARLY for our hike to Fáintìrean. The hall is quiet as a faint knock on my door indicates Eoghan is waiting for me to leave. I take my cloak from my wooden chair and sling it over my shoulders. Gálgalesh has gifted me a pack filled with sandwiches and two extra canteens, along with tonics and supplies to deliver to the village when we arrive. For a five kilometer trek, I am certain he has over-packed. Still, I draw the strap over my shoulder and look around my room one more time. I tug open my door to find Eoghan resting upon the frame with his heels kicked out casually. He wears his own black uniform with his pack—emblazoned with the Tinemallacht crest—pulled over his left side.

"Ready?" he asks, and I nod as I drag the door shut behind me. He straightens and holds out his palm invitingly. "After you."

Unsurprisingly, we make it out of the fortress and down the road without so much as a huff toward one another. I am still furious with him and have refused to speak to him unless absolutely necessary for days. I assume he does not mind the silence—prefers it, even, to the sound of my voice or my daggers hurled at his head. I figure I could hate him forever, and it would not so much as make him lose a bit of sleep. Nevertheless, I can still feel his lips upon mine when I close my eyes, and that has *me* losing sleep.

The forest is dark as night, and the moon has disappeared beneath the storm clouds that promise more ice and sleet. The gravel road from the prison is brown and void of snow, but around us stand enormous winter walls that make the path feel claustrophobic. Do the animals escape down the sharp cliffs just to elude the deluge that overtakes this mountain during the winter? Are the people of Fáintìrean infamously wild because of it? What other sort of nightmares hide amongst the land of frost and ruin?

By mid-morning, we have made it halfway to the village. Our pace is slow, much more so than I would have imagined for a quick jaunt across the summit. The cold fills my lungs, and the steep incline of the mountain road proves near impossible at a normal pace. As affected as I am, Eoghan seems equally unbothered. When we stop for water and breakfast, he lounges easily on the embankment. My nose and cheeks are pink with cold. I crouch on my heels to keep from placing myself on the icy perch next to him—to be anywhere but near him—and I feel myself longing for my cold prison room and squeaky old mattress. Even as we rest, we stubbornly refuse to speak.

I look around the forest, with its bare trees and lifeless grounds, and am reminded with a shudder of my last jaunt outside the prison walls. Why anyone would choose to live in this place, only Eoghan Kael knew. If I did not leave by next winter, I might take Gálgalesh's previous advice and beg for a swift death—that is, if I make it that long without going mad at all.

The final descent into Fáintìrean proves less taxing than the first half of our morning. We arrive by noon, the sky still black and the forest so very quiet and uninviting. The stone houses give off the first light we have seen since the prison gates as their windows glow yellow and orange. The smell of fire and warmth fills the air, and the faintest murmurs of families singing, laughing, and fighting trickle out from under the wooden doors of the cottages. For a village full of wild, dangerous people, it feels extremely normal, more homey than anywhere else has felt in months. Eoghan passes the first three houses inside the village walls but turns toward the fourth on the right-hand side of the road and ascends the short steps to the door. The windows are dark and the house is still. Without a knock or invitation to enter, he fiddles with the doorknob and pushes the door open, striding into the place familiarly and motioning with a jerk of his head for me to follow. I hesitate for a moment as I watch him from the bottom stair, but he simply drops his bag near the entrance and walks across the room to the hearth, lifts his hands, and lights a fire before walking back to the door.

"Go inside and get warm. I will be back in a few minutes with more wood for the fire."

He slides past me, back into the cold and around the side

of the building, where he disappears. Once he leaves and I am left standing at the entrance, I crane my neck to peer into the cottage, checking for life. Nothing moves besides the crackling fire Eoghan has conjured. No one seems to be home, and from the musty, damp smell coming from the place, it seems perhaps no one has been home for days or even weeks. I take the short steps up to the threshold and untie my muddy boots on the last step. Lifting my feet from the leather, I step cautiously through the open door and into the growing warmth and dim light. This is the one-room cottage Eoghan had brought me to the day he found me bleeding out in the snow. The leather armchair where Finn had sat remains near the fireplace, and a matching sofa sits against the wall across from it, a low table between the two. To the left is a tiny galley kitchen with a wood-burning stove, a matching dining table with two chairs, and a large, stone basin sink. Opposite the kitchen is one large bed—large enough to share—made of brown wood that shines in the fire's light. A matching bookcase and dresser round out the space. It is comfortable and clean, as though someone has done their very best to make a proper home out of this minute stone abode.

I make my way into the bedroom space—dropping my bag onto the floor as I do—and survey the bookcase curiously. Books on Draío history, weaponry, and lore line the shelves. I run my fingers across the leather spines, which have worn with age, almost all written exclusively in the forbidden language. Siarhinn, it was once called—it is probably still referred to as such across the sea, where its use does not come at a price, but now, we only call it for what it is: the forbidden language of our past. It would take me years to read through so many of them, even with my regular practice reading spells in Gálgalesh's quarters. I slog my way to the end of the line, my gaze trailing slowly on each new title—all of which I had never seen in all my days in the castle library. Forbidden books. I thought we had everything, but when they forbade the old language, they set aflame many of the tomes.

As I reach the last book, my eyes fall to something square and offset in the corner of the shelf, nearly concealed in shadows. I lean in for a better view and realize it is a photograph nestled among the leather and parchment. I place my fingers around the delicate frame and free it from its hiding spot. As the picture comes into view, I stumble backwards onto the foot of the bed and fall to a seat on the mattress. There, staring up at me from the dusty glass, are the three familiar faces of my brother Cai, Tiernan Damaris, and Eoghan Kael.

They are indeed smiling—no, they are laughing, their arms around one another's shoulders. My brother and Tiernan are no more than twenty-one or twenty-two years old in the photograph, making Eoghan at least as young as I am now. Eoghan is ever the same, with his dark tan and fiercely beautiful features I have come to recognize, and Cai's hair is still brown without the sun's mark. Tiernan remains bespectacled, but his face seems rounder, his features more boyish than I remember him. Together, they make a handsome trio of young men—a motley crew of allies.

I trace my fingers against the faces in the picture. How had they known each other, and where had they met? Had Eoghan, who always spoke poorly of Tiernan, once been his friend? When had they drifted apart? If my brother had known Eoghan Kael well enough to laugh with and embrace him, how had he never spoken his name? In all the times he had told me about Tinemallacht and the men he had met there, he had omitted Eoghan from his memories. Why would that be?

I jump nearly right out of my skin and gasp as Eoghan's

boots scrape against the floor. With firewood in his arms, he crosses the room and drops his wares into a basket in the far corner. He picks up one log from the top and places it in the fireplace, prodding it with a metal poker so the flames rise in the firebox. He wipes his palms to shake off the dust and then wheels around to find me, holding the picture weakly in my hands, speech slipping from my grasp. I watch as his shoulders drop a little at the sight. I know it's not anger in his eyes; even so, I can't help but feel as though I have intruded on something deeply personal, and my stomach churns uneasily as my hand goes slack in my lap. He crosses the room, and the silence between us becomes so palpable, it could be cut with a knife. As tears fill my eyes, I look up at him.

"Not exactly 'conscripted scum,'" he whispers as he takes in the image in the frame. "Military academy scum." He smiles a bit awkwardly as he tries to keep his tone casual, but the memory of me shouting those despicable words at him outside the dining hall tears me into pieces. "I was seventeen when I was accepted, the youngest in the history of Draío-coinnigh. Your brother arrived the same day I did, as well as Damaris." He points at the picture in my hands, and my lip quivers. "From day one, we were nearly inseparable. I don't know if any of us would have made it through the academy without the others. This photo is from our graduation day, the last day we were together before Tiernan took a position in the royal court and Cai and I headed to the training camps in Tinemallacht."

My head feels light, and my vision spins as my heart races in my chest. Eoghan Kael not only knew my brother, he had been friends with him. He had shared time with him—perhaps more than I had. Did they have secrets? Stories of glory and gaiety? All the times Eoghan had known me better than anyone should have...

"Gálgalesh said you knew who I was the moment you saw me arrive at Báscogar Prison..." Eoghan takes a seat beside me on the bed, and I feel the temperature rise slightly in his presence.

"How could I not?" His lip curls up to one side. "You look just like him. I am surprised no one else has figured you out yet."

I race through my thoughts, my questions, as my world breaks apart around me in fragments of understanding and confusion. "You dragged me into the dining hall and threw me to the ground because you knew who I was. You knew him and you hated me for being the one who survived. That is why you demanded Gálgalesh send me away—because you were angry at me for existing."

"Yes and no." There is no apology in his eyes, only truth. "I dragged you into that hall to demand Gálgalesh send you away, but not because I hated you for being alive. I wanted him to send you away because *knowing* you were alive meant there was no longer anything more important in this world than to keep you safe, and I was not sure...I'm still not sure that is possible. You leaving meant I would not know if you lived or died, and that is almost better than knowing. I hated you the moment you decided to stay, because now the only thing I think about every moment of every day is you and if my failure will cost you your life too."

My shoulders sink down to the floor. The leaders of the coup had watched the life fade from the eyes of my father, my mother, my lover, and my brother, all because they were useful or powerful in some way. They had not cared what happened to me—whether they broke me, defiled me, or killed me—because I meant nothing to them. My life meant nothing to them. Tiernan and Dedra had saved me because Tiernan had been my brother's friend, and he felt some sort of loyalty to him. Eoghan cares for my safety because of him, because he was important—because *he* should have lived.

I wipe a stray tear from my cheek and hand the picture to Eoghan. "I am sorry to have stayed. I know it's foolish of me." I rise to stand, and Eoghan remains still, gazing into the photograph as if remembering a friendship lost in time. "Whose home is this?" I change the subject as I shake away the tears filling my eyes again. "I'm wondering if they might have some tea."

Eoghan coughs lightly and rubs the back of his neck before abandoning the frame on the bed. "It was... Well, it is mine now, I suppose. There are tea and cups in the cupboard and some biscuits hidden in the bread box." He stands and removes his cloak, gesturing for mine, which he helps me remove before crossing to the door and closing it tightly, hanging our effects on two hooks beside it. "You can have the bed. I'll take the sofa."

―――

AFTER TEA and a much needed nap, Eoghan leaves me alone in the cottage while he goes to deliver medicine to the village elders. The house is cozy by now—much warmer than Báscogar has ever been, even in Gálgalesh's quarters. I lounge upon the brown leather sofa, my wool socks discarded and my feet kicked out in front of me so I can take in the fire's warmth. Apart from my tiny prison room, I have never lived alone. I have never made tea for myself or snuggled up with a book without someone tending to or scolding me. I take a moment to imagine what life might be like to live in such silent solitude, and I think I might be happy here. There is nothing luxurious about this place, apart from the freedom it offers, but I reckon that is the appeal of it. There is something in me that longs for the quiet, that does not care for retribution or power; a part of me that could slip away from the world and forget about the pain and heartache and leave myself behind completely.

But this is not my home; this is Eoghan Kael's. This is where he escapes to when he leaves the prison walls, when he refuses to be confined any longer. Why leave this place at all? What does the prison hold that brings him back? Why return to room 264 and live with the murders and thieves and miscreants? Do all the men sent on patrol to Fáintìrean have homes and lives in the village as well? Were any of them prisoners at all?

I replace my socks on my feet and cross over to my pack, still full of Gálgalesh's offerings. I grab the bag and then drag my boots from behind the door where Eoghan had set them to dry. I push my feet into them. They are still wet, but by now, I am used to the permanent dampness from the snow, and once I have laced them tightly up my ankles, I reach for my cloak.

The pure black that fills the landscape gives no hint of the day. The snow piles in drifts to clear the gravel pathways through the circular village like ghosts rising against the eternal night. I take the stairs down to the path, uncertain of where I might head. *To find Eoghan*, I tell myself. *Just find Eoghan.* I walk on toward what appears to be a central square with a bonfire in the middle, a number of people gathered around it. Heads turn slightly as I approach, each face pale and cheeks pink with cold, hair a light brown and round, chocolate-colored eyes. The villagers dress in white, as if attempting to camouflage themselves within the frosty surroundings. They take me in with mild interest, and I nod respectfully as I pass, my stark black clothes fading into the night, but I do not spot Eoghan anywhere in the street, so I continue on.

The stone houses are uniform in size, no bigger than the

one-room cottages, with a single bed and a bathroom. My mother would have gone mad at the sight of them. Her own rooms were the size of a block of these houses placed together. Even Dedra's cramped home in Gairdín could be a palace by comparison. The doors lay open on many of the cottages, and I wonder if the people of the mountain are unbothered by the chill of the air that keeps me huddled deep in my layers of wool. I peek into a few of the doorways, searching for a familiar face, and it takes me until I reach the far end of the village to locate him—his deep purr pouring out of the house nearest to the stone perimeter.

The door is ajar, just wide enough for a small amount of light to fall in a slim triangle upon the exterior steps. I ascend the steps quietly, peering through the small opening. A fire illuminates the room, as is customary in all the houses in Fáintìrean, and candles are scattered on the side tables next to the sofa. In the sitting room, a young woman hugs her knees close to her chest and rests her chin on them nervously. An older gentleman sits beside her with concern written across his face. His hands tremble in his lap ever so slightly, his fingers rubbing his opposite knuckle anxiously.

Just out of view, another woman moans in pain, and Eoghan shushes her softly. I lean forward, trying to see if I can make out the shadows cast long upon the wall, but I lose my footing and only catch myself just before I fall through the door. The two villagers on the sofa snap to attention as they turn to the commotion of my boots sliding against the stone. Clumsy. Useless. Always causing a scene. *Nice one, Maeve.* I roll my eyes and knock lightly on the door. There is no use hiding outside any longer now that they are aware of my presence.

"I was wondering when you would arrive," Eoghan's voice rises from the room, and I take his casual greeting as an invitation to enter. I push the door open ever so slightly and skirt around the corner to find Eoghan kneeling next to one of two single beds. His sleeves are rolled up to his elbows, and a young woman—only a year or two older than the one in the sitting room—is laying under heavy blankets, her brow damp with sweat and her eyes closed. Her hands tightly clasp Eoghan's own. "Just in time. Would you hand me a vial from my pack?"

I agree wordlessly and drop to my knees beside the bed. His pack is open on the floor next to him, a dozen vials of tonic identical to the ones Gálgalesh has filled my pack with stacked inside. I pull one free, and its milky white contents slosh back and forth against the clear glass. He frees his right hand from the woman's grip as he assures her quietly in the forbidden language and then reaches to take the medicine from me. I pull the cork and pass it to him, and he lifts it to the woman's lips. She only sobs and shakes her head, her lips pressed tightly together. He implores her to accept it, but her tears cascade onto her pillow, and she rejects it again.

"Muinsa," I whisper, and her eyes flutter open, finding me beside her. I reach out my hand toward her and wipe a trail of tears away from her temples. "Muinsa. Trust him."

She hesitates as she searches me, but I simply hold her gaze and run my fingers gently against her much-too-warm skin again. She leans into my touch, and my thumb caresses her cheek. She sniffs loudly—swallowing back her cries— and her lips part in acceptance. Thank the gods. Eoghan pours from the vial slowly until it empties completely and hands the empty bottle back to me. I replace the cork and drop it carefully into his pack once again. The woman's eyes fall closed again, and she weeps silently to herself. Eoghan picks up a drenched rag on the bedside table and wrings the excess water back into the accompanying bowl. Softly, he pats it along her forehead and scarlet cheeks as he whispers to her. He returns the rag to the bowl and then lifts her hand

and plants a kiss on the back of it. The edges of her lips turn up ever so slightly, and he lays her palm on the blanket as her breathing begins to ease.

"Thank you." He looks worn and tired, as though he has spent much of the afternoon and evening battling patients in their sickbeds.

"What is wrong with her?" My voice is little more than a whisper.

"A fever has spread through the villagers over recent months. It seems to only affect certain families and spares the others. We have not yet figured out why. The people of Fáintìrean cannot die, but it has caused a lot of suffering, and the relentlessly high temperature can threaten lasting damage to their minds if not treated."

"Is that why Gálgalesh has sent us here?" He nods. "I did not know the patrols from Báscogar care for the sick in the village."

"The Báscogar patrols don't. They trade common medicines for animal pelts and rabbit meat and provide protection around the Deep. The only other contact with the villagers they might have is when they bed the women—which isn't strictly against the rules, but some of the men are more dangerous than they look, even if it is only the smugglers and low-level criminals who are sent out on patrol. If they get anywhere near the village, they can be practically feral, so they are ordered to camp outside the walls and told the people of Fáintìrean are dangerous in an attempt to keep them away. It works for the most part, but Gálgalesh has had to punish one or two who didn't listen."

Kruz said they lose a few on patrol every year, but he never elaborated on their deaths beyond blaming the brutality of the villagers. As I look down at the innocent girl beside us, rage fills up in my chest. Those pigs. Gálgalesh should kill any man who lays a finger on these women as if they have an inherent right to their bodies. Eoghan gently nudges me with the tap of his arm against my own, and I escape my thoughts to bring my gaze back to his beautiful face.

"Gálgalesh provides care to the villagers, and a few of us who can be trusted have promised to do the same." Eoghan wipes his hands on his pants and rises to his feet. "The tonic should break the fever as long as they continue to allow us to treat her. Come on; let's leave her to rest."

I follow him back into the sitting room, where he explains the treatment to the woman's family. He promises we will arrive back in the morning to check on her, and the older man grabs Eoghan's hand firmly, bowing his head in appreciation. Eoghan returns the gesture, and the man gives me an appreciative nod as well. We collect our things carefully and then exit the small home back onto the gravel path. Eoghan walks close beside me in the darkness as the moon makes its first appearance in the sky. The blue-white glow casts a romantic light across the path, leading us back toward the bonfire in the square.

"That girl… Is she…"

"His daughter," Eoghan answers before I can speak my question. "They both are. Their mother was killed centuries ago. They are the only family he has left."

"Oh." I shove my hands into my pockets, my breath visible in the air in front of me. "I think it is nice that you help..." I stumble all over my words like a fool. What can I say? Eoghan Kael—whom I had thought might kill me more than once—is, in fact, wonderful and kind? Compassionate and gentle? I pull my cloak around myself, and Eoghan chuckles softly.

"*Some* stories about me are true, but not all of them." He leads us further down the path, and the faintest sound of music rises to greet us, growing louder with each step. "Are you hungry?" he asks and glances sideways at me.

"A bit," I admit, and my stomach growls loudly in betrayal. My cheeks heat, and I drop my eyes to my boots.

"This way, Princess."

He takes hold of me around the elbow with a smile and leads me to the commotion. In the center of the village, a group of fifty or more people have begun to gather. The intoxicating smells of breads, meats, and potatoes fill the air; smells so delicious, they make my mouth water. Not since I have arrived at Báscogar has anything smelled so appetizing. All around, people gather near the large bonfire, passing plates and toasting each other with steins of ale. Across the square, near the edge of the snow bank, a band is playing a folky tune that drowns out much of the chatter of the gathering, and I smile as I hear a few of the revelers sing along. Eoghan gives a friendly bow to three men seated at the very focus of the party, and they acknowledge him in turn, as if he is a welcome guest.

"The village elders," he whispers, his breath warm against my ear. I tip my head respectfully, and the three men smile at me and nod.

"What is this? A party?" From the delight on the faces of the villagers and the music in the air, this must be a day of grand celebration.

"The Fire Offering." He takes my hand and pulls me through the growing crowds; his voice is nearly a shout over the din. "To persuade the gods to ease the winter chill."

"Does the offering work?"

He shrugs his shoulders lightly. "Who knows, but why would anyone turn down a feast and dancing?"

———

"You seem happy." Eoghan leans into my side as I watch the fire burn in columns twenty feet high.

"I have never been so happy in my life," I concede. We sit in the warmth of the fire, enjoying the jubilant sounds of the fiddle and guitar, our stomachs filled with the most exquisite food I have ever tasted. Eoghan believes the taste is due to the dulling of our senses from months of consuming Báscogar's gray slop. Our faces are adorned with ceremonial ash spread in two fine lines across either cheekbone. Out of the corner of my eye, I watch Eoghan examine me with such great interest, and I begin to feel self-conscious, bashfully running my fingers through my hair. "What?"

"I have never seen you smile like this before."

"Well, I haven't had much to smile about since you've met me." It is the truth, but to be honest, I am not sure I have ever truly smiled in my whole life, not compared to tonight. "How about you? I believe you danced with every woman in the village tonight."

"Not every woman." I dip my head and shake it from side to side. "Oh, come on, Princess. One dance?" He nudges my knee with his own. "You'll regret it if you refuse. Tinemallacht men are marvelous dancers."

"And oh so modest." I throw my head back on a belly laugh. He bats his eyes and pouts his lips playfully, and I roll my eyes before throwing my arm toward him in defeat. "You're drunk, Eoghan Kael." He only shrugs and makes me laugh again. Angos help me, he is the most beautiful thing I have ever seen. "One dance. Just one."

He helps me to my feet with ease and leads me away from the towering fire. With deft precision, he pulls me to his body, and his right hand falls to my back, his fingers resting lightly against my lower spine. My hand drops to his shoulder, and he sways with me to the music.

"See? It is not so terrible to be near me without trying to

murder me." He spins us around with so much grace, I feel as entranced as I had been when watching him practice in the arena. Heat forms in my lower abdomen as I feel his chest press up against mine. "By the way, I've been meaning to ask —was kissing me so horrible that you felt the need to hurl your daggers into my back?" His voice is light and playful now, but I know the question is not rhetorical.

I focus my attention on the villagers dancing around us, as if not looking at him might make me forget his eyes have not left me for the last ten minutes. "I think kissing you was a mistake."

His movements slow, but his grip remains firm on my right hand and lower back. "And why is that?" He purrs the words, coating them with sensual desire and perhaps the tiniest bit of hurt pride.

"Because I do not enjoy being used as a pawn in some-one's plot for revenge. If someone is going to kiss me, I want them to do so because they want me, not to prove a point or get something out of me."

In all of two seconds, Eoghan has ruined what had been one of the best evenings of my life. Anger rises anew as the nearly forgotten kiss comes charging through my mind like an avalanche, and my lips tingle with the phantom pressure of his own. I tug at my arm, but he does not budge. Our bodies are nearly stationary now as he considers the scowl that has replaced my smile.

"Do you think I did not want to kiss you?" His words roll off his tongue like silk across skin.

"I felt how quickly you pulled away when Kruz passed and the show was over." I shake my head, and my arm falls from his shoulder to my side. My eyes search the party-goers dancing around us, completely oblivious to our quarreling. He's just trying to embarrass me now, like he did that day in the shower room. He will pull me in and hang me out to dry because he does not want me. I swipe at a ridiculous tear that has escaped my eyes and rolled down my cheek.

"Fuck Kruz Lanzo," he growls. "I have thought of nothing else besides kissing you since I first had you pinned underneath me in the training arena. I have gone half-mad not laying my lips against every inch of you." My breath hitches in my chest, and I feel all the color rush to my cheeks again. I cannot look at him, because if I look into his beautiful green eyes… "Maeve..."

"What?!"

I round on him, and as I do, he catches me and pulls my lips to his. I am falling, falling so hard, and I cannot see the ground. There is only Eoghan Kael, and whether he rejects me and cripples me with heartache or loves me—I do not care. My lips part, and as he deepens the kiss, I lose myself completely. He can have me, all of me, and I want him to. Oh gods, I want him to.

He pulls away breathlessly, his thumbs brushing against my cheek. "Princess—"

"Don't. Please don't call me that. Not now." I drag him back to me, and I wrap my arms around his shoulders as his fly to my waist. His tongue works its way into my mouth as I moan against his lips. "I need you," I whisper, and his body crushes into me, pulling me closer.

We only break free when our lungs are desperate for air. The Fire Offering no longer matters. The gods have had their fun. If I stop this boiling inside me, I might die. Eoghan's eyes flare with the same hunger I had seen the first time we kissed, but this time, it is not smoldering under the surface. No, it is raging through him. He releases me and grips my hand instead, nearly dragging me out of the square. The music fades as we reach the first houses at the entrance of the village, the fire in the fourth cottage glowing tiredly in the window. We hold ourselves back until we reach the top stair, and he pulls me over the threshold by the clasp on my cloak. It falls to my feet just inside the door.

I push Eoghan back to the bed, and he falls to a seat, pulling me to straddle him with his fingers in my belt loops. "Tell me to leave." He pulls me toward him and plants kisses down my neck to my collarbone.

"Why?" I groan as my head rolls back and my eyes close.

"Because if you don't, I am going to cross a line I told myself I would never cross. You have no idea how badly I want you."

He wants me, even though he said he never would. "Say it again," I whisper, my hips rolling into him.

He moans at the friction, and his teeth graze my skin. "I want you. Damnit, I *need* you."

I lift his head, my fingers falling into his hair. "I am not a conquest, Eoghan." I look deep into his green eyes, and there is nothing between us. No secrets, no reasons to hold back—only desire.

"No, Maeve. You're everything."

Our lips crash into each other as he lifts me to my feet. His hands are all over, and it is like electricity rushes through me with each touch. His fingers caress my thighs as he removes my daggers before unbuttoning my pants and rolling them down my legs. Swearing against my lips, he yanks at my boot laces to make quick work of removing my shoes, and I step back out of them, kicking my pants off onto the floor. He tugs at the hem of my shirt and pulls it over my head, his lips only leaving mine for a split second to throw the fabric to the ground. With expert ease, he hooks my underwear around his forefinger and pulls, dropping them to my toes. When he stands, his clothing falls away to meet mine. We are naked as we take each other in for one breath, then two.

Then, Eoghan catches me around the waist and lifts me

onto the edge of the mattress. I scream and giggle against his lips as I drop down onto the soft surface, and my ass bounces against the force of the movement. His hands trail smoothly from my hips down between my thighs. I feel my excitement grow as he touches me, and I almost whimper as he digs his fingers into my thighs to grip them tightly. He spreads my legs slowly, taking in the sight of me laid bare for him before he places himself between them, dropping to his knees.

"I realize how much you enjoy being worshipped," he teases, and I place my left leg over his shoulder. He kisses my thigh slowly as he works his way toward my center. My head spins as I feel his lips against my bare skin. I lean back on my elbows as he traces his tongue the full length of my entrance, and I fist the bedsheets as I drop my head back, my breath quickening. I feel his lips curl up into a smile before he blows lightly against my clit, causing me to shiver. Then, he takes me fully with his mouth, and I unravel.

I let out a moan of pleasure as he licks and teases, his fingers joining to play in unison. I reach for him, my fingers running through his hair.

"Eoghan!" I bite my lip as he rubs his thumb against my clit. My screams encourage him, and his mouth works me with enthusiasm. My body rushes with heat and pleasure as his fingers and tongue find a steady, torturous rhythm. Oh gods, he is good! I have never felt anything so frustrating and incredible, and I feel my senses slipping away further and further until I nearly forget to breathe. *More,* my body screams. *More, or I am going to die!* As if he can read my very thoughts, his fingers thrust deeper, and I gasp as he takes my clit into his mouth.

He drives another finger inside me, and my mind is no longer my own. Hurdling toward the abyss of pleasure and madness, my hips grind and my knees tremble, begging for more and more until he mercifully picks up the pace and urges me over the edge. The room goes black, and pleasure surrounds me as blood rushes to my ears. It's as though I am racing through the void of the universe, through the stars and the heavens, to my ultimate release, as if his tongue and hand are the only things in the world I can feel. I'm screaming, and I barely recognize my own voice as I release the last bit of my sanity. I fill the cottage with my cries, climaxing to Eoghan's expert touch that continues until my breathing slows.

"Satiated?" he teases as he rises, pushing me back into the center of the mattress.

"Not yet," I pant through deep inhales. He climbs on top of me, pinning me under his thighs, as he has so often done in the training arena.

"Good," he whispers against my ear. "Tell me, Maeve: does it excite you *now* to be under me? To have my mouth on you?" He leans forward and kisses down my neck to my chest, flicking his tongue against my breasts. "Did you think about it after I pinned you to that arena floor?" He grinds his hips into me, and I feel him slide between my thighs, his head pressing teasingly against my entrance.

"Mmm…" I have no words. What is speech anymore?

I can feel him smirk against my skin, and then he drives his hips into me. I feel him ease into me with a hard and steady pace. He pumps his hips back and forth, sliding deeper until he fills me, stretching me, claiming me. With each thrust, he wills me back to that edge, the place where names and dates and time and space mean nothing. And I am his completely. I want him to take me there, want him to lose himself with me.

His lips find mine, and I feel the heat of the fire inside him warm my mouth, as if he can breathe fire—as if he can command a whole world with the power of his lips. He nips at my lower lip as he pulls away, driving so deeply into me, I have to catch my breath.

"Easy now," he coaxes. "You're incredible, Maeve… You feel so good." I lift my hips, begging for more, and he increases his pace.

"I'm so close," I call out, the pleasure taking over once more. I might never feel this way again, but I have to. I have to—for the rest of my life, I need to feel this way.

I throw all my weight into him and roll us over so I am in control. His eyes flare wide, and I buck my hips down into him, arching my back as I seat him inside me. I reach for my clit, but he knocks my hand away as I ride him as hard as I can. He rubs me between his thumb and forefinger, and I reach back and squeeze his thighs to brace myself. He lets out a ragged moan as I rush to the cliff and dive off, pulling him over with me. It takes us a lifetime to come back down, and our bodies shudder and quake as we finally let go of the last of what was holding us back, that line he tried so valiantly not to cross, that voice telling me he did not want me. Because he does, and I want him too, more than I have wanted anything before. I fall limp on his chest as we struggle to ease our breaths.

"That was…" My cheek is upon his chest, wet with sweat, his hands tracing lightly up and down my spine.

"Unexpected?" he offers.

"I was going to say incredible," I amend with a breathless laugh.

"Incredible," he agrees.

We lay in silence as our bodies settle down, and then he pulls me to the mattress next to him before he wraps his arms around me. The cottage is freezing now that the fire has burned out, but neither of us could tell. We lay tangled in the blankets, our bodies closer than a whisper until we both give in and fall asleep.

CHAPTER TWENTY-TWO

The faint sounds of morning outside the cottage whisper softly to me as I slowly wake. Chatter and axes falling heavy onto wood in the dark distance somewhere reminds me something else exists beyond these walls, something besides the satiny skin of Eoghan Kael beneath my fingertips. I stretch, feeling two enormous arms around my middle, and the night comes rushing back to me in waves. Eoghan Kael had devoured me, enveloped me, wholly consumed me—and I had wanted him to. I had wanted nothing more than his hands and lips on every inch of my flesh.

Warmth radiates from him, heating me comfortably under a tangle of bed sheets. He stirs and groans, his lips against the back of my neck as his embrace tightly draws me into his bare chest.

"Morning." His voice is deep and husky, drenched in sleep. He presses lazy kisses down to my shoulder and back up my neck again.

"Morning." I roll over to face him—to make sure he really has not disappeared, that he is really here—and his eyes flutter open softly. His lips inch toward mine, and I pull away, just out of reach, causing his brow to tick upward in question. "I want to brush my teeth first."

He laughs quietly as his fingers trace down my spine. "I don't mind morning breath."

"You say that now." I shake my head and lean into the pillows.

"I grew up in the land of dragons, Maeve. You know nothing of bad breath until you meet one of them."

I laugh sarcastically and take him in. He is beautiful as his hair falls around his face, his green and gold eyes shining with his first glassy morning gaze. I raise my hands to his face, my thumbs tracing over the contours of his jaw, the fullness of his lips that had tantalized and taken me just hours ago. I run the pad of my finger along the small scar above his left eye. He, Eoghan Kael, had chosen me. Not to prove a point and not for others to see, not for any worldly gain of his own—he had chosen me because he desired me completely. He had chosen me because no one else could have satisfied him in that moment but me.

"What are you thinking?" He smiles and nuzzles my hand. I shake my head, afraid to think it or voice it in case it ruins everything. I cannot tell him how I feel when I am still figuring that out myself, the feeling so unlike anything I've ever known before. I decide on something else completely.

"Have you bedded other women here, like this, Eoghan Kael?"

"Yes," he replies with an easy laugh, and when my mouth falls open, he nips at my lip. The sheer lack of emotion he displayed towards the fact that he had shared this mattress with others was astounding. How can he say it as though it means nothing to have me in the same bed? "Don't look at me with surprise," he says. "I know I am not the first man to have had you either."

"But not in this bed." I push him away, my hands on his chest, but he pulls me in, kissing my jaw playfully.

"Well of course not. This is not your bed." I scowl back at him, and he sighs and rolls his eyes. "I am sincerely sorry for the women I bedded before you captivated me so entirely. I am sorry you pushed me down on the bed and I thought of nothing else but feeling you around me. Next time, I will take you on the floor." He moves his mouth close to my ear and drags his teeth softly along it. "Or the sofa. Or the kitchen counter. Anywhere will do." My breath hitches in my throat, and I want him now—anywhere, everywhere. But, as if knowing the power he has over me, his arms loosen, and he lets me go, a cold rush of air dampening the mood. "Just not right now. We need a fire and breakfast, and then I need to head back into the village to check on the sick. You are free to come with me if you would like, or you can stay here in the warmth."

He moves to the side of the bed and stands, and I take in the sight of his toned body again. This time, I allow my eyes to linger on every curve of his muscles, from his shoulders, down his back, his ass, his large thighs. Every inch of him is delectable. Even Rian, who had been the only man I had ever seen naked before I came to Báscogar, could not hold a candle to him. He had been soft in places where Eoghan's body is chiseled, as if made by the gods out of marble to display the perfection of the male physique to the world. Not to the world—to me, only me, in this tiny cottage with darkened windows and bed sheets falling from the mattress onto the floor.

My eyes track lower down his exposed skin, and I notice a dark image etched into the outside of his right thigh, but it is too dark to make sense of it from where I lay. I drag myself toward him and run my fingers across his skin. He looks down at me, wincing slightly from the icy touch. A skull engulfed in flames—the Tinemallacht crest, just as Cai had hand-tipped on his arm.

"My brother had one of these as well…on his arm, though." The lines are imperfect, just as I remember Cai's to be, but the care is obvious in the workmanship.

"I know." Eoghan's voice is soft and understanding, though there is sadness hidden there too. "I was there the day he got his. He had told me it captivated you when you had seen it."

My head jerks upward. "He told you about me?"

"I almost could not get him to *stop* talking about you." He finds his pants in the discarded pile on the floor and steps into them, and I drop my hand from his thigh as he does. "You would have thought you were the sun and everyone simply spun around you, vying for you to shine upon them." He crouches down beside the bed. "Now, I think I'm starting to understand why." He leans forward, too quickly for me to get away, and plants a kiss on my lips. "Go bathe, dragon breath. I'll handle breakfast."

———

FOR MOST OF THE MORNING, I accompany Eoghan on his rounds through the village to administer medicines to the sick. When we reach the house near the far perimeter, the father greets us at the door and takes us to his daughter's bedside. Her fever has subsided, and they have been able to keep her comfortable through the night. Eoghan drops onto the floor beside her bed and notes the color that has returned to her face and the calm in her expression.

"How are you?" he asks her quietly in the forbidden language, and she mumbles a reply too low for me to hear. "Good." He rubs his thumb against her forehead as she wraps both of her hands around his other wrist. He breaks her gaze for just a moment to instruct me to find him another vial of tonic, and I rummage through my pack to pull one free. He takes it from me, and without so much as one word of coaxing, the girl opens her mouth. "Good girl," Eoghan encourages, and when she has drunk it down, he pats her hair softly.

I turn away and move toward the sitting room as the moment becomes almost too intimate for me to bear. Eoghan Kael, the man I thought I knew, is gone, and the man who has replaced him is so spellbinding—so perfect—the only reasoning I can accept is that he is not real at all, and I will wake up in the morning to find all of this to be a dream and be back in Rian Doherty's arms. At least then, life would once again make sense.

He joins me after one last goodbye to his patient and intertwines his fingers with mine at my side. We bid our host a farewell, and Eoghan walks with me to the door. As we exit onto the gravel pathway, I squeeze his fingers harder in my own. Rian never liked to hold my hand; he called it a childish thing to do, as if our hands clasped together might have been as beneath him as building castles in the sand. I never understood why, but as Eoghan's thumb grazes softly against the back of my own in reassuring strokes, I wonder what could ever be more lovely.

"What of the rest of the day?" It is still quite early, and Eoghan will not have to check on any more patients until the evening.

"Well, this evening, I have some business to attend to, but for now, Gálgalesh has instructed me to continue work on your sparring. "

"What business do you have tonight? May I join you?" We pass by two women who giggle and hide their faces as Eoghan Kael smiles and nods at them in polite greeting. I never realized just how gentle his eyes could seem when he isn't trying his best to kill you. He was a savior in this village, not a threat, and everyone saw him as such.

"No, you cannot." He says the words as though the matter is as simple as that, as if he could settle it without discussion at all.

"Why not?"

"Because it does not concern you, Maeve. You can stay in the cottage, and I promise to come straight back to you as soon as I am done." I stop walking, and my arm tugs forward lightly before Eoghan realizes I am no longer at his side. He turns toward me and takes in the scowl on my face. "Why are you angry?" he asks critically, as if I have done something to annoy him and not the other way around.

"You cannot bed me and then keep information from me. That is not how things will work between us, Eoghan."

"I made you no promises last night." He is right, I know he is, but he does not have to be so cold when he speaks to me.

"Do not speak to me as if I do not deserve your honesty."

"Have I lied to you?" He steps back into the space between us, and I back away, but he closes the gap again. His scent of sandalwood, bergamot, and warm cedar embers mesmerizes me, as though each inhale of him wipes out every thought apart from being near to him. *Get a grip! He's hiding something from you, just like everyone else.* I put my hand between us on his chest to block him from stepping any closer—if he even could.

"You will not tell me your business or allow me to come with you. At the very least, you do not trust me."

"Your idea of trust is simply you knowing everyone's business, regardless of whether it concerns you. This does not concern you, *Princess*."

That title again, the one that bites like vinegar on his tongue—the one that raises the invisible barrier between us.

I loathe it as I watch the stone mask fall into place. He disappears behind it, and I feel as though we are back at the prison once more, where he wants nothing to do with me. I drop my hand to my side, slipping it away from his reach. It was a mistake for Gálgalesh to send us here as if we could act civilized for even a moment. He has kept so many secrets from me since I arrived in Romiodóg, it is silly to think he would not continue to do so.

"Fine." I continue toward the cottage, leaving him behind. He looses a frustrated growl and stalks off after me.

"Maeve, stop." I refuse to slow my pace, and I feel him catching up to me. He catches my elbow, and his touch is soft, almost pleading. "Maeve. Stop it."

I halt, and I am not quite sure why. Maybe it is the frustration in his low, powerful voice. Maybe it is his touch that sends currents through my body like nothing else in the world ever has. Maybe it is simply because he followed me, as though my leaving makes any sort of difference to him at all. He could let me leave, let me lock myself away in the cottage. It is what he asked of me, after all. He could let me leave Fáintìrean completely, and he would not have to explain himself or continue our quarreling. He could be through with me...but he does not want to be.

He pulls me back, turning me to face him. He lifts my chin so our eyes meet, and his are bright, his brows pulled together tightly. "Why did you walk away?"

"Because I don't want to fight with you, Eoghan. I want you to think more of me than just a spoiled princess who demands her way. I want you to trust me, but I cannot force you to."

He rubs the clasp on my cloak between his fingers. "There is much more than you and me in this. If I could, I would tell you anything you ask of me, but it isn't my call. Not this time." I can feel my core warming again at his touch, and it takes everything in me to remain upright. "*You* have to trust *me* as well. Can you trust me? Can you trust I will tell you all you need to know?"

"I cannot live with secrets, Eoghan." It is the only thing I can say. No matter how much I want to relent, my life has always been full of secrets. Hell, I was kept a secret from the world for much of it. I am living in secret now! I cannot have it between us. He studies me, searching for any give in my expression, and when he finds none, he sighs solemnly.

"I'm sorry then."

I'm sorry then. As if there is nothing to be done and nothing else to say. He has given up so quickly, without an ounce of compromise. He chose to push me away instead of being straightforward. How silly of me to think the answer would be anything else. One night could not change how he saw me, not really. No matter that I felt something I had never felt before when he touched me—like I was safe, like I was made just for him.

He frowns as I pull away from him, but he does not follow me back to the cottage. I slam the door behind me and fall onto the bed, the blankets still smelling faintly of him. I will go back to Báscogar and demand Gálgalesh send me away, send me anywhere—to the ends of the Earth and further still if he had to. I'll find a way on my own to kill the ones who murdered my family. There is no way I am spending another moment with Eoghan. I am embarrassed to even look at him. Perhaps I had miscalculated what last night meant to him. He still hated me for being here—he might have planned to convince me to leave when we returned anyway. Now, he would get what he wanted, because I am a stupid girl with a crush and ridiculous notion that anyone could see me as something more than a liability.

I wait in the quiet darkness for Eoghan to return, but he doesn't for the rest of the day. The fire goes cold in the hearth as the hours fade and my stomach aches with hunger. What have I done? Why couldn't I leave well enough alone? Gálgalesh was right: I have no right to anything at all—I just assume I do because I have never been deprived of anything in all my life. I walk to the bookcase and pull the photo from its hiding spot once more. I had become a weak, whining woman who could not hold her own, and Cai would have been embarrassed by me. What would he say if he saw me now? Why could I not trust Eoghan Kael? If Cai had, then certainly, he was worthy of my trust—Cai had never been wrong before. Could I not live with knowing he was beside me, helping me to succeed?

The front door creaks open softly, and without turning to it, I let out a heavy sigh of relief. "I wondered if you would ever come back," I say into the black that has fallen over the cabin as his boots thud heavy on the floor, drawing nearer to the bed. He doesn't respond. He must still be angry with me. How could he not after I'd thrown such an enormous tantrum in the middle of the village because I had not gotten my way? "I'm sorry, Eoghan… You're right: I need to trust you too. If you did not care at all, you would have killed or exposed me the moment you realized who I was; but you didn't, which proves more than telling me your secrets could." The footsteps round the corner slowly, and I rub my thumb across the photo in its frame. He stops inches from me, his boots almost disappearing in the shadows of the room, but still, he refuses to speak. "Say something. Please."

I twist my gaze skyward, and fear courses through my veins, making my blood run cold.

"Well, well, well. I guess proper introductions are in order, Princess." A malicious grin falls across Kruz Lanzo's face as he stands over me, so close, his knees touch mine.

I shoot backwards across the bed, throwing the frame from my hands. I dart toward the window above the headboard, but he launches for me and wraps his arms around my waist, pulling me back toward him. I thrash and kick furiously, trying to break free, but he steps forward and wraps his legs around mine, holding them down. *I will claw his eyes out of his head.* I scrape my nails down his arms, and he flinches as I draw blood, but his size is immense, nowhere near a proper match for me as he pins my arms to my chest with one of his own. I writhe beneath his weight, trying to remember anything from my sparring lessons to help me break free. Nothing helps. Kruz could have always bested me in training; it had been a mercy each time he hadn't—a mercy he would not show me this time. With his free hand, he reaches into his pocket and pulls out a cloth, shoving it into my mouth as I make to scream. It is instantly bitter on my tongue, and I try to spit it out, but he presses his hand over my lips, forcing it to remain. I cough as the taste chokes me, my mind feeling heavy and fogged as darkness rings my sight. *He's drugging you,* a faint part of my mind whispers. *You have to get away from him. You have to get to Eoghan.* I try to kick and thrash in his grip, but my body refuses the command, and my limbs become heavy, dragging me towards the ground as my eyes fall shut and everything goes black.

———

I WAKE to the wind whipping across my face, and I blink my eyes open heavily. My head is throbbing, and as I look around in the darkness, all I can see are trees rising like shadowy figures of childhood nightmares. I am laying on my side in the snow at the base of one of them. In front of me, Kruz Lanzo sits, sharpening a long hunting knife against a smooth gray stone. I groan as I push myself with difficulty to a seat.

"Ahh, awake now. Sooner than I expected—that's a pleasant surprise at least. I suppose Gálgalesh's sleeping drought is not as pungent as I thought."

I rub my head and blink my eyes. There is no light around us; we must be far enough away from Fáintìrean for the sounds of the villagers and fires to fade away yet not near enough to Báscogar to spy the pale glow of the guard towers. Kruz seems unbothered by our solitude as he continues to pull the knife across the stone in front of him.

"I can see you are still rousing, so perhaps I should start. I will say, when I discovered you and Eoghan Kael had taken a little outing to Fáintìrean, I was not expecting *all* I found. Though last night's copulation did not surprise me much—I suspected Kael had taken you as his whore for a while now." His lip curls up into a menacing smirk. "He has you screaming his name like a good little pet, doesn't he?" Last night... He had seen us last night... "Tell me, did you like slumming it with the Fire Cursed, Princess Maeve? Did it make you feel wicked? Dangerous? After all, I heard Tine-mallacht vermin were as off limits for the royal family as foreigners. Don't want to taint the bloodline with a dragon's curse." My eyes darken with rage.

"Fuck you," I snap, my tongue still heavy with sleep. "I hope Donn takes you to the very pits of his hell."

"Oh, I'm sure he will, but I'll offer you up to him first: the damned princess of the conqueror's kingdom. He might just reward me for sending you to him," He presses the hot blade to the snow, and it hisses and steams angrily. "I will say, you did a fantastic job fooling me. I even felt sorry for you—poor *Alana,* who had been sold to work in the castle. Did you come up with that one on your own, or did the faerie help you? I'm sure you're just the right kind of bitch; pretending to be a slave did not phase you at all. I did find it odd you knew nothing of the world, but I thought maybe you were just simpleminded, and I pitied you more. To think, I actually started to like you, started to think maybe the gods had done me one favor by sending you here to me…only to find out they gave me the best gift of all."

He slides like a serpent over the snow toward me, the knife still dangling in his hand. The bastard hasn't even bothered tying me up—but I figure it would be a waste anyway, seeing how he has given me a poison that has nearly paralyzed my limbs. He lifts my left arm by my wrist and cuts away the sleeve of my shirt to expose the smooth skin on the underside of my arm.

"You see, I have dreamed—for twenty years—for the chance to enact my own revenge on your father for locking me away on this gods-forsaken mountain. I have dreamed of nothing else for *twenty years*. And now, perhaps my pleading has finally reached their ears, because they sent you right to me, dropped you right into my hands all those months ago, and I did not even know it."

"I-I-I am not my father. I was born twenty years ago. I had nothing to do with your imprisonment in this place."

"Yes, that is true." He nods his head and feigns pity for a moment before continuing in a low and dangerous voice. "But Maeve, do you want to know what is also true?" He takes his knife and drags it across my exposed skin, tearing into my flesh as blood flows red and hot. I cry out as the white-hot pain sears through my arm. "You are his blood, and I'll take what I can get. Besides, all of you are the same. You care only about yourselves. You feel for nothing. You kill and you use for your own benefit, and you know no better because that is how it has always been." I try to move, to run, but my body barely shifts in its seat. "Such a shame the others had a quick farewell. I would have taken my time— just like I am going to do with you."

My heart is beating out of my chest. I need to get out of

here now, or else Kruz Lanzo is going to flay me alive. I try to wiggle my toes in my boots, but they move so slowly and lamely, I'm sure I cannot move to stand. It could take only gods know how long before I can. He has me right where he wants me. I'm at the mercy of Kruz fucking Lanzo. I've killed a faerie, but I'm going to be murdered by a smuggler who kisses like a woman has not touched him before. Could anything be more pathetic? Blood flows freely from my arm into the white snow, and I know it is only a matter of time before that slows me too. I have to get away from him *now*. I pull at the thread of magic weakly humming inside me. It has been dulled by the drought Kruz has given me, but if I can just conjure something, it might buy me some time. *Think, Maeve, think! You cannot be killed by Kruz Lanzo!*

Last week, in Gálgalesh's office, I was working on offensive attacks, something that might help in a fight. I had managed to use the spell that forced Gálgalesh back into the wall of his office—and had him cursing my name. If I could pull the magic toward me, I might be able to conjure it now. I can feel my hands and feet begin to tingle as they awaken, the first signs of life in my drugged body. I'll have to hurl myself into the forest as the magic hits him and hide somewhere, hoping he will not find me. The feeling of pins and needles tells me my legs are heavy but awake. If I am going to do it, it has to be now!

I close my eyes as Kruz continues to babble on about how he is going to make my death worth his while. *Find the magic. Please hear me! Please help me!* I reach and lay my request bare. It is weak as I feel it travel down the line...too weak. My brain is too clouded to concentrate on the thread. *This isn't going to work.* The thread goes quiet as my request travels into the darkness and out of reach. *I am going to die. I am going to die, and Eoghan isn't even going to know I am sorry. He's going to think I ran away. He will never know I...*

No. I will not die like this. I will kill Kruz if I have to, but I will *not* die! Something deep inside me boils over. It's a new feeling, a dangerous one that has nothing to do with the thread of faerie magic in me, but I am alert, and my mind feels stronger a moment before as pure rage sears my veins. I send out the request down the thread again, with more command this time, and a wave washes over me—a response. I concentrate, and for once, I am happy faerie magic does not need the dramatics of arm motions or chanting under one's breath. I inhale, and then I set it free...

I am on my feet as Kruz tumbles sideways into the snow. There is little power behind the spell, only a fragment of what had been wielded in Gálgalesh's quarters, but I run as hard as I can into the woods without stopping or looking back. Kruz cries from somewhere behind me, and though my legs feel like they weigh four times as much as they do normally, I press on.

"No!" Kruz yells, and too soon after, he is on his feet, charging after me. *Keep running. Don't stop. You're dead if he catches you.* I will my burdensome legs forward, and my feet slap against the snow as I make my way into the thicket. Ahead, I spot a tree with a wide hole at the base. *If I can slide through it, I might be able to get far enough out of his reach.*

Not much further now; I'll take it at a running slide. I kick my legs out in front of me and leap, but the full force of Kruz barreling into me knocks on my side, thrown me to the ground with a hard thud against a hidden rock. His arms fly out in front of him, and he wraps his hands against my throat, squeezing so hard, I gasp and see stars. He is strangling me, and though my hands grab at his wrists, he presses his full weight further onto my windpipe to shut off my airway completely.

"Release her!" It is not a purr but a shout this time from beyond my view, the voice of my savior I have come to adore. Kruz hesitates at the sound of Eoghan's command but does not ease his grip; rather, he lays in deeper, pressing further to constrict my breath. I am going to die—I can feel it envelop me. I can feel my lungs constricting as they plead for air. "I said: *release her*!"

Eoghan grabs Kruz by the back of the neck and pries him from me, as if he's nothing more than a child. Kruz's hands disappear from my throat, and I cough and wheeze as I roll to my side. Eoghan lifts him off his feet, turning him to face Eoghan's bared teeth and frightening glare.

"Let me go, Kael," Kruz pants, but Eoghan grips him tighter. "She is nothing but a leech. We owe her nothing, and she should have died that day with the others."

"You will *not* harm her." Eoghan's eyes are deadly. I've never seen him so angry—so much like the killer the prisoners talk about.

"I'd be doing you a kindness now that you've had your way with her. Maybe I'll have my way with her too before I watch the light leave her eyes."

"*No*," Eoghan snarls.

"Oh, I forgot. You've made her your whore. Don't you know, Kael? Whores are meant to be shared. That's their purpose: to be used. It doesn't even matter if I am a common foreigner; if she'll fuck you Tinemallacht bastards, she'll fuck anyone."

Kruz shoots his hand to his belt, and I shout for Eoghan as Kruz unsheathes a dagger at his side. Eoghan is faster. With lightning fast reflexes, he grabs Kruz around the temples and twists hard—a deafening crack echoes through the silence. The dagger hits the snow as Kruz's body does; it lands next to me, and Eoghan stares down at it, fire in his eyes.

CHAPTER TWENTY-THREE

I clutch my hemorrhaging arm as I take in Eoghan's furious and deadly countenance of pure rage. His eyes fixate like stone on the vacant expression on Kruz's lifeless face. He had come as Kruz Lanzo had tried to strangle the life from me. He had killed him—to protect himself? To silence the hateful words Kruz had spat at him as he called him vermin? No, as Eoghan's glare makes its way from Kruz to the snow stained red with my blood and finally to me, his eyes soften, and I know it was not for his benefit at all—he did it for me.

"Kael!" Gálgalesh's voice rises from a few yards away, and we both turn to see him racing toward us through the trees. "Do not touch her!" There is panic in his voice as he reaches us, and he stops and places his hands on his knees, breathing raggedly.

"What's the matter?" Eoghan's eyes dart between us, but Gálgalesh's own haven't left the slice in my arm. He summons a vial of healing potion from his pocket and pushes it toward me without touching it; then, he takes a rag from inside his cloak and a canteen, dousing it with water before throwing them both into the snow next to me.

"Drink and then clean the blood from yourself. Your blood smells peculiar. I cannot place it." I do as instructed, and the wound on my arm closes after a moment. I wipe down my arm until the blood is gone, and Gálgalesh indicates for me to place the rag in the snow and move away. When I do, he looks at Eoghan. "Burn it." Eoghan doesn't hesitate, and almost as soon as he throws his hands out, the rag catches fire, the snow melting to nothing beneath it. We watch in silence as the rag turns to ash. "Take her back to the village and have her bathe. Woman, do you have a change of clothing?" I nod. "Have her burn those in the fire when she's done to be safe. Finn and River were not far behind me. They can help me with this." He indicates to Kruz.

"He figured out who I was." My voice cracks as I speak for the first time. "He figured it out when he followed us to Fáintìrean."

Gálgalesh lets out a heavy sigh, and that primal sound from somewhere in Eoghan's throat vibrates between us in a low, almost possessive way. "Well then, we are fortunate he did not make it back to Báscogar. I was notified this morning that he had deserted. I did not think he had followed the two of you, but his interest in you had been apparent." He looks up at Eoghan, and it is as though he might have shoved him for the way Eoghan shakes his head and looks up in renewed awareness. "Go, now. Before we have to explain anything to the others."

———

I sink down into the tub as the steam rises around me. As my luck would have it, Kruz had been dumb enough to stay close to Fáintìrean, and it only took Eoghan seeing the light from my conjuring to know where we were in the surrounding forest. A lucky shot. I run my hand against my neck, where the shadow of black and blue bruises that formed under the force of Kruz's crushing grip remain tender to the touch. If Eoghan had not finished his meeting and realized I was not in the cottage, if he had not come looking for me, I would be dead now. Four times now, I have cheated death. Donn must be furious.

I take my time washing up as I savor the luxury of a private bath. There are so many things I will miss when we go back to Báscogar, the private bathroom being one of them. I dress in my extra black shirt and pants and wrap my now-tainted clothes in my cloak. I do not know what Gálgalesh scented on me, but whatever it was, it scared him enough to sacrifice the only warmth I have against the cold. I exit the tiny bathroom and see Eoghan lounging on the sofa, his chin resting on his palm and his elbow propped up on the arm. He wears black pajama bottoms, and his chest is bare. I pause as I take him in, the sight of his perfect body heating me to my core. It is almost obscene to look at him like this. I cross the cottage and stop in front of the fireplace. Eoghan looks up when my footsteps approach; he watches me, the reflection of the warm glow in his eyes.

"In here?" I hold my bundle of wasted clothes to the fireplace.

"Yeah, in there."

There is a small fire burning pleasantly warm in the hearth. I toss my clothes onto the hot logs and watch as the fabric smolders and glows orange as the flames engulf them. Eoghan stands from the sofa and looks down at me. He towers over me by more than a foot, and I never noticed how comforting the difference could be until now. My protector who can shield me from harm. I slowly turn away from the blaze and see him, his face bathed in firelight. The hardness of his eyes is nowhere to be found, and the rage there when he appeared in the forest—that had stayed the entire way back to the cottage—has been replaced with concern and… sadness? I close the gap by an inch, and he mirrors my step. Another, and he moves with me until my toes touch the tips of his own. His lips part as he looks down at me, and we both throw our arms around each other. My feet leave the ground, and he drags me into his arms as his mouth envelops mine in a kiss.

"Eoghan, I am so sorry—"

"Shut up," he snaps against my lips.

"What?"

"Shut up," he says again and kisses me hard. My hands snake up into his hair, balling into fists around the strands as his lips crash into mine. He does not seem to notice. It is not until we are gasping for breath that he pulls his mouth away. "I thought you had left." He is panting to catch his breath as he speaks, but he doesn't move to loosen his grip on me. "And then I saw the bed, and I thought… I don't know what the hell I thought! Damnit, Maeve, do not ever scare me like that again!"

"You came after me," I breathe. "You could have left me, but you came after me."

"I told you already: nothing else matters in this world but keeping you safe." He places my feet back on the floor but does not remove his hands from my waist. "I think it's time we had a talk."

He guides me to the sofa, and I sit before he walks away toward the kitchen and out of sight. What the hell? Why did he leave? I crane my neck to find him, but within moments, he reappears with a bowl in his hand. He makes his way back to the sofa and holds the bowl out to me. Food. He has brought me food. The smell of hot stew fills my nostrils, and I take it from him eagerly. I have been hungry since before Kruz arrived, and my stomach groans loudly in response. He nods and sits opposite me in the leather armchair and watches me as I eat.

"So…" I look up at him, the spoon held tightly between my fingers.

"Eat." He smirks. Like hell is he going to initiate a conversation and then avoid it completely!

"No." I drop the spoon into the bowl, making broth splash over the side and onto the floor. "Start talking. I'll eat as you do."

Eoghan sets his heels on the small table in front of us as he sighs dramatically. "You are such a stubborn little thing." Want to see how stubborn I can be? I cock my eyebrow expectantly, and he rolls his eyes, his amusement evident. "Fine. Where do I begin?"

"Let's start with where you were this evening." I lift the spoon to my lips but drop it back into the bowl. "And don't just say you had a 'meeting'; you've already told me that. What meeting? Why are Gálgalesh, Finn, and River here? Why did I have no clue?"

Eoghan's green and gold eyes almost glow in the low light of the fire—of course they do. That is *his* fire burning hot in the corner of the room. "I *did* have a meeting—and the others were there as well. They arrived just before it started, actually. The village is better than the prison to meet, fewer prying eyes and nosy bystanders." He shoots me a knowing look; I mock him wordlessly, but I remain quiet as he continues. "Some of us meet to discuss plans and training and rumors from back home or the Capital. Not that it matters much anymore."

"That's not an answer, Eoghan. An answer should give understanding, not create more questions."

"I'm trying, Maeve."

"Does this have to do with the 'Leader'?" His eyes widen, and his body goes rigid in his seat.

"What do you know about the Leader?"

"Only that they are the only person anyone can talk about. In the Borderlands, everyone kept talking about the Leader's death. Gálgalesh would only take me in when Tiernan brought the Leader up, and when I arrived at Báscogar, Gálgalesh told me the prison was the Leader's training ground. His own personal army of those too dangerous to serve but too good at killing to be wasting away... Is that why you are at the prison?"

"Gálgalesh has a way of making everything and everyone sound terrible and threatening. I guess a part of what he said was true, though: the prison is a training ground of sorts." He rubs his jaw as though agitated.

"For my father? Was he building up a personal army?"

Eoghan looses a laugh that makes me feel stupid and insecure. I set the bowl on the table and wring my hands in my lap. "No, of course not. He had an army of thousands at his disposal, and he ruled with an iron fist, whether everyone hated him for it or not. He had no use for hiding."

"Oh," I whisper. "Then someone else... One of his army commanders? I heard a few of them were executed after the..." I can't finish the thought.

"Come on, Maeve. You're not going to make me spell it out for you. Four years ago, I agreed to come to Báscogar to train a group of the best fighters in Draíocoinnigh. Not as a prisoner, but to build a safe space away from the watchful eyes of the kingdom where we could prepare against an imminent threat to all of us. I came only because I thought if

I did, I would be saving the most important people in my life."

My mind is racing. What threat would be so great, the king's army could not handle it? Who would have the power to build an army of their own? Why would Eoghan—the youngest person in Draío history to fight in the king's army as a commander—choose to be part of a breakaway militia?

"Cai..." I am going to be ill. I am going to lose the contents of that stew right on this very floor. "Why would he do that? What threat did he think was so terrible, he needed his own army?" My brother had risen an army in secret while pretending to serve the kingdom. Usurpers do those sorts of things...and Eoghan had helped him. "Was *he* planning his own coup? Did *he* do this and miscalculate the outcome?!"

I throw myself to my feet. I want to cry and scream and vomit, and I am left paralyzed, not knowing which to do first. "What?! No! Calm down. Cai did *not* plan a coup against your family and get himself killed. He would never do that, especially if it meant putting you in harm's way."

"Why then?" I bear down on him now. "Tell me why he— and you—decided to sneak behind my father's back and build a secret militia!"

"I don't know. He never told us. He never got the chance. I think even he was still figuring it out when he... Well, when he was killed. But I swear it, he did not do this. He would never do this."

"And you trust him on that?" I feel like I cannot stop moving or I might combust. I tap my foot hard and rhythmically against the floor.

"Don't you?"

I pause as Eoghan's words hit me like a ton of bricks. Cai, the only friend I had ever had, the only person in my life who did not ignore me or use me or lie to me. Did I trust him enough to believe he had not tried to kill us all for power and greed? I close my eyes and inhale deeply as the memory of him in his Tinemallacht clothes and his makeshift bed on the castle floor flood my mind. He had no interest in being king—no reason to plot and kill for control. I open my eyes and sink down onto the floor in front of Eoghan.

"So he sent you here to train. Finn and River too?"

"All the Tinemallacht men at the prison and a few others as well. We recruited a couple of prisoners when we arrived. Not most of the men there, but a small amount hidden amongst the winter camp." Hidden in the prison; and here I thought I was the only one. "Most prisoners at Báscogar would kill a royal on sight rather than fight for them." The understatement of the year. "But Cai was different in a lot of ways, and some of the men recognized that."

"And now that he's gone?"

"That's why we meet: to decide what the hell it is we do now. Whatever the threat is, if it is still out there, we would like to stop it—but we just don't know what it is or how much time we have. With you alive, maybe there's hope that not all of our work has been in vain."

"And how many of them know I'm alive?" Eoghan's mouth ticks up in a half-smirk.

"You don't trust anyone, do you, Maevie?" He runs his hands down my leg gently. "Gálgalesh has been true to his word: no one else knows. And believe me, after today, I am keeping you a secret until you are as far from this mountain —maybe this continent—as you can be."

The possessiveness in his voice takes me by surprise.

"Thank you, by the way, for saving me." I feel the roughness in my throat as I speak, a constant reminder that Kruz had almost murdered me less than two hours ago.

"I was going to kill him the next time he laid his hands on you regardless. He just sped up the process." Heat rises in my cheeks. Amazing how easily he can make me blush. "You're doing that thing again."

"What thing?"

"Where you make me wonder how I am ever going to spend another moment not thinking about you." I cannot be redder if I tried. "Like I said, you might be the most dangerous little thing in the entire prison—maybe the most dangerous thing in this whole world."

CHAPTER TWENTY-FOUR

Gálgalesh, Finn, and River enter through the cottage door with a loud bang. A heavy wind whips across the sitting room, making the fire flicker in the hearth.

"You could knock…" Eoghan doesn't even look toward them as they close the gap between us, but he continues to smile as he holds me transfixed in his stare. "What if we weren't decent?"

"Wouldn't be the first time." River drops onto the couch, and Finn follows as Eoghan rolls his eyes. I turn to look at the fire. I am going to have to get control of myself around Eoghan at some point, or else I am going to embarrass myself like a child every time he smiles at me. Gálgalesh enters the kitchen and serves himself a bowl of stew before addressing us.

"Kruz Lanzo has been taken care of," Gálgalesh says as he reappears. "Tomorrow, when you return to Báscogar, I want no discussion of him. He has deserted the prison. When they find his body along the ridge line, no one will be the wiser. No one will ask questions."

The three men are silent, but they nod in agreement, and

I cannot breathe for a long moment. Kruz is dead, and it is my fault. All he wanted was to return to Iranndair and see his family; he never would get the chance now. I can't help but feel the heaviness of guilt build in my gut, as though I had taken that from him in some way, despite what he tried to do to me. I am so tired of death—to my very bones, I am tired of it. I do not think I could bear another person dying beside me or because of me; alas, I am beginning to believe the more I cheat death, the more it will close in on me. Eoghan drops his feet to the floor and leans forward in his chair. A tear tracks down my cheek, and he rubs it away with his thumb.

"We don't cry over bastards like Kruz Lanzo," he whispers, just between us. "He deserved what he got and worse."

"Gálgalesh says Kruz attacked you while you were alone." Finn is talking to me now, but I can barely hear it over the ringing in my ears. "What did you do to piss him off so badly?"

"Me."

Eoghan sits back and winks at me, and I let out a ragged, watery laugh. River sighs audibly behind me, and I don't need to look to know Finn has slunk back onto the cushions. Gálgalesh expresses his disapproval by clicking his tongue, but Eoghan is amused, as playful as he had been last night when we celebrated the Fire Offering, and if I had not fallen then, I sure as hell would have fallen now.

I should be furious with myself. Only six months ago, I had been engaged to Rian and now... Well, now, so much feels different. *I* feel different. This feels different—when Eoghan touches me or looks at me... I don't think I'll ever have the words to describe it. And to top it all off, Eoghan had killed Kruz Lanzo because of me. I'm not sure how to reckon with that one. Would I always be such trouble? Would he tire of saving me? When will I stop having to be saved?

"At any rate, it does not matter what Alana has done to warrant an attack from Lanzo. He has been taken care of. I do ask that when you return to the prison tomorrow, you keep...whatever is going on between you two to yourselves. Rhodes, Hayes, let us go. We have much to do before morning." The two men stand and dutifully file out the door. River shoots Eoghan a mischievous grin as he leaves, and Eoghan scowls at him, feigning annoyance, before his friend disappears over the threshold. It is clear a silent conversation just took place, one I will ever know a thing about. Gálgalesh makes to follow them with a fresh bowl of stew still in his hand, but he stops before he makes it to the top step. "We found this rag in Lanzo's pocket. It seems he stole a sleeping drought from my quarters." He pulls it from his cloak with his free hand and holds it up so Eoghan and I can see. "Woman, did you wield against him before you ran?"

"Yes..." What else could I do?

"You should not have been able to do so while under the effects of that drought. Curious... I believe I have once again underestimated you."

He continues out the door, which shuts on its own behind him.

***

WE LEAVE around mid-morning to return to Báscogar after Eoghan does one last check of the ill Fáintìrean villagers. He drapes his cloak over my shoulders—since mine was sacrificed to the fire last night—and we leisurely make our way back to camp, cherishing the peaceful, uninterrupted moments together before the prison walls close in on us.

"Follow me," Eoghan beckons as he veers off the gravel pathway into the trees. I pause. I never want to go into the forest again. I never want anything to do with those foreboding trees and darkness that almost swallowed me up twice now. Eoghan takes my hand in his, but he does not drag me away from the road. "Do you trust me to keep you safe?" I nod once as I gaze past him into the trees. "Then trust I won't let anything happen to you in there now."

Trust. That word echoes around me again. I need to trust him. He has saved my life more times than I deserve. I can trust it in his hands. He is safe, and he is going to keep me safe for as long as he is with me. I know that. It is the only thing I have ever known for certain in my life. I take a step toward him, and he entwines our fingers as he guides me through the snow.

We walk until the gravel road is no longer visible in the darkness, until the black of the sky and the white of the snow are the only things we see. Romiodóg is the most oppressive, unwelcoming place I could ever imagine. Similar to the dungeons of Caisleán Rialú, it is cold and damp, and the unforgiving horrors experienced here haunt me at night. I hate this place more every day. My throat tightens as I swallow hard, and my hands begin to tremble as we pass through a small clearing that reminds me of the one Peadair had brought me to so he might kill me and my screams would not be heard. I can't be sure of the place, though; everywhere looks the same when drenched in white.

"I am right here." Eoghan's voice is so delicate and soft, it feels as though he has wrapped himself around me with just his words. "Not much further."

We wind through the trees, and I marvel at his sense of direction. For all I know, we could be heading south toward the Borderlands and nowhere near Báscogar. *Trust, Maeve. You have to trust him.* Just as I begin to become wary of our trek through calf-high sleet and icy, Eoghan leads me up another short hill, and we stop and gaze down at the valley below.

Green. All I can see is green. As my eyes trace the wintry hillside sloping down into the valley below, I gasp at the luscious contrast of color peeking out beyond the blanket of white. At the bottom of the valley sits a lush pool of blue, crystal clear water, night-blooming flowers in purples and whites speckling the grass. Life. Life in this barren land. Eoghan urges me forward, and as soon as our boots step out of the snow and onto the turf, something shifts in the air, and my eyes grow wide in surprise.

Warmth. As though we have walked into a spring evening at the Golorgleann flower fields, the temperature around me rises significantly. Though not as warm as the endless days of summer, it fills me from the inside out with joy as my teeth cease their boundless chattering and my hands begin to thaw. Eoghan reaches toward me, motioning for the cloak, which I pass to him gladly as we reach the valley floor. Compared to the cold at the top of the hill, this could be considered sweltering.

"What is this place?" My mouth falls open as I take in the spring oasis, and Eoghan takes a seat in the grass, beckoning me to himself. I drop down beside him, expecting the grass to be wet, but it is soft and dry beneath my fingertips.

"This is the wonder of Romiodóg," he begins as he plucks a flower between his fingers and places it behind my ear. "The reason the people of Fáintìrean can survive the endless winters and trade animal furs and meats. It's a refuge fueled by magic, where winter can never reach and every animal on the mountain comes to be watered and fed. A gift from the gods, they say."

"And why isn't it overrun with people? Where are all the men out on patrol?" I look over my shoulder, half-expecting a party of Báscogar prisoners to storm the valley.

"It's a secret," he whispers, and I feel his lips against my ear. "My gift to you, to apologize for not sharing my secrets with you before. It won't happen again. Everything is yours. Forever."

His hand cups my right cheek as he presses his lips onto my left one. *Everything is yours. Forever.* No reservations, no stipulations. He is giving himself to me completely. I want to melt into his arms, and if not for the wonder of this place and my desire to spend every possible moment I can taking it in, I would.

His lips and hand fall away, and he unties his boots before leaning casually back onto his elbows and kicking them off in front of him. I find my breath again after realizing I had forgotten to inhale when he touched me. I have reached the highest heaven, and Eoghan and I are the only two people there. Nothing in this whole world could be more perfect, not even if I was back in my favorite grassy spot on the castle grounds. I turn to Eoghan, and his soft smile sends chills right through me. I pull my knees into my chest and rest my head on them. I want to know everything about him. I want to know his favorite color and his favorite smell. I want to know what makes him smile. I want to know even the worst things—the terrible things that wake him from his sleep so I can kiss them away.

"Eoghan?"

"Hmm?" He closes his eyes as he lounges beside me.

"The first day I was at Báscogar, did you really see me climbing from the window?" I watch as his mouth ticks up at the side, and his green eyes open, dazzling devilish.

"I ventured a guess. Finn, Sullivan, and I were entering the shower room, and I noticed your toiletries on the counter, your clothes on the bench. I couldn't see anything through the steam until you knocked out that window, but I diverted my eyes when your shadow became visible. I stood there nearly breathless, waiting to hear you scream as you fell, trying to figure out what I could do if you did, but then I heard you fall through your window, and I knew you had been crazy enough to make it." His shoulders bounce as he laughs. "It was terrifying and stupid, by the way. Don't do it again."

He'd been scared of me dying, even though he hated that I was there in the first place. Even so, he had had the decency to look away. "So you didn't see me climb through the window?"

"No, I didn't." He runs his fingers through the grass, and I watch as they grasp a handful before loosening and flexing. "Would it have been so terrible if I had, though?"

I ponder the question for a moment. By now, he has seen everything anyway, laid out on full display for him. "No, I suppose not… It's just that, until now, no one other than Rian had seen me that way."

"Ahh." I feel his body heat next to me, but he takes a breath, and the temperature drops again. "You really loved him, didn't you?" I nod, though something inside me hesitates to answer. "Did your father approve when you told him?"

"Don't be ridiculous. He almost killed me for it."

"Why? He didn't like him?"

"Falling in love was not allowed for me. That was the rule. Not that I had many men to choose from in the palace, but I wasn't allowed to love a man or kiss one…or… Well, it just wasn't allowed, but I broke all the rules because I refused to be a lonely old spinster locked away in a castle for the rest of my life." My fingertips brush along the fabric covering my stomach as I remember the day Rian and I had told him of our engagement, and my hand clenches into a fist somewhere above my navel. Eoghan takes my hand into his own, and I soften at his touch.

"He knew you'd be irresistible to anyone who met you." His thumb brushes against the back of my hand. "At least you fell in love with a rich man. He might have actually killed you if you fell in love with a Fire Cursed like me."

What a terrible truth. I don't want to think about just how right Eoghan might be, just how forbidden it would have been to have his hand in mine back then. I clear my throat.

"What about you? Have you ever been in love?"

"For a day or two, maybe. Nothing that lasted long enough for marriage." Even that makes my heart fall into my stomach. "Marriage in Tinemallacht is more important than it is in the other territories, though. When someone marries in Tinemallacht, they participate in a fire ceremony where their hearts are entwined. There's no remarriage, not even at the death of a partner. You only get one shot at it, so it's not taken lightly."

"And you never…?" I find I'm almost sweating as I wait for his answer.

"No, never." The pressure in my chest falls away, and I stifle a sigh.

"Well, I'm…" I pause. What was I? Happy? Relieved? *A moron,* I hiss to myself. *An absolute moron.*

Eoghan smirks next to me, and my face heats in embarrassment. I bury my forehead in my knees, wishing I could go back to the beginning of the conversation and say absolutely anything else.

"What's the matter?" he coaxes, but I shake my head. "Come on, you're flushed. What is it?"

"Leave me alone; it's hot." I laugh despite myself and bat my hand toward him. "I'm in wool clothes, and the temperature is stifling."

He studies me for a long moment and then nods his head before jumping to his feet and walking away, leaving me in the grass. I stumble to stand, my mouth agape as I watch him go.

"Where are you going?!" I shout after him, and he turns

without slowing down. His hands grip the hem of his shirt and pull it over his head before discarding it on the ground and moving to work the button of his pants.

"It's hot! I'm going for a swim!" He drops his pants to his ankles and kicks out of them smoothly, leaving him only in his underwear and socks, which he discards teasingly. "Are you coming?"

He turns his back on me again, and I watch his perfect ass as he walks to the edge of the turquoise pool and slides down beneath the surface. Shit. If I don't go in after him, he'll think our conversation scared me off. But then, if I do, I'll be exposing myself again to him, and with the heat radiating through me, I run the risk of losing all my self-control while being so vulnerable with him. He emerges from the water and wipes his hand through his hair as he beckons me to join him, and something inside me tells me I want to—I need to.

I tug my heavy shirt off and untie my boots before shrugging out of my pants now sticking to my sweat-drenched skin. The air caresses my body, and I close my eyes at its delicate touch. I push my underwear down and off into the grass, and then I make my way to the pool.

I haven't swum since the summer in the castle pond. This is different. The water feels like starlight on my skin as I sink down below the surface. After the initial shock of cold, the pool seems to adjust to my body and warms to my core temperature, suspending me in what feels like nothing at all. Magic. Magic that goes beyond anything I can imagine.

"Amazing," I whisper as I feel two arms wrap around me. I turn to face Eoghan and drape my arms around his shoulders, feeling the dampness of his skin against my fingers.

"*You* are amazing."

He presses his lips to mine gently at first, but my lips part, and I feel his tongue against mine as he deepens the kiss. I trace my nails lightly against the nape of his neck, and I feel him shiver and pull me closer. I want to stay here forever with him, just like this.

He pulls away, and my chest heaves heavily against his as I gasp for air. I didn't even know I needed to breathe until he let me go.

"Kiss me again," I beg as his hands trail down my spine, holding me to him in the infinite nothingness of the pool.

"No," he laughs, bringing his nose to the spot between my collarbone and neck.

"Why?"

"Because if I kiss you again, I'll never want to stop. I'd let the world come crashing down around us, and I wouldn't even flinch."

And then, as my heart beats out of my chest, his lips meet mine.

———

WHEN WE FINALLY MAKE IT through the gates of the prison later that afternoon, Eoghan walks me to my room, his cloak once again pulled over my shoulders to stave off the bitter chill. There is something different about him as we walk through the dark and damp halls. His shoulders are square, and his jaw sets into a hard line. The Tinemallacht warrior of Báscogar—feared above all else—has arrived once again, a mask falling into place to hide the man he really is from the other prisoners. Even I feel a slight unease as I take him in, and it is only the faint stroke of his pinky against mine that reminds me the man from the cottage and the secret spring valley is still beside me.

We reach my door, and he places his hands against the wall on either side of my head as his gaze holds me. "Thanks for your help on patrol," he says as a group of prisoners move past us in the hall, and I realize he is shielding me from their view. A jealous dragon, isn't he?

"Any time, Kael." I grab the front of his shirt, tugging lightly, and he responds by inclining his head to hover his lips over mine. I am completely engulfed in his warmth, scorched by the passion that radiates through him—the undeniable mark of his undoing.

"Remember what Gálgalesh said," he whispers, but he doesn't back away.

"I don't care what Gálgalesh said." I drop my voice until it is barely audible between us. "It is taking everything in me not to drop to my knees right here in this hallway and—"

His right hand flies from the wall to cover my mouth, his eyes growing wide. He is more concupiscent than I have ever seen him, and I laugh against his palm. He takes in a deep breath and drums his left fingers against the stone beside my head.

"You're going to be trouble, aren't you?" I shrug innocently. I quite like seeing him this unraveled for me, especially after all the time I have spent going mad at the sight of him. "I need to go train, and you need to rest. Go and be good, and I will be back before dinnertime." He removes his hand from my mouth. "Besides, I'd prefer we didn't have an audience when you drop to your knees for me."

A jealous dragon, indeed. He turns the doorknob behind me, and the door creaks open. I release the front of his shirt, and he straightens to full height before I disappear into my room.

I don't remember it feeling so dark, so cramped, so dreadful. A taste of freedom will do that to a prisoner, whether the cage is simply for show or not. I walk across the darkness deftly, as I know every inch of the space by heart now, and look out into the darkness, wishing to be back in the cottage laying across the sofa by the fire. Ice has formed on my windowsill from the winter freeze that moved in this morning. There is definitely no warmth to be found here. I throw the cloak from my shoulders and myself onto the mattress. My eyes feel heavy as the long nights in Fáintìrean without sleep begin to catch up with me. I press the heels of my palms into my eyes and rub them until I see stars. I had woken up three times last night in a fit of screams as I fell to Kruz over and over in my dreams. Eoghan had slept on the sofa, rushing to my bedside each time, shushing and calming me until I drifted off again.

I take in my tiny bed, so uncomfortable and cold, and I pull the blankets around me. Sleep. I'll sleep until dinner, and then I will find Eoghan to warm me again somehow, even if we need to ignore Gálgalesh to do so.

———

Bang! Bang! Bang! I could not have slept for more than an hour. The hall outside my room is still loud with passersby. Dinner must not have been served yet, as the halls are nearly empty at dinner time...and right now, it sounds as though every resident has gathered outside my door. *Bang! Bang! Bang!* Three terrifying and urgent knocks rattle against the wood—the same ones that had shaken me awake moments before. I stretch my arms out groggily and push my feet to the floor. I'm moving at a snail's pace. I haven't had enough rest to wake quite this abruptly. *Bang! Bang! Bang!*

"I'm coming!" I shout at the door in a husky voice coated in sleep. I yawn and pull the door toward me, and Eoghan barrels into the room. He looks agitated and worried as he pushes me back toward the bed, shutting the door behind him so quickly, I cannot quite process my footing, and he has to grab my arm to keep me from stumbling back. "What's wrong?" He's searching my desk drawers and the small side table by my bed, but he comes up empty-handed. "Eoghan, what's going on?"

"Your boots." He grabs my shoulders with a gentleness that does not match the frenzy of his movements as he urges me to a seat on the mattress. He crouches in front of me and pulls my boots to him before shoving them onto my feet and lacing them quickly. He grabs his own discarded cloak and throws it over my shoulders, buckling the metal fastener near my neck. As he stands, he takes my hand in his to pull me to my feet and toward the door, but I dig my heels in. Why isn't he speaking to me? What has him in such a rush, he cannot even take a moment to tell me what is wrong?

"Eoghan…" He turns to me and finds my gaze for the first time since he bounded into my room. "Tell me what the hell is going on."

"Three of the king's men arrived at the gates twenty minutes ago. They are calling for an audit of the entire prison, with every prisoner accounted for."

"The *king*? Eoghan, the king is dead!" He hasn't let go of my hands, and I can feel him tugging at them lightly, trying to get me to move.

"The *new* king, Maeve, and we are not on the prison roster. They cannot find us here. If they start asking questions…"

Understanding washes over me. The usurpers have finally crowned their king, and they are now coming to call on the prisoners of Báscogar. If anyone recognizes me, I'm dead. If Eoghan and the other Tinemallachts are caught in the prison when they are not on the roster… Well, maybe death would be better than what might happen to them. I untuck my boots from under me, and he drags me out of the room behind him.

There is utter chaos in the halls. Every prisoner is indeed running through the corridors, either trying to make their way to the prisoner count or to hide the contraband in their rooms in the case of a check. Eoghan grips my hand with so much force, it makes me wince, and he keeps me tucked close to his side as he rushes down the crowded hall toward the eastern tunnel so many have used to try to escape the prison. I was told by Kruz once that it lets out on the jagged cliffside, and although no one guards it, it is almost certain suicide to try to traverse the icy, relentless terrain. Eoghan could navigate it, though; I have watched him enough in the training arena to be fairly confident of that. I, on the other hand, might be a different story.

We break free of most of the crowd, who had begun to make their way to the central courtyard. Eoghan grabs the hood of the cloak and throws it over my head.

"Keep your head down," he mutters under his breath. He doesn't slow our pace to the exit.

"Where are the others?" I whisper back.

"They already made it out. Probably on their way to Fáin-tìrean by now."

My heart eases a bit in my chest. The others are fine; they had made it out. Now, we just need to make it to the tunnel, and we will be out too. We round the corner, and the pathway begins to darken and slope downward. Eoghan grips my hand tighter, and I pray we get out of here before he breaks my fingers with the effort. We take another right, and I can see the faint glow of the metal gate at the edge of the tunnel. Eoghan picks up pace, hurtling us toward the white snow on the other side, maybe fifty yards ahead. Forty. Twenty-five. Ten.

"And where do you think you're going?"

Shit. The rough drawl of one of the king's guards sent to Báscogar halts us just feet from the tunnel's exit, and both of us stay silent as we listen to the guard's boots against the stone of the tunnel floor. The light is so dim here, I can barely make out Eoghan's face. A small mercy. If we can't see each other, perhaps the guard cannot see us. Eoghan runs his thumb across my hand and then drops it and turns clear around, away from the gate.

"As soon as you get a chance, run," he breathes before taking a step toward the man. Oh gods, no! He is not going to be valiant on my account. Like hell am I going to let him stay while I run away, not when he has saved my life a handful of times in as many months. I'm tired of running—tired of others being hurt or killed as I get away. I turn on my heels, and his breath hitches in surprise. "What are you doing?"

"I am not leaving you here," I hiss back.

"Leaving, are we?" The guard takes another step forward.

"We have patrol duty on the Eastern Ridge Line." Eoghan's voice is cool and calm, but his body is tense. I find his fingers once more, but he pushes them away softly. *Don't make them think you need protecting*, I remind myself. I straighten as the guard approaches me.

"Patrol has been canceled on account of the king."

"I see no king here." The deep purr of Eoghan's vibrates through his chest as he stands his ground. He's bigger than the man in front of us, and in a hundred fights, I would bet on Eoghan to win. But it isn't just strength we need on our side—we can't make a scene and draw attention if we are going to make it out of here alive.

"You would not see royalty in a place like this, would you?" I almost laugh out loud at the words. If he only knew just how wrong he was. "Everyone is to be accounted for in the courtyard, even the girl." *The girl.* His words are dripping with something that makes Eoghan growl under his breath. It's hard to reckon with my slight frame. I look weak and fragile beside the men of Báscogar. "If you refuse, I've been given permission to take your heads. We don't need you breathing to count your presence." I look toward the ground and see a small executioner's ax swaying back and forth as it hangs from his belt. He turns to the side to clear the way and motions for us to move. "After you."

We slowly begin our walk back up the eastern tunnel, the guard just paces behind. We hadn't made it out, and we both know what this means—not just for us, but for Gálgalesh as well. Our boots echo down the corridor, and with each step, the light finds us, dim as it is, growing warmer as we go.

"Do not say a word." Eoghan walks so close beside me, his warm arm brushes against mine. "Not one word."

We turn down the main hallway, and a crowd begins to form around us. The guard at our backs pushes us forward through the men lining up for the count, into the blackness of night and the white banks of snow in the courtyard. Though the road up the mountain has opened once more, the eternal night is still much too dark to make out anyone properly. Another mercy. The guard stops us in the center of the courtyard in front of another man with a roll of parchment in his hand. I recognize this one as who pulled me from the fireplace on the day of the coup. Though he has now bathed and dressed himself in a clean uniform, I'd never forget the scars on his face.

"Caught these two trying to escape," the guard behind us says to the other, and the scarred man's head cocks to the side as he takes us in. I drop my gaze further, Eoghan's large cloak hood swallowing me up.

"Did you now?" His raspy voice grates across my skin, and I ball my fists as my hands start to shake. I can feel his eyes glued to me, examining me. "Names?"

"This is ridiculous; the king does not run Báscogar. The Warden runs it." Eoghan is going to get himself killed just to keep me safe.

"Things are changing now. The king believes the previous

person in charge neglected this prison, and he has taken it upon himself to rectify the situation."

"Yet he sends his henchmen to pay us a visit instead of doing so himself. Doesn't sound like much has changed."

I wish he would stop talking, close that beautiful mouth of his and just try, for once, to not be the hero.

The man turns to Eoghan and takes a step toward him. "Names?" he says again through clenched teeth.

"Fuck off," Eoghan snaps, and like lightening, the man rears back his hand and hurls it toward Eoghan's face. He connects with Eoghan's jaw, the sound of fist colliding with flesh making me sick. Eoghan barely moves—doesn't even stumble—as he takes the assault. "A henchman and a bully. I'd expect nothing less."

The courtyard is silent, as if everyone is holding their breath as they watch the scene unfold. A pin could drop, and everyone would hear it. Even the owls have stopped their calls in the trees. If I could hit him too, I would. I nearly whip around and shout at him to be quiet when the sound of smooth, easy steps from behind us breaks through the silence.

"It is unkind to strike a prisoner under another man's command—even if he does deserve it." Gálgalesh strides up beside us, and the man backs away from Eoghan as if he fears the faerie. Of course he does—why wouldn't he? Faeries kill men of all ranks and size. They are the nightmares of this world become flesh.

"I need their names." The rasp of the man's voice fills the air around us, and I realize for the first time that Gálgalesh is silencing the space, keeping the others in the courtyard from hearing us—that vexatious faerie magic these men know nothing about.

"This is Alana." I feel Gálgalesh's fingers settle on top of the hood, holding my head down so they cannot get a good look at my face. "A slave girl who deserted the royal house-hold. And this foolish man is Eoghan. He came to us after killing six men about your size with his bare hands. Nasty beast of a man. I would not tempt fate hitting him again if I were you—but I do value my life quite dearly." I can almost feel Eoghan's satisfied smile fan out across his lips.

"I have no Alana or Eoghan on this list." The man shakes the roll of parchment in his hand.

"Of course not—they arrived here shortly after we sent our last rolls to the Capital. There would be no official record of them yet. If you would follow me, however, I have the updated rolls in my quarters, and I would be delighted to show you exactly where they are." Gálgalesh removes his hand from my head, but I do not dare look up. The man who caught us in the tunnel tries to grab us by the elbows, but Gálgalesh steps toward him, and he backs away too. "Leave them here; they are not worth your time."

"But they were escaping out of the tunnel!" the man complains.

"Nonsense." Gálgalesh lets out a wicked laugh. "I sent them to guard the tunnel from deserters. They were there on my orders."

"But I saw them leave—"

"You saw *nothing*," Gálgalesh's smooth voice is dangerous now. "Did you see them open the gate to leave?"

"Well, no but—"

"Then how can you be sure you did not disturb them on orders from the Warden to stop others from escaping?"

The scarred man sighs. "Idiot!" He pushes past us to his partner. He raises his hand and smacks him hard across the face, making the first guard whimper and retreat further. "Let's get these damned rolls and get on with it."

He shoves the other man back through the courtyard to the corridor. "Meet me at the praying tree in an hour,"

Gálgalesh murmurs under his breath before he leaves us where we stand in the courtyard, the sound of the crowds rushing back in his wake.

———

EOGHAN and I sit at the foot of the praying tree in silence as we wait for Gálgalesh. Dinner had been a blur as we sat alone at our table in the far corner of the hall. The tension and silence was palpable, and neither of us could stomach much of the tasteless gruel on our plates.

Eoghan rubs his jaw tenderly next to me. There is a little bit of swelling there, his lip split from a ring on the scarred man's finger, but he is lucky that is the worst of it. I hadn't really considered the future of Draíocoinnigh after my father's death. It had occurred to me another would take his place, but being so far from Gairdín all these months, I've started to forget there is anything beyond these walls, forget there might have been something more at play than just death. How naïve of me to think someone could look such power in the eyes and not want it. Who wouldn't take it if they had the chance?

The sound of Gálgalesh approaching shakes me back to the present, and I stand as he reaches the altar at the tree. I make to speak, but he holds up his hand to silence me, taking out a small bowl and canvas pouch filled with incense. He pours the contents into the bowl and lights a match, causing the herbs to smolder and catch fire. The smell of patchouli and cedar fill the air around us, and Gálgalesh closes his eyes. Gods be damned, I want him to speak. I care nothing of the ceremony of tributes and sacrifices to gods who never hear us or refuse to listen. I long for him to assure me he has dismissed the king's guards, that the Tinemallachts will come back, bringing safety to this place. He doesn't say a word, simply praying in silence until the incense is nothing but smoking ash. He lifts the bowl in his hands and turns it over, dispensing the black cinder: CM GD MUINSA. He reaches in his pocket and pulls out a cloth to wipe the soot from his hands.

"I have been a prisoner of Báscogar since the humans turned on the faeries and outlawed the use of faerie magic in human communities one hundred and seventy-eight years ago. I was a healer at the time, creating tonics and potions for faeries and humans alike. The rulers of this land saw my tonics as dangerous and warned me to stop treating humans in Draíocoinnigh, but I could not do that. There were too many who were sick, and healing magic is rare among human alchemists; true healing magic without tonics is almost unheard of." He indicates to me before continuing. "I continued to heal where I could, mostly among the mountain regions far from Golorgleann, but they eventually caught me as humans flocked to me, and they gave me a life sentence here.

"Then, a century ago, I became the Warden of Báscogar. It was a foolish thing to do. Upon the death of the Warden, five contenders are granted the opportunity to fight to the death for the position in the training arena. Knowing I had magic and strength on my side—and knowing the position would give me occasional leave from the prison and an opportunity to see Peadair again—I took a chance. It was silly, really—as if any human could possibly be a match for a faerie—and I won with little trouble at all. As Warden, I saw a renewed opportunity to bring healing and care to the people of Draío—*my* people for the past three hundred years. I began selling my tonics on the black market, making friends with the drug smugglers and thieves to move as much through the kingdom as I could. I took no gold for my wares, giving it all to those who helped me.

Peadair helped from the outside as well. That was where I met Tiernan, a decade ago at least, smuggling Ama for spare gold.

"As much as I love Peadair, he is an unpredictable creature with a penchant for money and jewels. While passing along my tonics, he began selling Ama on the side. Outside the Borderlands four years ago, they apprehended him for selling a particular Ama—I've been told maybe you had a taste of it once during a time of need."

"Tiernan," I whisper, and Gálgalesh nods solemnly.

"Of course *he*, the brother-in-arms of the heir apparent, had come out unscathed. However, a group of king's guards brought Peadair to Báscogar prison, with the Prince of Draíocoinnigh escorting them, for a life sentence, punishment for selling the wretched drug. Do you know what the punishment is for possession of Ama?"

I gulp. "Even locked away in the castle, they teach us the price of selling our souls to the highs of alchemists—fifty lashes to the back."

"That's right. Administered by the Warden of Báscogar Prison. Fifty lashes could kill anyone, even a faerie. The punishment is designed to kill, not just to prove a point." He pauses, and his breath flows heavily through his lungs. "Peadair was tied to a wooden stake in the training arena at dawn, the guards and Crown Prince the only audience to watch as my trembling hands lifted the scourge high. I had administered a number of lashings before, but this particular morning, the scourge felt like lead in my hands." I remember the heaviness of the weapon as Gálgalesh thrust it into my grip. It felt like a magnetic pull was dragging it down to the floor, and me along with it. "I said my prayers to the gods of my homelands, and then I let it snap through the air—but someone stepped in its path before I brought it down to meet Peadair. Woman, there are not many rules governing our home here at the prison, but do you know our rules about taking one's punishment as our own?"

"Half the punishment of the original order to the one who has taken their place, and the one who has been spared must swear a life debt to their savior." Eoghan's voice is low and even as he too listens to Gálgalesh with quiet interest.

"Yes. Your brother, Prince Cai—the Leader, as he would come to be known by those who knew him best—showed mercy to not only Peadair, but myself that day. Tiernan had told him of me and the sentence he had saddled upon Peadair, and he ultimately bore the price. He received twenty-five lashes, and in return, he asked me for a debt: to help save the kingdom of Draíocoinnigh. Before he left, we made this carving as a reminder of what he had given and the bond we now share. He never returned to Báscogar; he much preferred Fáintìrean and the villagers there who took him in as one of their own. But just months later, Eoghan and the Tinemallacht men arrived and began their training in secret behind these walls."

Cai had saved Peadair's life—not only saved him but had taken his punishment for his own. My chest wells with a mixture of pride and devastation, and my eyes grow heavy with tears. I look to Eoghan, who meets my gaze, and without a word, I know this is a story he knew. This was why, with perfect conviction, he and everyone else could say they trusted Cai blindly—because Cai was good. I let the tears fall wherever they may for as long as they will come.

"I'm…I'm…"

I cannot find the words. Sorry? For what? Not knowing the most decent one of us all was, in fact, decent—or that he was now dead and, because of his decency, everyone is now saddled with me? Gálgalesh shakes his head, his own eyes silver with tears.

"Do not weep. It dishonors his sacrifice." He wipes a tear

from my face. "Peadair and I, as First and Second Wardens of Báscogar, have received a summons to the Capital for meetings with the new king. In our place, the king has ordered a brutal man named Drustan Anwyl to serve as the Interim Warden. I have ensured both of you are listed on the prisoner roll, but it won't be long before Anwyl realizes neither of you are actual prisoners. He was not in the Capital during the coup, though, and will not suspect your real identity. I have sent a raven to the village to keep the others away while I am gone." His expression darkens as his eyes move between us. "Stay together. Eat together. Sleep together. Train. Whatever you do, woman, find a way to kill these bastards for all of us —for the Leader." As he finishes, Peadair arrives at the stone archway. He does not move into the courtyard; when Gálgalesh turns to see him, he nods once toward us. "I must go. Do as I say."

He makes to exit, but I grab his arm. He looks down at my hand, but before he can protest, I throw myself around him in an embrace. "Be safe." It's the only words I have for him. Nothing else feels like enough. In a world where Gálgalesh has seen and been through so much, words seem hollow and useless.

"I'll be back in a month. Try to be gone before I return," he whispers against my ear before releasing me. Eoghan takes my hand as we break away from one another, and Gálgalesh turns away, leaving us and the prison behind.

CHAPTER TWENTY-FIVE

It has been hours since we returned to our rooms, and yet sleep eludes us. Eoghan and I lay silently in his bed, his arms around me as my head settles against his chest. Gálgalesh and Peadair have left Báscogar Prison; all our closest allies in this place have fled for their lives and escaped —we are now truly prisoners here for the first time. The pit of despair in my stomach becomes a crater as I realize if it had not been for me, if I had not hesitated or questioned… If I was not here, Eoghan would have escaped too. He stayed behind to rescue me. Another rescue—another reason to despise my existence. Could I blame him for it after all that had happened? I wish I could be anything else in the world other than the useless woman he has to save all the time.

His chest heaves steadily, quietly, and heat radiates from him, making the room more than bearable. I have never been to his quarters before, and even though they look similar to mine in many ways, Eoghan's personal touch is evident everywhere, from the collection of weapons near the door to the Tinemallacht insignia on any item not provided by the prison. I love it in here, in our own little hideaway, far from anyone else. As his fingertips dance feather-light across my skin, I imagine we are back in the cottage, laying together under the blankets. We should have just stayed. We should have given up on our goals and promises and stayed in Fáin-tìrean—in that cottage where we found each other.

"What do we do now?" My voice is just a whisper, like the last bits of smoke rising from a dying fire.

"We stay alive." Eoghan's fingers entwine with mine protectively, and I am aware he might never let me go now that Gálgalesh has gone. "Like Gálgalesh said, we will stay together, and the first chance we get, we will leave this place behind and meet up with the others."

"And then what?"

"I don't know, but we can figure it out together."

There is movement outside the door in the corridor as the other residents of the prison begin to stir. It must be morning already. I disentangle my hand from his and wipe my eyes as I yawn against Eoghan's chest. Before we made it back to our rooms last night, we were instructed to meet in the dining hall for breakfast and new duty assignments at dawn. I roll away from him and swing my feet to the floor and sit up at the edge of the bed. Eoghan reaches for my waist to pull me back toward him.

"You haven't slept. Stay in bed." His protests are an exhausted purr and I wonder about the last time he had some proper sleep himself.

"We must report to the dining hall. We have no time to stay in bed." I shake him off, and he lifts his head from his pillow, hand running through his hair lazily. "We can sleep after we eat." He pushes himself from the mattress and climbs off the bed around me. He drops his pajama bottoms to the floor and pulls on his black prisoner's uniform before he steps into his boots. When he's finished lacing himself in, he crouches in front of me and laces up my own.

"I can do that myself, you know," I complain when he taps the toe of my boot, as Tiernan had done after he laced me up.

"I know you can—you're the most capable, strong woman I have ever met. Just give me this one pleasure of treating you like the princess you are before we walk out this door and I have to try my best to not break anyone who does not bow down to you in praise."

He helps me to my feet, and we leave the room together, with Eoghan walking so close to my side, I can barely move without bumping into him. He's protective, and I know that despite our best efforts to hide our affection, there is no doubt in anyone's mind that I am his now. We make it to the dining hall to find a queue of men waiting to enter. With Gálgalesh gone, no one knows what to expect of our temporary warden. Once we get inside the—only slightly warmer—hall, Eoghan follows me to the serving stations and then our table. Empty, again. I remind myself that the others are safe; they are just a few kilometers away in the village, waiting to return. River and Finn are fine. Gods, I hope they are safe. I look to Eoghan, and I see the mask he always wears so perfectly in the prison walls crack just the slightest bit. I know he has had to reassure himself the same as I have. He has given everything to be here with me; he has sacrificed everyone he loves for me. That hardly seems fair. I wipe my eyes as I dig my spoon into my porridge.

We sit side-by-side and let the low grumbling of the room surround us. Rumors abound of Gálgalesh being permanently replaced and of the new king tightening his hand on the prison. I keep my head down toward my tray, hating every word, wishing I could shove my fist into something and beat it until this hatred and loathing subsides. Heavy footsteps reverberate through the room, and the chatter quickly dies down to a whisper before disappearing to nothing at all. I lift my head to see a guard I recognize from the duty rotation in the towers and a man I can only assume is our new warden, Drustan Anwyl. He is broad in stature, and though he stands a few inches shorter than Eoghan, he is quite tall. He has sandy blond hair that reaches his shoulders, and his eyes are pale gray. He might have been handsome once, if not for the brutality of the scar running from his hairline and across his face to the opposite side—right down to his chin—and his smile is dangerous, like a serpent ready to strike.

He steps to the center of the room—the guard at his side—and clears his throat loudly against the silence.

"Prisoners of Báscogar, allow me to introduce myself." His voice runs through me like a chill down my spine, the hairs on the back of my neck rising. "I am Drustan Anwyl, your new warden…for the time being. You will address me as sir when or if you are allowed to speak to me. While I am here, I will be overseeing some changes in your duties, training times, and leisure. First," he surveys the faces of the prisoners with square shoulders, his hands in his cloak pockets, "breakfast will be served at dawn each day, and duties will begin one hour after that. If you fail to report, you will be punished. Three failures will see you lose training opportunities for a week. Second, lunch will be served at noon each day, and then duties will resume until three. Training will be available from the end of your duties until dinner at five, and then you will have evenings free until lights out at nine. Random bed checks will be conducted by guards to ensure all prisoners comply with protocol.

"Third." His voice is grating and makes me feel uneasy as Eoghan grips his fork like a weapon in his hand. "There will be no drinking, gambling, or music—as I have been told the leadership here has been lax in enforcing the rules for a long time. Additionally, there will be no patrols outside of the prison walls, as the towers themselves are sufficient. Finally, everyone needs to surrender all weapons to me in the central courtyard by this evening. This includes any training swords, daggers, and short knives you may possess." He looks around the room at the stunned faces of the prisoners, all too speechless to protest, and a wicked smile tugs at the corner of his lips. "That is all."

He walks toward the serving stations, and the chatter of the room renews in desperate, worried tones. Prison duties will begin again, training will be limited, and our time together will be non-existent, with bed checks in place, no weapons to protect ourselves in these walls. I will be lucky to survive a week.

I feel Eoghan's hand slide across my thigh, pulling me away from my thoughts, and his fingertips press down lightly as Drustan Anwyl approaches our table. My eyes shoot upward to meet his as he beams down at us, making my skin crawl.

"Alana, is it?" My mouth is so dry, my tongue sticks to the roof, and I nod my head once silently. "Your duties will be with me in the warden's quarters. I trust you know where to find them." A pointed question he needs no answer to. "Eoghan, you will be on overnight duty in the South Tower from three in the afternoon until sunrise. You may rest and have your leisure time in the mornings while the others take first duty."

I feel Eoghan's fingers move across my leg, and I realize he has gripped the hilt of the dagger strapped to my thigh. His body is rigid, his stare lethal. "Alana and I serve our duties together or not at all." Eoghan's voice is a low thrum of the dragon inside him, ready to devour his next meal.

"So I have been told by the last warden." Anwyl's eyes narrow as he bends down toward our table. "No, Alana will serve her duties in my quarters, and you will serve in the

South Tower. I do not have to remind you there are penalties for disobedience, do I?"

I grip Eoghan's wrist, keeping his hand against me as he tenses. "No." My voice is like sandpaper. "We understand."

Anwyl's smile widens. "Very good. One hour, and then I expect to see you at my quarters. Eoghan, get some rest. You'll need it."

Drustan turns from us on his heels and walks toward the double doors leading to the corridor before he disappears behind them. Eoghan pushes his tray away, and it slides off the edge of the table and onto the floor with a hollow metal clamor. He runs his hands through his hair and rests his elbows on the table, his breathing heavy.

"Eogh–"

"Do you understand what he is doing?" Eoghan snaps, and I throw up a silencing charm at full tilt to keep the others from listening in. "He knew as soon as Gálgalesh stepped in yesterday that something was different about us. He's trying to separate us, keep us as far away from each other as possible."

"I know." I lower my voice despite the privacy the faerie magic affords us. "But there's nothing we can do now. We just have to make the best of it until Gálgalesh gets back."

"I can't protect you when I'm on night duty and you're in his quarters all day." Something like anxiety changes his tone, and I squeeze his hand against my thigh.

"It'll be okay, Eoghan." I'm not sure of my own words at all. I want to be, but Eoghan has saved me twice now. I can't reason away his worry as my heart pounds through my chest as I speak. If only we had some way to communicate wherever we were, maybe we both could feel better about our separation. "There is a spell I read about when I was studying with Gálgalesh that can send messages to another person, a message that is indecipherable to anyone else, through physical space. I have the instructions in my desk. If I can master it, I can tell you if I'm in trouble and where I am."

"*Can* you master it?" Eoghan stares forward at nothing in particular, his forehead resting on his palms.

"Yes." He might have had to save me from Kruz, but my faerie magic has grown stronger every day—much to my own and even Gálgalesh's surprise.

Eoghan nods and drops his hands to the table before sighing loudly and beginning to rise from his seat. "One word is all I need, and I swear to Danu, Anwyl is dead," he promises with his lips against my temple, his warm hand caressing my throat with a featherlight touch. My hand meets his wrist, and I feel his pounding pulse under my fingertips. He places a shadow of a kiss against my hair before he straightens and leaves the dining hall.

———

FIFTY MINUTES LATER, I reach the door of the warden's quarters—Gálgalesh's rooms—and stand silently before the splintering wood, almost expecting it to swing away on its own accord to reveal Gálgalesh at his desk, a letter or a map splayed out on top of it. The door does not budge. I raise my hand to the uneven surface and knock against it three times.

"Enter," Drustan Anwyl calls from somewhere inside, as if he doesn't want to waste his time greeting me. I turn the doorknob and push as the door gives way to the familiar room. Drustan Anwyl stands at the desk, attempting to pry open the drawers that appear sealed shut. Faerie magic, no doubt—although Drustan would not suspect such spells and charms in a place like Báscogar. When he hears my footsteps cross the threshold onto the threadbare rug, he turns, and unease washes over me. "Alana. I am happy to see you can follow orders. Please come in, and close the door behind you.

This place is so damn cold, I think I might freeze to death here." He scowls in the direction of the hall. "I prefer Tonn-fórsca to Romiodóg in every way."

"Tonnfórsca?" The coastal territory where Rian lived, where I might have lived if everything would have turned out differently.

"Yes, Tonnfórsca; the place I call home. Have you been?" I shake my head, noticing the slight accent in his voice for the first time. "Not as dreadful as these mountains, I assure you. Come further into the warmth of the room." He motions with his hand, but it feels like a command more than an invitation. "You are so pale, you look like ice." He looks me up and down, and his eyes stop below my chin. "That is not your cloak. Why are you not dressed in proper prison attire? I was told all prisoners are issued a set of prison clothes, including a cloak, but this one drowns you."

I look down at the heavy fabric draped around my shoulders and pooling on the floor. I had forgotten I was even wearing Eoghan's cloak until now.

"Mine was destroyed..." I hesitate as he eyes me curiously. "I haven't gotten to the outfitters for a new one."

"Well, tomorrow, I want to see one that fits. There is a penalty for not dressing properly, and whoever lent their cloak to you might be in danger of punishment for being improperly dressed as well." Another pointed statement that does not require a response; we both know exactly who the cloak belongs to. "Set it aside and come help me. I have work for you."

Mundane, horrible work is what Drustan Anwyl has in store for me. For the first session before lunch, he has me read out a list of all the prisoners' names, their magic, and their crimes as he notes the prisoners who are of particular interest: murderers and mad men, sentenced for violent crimes against others, or those with unique wielding abilities. Gálgalesh must have provided this list to the king's guards before he left, as Eoghan and I are both listed—although our magic remains a mystery in both cases.

At lunch, Eoghan does not meet me in the dining hall, and I sit for quiet minutes, pushing around the food on my plate before leaving to find him. I make it to the end of our corridor before being stopped by a guard with no neck and a much too small head upon his large shoulders.

"Where do you think you're going?" He blocks my path down the hall so completely, I can barely see past him at all.

"To my room." I push at his arm, but he does not budge.

"No one goes to their rooms until after their afternoon duties. Warden's rules."

Of course not—not if Eoghan was meant to be there, at least. I try to force my way through once more, but he does not give in. With a huff of expletives under my breath, I turn away and head back to the warden's quarters.

The afternoon session is no better than the morning's. When I arrive, Anwyl hands me the scroll of parchment from the previous prisoner records—the true Báscogar records—and makes me read off each name as he looks for discrepancies in the entries. The only missing names are Eoghan and me.

"Curious," Drustan muses, and his voice makes my jaw clench. "You and Eoghan both arrived after the last census, yet these were sent just prior to the roads closing this winter." Another non-question we both know the answer to perfectly. "Did you arrive together? Were you caught together?"

"No." What answer could I give that would not ruin Gálgalesh's work to keep us safe within these walls? "We came here together, but we weren't caught together."

He nods, but there is something else in his eyes. "And the previous records didn't list your magic. Why is that?"

"I-I-I have no magic." My voice shakes at the half-truth as I feel the hum of the faerie magic speaking to me. He has no reason to suspect it, and he might kill me if he finds out. "It was siphoned from me as a slave."

"Hmm." Anwyl turns back to the parchment in his hand and makes note of something lazily. "Fine then; you may leave for today. Oh, and leave those daggers strapped to your thighs on the table."

My daggers. Of course. Everyone is to surrender their weapons by the end of the day. He waves his hand without looking at me, and I collect Eoghan's cloak from the sofa, unsheathe my daggers agonizingly and set them on the table between us before nearly racing out of the room. If I am early, maybe I can catch Eoghan before he leaves for his duties at the South Tower. I need his arms around me and my hands in his hair. I need to know he is all right; that everything is going to be all right. I stalk down the low-lit corridor toward the portico, and a cold mountain breeze whips across my face as I turn the corner and take in the black sky. It is later than I expected—significantly so. I grab the arm of the prisoner walking past me, and he halts, alarmed.

"What time is it?"

"Half-past five," he grunts and shakes me off him before pushing past me again.

Half-past five. I had missed Eoghan, had stayed hours longer than we were told we would have to. Where had the hours gone, locked away in Drustan Anwyl's quarters? Training time was gone, and dinner was through. Eoghan had been right when he said Anwyl was trying to keep us away from each other, and he was already succeeding. I feel a cold, hollow part of me sink in my chest, and I sigh as I make my way back toward my room alone.

———

I WAKE at the first signs of dawn, stretching against my pillow and looking around my room expectantly. Eoghan has not made it back yet from his guard's shift. I roll away from my pillow and push myself out of bed, dragging myself to my feet.

Today's duties are as tedious as the last. I spend the morning shining the warden's shoes and cleaning the quarters as Anwyl watches me from the desk. His eyes never leave me, and his voice grates against my skin as he shouts demands to clear the faerie filth from every corner of the room. It's a test—that is easy enough to see—to discover if I really was a slave girl in the Royal Household. *I'll be damned if cleaning gives Gálgalesh up*, I seethe as I wipe sweat from my brow. It is not until lunch time that Anwyl becomes bored with the game and lets me rest.

Eoghan does not arrive again at our table during lunch, and it takes everything in me to not use my magic to barrel through the guard blocking my way to find him. Where could he be that would keep him away?

When I arrive in the afternoon at the warden's quarters, Drustan Anwyl hands me a scroll and gestures to the sofa across from where he sits in an armchair, his feet up on the table. I unravel it slowly, my own familiar handwriting mixed with Gálgalesh's against the parchment.

"The food supply count." I scan through the list I had so carefully organized just months ago, before I began my training in secret.

"Interesting. I was not sure you would know what it was. The count appears to have been taken just before you arrived at the prison." By all accounts, I should not know what this is. He knows that, but it is obvious enough with the lists of foods and quantities that I might not have made such a grievous error.

"They do the same at the castle," I recover, pushing it back toward him, but he refuses it. "What does this have to do with anything?"

"Well, I thought perhaps you might be able to help me. The calculations seem to account for more people than there are prisoners at Báscogar."

"So? Would it not be prudent to account for new prisoners in case they arrive before the next supply run?"

"Perhaps. But in the winter, a prisoner transfer is unlikely here. One might calculate, given the harshness of the climate and the prisoners themselves, for *fewer* people than they started with last supply run." He takes out the scroll from yesterday and a pen and passes them both to me. "I would like you to run the calculations again, against the list of prisoners at the time of the supply run, and help me make sense of them."

I take the pen from him, my hands shaking. Regardless of what I say, my handwriting will give me away. He knows it and so do I. His mouth is nearly dripping with venom as he sizes me up and plans his attack. I pass the pen to my left hand and drop my fingers to the parchment, working out the characters as I go, attempting to make it look easy as my right hand screams for attention at my side. I ignore the urge to give up, and the process is long and slow, Drustan Anwyl watching me curiously with every pass of the pen.

Hours later, my fingers are cramping and shaking against the parchment full of manipulated calculations. He finally sighs and presses himself up from the chair.

"Go," he says, and, without another word, he walks away into the bathing chambers.

I leave in silence, my hands throbbing and my head aching. I do not even have to see the sky this time to know I have missed dinner again...and my chance at finding Eoghan.

————

I GASP as I am shaken awake by two arms wrapping around my waist, the warmth of a body against my back.

"Shh, it's just me," Eoghan whispers against my neck, and my eyes fill with tears of relief as I turn to face him.

The room is dark—it can't be later than three in the morning—and his face is obscured in the shadows. But even without being able to see clearly, I can tell there is something wrong. I throw out my hand, and the candles in the room light, casting an orange glow around us...and I nearly scream as I take him in. What have they done to him? Oh gods, what have they done?! Eoghan's face is black and blue, and his left eye is nearly swollen shut. His jaw has a lump where a fist has collided with his face, and there is a deep cut in his puffed up lip. He is almost unrecognizable in the light, and as our eyes meet, he shrugs his shoulder and winces slightly with the movement.

"What happened?" My fingers hover over his face, not sure where to touch him.

"Oh, this? Don't worry about it. You should see the other guy." He tries to smirk, but pain sears through him, and his expression is more of a grimace.

"Eoghan..." I reach my hand toward the drawer next to my bed, and it opens, a vial of Gálgalesh's healing tonic flying through the air toward us. I catch it and uncork it to offer to him. He takes it from me and empties the liquid into his mouth, and within moments, his wounds begin to disappear. "Who did this to you?" I demand as his face becomes familiar again, my hands resting on his cheeks.

"Do you have my cloak?" he asks casually in reply.

"They did this to you because you didn't have your cloak?!"

Eoghan shakes his head. "No." He points to his left eye, where the swelling is slowly lessening. "They did *this* because I didn't have my cloak. The others are the result of my complete lack of respect for authority, but they could do worse than me when it comes to Tinemallacht warriors."

This time, he does laugh to himself. I graze his cheeks lightly, and my lips pull down in a frown. I find little amusement in anything he is saying as I study his face.

"You're going to get yourself killed." I drop my hands from him, and my brows pull into a scowl. "I thought we decided to stay alive?"

"We did, and that is precisely what I am doing—keeping you alive." He exhales, and his hands loosen around me just enough so he can pull away and examine me thoroughly. "Are you hurt?" He runs his hands down my sides, and my heart pounds at his touch.

"No, they haven't touched me," I breathe, my voice cracking. "Anwyl is suspicious of Gálgalesh. He's seen right through his scrolls. He keeps asking me questions about the prisoners."

"You too?" Eoghan's hands are trailing now, less for examination and more for the pleasure of lazy caresses against my bare skin.

"Have you seen him?" I run my fingers through his hair. "He's visited you on duty?"

"I wouldn't call it duty per se. More of an interrogation. He arrives just after dinner and asks me about Gálgalesh and my time here...and you. He's not fooled, but I'm not sure he has figured out why we are here—just that we shouldn't be, that Gálgalesh has something to do with it." His green eyes stop trailing as they reach mine, and his expression softens.

"Two days, and I have gone half mad not being able to see you."

"How did you get away? I thought your shift was until dawn."

He presses his lips to mine and kisses me softly, gently, as though holding himself back with all the self-control he can muster. My lips part ever so slightly, inviting him in, but he doesn't take the bait. He pulls away, and I whimper at his retreat. "Suffice it to say, the guard on duty will wake up with a headache and a sore jaw in the morning."

"Eoghan, you can't! Anwyl will punish you for that!"

"Let him," he whispers, nipping my lip lightly and kissing me again. "I had to see you, make sure you were okay."

He pulls me in, and I wrap my arms around him. He's in trouble, and next time, his wounds will be worse than today; but for now, all I can do is breathe him in like the first drop of water in the desert. He's intoxicating, and as soon as he touches me, everything falls away. His mouth is on me, searching across my jawline and down my neck to my collarbone. I should send him back to the South Tower and make him leave, but I can't think of anything but the feeling of him as he trails his tongue down my chest.

"I've been practicing that spell so I can communicate with you when we aren't together." My words are pants as he reaches my breasts.

"Mmm?" he questions. "And?"

"I still need time." The room is like sitting in the sun in the middle of summer now. "But I think…I think I can do it."

"I trust you." His mouth threatens to move lower as he pulls his shirt away, and I'll let him. I need him more than I've needed anything in my life.

Like being thrown into an icy river, two knocks on the door pull us apart, and the room turns frigid again. Eoghan swears under his breath and rolls away from me. He picks up his shirt and tosses it onto the bed with the clothes I discarded earlier in the evening, and I scoop them up, tugging them over my legs and head. He waits until I am fully clothed before he reaches for the doorknob.

"Lights out and pretend to be asleep," he commands softly, and I wave my hand to pull the light from the room before leaning back against the pillows without hesitation. He pulls the door open just enough to peer out of it. "Can I help you?" His voice rumbles through his chest.

"I thought I might find you here," Drustan Anwyl's voice is an amused and wicked hiss. "And Alana as well, I presume, seeing as this is her room."

"She's asleep." He closes the gap in the door further so there is only a sliver of light shining against the wall.

"And you are without your shirt while you're supposed to be on duty halfway across the prison. Yes, that makes perfect sense. At any rate, you will rouse her, and you will both follow me. Now."

"Fuck off." Eoghan moves to shut Drustan Anwyl out completely, but he throws his hand up, holding the door in place.

"That was not a suggestion." Footsteps behind Drustan Anwyl tell me he has brought at least two guards with him. I push up from the bed and pull on my boots. I grab Eoghan's shirt and cloak and shove them into his hands before throwing on my own.

"Let's go." I yank the door away and walk past Eoghan into the hall. He rolls his eyes and follows behind me, threading his arms and neck through his shirt.

"Very good. At least someone has some sense between the two of you."

Anwyl turns from us with that smirk that makes my skin crawl and starts down the hall. We follow silently behind him, and Eoghan grasps my hand protectively at his side. We walk until we are far from the sleeping quarters, and it is only then Drustan Anwyl stops, and his guards close in behind us.

"It is a foolish thing to do, leaving your post without permission. Tell me, was she worth it?" His eyes take me in as his lips pull wider, hungry and wild. "I bet she was. I wondered why Gálgalesh had never let a woman prisoner in before, but now I see how tantalizing one might be." He reaches toward me, but Eoghan steps between us, pulling me behind him. "What a protector you have, Alana. Remind him who I am and how quickly I can end his miserable, Fire Cursed life. I have every right to execute him, and the king would not even bat an eye." He laughs, and I tug on Eoghan's arm to pull him back. "But, since it seems you two are the ones keeping secrets here—secrets I need answers to, I am going to spare him…for now."

He hauls his fist forward and barrels it into Eoghan's stomach. Eoghan folds over on himself as the punch knocks the air from him. "May I remind you both that I will not tolerate insubordination in *my* prison. Whatever you think you are doing here, it is now through. Eoghan, you will return to your station at the South Tower, and you will serve the morning shift as well before your evening shift begins. Failure to do so will be a decision you pay for in blood. Alana, you will be staying in the warden's quarters with me until further notice. I think we can agree you need to be kept under a watchful eye. The prison is a dangerous place for a woman, after all."

Eoghan straightens to full height and rounds on Drustan Anwyl. "You touch her, and I will rip you apart."

Drustan's smile does not so much as falter as he grabs my free hand and pulls me toward him. Eoghan's grip tightens almost painfully, and I can see in his eyes the same fire that was there moments before he killed Kruz Lanzo. Still, he can't kill Drustan Anwyl, not if we do not want to die at the hands of his men seconds later. I untangle my fingers from Eoghan's, and his expression changes from rage to confusion.

"It's fine," I say quietly, but we both know that isn't true. "I'll be all right."

Anwyl drags me to his side, his eyes never leaving Eoghan. "Again, be thankful she has some sense." He turns his attention to his guards. "Take him back to the South Tower. If he fights you, you have my permission to kill him, but bring back his head for my wall."

Without another word, he waves them off, and the men grab Eoghan around the elbows, dragging him in the opposite direction. There is nothing I can do; he'll be beaten or worse for his actions, and I can only watch as he disappears down the dark hallway.

CHAPTER TWENTY-SIX

"Come now, Princess. Please, take a seat," Sir Oli Raven ushers me into a small office in the dungeons of the castle. It is cold and damp and lit by an orb of magic commonly used to light the rooms of the castle in a soft, white glow. Built into the stone walls are cabinets reaching from floor to ceiling with dark wood frames and glass fronts. On the shelves sit vials of potions in greens and golds and blacks, all swirling of their own accord. Poisons and medicines mingle behind the glass, a dangerous gamble for anyone but the Potions Master.

He guides me to a chair in the middle of the room, its arms a cold steel with leather straps slung across them. This is the chair of my waking nightmares; the chair that reminds me I am merely a specimen in this place, something to poke and prod. I sit obediently as he pulls the straps around my biceps and wrists to lock them in place. To the left, against the wall, sits a cabinet so like the others, but I know no potions will be found there. The vials are crimson behind the glass, the liquid still; my blood, the Life Bringer, sits waiting to be consumed by the greedy or needy inside these walls.

"Today, we have a few items on our list." There are always a few experiments on Sir Oli Raven's agenda when he brings me *down here alone. "We will need to fill fifteen new vials this week, per your father's request." I can feel my veins tighten at the words. They have been drained once a week in this room for as long as I can remember. As I look over at the vials sitting like trophies behind glass, I wonder when he will have his fill and relinquish me. I imagine that day might never come. "But first, we will continue our study of your unique magic and its usefulness to our king."*

For the past month, Sir Oli Raven has been experimenting with various parts of my body that might give the one who comes into contact with it my healing magic. Mostly, he has plucked out my fingernails and taken samples of my saliva for consumption. Although last week... I shudder and close my mind to the thought of what he did to me in this cold, damp dungeon. I refused to cry as he held me down with my back against the stone floor, my dress pulled up around my stomach, my eyes tracing the walls as I counted the minutes until he let me go.

I never cry in this place. I never let him see the pain persist or any weakness as he plays his games. He would enjoy it too much if I did.

"What will it be this time?" I try to keep my voice light and calm, even a little bored.

"Oh, nothing too terrible." He is almost giddy with excitement as he ambles over to a drawer at the far end of the room. He draws it toward himself, rummaging through it. It is not until he pulls out a long knife—one used by the chefs in the kitchens to carve meat from the carcass of an animal—that he speaks again. "The king is curious about the connection between your flesh and your magic. He wonders, perhaps, if the magic lives inside your blood exclusively, or if... Well, perhaps we need to worry about someone cooking you up for supper."

He laughs as he turns toward me, the knife in his hand, and closes the distance between us. He presses the blade against the backside of my forearm, and I flinch as I instinctively attempt to pull away, but the chair holds my arms in place.

"Don't," I protest weakly, though my pleas have never stopped him before.

"Do not worry, child. It will only hurt for a moment. Remember, you are stronger than the pain. Your body will protect you—heal you."

He presses the blade into my skin, and I bite a hole in my lip to keep my screams from filling the dungeon. The pain sears hot through me as flesh is cut away from bone. I see red pour out into a bucket below the arm of the chair, and I become sick at the sight. Mercifully, my body lets me sink down into the black abyss as my consciousness leaves me.

"WAS Gálgalesh a sympathizer of the last king?"

Drustan Anwyl's voice comes from somewhere in the dark corner of the dungeon below Báscogar. I am not sure of the day or how long I have been here because of the lack of windows in the room; although, by the feeding schedule, it appears that food—in the form of a single apple or piece of bread and a glass of water—arrives in the mornings and along with it, Drustan Anwyl. In the evenings, only the guards pass a tray across the stone floor before trapping me in darkness again. I gave up counting after a fortnight. Two days after I last saw Eoghan, Anwyl dragged me down here just after breakfast. I had assumed it would be punishment for sending a raven to Gálgalesh in the Capital and had reasoned he might keep me here for a day or two to teach me about his own authority. After three, though, when the guard swung open the door and threw my one full meal of the day onto the dirty floor, I knew I was not leaving.

Drustan has visited every day since they brought me to this place, interrogating me repeatedly. The questions are always the same. Today is no different.

"As I have told you every time you ask, I do not know," I hiss at him, and a shadow of a towering figure moves in the darkness, slamming into me and throwing me back. I gasp and cough as I fall to the floor from the force of the blow.

"Has Gálgalesh been planning any retaliation for the death of King Cashel?" His voice is calm and patient.

"I don't know," I wheeze, and I brace myself as a hand with the force of a cannon pummels into my right cheek. I can feel blood flowing freely into my mouth, and I spit it out in front of me.

"I have told *you* before: tell me what you know about Gálgalesh and what he is hiding, and this can all be over, Alana. Tell me why you and your precious Eoghan are here, and I'll let you go."

I'm here to kill the ones who killed my family, my brain screams. *I am here to kill you.* If I could stand, I'd kill him this very instant. I stabilize myself with my hands against my knees and draw in a ragged breath.

"Bring Eoghan here, and I will tell you everything." A lie, of course, but if I could just see him and know he's all right… we would probably both murder these men together. Alone, I'm not sure I would be a fierce opponent. Even my faerie magic is dulled and starved in this place, and I am almost unable to conjure at all, certainly not anything that could help me escape.

"We have been through this. Tell us first, and then you can see your boyfriend." Every word that leaves his mouth makes my skin crawl. "Don't worry, you are both too valuable to kill. He is safe under my guards' watchful eyes."

"I want to see him first." I feel a hand swipe toward me, but I evade it, using up the last bits of my energy. I groan as I roll across the floor and feel the extent of the injuries to my shattered and broken body.

"*No.*" He sounds annoyed now, the sign he will soon leave

me to his guards to rough up before they too exit the cell for the rest of the day. He always gets frustrated before he leaves. With satisfaction, I realize today, his patience has worn off quickly. "What has Gálgalesh been hiding here? Supplies? An army? *Tell me!*"

"I'd rather you kill me."

I've done it now. I hear him stand from the metal chair his guards drag into the dungeon each time he visits, and his footsteps echo against the walls as he makes it to the door. He knocks on the wood, and the guard on the other side drags it away, illuminating his silhouette as he greets him with a torch in his hand.

"Disappointing," he says over his shoulder before he exits the room.

The door closes behind him, and as it does, fists and boots find me in the dark. They are always swift to their punishment, bringing me to the brink of death as if seeking to break the record for how quickly it might come. It reminds me of that day when the crowd pulled me down into the dirt, trying to beat the air from my lungs. The guard grabs me by my shirt, and I lay limply, my arms splayed out toward the floor. He brings his fist to my face over and over again, and I can feel my nose crack under the force of his blow. If the gods were good to me, they would let me die. Instead, I silently beg for the relief of the impact knocking me out. They always stop when they think they've killed me, and I wake after a few hours to find myself beaten but still here.

"Stupid girl." The guard's voice startles me just as I am about to go under. I heard it somewhere before, but I cannot place it. "Just make something up."

He hits me again, but this time, he pulls his punch. He releases me, and I fall onto the stone floor. He crouches beside me, his immense mass imperceptible in the darkness.

Without a word, he slips the head of a small vial between my swollen lips and empties the contents into my mouth. Healing—at least of the superficial injuries—rushes through me. I hear the vial fall into his cloak pocket and clink against another before he leaves me sprawled on the rocks.

———

"FIND EOGHAN," I whisper as I lay in the darkness, reaching for the tethering magic. If I could just find Eoghan and tell him where I am, maybe he would come find me. How I would know I found him, I'm not sure. I'm not sure I know how the magic works at all, but Gálgalesh has not offered any spells for two-way communication yet, so I have resolved that begging the magic to do what I need is my best and only option. I pull my eyes together in concentration and cling tightly to the magic humming quietly inside me. "Find Eoghan and tell him where to find me."

The loud metallic clanging of the door lock instantly makes me sit upright, and a small triangle of orange light fans out across the floor as someone pulls the door away. A tray with a piece of bread, a silver cup of water, and...a thin roll of parchment next to a nearly burned-out candle is slid across the floor. There is maybe a handful of minutes left on the wick at best. I rush to the tray as the door closes, and darkness envelops the room again. I dive for the candle and feel around the tray. No match, but that's no matter—I have enough strength for this. I push all my concentration toward the candle, and it erupts in a warm glow of flame. I reach for the parchment and unfold it.

YOU ARE BEING HELD IN THE DUNGEON JUST BEYOND THE SHADOW LURKER'S CORRIDOR. HE WILL ENTERTAIN BARGAINS FOR FAVORS IF YOU OFFER HIM SOMETHING HE WANTS.

The shadow lurker's corridor, where Kruz Lanzo had brought me the first full night after I arrived at Báscogar. Shadow lurkers retreat from the flames of torches and the sunlight; according to all the tales, safety is found only when one carries the light with them. That is why the shadow lurker tried to attack me when I left the party alone without a torch, why torches fill the halls outside this dungeon. It still lives, and it is only steps away now.

I catch the edge of the parchment with the flame and let it burn with the candle. I know nothing of shadow lurkers other than their desire for human blood and their dependency on Ama. Neither is something I could give him in a bargain. I have nothing to help me get out of here. What silly information to give, as if it is of any use to me at all. I push the tray away furiously, and it slides roughly against the wall, where it clatters against the hard surface—just another obstacle in my way if I ever do get out of here. I move back toward the metal bed in the corner and lay down across the cold surface.

———

"Wake up now, Alana."

A distant voice whispers to me from the empty black void. There is nothing, nothing except darkness…and pain. The shadow of it is like a headache threatening to take hold. I do not know my name, nor do I have the capacity to care. I am resting in the black, falling toward nothing forever…

Water envelops me, and I gasp as I feel it rush through my nostrils and into my mouth, drowning me. My eyes fly open, and I feel hands around the back of my neck and head, holding me down in a bucket of icy water. The pain that had hovered just around me, now floods through my body. I struggle and tremble, trying to escape, but they have bound my arms and legs to a chair, securing me in place.

The hands tighten around my now nearly chin-length hair and yank my head up from the flood. I sputter and spit as I pant for air.

"Welcome back." Drustan Anwyl is just a shadow in front of me in the darkness, but his voice sets me on edge. "Now will you cooperate? You really are no use to me unconscious, but, apparently, civilized conversation does not seem to get through to you. I need answers. I will not accept anything less this time. You have wasted my time for far too long."

The guard releases me, and my head falls forward. They've given up on what Drustan Anwyl calls their 'polite tactics' and are no longer just leaving me bruised and bloodied on the cell floor. After our last interrogation, where I repeated once again that I know nothing of Gálgalesh's plans, Anwyl has resorted to alternative forms of torment. My fingernails were the first to go as he pried them one-by-one from their nail beds. I only vomited twice from the pain. This time, it seems his weapon of choice will be water. It cannot be long until this breaking finally takes me, and I will welcome it gladly.

"Tell me what Gálgalesh was hiding for King Cashel."

I am so tired of these questions. For weeks, I have been asked the same useless things. Things I do not know. Things I would never tell him even if I did. "I do not know!" I bite back as I feel the hands wrap around my neck again.

"The thing is, Alana, you must know, or you would not be here." He crouches beside me and runs his fingers against my cheek. I shrink away from his touch, and he laughs in quiet amusement. "It's a shame, really. I was looking forward to you. You could have had comforts in this hell of a fortress. You could have even left here one day with me. Alas, you continue to lie for that filthy faerie who will never make it back from Gairdín." He leans in so only I can hear him. "Or are you lying for Eoghan Kael, Tinemallacht's wonder warrior? Perhaps our new king might like to rewrite his fate as well." He stands and wipes his hands on his pants. "I am bored of this. Untie her. We will be back tomorrow, and I want answers. Answers, or both you and your precious lover will lose your heads."

He leaves the room, and the guard stays behind me, fiddling with the ropes.

"You are an idiot," he hisses at me, taking another vial from his cloak and emptying it into my mouth, just as he has done day-after-day. "What good are we if Kael dies? What good is Kael if *you* die? Lie. To. Him. Did you not read my letter?"

"Of course I read it!" I yank my wrists free as he loosens the binds and massage them tenderly. "It was useless! How would I bargain with a shadow lurker? Offer him my blood?"

"Or someone else's! The shadow lurker has taken more than one life that has asked too many questions in this place. He likes to help keep secrets; it is the only way he will enter into a bargain—but it must be worth keeping. I have a feeling you are here because Gálgalesh believed yours was exactly that." He straightens and empties the bucket into a grate in the floor. "I will not be on duty tomorrow. Do not get yourself or Kael killed while I'm gone!"

He dumps me roughly from the chair and carries it to the exit. As he opens the door to leave, the light streaks across his face, and for the first time, I recognize him as one of the men seated at the table during the secret meeting Gálgalesh had caught me eavesdropping in on. He gives me a final stern look and leaves the room.

———

I AM up the entire night, mulling over my plans in my head. Everything must work out perfectly. If not…well, it is not only my life on the line. I grab the tether of magic and pull hard, and it wakes with a loud, expectant hum. *Find Eoghan and tell him where I am*, I think to myself. *Find the Dragon of Báscogar. Find Eoghan.* I repeat it one, two, three, fifty times as I beg the magic to help me. I do not remember the spell after days of relentless agony clouding my brain. I cannot think clearly enough to put the symbols into sequence, but I reach anyway.

Morning comes with a knock on the door only seconds before it flies open to reveal Drustan Anwyl as he walks into my cell alone. His guards remain just beyond the threshold, and I notice my mystery savior is absent, as he had said. I stand and hold out my hands as though in surrender.

"Well?" Drustan Anwyl shuts the door tightly behind us, plunging the dungeon into total darkness.

"I'm ready to show you now." I keep my voice timid and quiet, as though I am shamefully letting go of a secret I kept for too long.

"Show me what?" He takes a step closer, and it takes everything in me not to back away.

"What Gálgalesh has been hiding for King Cashel—what *we* have been hiding." If I cannot make him believe I know nothing, perhaps he can believe I know something.

"And where might he be hiding it?"

"I'll take you to it." Even in the dark, I can sense his expression change to doubt. He *has to* believe me. If he doesn't, there's no hope of getting out of here. "I am finally willing to give you answers, and now you don't want them because you are afraid to let me out of this dungeon?"

He studies me for a long moment, and I can tell he is weighing the risks of letting me go. He had never planned on it from the start. "Fine. You will take me to this hiding place, but you stay ahead of us so we may watch you the entire time." I nod in agreement, and he grabs me by the elbow and pushes me toward the door.

When he opens the dungeon door, the low light of the torches is nearly blinding. I haven't escaped the darkness in weeks. I blink my eyes, willing them to adjust, and I wonder if I will make it down the hall at all, but I have to. For Gálgalesh and Eoghan, I have to.

"Give her a torch," Anwyl snaps impatiently at the other two guards. Wonderful; I did not even have to beg. "Now walk slowly, but do not waste our time. I do not have all day, and you have wasted weeks now with your posturing. I will savor your blood as your head rolls from your shoulders if you do. Do you understand?"

If Eoghan was here, he would tell him to fuck off, and I have half a mind to do just that. Still, I remain totally silent as I take the torch from one of the guards and turn to face the long corridor. I start my slow stroll, unsure of where I am going. If this is going to work, I cannot leave this hallway. I take each step as if counting them, dramatically waving my finger as though the stones on the floor have any meaning at all. The other three men walk just a few paces behind, following my steps absurdly. I almost laugh as I listen to them mutter to one another, but I bite my lip and continue my trek.

I reach toward the magic tether again, searching desperately for someone else. *I need to talk to the shadow lurker,* I request into the thrumming of its power.

"Yes, oh disgusting one? How foul you smell! Not as delectable as last time." The shadow lurker's voice is so close to my ear, I marvel at my inability to see him.

Can you hear me?

"Of course I can. Whose magic do you wield? Not your own, I am sure of it."

Not important. I need to ask you for a bargain.

"Intriguing." His breath is hot and rotten, but I keep my eyes straight ahead.

If I tell you a secret, will you trust me to uphold our agreement?

"Ah, you have been told I do nothing without a secret first," he hisses, his voice echoing around me. I feel him so close, I am unsure why the others cannot see him either. "If the secret is worth keeping, perhaps."

I am Maeve Moran, the Lost Princess of Draíocoinnigh. My healing magic was taken from me, my blood smells of death, and I am here to learn how to murder the ones who killed my family.

"Ah, so that is why... You are a wicked and disgusting one indeed! Make your bargain, and your secret is safe."

"Pick up the pace, Alana," Drustan calls behind me, and I wave my hand in the air as if I am listening.

If I give you these men, will you kill them all and leave me to go free?

"All three?" The shadow lurker sounds as though his mouth has begun to water.

But you must kill them. There is no way out if they are not all dead. There is no way out if he hunts me down too.

"Delicious." The words roll velvet smooth across his blood-stained tongue. "You have my word, Princess. You may go free, and I will rid this prison of these men."

I nod, not knowing if thank you is the appropriate response to someone agreeing to *murder*. I take two more steps and stop suddenly, the other men halting and tripping over themselves. I do not turn to face them. Instead, I fix my eyes straight ahead toward the unlit corridor.

"Well?" Drustan Anwyl snaps behind me, and I catch a shadow move just off to my left, lurking dangerously closer. "Do not tell me you've forgotten where it is hiding?" He scoffs.

"No." My words are slow and pointed. He deserves every

last agonizing one. "I just wanted to say..." The shadows grow larger, nearly pushing in on the torchlight. "Gálgalesh will be sorry to have missed your death, but I will enjoy it immensely."

I throw out my hands, and every flame extinguishes in an instant before I am running. As fast as I can, I throw myself down the corridor as the shadow lurker draws in for the kill. I race to the end of the hall as the screams begin to rise, shrill and terrified. I do not stop, *cannot* stop. I fly straight into the wall, but I am ready for it, only skimming the corner as I whip myself through the dark.

EOGHAN, I shout down whatever line the magic has formed. *EOGHAN, HELP ME! FIND ME AT THE WINDING STAIRS!*

I run and run until my lungs feel like cement and my legs feel like jelly, and then I run some more. I push up the sloping passageways until I see the faintest light—the first signs of safety—beckoning me ahead. And then, there are footsteps racing toward my own, and I feel arms wrapping around me as my body collides with a solid wall of familiar warmth.

CHAPTER TWENTY-SEVEN

I t's Eoghan. He's here and he's…he's burning up! His skin is scalding as he wraps his arms around me, and I jump away from him with a yelp. Immediately, his arms fall from me. He swears loudly to himself and mumbles an apology.

"Are you all right?" He shakes his hands as if airing them out and then grabs my face. Cooler, much cooler. "Where is he?"

The screaming has faded with the men I left behind, but my breath is ragged, and my lungs ache with each inhale.

"They… are… gone," I wheeze. The shadow lurker has kept his end of the bargain. Drustan Anwyl and his guards would no longer walk these halls. Eoghan pulls me gently into him in the darkness, his body more welcoming than dangerous this time. I feel the scratchiness of facial hair as he kisses the top of my head, and as my arms lace around his middle, I feel his clothes caked with sweat and blood and dirt just like mine. They must have had him locked away too.

"I thought you were dead—they told me you were. But then I heard you call out to me…" His voice trails off, and it is a pure fury that silences him so thoroughly, tremors run through his body.

"Where were they holding you?" There are lacerations on his sides, but the wounds do not feel deep. I grip him so tightly, I think I might slice him in two, but he does not try to retreat.

"The South Tower, since the day they separated us. They assigned Bode to be my guard, and he went easy on me when the beatings came. He'd only break me to the point that Gálgalesh's tonic would heal me before the next round. I asked him about you, but he said Anwyl kept our guards separated so they couldn't pass information between us. I guess he wasn't a total idiot, at least. Bode thought maybe one of the others was assigned to you, but we couldn't be sure." He catches my chin lightly between his fingers and lifts it so we can see each other properly. "I knew you could do it. If you were still alive, I knew nothing could keep me from finding you."

"How did you escape?" I ask, and as I do, I catch his wrist out of the corner of my eye. It's glowing faintly green with the remnants of a Faebond burn. "They held you in Faebond?!"

"They tried." I could kill him for his casual smirk, as if he wasn't on the brink of death just minutes before. I scowl and grab his wrist to examine it, finding the burn still fresh.

"How?" I point to the burn mark on his wrist.

"I burned through the Faebond when I heard you calling me."

Burned through the Faebond. That is...not possible. Faebond neutralizes magic. That's why it is one of the four high crimes to use it against another wielder. "Faebond is the only substance in the world that disables every type of magic. You cannot wield when bound with Faebond."

"I cannot wield in these walls either, but regardless, the

heat remains, and when I heard you pleading for help, nothing else mattered. The bonds melted off my wrists." I make to ask more questions, but he cuts me off with a tender swipe of his thumb along my chin. "Are they dead?"

"If the shadow lurker has sufficiently feasted, they are."

He nods once, and his body relaxes just slightly, though his jaw remains clenched and set, the muscles in his throat tight as he swallows.

"Good—although I would have liked to have gutted them while they screamed." He steps away from me, his hands still shaking slightly as he entwines his fingers with mine. "Come on. Let's get out of here."

He leads me to the stairs, and I notice the black footprints of his melting soles as we climb. He pays little attention to anything around us and pulls me to his side protectively. We don't speak—we can't seem to find the words, and for the first time, I feel how raw my throat is, how dirty my hands are, how weak I feel. I haven't had a proper meal in weeks or washed in just as long. I'm starving, filthy, my body threatening to collapse. But Eoghan is there, holding me steady, as if he too is not starving and exhausted and pained in every way.

We reach the dorm corridor, and he pushes open our doors, collecting the small baskets of toiletries and towels we both keep by our desks. We continue toward the showers, and he presses his shoulder against the wood door, revealing three men standing naked near the sinks. Their heads snap in our direction as we stumble in—too thin, too dirty, too sick, a horrifying image that keeps them staring.

"You have two seconds to leave before I break all your necks," Eoghan says flatly, and I know, this time, it is not a joke.

The men rush to collect their things and race out of the room without even wrapping towels around themselves.

Eoghan drags the bench across the entrance and points toward the showers.

"You first."

He pulls off his shirt and turns to the sink, taking a razor from his toiletries kit. I strip down and enter the shower without glancing at the mirror. I don't think I could bear it this time; the image might finally break me. I turn on the water and let the dirt and blood roll off me, rinsing the battlefield away. As I close my eyes and allow the water to run across my face, I think about the times Cai must have done the same after coming back from the fights against the Iranndairian soldiers. Eoghan would have been at his side each time— blooded and perhaps wounded, but ultimately victorious. How did they come back from this? How could they stare death in the face, whisper its name, and then march right back to the living as though they had not been to Donn and back?

I run my hands across my face and reach for my soap as the sound of another shower turning on meets my ears. Was Eoghan giving me privacy, or did he need it for himself? Was he afraid to be near me? Was he disgusted by my frailness? Was he tired of the trouble I brought him? I finish washing up and turn off the tap. I grab a towel and wrap it around myself, water dripping from my hair down my back. I move to the sink, rummaging through my basket and brushing my teeth while surveying myself in the mirror. My ribs show through my skin more prominently than they had before. Despite my wounds healing, there are still a few lasting marks the tonic couldn't completely eliminate, and my eyes look sunken and black with fatigue. I stare for as long as my mind dares, taking in the stranger staring back at me. I am no longer the princess locked away in the castle with no knowledge of the world or the evil that exists. I have met its gaze, wrestled with it until it let me go... Sometimes, I have been the evil myself. I know I can never go back now, and even if I did, it would be different—tainted with an understanding I never wanted and never asked for but can no longer forget.

I turn toward the showers, steam filling the room, and I see Eoghan slightly ahead, obscured by the mist. Three weeks he has been held up in the South Tower, thinking I was dead, and yet he did not give me up to Drustan Anwyl. Somehow, he had hoped against hope there was something left to save, work left to be done—just as he remained hopeful when Cai died, ceaseless hope despite all that he had been through, despite the evil that he too faced. I wonder how anyone could be so untarnished by this place. I move closer, watching as the water cascades down the muscles of his back and the curve of his ass.

"You're staring," he muses, his back to me, his hands sliding through his hair.

"It's difficult not to." My eyes trace down his body and the angry cuts on his sides. I notice fresh scars on his back and realize someone has whipped and beaten him so badly, even the tonic couldn't properly heal him. "It's my fault, isn't it?" I stand at the edge of the shower, the water bouncing off the stone onto my feet. "You would have been all right if it wasn't for me."

Silence—nothing but long silence envelops us, amplifying the sound of water smacking against the floor. Eoghan removes his hands from his hair and slams one against the control on the wall, the shower cutting off at his command. He turns toward me and takes a step closer, his body on full display, closer, closer, until he is towering over me.

"Do you think I could bear one moment knowing you were here without me? I'd gladly take any amount of hell to make sure you were safe. Do you not understand, Maeve?

There's nowhere I wouldn't go—nothing I wouldn't do for you."

He grabs me and presses his mouth to mine, kissing me deeply. My towel drops from my grasp as my arms snake around his neck and into his hair. I'd missed the fullness of his lips, the taste of his mouth, more than I had even known. His voice is my favorite sound. Sandalwood, bergamot, and cedar are now the only scent I can smell. He is the only thing I can see. I need him more than water, more than sunshine, more than air. He lifts me as my lips part, and his tongue finds its way inside my mouth as my legs wrap around his waist. I can feel the heat of his body against our wet skin, his hands cupping my ass to hold me tightly against him. He presses my back against the shower wall and breaks away for air before his lips find the hollow between my neck and collarbone.

"Do not for a second think there was anything you could have done or said to have made me leave you. I would burn down this world before I lost you."

His mouth moves to my breasts, and as he begins to kiss and suck, I lose my ability to breathe. There is no way to be close enough to him, to stop how my body aches. I want my hands on him, my mouth, my tongue. "Oh gods!"

He smiles against my chest and lets out a deep laugh. "Let me take my time with you. You're so impatient." He uses the wall and his hips to pin me in place and frees his hand to stroke my entrance as he passes his thumb lightly against my clit. My legs nearly lose all strength at the sensation, and my head rolls back against the wall.

"You feel incredible around my fingers," he says as he thrusts one and then two inside me, building a slow, steady rhythm that threatens to drive me mad. He gently grazes my nipple with his teeth, and I let out a gasp of shock and pleasure. There is nothing anymore. There is no prison, no death, no pain. There is only him—us—as one.

"I—" I don't want to say it and ruin everything. His lips move back toward my neck, and he uses his free hand to grip my hair gently, pulling my head back for better access. "I—" He hooks his fingers and picks up the pace to massage the sensitive place inside that has me tightening around him. I feel my body tremble in warning of my building climax.

"I love it when you bite your lip as you're about to come." He rubs his thumb in lazy circles as he speaks but denies me the winning touch, making me moan and pant for more.

"Eoghan," I nearly beg, but he has me at his mercy and he knows it.

"What were you saying?" he coaxes and slows his fingers to an agonizing thrust that teases my orgasm while keeping release just out of reach.

"What?" My mind has emptied of anything but the desire to be closer, to have him deeper. He maintains a teasing pace and his eyes find mine as his lips stop moving. He waits for me to continue and if I don't say it now, I might just combust. "I… I love you, Eoghan."

It is almost a whisper, and his hand freezes completely. I shouldn't have said it—it was stupid to—but if this isn't love, I do not know the feeling at all. I have never felt this way about anyone in my life—that if Eoghan is not here, nothing in the world matters. He has changed everything from the second I first saw him, though his eyes held nothing for me but disdain. It has been only him; it will always only be him. I swallow through my heavy breathing, hoping for anything but the mood to turn cold. Then, the fire in his eyes rises, and the room becomes a furnace.

"Fuck, I love you," he moans, and then he crashes his lips to mine as he replaces his fingers and thumb with his cock. He pushes inside me, the welcome stretch making me moan into his mouth. "I want you." His voice is a low, guttural growl as he withdraws from me, only to drive deeper with the next movement of his hips. "I fucking *need you.*"

My eyes fall shut as I am overcome by his scent, his cock, his mouth—all of him, pulling me toward that pleasure building deep inside me. *More. I need more.* I bite down on his lip, and he smirks as he drives home completely to the hilt. He overwhelms me with kisses as he angles me so my clit rubs against him with each thrust. With the next long plunge, I lose myself to the ecstasy and cry out as I tighten and then release around him.

"Maeve…" He grinds his hips into me as that primal part of him unleashes, setting the pace that will bring him to the height of his satisfaction. He presses his mouth to mine as he comes for me, and my body goes limp as I ride him to the mountain top of our pleasure.

My legs fall from around him to the floor, and he grips me to hold me upright. I lean my head forward against his chest, my hands caressing his sides as he plants a soft, breathless kiss on my head. "So much for the shower," I laugh.

"I knew I wouldn't be able to keep my hands off you for long." His fingers pass over me lightly, as though he is controlling every movement to keep from pressing me up against the wall again. "Oh, I'm in trouble now."

"Why's that?" I raise my head just enough to see him.

"Because I am in love with my best friend's sister, and I don't even have the decency to feel bad about it or to let her go." Now it's my turn to freeze as his eyes fill with the most tender expression I have ever seen, holding me to him as though his soul has wrapped itself around mine in a lover's knot. "I've known for too long now and pushed it aside, thinking you might not feel the same, but I love you, Maeve. If I have to bring this entire kingdom to its knees for you, just say the word, and it's done. I am yours for this life and the next, because there is nothing if it is not with you."

I don't know what to say or do. Could anyone love so much that their heart melts in their chest? I do not know, but if it was possible, I might just take my final breaths soon. I had given my heart to someone who said the words as though they were worth less than a copper coin. Eoghan says them as if they hold the key to his existence. I bring my fingertips to his face and rise on my toes to gently press my lips to his. He lets me guide our desire, matching the softness of the kiss.

"What happens now?" I whisper as we break away. With us, with Báscogar—the question is one and the same.

"Well, we can get the hell out of here and hope we make it to the tree line before someone comes after us for Drustan Anwyl's death…or we stay and wait for Gálgalesh to return and hope no one blames us for Drustan Anwyl's death."

I pick up my towel and wrap it around myself. "How did we get so lucky to choose between the two?" Either way, we are dead in the end.

"I'm with you, Moran, to the end." And as we gather our things to leave, I know it's true.

CHAPTER TWENTY-EIGHT

By the time we get our clothes on and leave our rooms, it is after quiet hours. The halls are empty save for one or two of Drustan Anwyl's guards lurking in the dark. None of them seem to have missed him this evening or suspected his disappearance, a sign that we might not be found out tonight. There is little doubt, however, that the guards are on edge and alert, as if expecting something. What has happened since Anwyl locked us away? There's something so different about this place, and I cannot quite place it. The air of the prison is thicker, expectant, even.

Eoghan leads us silently through the corridors, avoiding the patrols with expert precision as we head toward the kitchens. I follow along silently. Since I arrived at Báscogar nearly six months ago, I have rarely walked the corridors at night, save for the first night I encountered the shadow lurker and the night I was taken from my room by Peadair. I scarcely know my way around as it is, only exploring the most necessary parts of the fortress and staying away from dark corridors and quiet corners for fear of losing my life. Eoghan has no such fear. He is the most dangerous predator in these walls. and nothing would dare test him—that is, if they want to keep their heads.

We wind down the darkened passageways and trap doors leading to the belly of the prison, and when we reach the empty kitchen, Eoghan rakes the cabinets and ice boxes for food. He taps on a cabinet labeled FOR THE WARDEN OF BÁSCOGAR and, with a devilish smile, pulls it open. Inside sit tins of fish from the Tonnfórsca harbors, edible flowers from the Golorgleann flower fields, purple sprouts and black mushrooms from the farms to the East, and wine from the Druí colony in Gálamáistir. It's food of the wealthy, luxuries that, for so many years, I would have seen as common place but now know to be more valuable than gold—especially in these unforgiving mountains. Eoghan empties the cupboard and moves toward the stove, pulling a pan from the hook above.

"A feast fit for a princess," he whispers as he lights the stove and heats the pan.

I watch as he pulls out a knife and slices the flowers at an angle, preventing them spoiling with the poison hidden inside. He chops the mushrooms in cubes as the chefs of Caisleán Rialú always had and throws them into the heated pan with a splash of wine. An expert in war and also in the kitchen.

"Where did you learn to cook? I was always told Tinemal-lacht didn't receive the same food we did in the Capital." He passes me the bottle of wine, and I take it from him and bring it to my lips.

"Some rumors are true, but most are not. Everything depends on what family you are born into, just like every-where else." He's concentrating now as he drains the tins of fish. "Although, tinned fish is a delicacy saved for special occasions. Appropriate, I suppose."

"Oh? Is today a special occasion?" I let the alcohol coat my throat pleasantly and savor the taste I haven't had for months.

"Every day you survive another attack is a very special occasion."

The room fills with the sweet aroma of honey and perfume as he adds the flowers to the mix. I close my eyes and bask in the welcome scent, and my mouth begins to water in anticipation. He adds the fish to a second pan alongside the first before he takes the bottle of wine and knocks back a drink himself. As the dish heats and nears its finish, he adds the purple sprouts and some sliced nuts he found at the very back of the cupboard—an import from Oleaíncudd, where the heat is most suited for nuts and exotic fruits. Then, he takes two trays, silver and dented, from the piles set aside for tomorrow's breakfast and divides the meal between us. He hands me one tray, and I swallow hard.

"It feels like the last meal before an execution," I admit as I grab a fork. The smell is better than I even remember from the meals at the castle, and my stomach grumbles loudly.

"If it's our last meal, we might as well enjoy it." His lifts a forkful to his mouth but waits for me to take a bite. I oblige, even if the food feels so out of place in the prison, I can hardly make sense of it. The minute it reaches my tongue, however, everything melts away besides the symphony of tastes that make me roll my head back and moan in satisfaction. Eoghan lets out a soft laugh. "That good, huh?"

"How is it possible that you are good at everything, Eoghan Kael?"

"Everything? Oh, I doubt I am good at *everything*." He takes a bite and rolls his eyes dramatically, a smile dancing across his lips.

"*Everything*. Fighting, saving, cooking, fu—"

"All right, you've made your point," he cuts in, pink rising in his cheeks. I can't believe I can make him blush when everything he does brings me to my knees. I lick my fork and wink at him, the temperature rising in the room before diverting my eyes back to my tray.

"You said in Tinemallacht, everything depends on what sort of family you are born into." I pause, not wanting to sound as though I am searching for anything more than casual conversation. "What sort of family do you come from?"

Eoghan leans against the counter coolly as his eyes take me in. He hasn't stopped doing that since he admitted his feelings for me in the shower room. Those beautiful green-gold eyes have me melting into them. "What sort of family do you want me to come from?" he purrs, but his words are guarded. "Am I rich? Highborn?"

"I didn't mean it like that," I begin, but he snorts and shakes his head, his fork clinking lightly against his teeth as his bites down against the metal.

"Yes, you did, but that's a fair question. I should have at least pretended to not know what any of these ingredients were if I didn't expect you to ask. My father's parents were the last Lord and Lady of Tinemallacht—before the king rescinded the title and stripped Tinemallacht of all noble claims when I was six. He was angry when my father, who was the general in command during the Second War against Iranndair, failed to secure absolute victory and overthrow the Iranndairian government for the Crown. So yes, I am highborn and enjoyed some pleasures of my name—but that means nothing now, besides the honor of providing you with a good meal."

"I'm sorry—about your family and about my own, I suppose..." How he must have loathed us as he grew, knowing we caused so much loss.

Eoghan shrugs. "There are more things in this world to enjoy than power and status. Besides, the sun still shines the same in Tinemallacht whether you live in a palace or not. I prefer the desert houses to the palaces of Bastain anyway."

Bastain, an oasis in the unrelenting desert where the Falacht River peaks out from under the depths of the sand. Cai once told me the pale palaces of adobe, clay, and plaster, with their bright tiles and horseshoe archways, made Bastain the jewel of Draíocoinnigh.

"Do you miss it?" I finish my meal and place my tray on the counter beside us as Eoghan ponders my question.

"I did." He nods. "Until I met you. Now, I'd gladly stay here if you prefer the snow to the desert sun."

His knee knocks against mine lightly. I'd never ask him to stay here—or even in that tiny cottage in Fáintìrean with me—but I knew he would.

"I'd like to see it—your home. Cai's home." The place that had stolen my brother's heart so completely, he had never wanted to come back. "Would you take me?"

"Just say the word, and we will leave. I'd love to see you with the sunlight kissing your face. I always knew the view was missing something; now I'm sure it was you."

I blush again before I pull him to me, and his arms wrap around my waist. I lay my cheek to his chest and nestle into his warmth. In another life, there was no Rian or the throne that so enamored my family and took my brother from me. There was no prison, no death, no titles, no wars. There was no one but Eoghan Kael, and I never had to know what it was to fear him or hate him or miss him until I felt I might die. In another life , I never had to wonder about his secrets or the hatred in his eyes. They were only soft and without fear, open to me completely. In another life, I never had to wonder at all. We could just stay like this, and that would be enough for us. The lives we never got to have ache in my heart, as if they were snatched away from us before we could experience them.

He runs his hand through my hair and plants a kiss on the top of my head.

"Say it again," I whisper.

"Say what?" He smiles against my hair.

"That you love me. I wonder if I might have imagined it, made you up in my mind. That perhaps I fell in love with you so deeply, I was desperate to have you love me back."

He brings his hands to my waist and lifts me onto the counter so we are at eye level with each other. His entire face glows as if he is the flame and I am the moth. I am intoxicated by him, captivated so completely, I can barely comprehend how he can be real.

"Maeve Moran, my princess and my queen." He takes me in, and I feel a tightness in my throat. "I love you more than I have anyone in the entirety of my life…and that terrifies me yet excites me to no end. I love when you smile and when you frustrate me so much that I might go mad. I love when you kiss me and your lips part, asking me for more. I love when you are stubborn and throw your daggers at my head. And I love when you tell me you love *me*, because I never thought that I'd be lucky enough to hear those words from you. My world fell apart the moment I met you, and I have never been happier to watch it shatter into a million pieces."

His stare is endless, his eyes so soft and unguarded, I feel as though I am holding his heart of glass in my hands, scared it might break. I make to open my mouth to speak, but outside the kitchen door comes the faint sound of footsteps that snaps our attention away from each other.

"Time to go." Eoghan takes my hand and leads me to the far side of the kitchen to a small door hidden in the wall, our trays and pans left on the counter. I stop and pull the tether of Gálgalesh's power toward me; the dishes rise and fall with a splash into the stale water left in the sink by the dinner crew.

"You're getting really good at this magic thing, you know," Eoghan teases as he pushes me through the opening in the wall, sneaking in behind me just as the kitchen door creaks open and we disappear down the black corridor and out of sight.

———

THE SAND WHIPS around me in a cyclone of red and brown as I walk under the awning of a flat roofed clay house indistinguishable from the dunes surrounding it. Its welcoming tile entry is terra-cotta red, images of dragons etched into the surface depicting moments of battle and peace from a history lost to time. A light scarf wraps protectively around my head and the lower half of my face, my pants and shirt a loose beige linen to keep me cool in the unrelenting heat.

Tinemallacht. The desert home of the great, the brave, and the strong. I reach out for the doorknob, sand piling up against the bottom of the tightly sealed door. I turn it, and it gives way to a shaded room, where a woman lays in the bed, her honey hair with sun-bleached highlights falling across the pillow and along her back as she sleeps, a baby on the mattress next to her. He is a little boy, not more than a year and a half at best. I move closer, watching their chests rise and fall slowly as they dream. The child is so delicate and small, and I wonder at him, how he naps without worry of anyone watching. Quietly, I make my way around the woman's side for a better view. His face is so familiar, yet I cannot place it. I reach across the bed for him, and my fingers wrap around his small, sleeping body, lifting him into my arms...

Eoghan snaps upright as the loud toll of the warning bell chimes through the prison. I look around and rub my eyes in the faintest gray light—morning has indeed arrived. Eoghan's fingers run featherlight against my naked back as I push myself up from the mattress.

"What's that?" I yawn.

"They are directing us to the courtyard. Someone is approaching Báscogar, and they want us all there when they arrive."

"Gálgalesh? It's been nearly a month since he left. Do you think he has returned?"

Eoghan's eyes darken. "I don't know. I never expected him to make it back from the Steel Citadel, and I don't think he expected to either. I'm not sure anyone would alert us of his arrival regardless."

"Who then? More of the king's guards?" The cool air in the room has me pressing against Eoghan for warmth.

"Maybe. They might have found Anwyl's body and alerted the men in the village at the bottom of the mountain. I overheard two of my guards talking about the men he had positioned there in case prisoners attempted escape."

The bell chimes loudly overhead once more, and the window shakes at the sound. Such a fuss for a handful of guards arriving? I had not been to many places outside the castle walls, but even inside them, I knew the king's guards preferred not to announce their arrival. I doubt Drustan Anwyl's men would be any different.

Eoghan disentangles his limbs from around me and rises from the bed. He steps into his pants and pulls them up to his hips before buttoning. I crawl to the edge of the mattress and stand next to him, the blankets falling away. He pauses as he catches the sight of me naked before him. If he could devour me with his eyes, I would already be gone. He rakes his teeth against his lower lip and then yanks the wardrobe open quickly, pulling out his black shirt.

"You have five seconds to throw on something or else I am laying you back down on the mattress, and we are both going to get a beating for not reporting."

"Is that a promise?" I tease, and he grabs my chin softly, angling my mouth upward before his lips touch mine.

"Yes," he whispers. "But I don't feel like killing the man who punishes you, so get dressed."

He kisses me softly and then releases me to throw his shirt over his head. I pout for a moment and sigh pathetically before reaching for my own clothes. He waits until I finish, only loosing a low, guttural moan when my fingers linger on the band of my underwear for a moment longer than necessary, tempting him to take me back to bed. When we finish dressing, he laces his fingers with mine before we exit the room, filing in line with the others down the corridor. We make it around the first bend when Bode, a young prisoner from Romiodóg with stunning gray eyes and pale features, files in next to us, and I remember he had been a guard charged with Eoghan's imprisonment, had helped him as the guard charged with my own had helped me.

"You left me a mess to clean up yesterday," Bode whispers.

"Did anyone suspect?" Eoghan mumbles under his breath, and Bode shakes his head almost imperceptibly. "Good. Thank you. Have they found Anwyl?" Another shake of the head, and Eoghan nods. "At least we have that. What's this about?" Eoghan's fingers tighten around mine protectively.

"Not sure yet, but stay in the shadows. Anwyl had to have alerted the Capital, and whoever is on their way might be here to take you back with them."

Eoghan inhales audibly through his nose as his shoulders square. "Stay with us?" he asks, but Bode declines with another infinitesimal movement.

"There are too many guards who will be expecting me. If anything goes wrong, meet at the Eastern Tunnel."

Eoghan nods, and Bode disappears, following the crowd to the stairs toward the courtyard. Eoghan veers left, and I follow closely at his side. We make it to the portico, where the arching stones create open windows along the perimeter of the courtyard from the second floor. Below, I can see the other prisoners filing in and registering with Anwyl's guards. I watch as Bode reaches the others and whispers to the man with roll call duties. He points toward the South Tower, and the man nods before making two marks on the scroll of parchment in his hand. I back away from the arched window, falling into the shadows while retaining my view of the quad's snowy center.

The front gates creak open loudly, and the courtyard, once buzzing with hundreds of voices, falls silent. Footsteps echo through the prison, and I try to count the pairs. One set clanks against the stone from the metal soles of the Royal Court—impractical in these mountains, but no doubt worn for that exactly: to know someone of high rank is approaching. Three pairs of guard's boots… No, five pairs of guard's boots and one pair of leather riders that tap softly, almost unnoticed against the ground. The shoes of someone important—a king or a duke. But there are no dukes in Draíocoinnigh, not anymore. None would have survived the coup, not unless they had started it themselves.

Two pairs of boots and leather riders fall silent as the others move forward, and the shadowed figures of an average-sized man flanked by three much larger guards appear in the entrance of the courtyard. They pause, and the man in front takes something round from the guards before marching into view.

My heart falls from my chest. Sir Oli Raven, my father's trusted Potions Master and Experimenter, steps forward into the clearing, cradling something at his side obscured by his heavy cloak. He sports a gold insignia on his breast, signifying he traded his position to become the new king's Hand. My father's most trusted and loyal servant was part of the effort to take his and the rest of our lives—he had experimented on me, defiled me, tortured me, drained me of my life source, and then simply watched as the crowd pulled us apart. Anger wells up from deep in my stomach, and it takes everything I have to not race down into the courtyard and slit his throat the same way they slit my mother's—Cai's.

I disentangle my hand from Eoghan's and move closer as Sir Oli Raven turns to face our way. He raises his arm, and as his cloak falls away, my hands fly to my mouth in horror. Gripped between his crooked fingers is a handful of ashen blond hair, and below it, dangling lifeless and pale, is the head of Peadair, severed clear from his body. The courtyard rises in a roar of shock and anger at the sight of the faerie's face, his eyes cold and lifeless. Sir Oli Raven swings his arm and releases Peadair's head, which falls in front of Bode and the other guards with a disgusting smack before it rolls against the stones.

"Prisoners." He lifts his voice, and bile rises in my throat at the sound. "I have been sent here by order of the king to inform you this prison is now under the control of His Majesty. Your warden, Gálgalesh Devenallt, and his second warden, Peadair Okenshem, have been convicted of treason and sentenced to death. As a show of mercy and good faith, we have returned Peadair to you after he paid for his crimes. Your warden has escaped and is being sought after in all five territories. Rest assured, we will find him soon."

The voices in the courtyard are nearly earsplitting now. Peadair's life has been taken. Gálgalesh is on the run and wanted by the Crown. He could be anywhere by now—in the Borderlands, in Dún, or even on a ship headed across the sea to Trader's Bay. Regardless, he will not return for us—he cannot. I pull on the tether of magic, and it sings to me. Will it know if he's caught and killed, or will the magic die with him?

Sir Oli Raven looks to his guards as the cacophony of shouts and protests continue.

"Quiet!" one guard yells, and the crowd shouts back at him with profanity and threats of violence. Sir Oli Raven sighs in boredom, nodding as the guard drags a prisoner from the crowd into the center of the courtyard. "QUIET!" He shouts again and runs the blade of his short knife across the prisoner's neck. Blood flows in torrents to the ground, and he throws the man down with it—choking and gasping as we watch on, silence and terror washing over us.

Sir Oli Raven waits for the man to fall still. "As I was saying—we will find the faerie Gálgalesh Devenallt, and he will meet his end in time. For now however, the king has asked me to come and to extend an offer to your Interim Warden, Sir Drustan Anwyl, to take Gálgalesh's place. Now, where is he?"

Anwyl's guards look to one another, murmuring amongst themselves. Bode turns slightly in our direction and then turns back, as though he too has no knowledge of the warden's whereabouts.

"No?" Annoyance more than surprise coats Sir Oli Raven's expression as he rolls his eyes. "Stayed in bed, I imagine. A fool. I told the king…" He turns to whisper to one of his guards. "Find him, *now*."

Bode backs away and follows Sir Oli Raven's guard back through the fortress. Eoghan has been still for far too long, but his body heat tells me he is still behind me.

"You know him, don't you?" His voice carries the deadly bite that used to make me fear him.

I nod. "He was my father's Potions Master, responsible for taking vials of my blood for my family…among other things." My hands shake, and Eoghan's breathing quickens. I feel the corridor turn into a sauna as Sir Oli Raven continues to speak.

"Now, as Anwyl is roused, I have come here with another —by order of His Majesty the King." His voice has returned to its official cadence. "Prisoners of Báscogar, may I present to you, for your fealty and appreciation, the Crown Prince of Draíocoinnigh."

My muscles tighten, and I cannot move, cannot blink, cannot breathe. Two sets of boots echo off the ground as the leather riders tap along, keeping pace. The usurpers have crowned their king, and his son has come here to show his might—maybe to find allies in this place riddled with lives ruined by the fallen king. Each footstep makes my blood run colder until I feel little more than ice in my veins—ice wrapped in dragon's fire. The shadows of their bodies fill the entryway and step into the courtyard.

In the greens and blues of the sea, gold bangles filling his arms and his hair pushed back from his face, I feel an arm wrap around my waist, pulling me away from the archway, and one hand fall over my mouth as I let out a scream. The usurper. The traitor. The liar. The thief. The one my very soul cries out to kill. There, standing in the courtyard—his heart beating surely in his chest—is my fiancé, Rian Doherty, the newly crowned Prince of Draíocoinnigh.

ACKNOWLEDGMENTS

The Land of Frost is the start of a love story that has helped me to fall for writing again while taking me to worlds I have only ever dreamed of. When I say this book has been an amazing, whirlwind journey, I cannot emphasize enough all that it has done for me. This book will hold a special place in my heart forever.

I would like to thank the following people for all they have contributed to *The Land of Frost*'s creation:

To my family: Jess (dad), Dawn (mom), Jess, Kellen, and Wyatt. Thank you for always supporting me through this process, for loving me despite the long hours I spent cooped up, missing time with you so that I could write.

To Megan Brebner, my best friend and biggest fan. Without you, this story would never have come to be. Thank you for being my constant stay from Gairdín to Báscogar and all the places yet to come.

To Tyler Brebner, Kevin Easley, and Freddy Lopez. Thank you for listening when I have something to say. Thank you for seeing me when I feel unseen.

To my Social Media Intern, Judy Green. Thank you for sticking with me and helping *The Land of Frost* find its readers.

And last but not least, I want to thank my Creator for blessing me with the words to write this novel and the courage to bring it to the world. I am forever grateful to You for all You have done in my life.

THE STEEL CITADEL SERIES
GLOSSARY

538-539 TC (Tar éis Concwas)

The events of the Land of Frost takes place 538 years after the conquest of the continent by the Ancient Fathers and the establishment of Dún, Iranndair, and Draíocoinnigh.

Draíocoinnigh

Drayo-cone-knee

The Kingdom of Draíocoinnigh occupies more than sixty-five percent of the Continent of Thoirmór (*Hairshmore*) and is made up of five distinct territories, each with their own unique landscapes, architecture, industries, and resources. The kingdom is bordered to the north by the kingdom of Dún and to the south by the Republic of Iranndair.

Calendar

The story follows the calendar established by the Ancient Fathers, a twelve month calendar beginning with the new year on the first day of the month of Ennáir. The months are as follows: Ennáir, Feabrah, Márta, Aibreán, Beltané, Meitheam, Lúil, Lúnasa, Medi, Hydref, Samhain, Noll.

Seasons

The continent of Thoirmór enjoys four distinct seasons: Winter (Noll, Ennáir, Feabrah), Spring (Márta, Aibreán, Beltané), Summer (Meitheam, Lúil, Lúnasa), and Autumn (Media, Hydref, Samhain).

KINGDOM DETAILS

Providences:

Golorgleann

Go-lore-glee-on

Golorgleann is the central, capital territory of Draíocoinnigh, and the wealthiest of the territories in the kingdom. Known for its flower fields, grain, and produce, this region supplies the kingdom with much of its freshly grown crops, giving it its name meaning "Copious Valley".

Tonnfórsca

Tone-for-sca

Tonnfórsca sits on the central, western coast of Draíoconnigh and provides the vital maritime trade routes across the Murcean Sea Trader's Bay in the Kingdom of Oleaíncudd.

Gálamáistir

Gala-maish-ter

Gálamáistir to the east is a small, yet vital territory which houses Draíocoinnigh's coveted military academy within the heart of this densely forested region. With near-constant high winds, the region is best known for its airship pilots who traverse the kingdom's skies... at least where the dragons do not.

Tinemallacht

Tine-mal-ackt

Found in the red sand desert to the south that reaches from the Murcean Sea in the west to the Bay of Dragons in the east, Tinemallacht is known for its formidability and brutality. Devoid of surface water, except where the Falacht River rises above the sand in the Oasis of Bastain, and overrun by dragons, Tinemallacht is home to the Fire Cursed warriors of legend... and terror.

Romiodóg

Roh-ma-dahg

The poorest of all the territories, cursed by an eternal winter and darkened sky of night overhead, Romiodóg is often overlooked by the other provinces of Draíocoinnigh. Though its exports of iron ore and steel are the heart of the kingdom's wealth, its merciless mountain range that houses Báscogar Prison, is feared beyond all else. One would be remiss to seek shelter in such a gruesome place.

Neighboring Nations:

Dún

Duhn

The faerie kingdom of Dún lies to the northwestern border of Draíocoinnigh and is counted as a malevolent foe. The kingdom consists almost entirely of tent encampments overseen by the most brutal of each camp and determined by shows of strength and fights to the death. The kingdom is governed by a king, chosen in the same terrible manner, and a council of elders who maintain their seats for a term of three hundred years.

Iranndair

Ear-an-dare

The white sands of Iranndair touch the southern borders of Draíocoinnigh. Known for their production of magical strongholds, Iranndair is the most constant threat to Draíocoinnigh's peace causing three separate wars since the reign of King Fergal beginning in 335 TC. Home to human magic wielders and fomorians—ancient, blood-thirty giants from across the seas with bodies of humans and heads of goats— the Republic of Iranndair is the last place one might find themselves seeking shelter or friendship.

The Borderlands

The unincorporated territory of the Borderlands, nestled in the center of Draíocoinnigh. Though the quickest and most direct path between the Romiodóg and Draíocoinnigh's other five territories, its perilous, ever-changing forests and creatures of nightmare that call the territory home make the journey one that might break the traveler before they might it to their final destination.

Oleaíncudd

Oh-line-cood

Across the Murcean Sea to the west, on the continent of Thiarmór (*Here-More*), Draíocoinnigh's only ally and trade partner can be fond. With gorgeous seas of turquoise and the infamous Trader's Bay, Draíocoinnigh's merchants find rest and more than their fair share of gold on these shores.

MAGIC SYSTEMS

Human Magic

There are two types of human magic: Common and Individual. Though the strength of the magic depends on the wielder and their own gifts and aptitude, all human magic is limited in scope and strength. There are two main weaknesses to magic: its ability to be siphoned from another and Faebond's suppressing powers against it. The magic of humans cannot be transferred to another, unless siphoned.

Faerie Magic

Unlike human magic, faeries only enjoy one form of magic amongst them. It is nearly limitless in scope and strength and much of the common faerie magic contains elements of the individual magic humans might wield. Siphons cannot steal this power from a faerie and its only perceived weakness is to Faebond that can suppress it completely. Faerie magic can be transferred to another living being—creature or human– through the entering of a blood bond which connects the faerie wielder and the recipient for life. The extent of such a connection is not well known.

Dragon Magic

Dragon magic also only enjoys a single form manifest in their fire. This too is almost limitless in scope and strength. At the end of a dragons life, they choose a human wielder from the Desert Region to carry their magic on into the next age and this is where the Fire Cursed of Tinemallacht get their name.

Mystic Magic

Not much is known of the magic of creatures within the borders of Draíocoinnigh. From merrow to shadow lurkers, they each possess a unique amount of power. One might heed warning before tempting the gods and testing such abilities veiled in mystery.

RELIGION

Religions of Draíoconnigh

Polytheism

As a polytheistic society, Draíocoinnigh and its providences worship twelve separate gods and goddess by region, family tradition, and cultural acceptance. Each god is honored with their own temples found throughout the kingdom and overseen by Highdruí, a class of religious leaders bound to specific deities to seek safe passage for others to House of Donn. While each god demands their own customs of tribute and sacrifice, worshipping any god might come at a price.

Atheism

Though belief in the gods is widespread throughout the kingdom, it is certainly not mandated. Even the Moran Family Line is counted among the nonbelievers in the kingdom. Do not count on finding King Cashel kneeling at the altar of Danu or Dagda.

The Gods and Goddesses of Draíocoinnigh

Angos

Goddess of Love

A favorite among the lovesick and mothers the kingdom over, Angos is honored yearly with the Festival of Grá and with incense burned in the room of a woman or man hoping to meet their match. She also demands a sacrifice of blood by believers at their ceremony of marriage; but what is love, if not a deep cut to one's palm… or heart?

Anu

Goddess of the Earth

Protector of the fields and goddess most-high to the farmers of the Golorgleann providence, Anu, the goddess of the earth is said to bless Draíocoinnigh with their edible flower crops and sweet fruit in the summer months while bringing grain and other staples that keep the kingdom without need of rationing, even as the winter months take hold. Anu is said to enjoy incense, the annual Golorgleann flower festival and the blood of a calf spread upon freshly plowed fields.

Bailor

God of Pain and Destruction

The god Bailor is a terrifying god, and patron protector of the territory of Romiodóg. The god of pain and destruction is best honored with incense burnings, festivals that include shows of strength and brutality, and of course human sacrifice.

Brigid

Goddess of Fire

Red tongues of fire are said to tumble from the goddess' scalp like tendrils of crimson hair. It is no wonder Brigid is widely worshipped by the Fire Cursed of Tinemallacht—or was, until the dragons burned her temples down. Her remaining devotees seek her favor with the burning of incense, fire festivals, and the sacrifice of sheep by dragon fire.

Cernunnos

God of Forests

The god most honored throughout Gálamáistir's borders is Cernunnos, the god of forests. Ironically, the god of the trees also demands a fire sacrifice, leading to Gálamáistir's annual burn and the black scars along the territory's vast rolling hills.

Dagda

God of Good; Earth and Harvest

The only god that does not demand or accept sacrifice, Dagda is also the only god counted by believers as *good*. Incense burning will do at the temple altar yearly and good fortune comes to those looking for Dagda's favor at the Festival of Áthas, held after graduation each year at Draío-coinnigh's military academy, where no one needs more favor or luck than the newly graduated officers heading off to war.

Danu

Goddess of All Things

Seen to be the lead goddess over all, Danu is worshipped throughout each territory of the kingdom and welcomes a variety of worship practices including incense burning, festivals of dedication, and sacrifices made at her temples.

Donn

God of Death

Donn may, perhaps, be the only god recognized by believers and nonbelievers alike. It is said that when the dead arrive at the House of Donn, the god himself greets them on a mare of white, guiding their souls through the veil of this world and—if one has found favor—to the realm of Magmé for the rest of eternity. The Parade of Spirits honor Donn and the dead in Gairdín each year.

Lir

God of the Sea and Merchants

The Sea God, Lir, is beloved among the merchants of Tonnfórsca as he guides their ships across the Murcean Sea. They pay him handsomely with a tenth of their earnings left on his altar, and the highdruí of his temple are known to be the only in all of the kingdom to wear robes of silk and threaded with gold; though, surely, neither good fortune is connected.

Lugh

God of War

Lugh is celebrate throughout the kingdom as the god of war. Many credit the success of the First and Third Wars with Iranndair on his hand and the failure of the Second on the lack of tribute by General Kael of the Tinemallacht Forces.

Macha

Goddess of Protection

Said to be the sister of Dagda, Macha is worshipped throughout the territories, but nowhere more than on the front lines of battle. Sacrifices are given, incense burning, and prayers raised, though one never knows if they have been granted favor until morning comes the next day.

Taranis

God of Lightning/Weather

For favored winds and clear skies to fly, the believers of Draíocoinnigh turn their worship to Taranis, the god of the weather. His temples are the only to not boasts roofs, though they have yet to find a single cloud above them thanks to the ample sacrifices given in Taranis' name each year.

LANGUAGES

Anqonda

On-kwan-da

The language of the faeries, Anqonda is easily recognizable among the humans of the continent for its agglutinative word structure and sharp clicking sounds that mark the letters "c", "q", and "x". There is no human in modern history that can speak the language and for that it has become largely taboo throughout the kingdom… even as taboo as faeries themselves.

Siarhinn

Sheer-hin

Known as the Forbidden Language to the citizens of Draíocoinnigh when a kingdom wide ban was enacted in the first year of King Fergal's reign, punishable by death, the language is spoken in secret nearly two hundred years later by approximately half of the population. The language is spoken by humans and faeries alike and it is said to be the language of the First Settlers and the Ancient Fathers. All tomes written in the language were burned by the King. Rumor has it, copies were kept in secret in Tinemallacht and the mountain villages to the north. Siarhinn is known in Draíocoinnigh and Oleaíncudd; however, it is not taught in Iranndair.

Common Phrases/Terms in Siarhinn:

- *Iy Donn, d'anam* – For Donn, your soul
- *Feallwr* – Traitor
- *Tha grá di* – I love you
- *Muinsa* – Trust
- *Dualdanas, Urrir, Ghlóiriant* – Duty, Honor, Glory

SOCIAL SYSTEM

Societal Classes

Draíocoinnigh is divided into five distinct class systems, the first and highest consisting of the rich and the lowest consisting of creatures and non-human beings.

First Class: Rich

This class is mainly reserved for the royal family and those with titled lineage (Highborn). There are Four Seated families in Draíocoinnigh and around twenty lesser titled families, many of which reside in the capital of Gairdín. Others, such as wealthy business owners and merchants might find favor within the class system as well, though they might not hold a title, their considerable wealth will afford them respect and an invitation to some of the most coveted tables. This is the smallest and most elite class within the Draíocoinnigh class system and though not impossible to reach, it is extremely difficult and demands a great deal of gold to obtain.

Second Class: Common

The commoners of Draíocoinnigh make up the largest portion of the population. Bakers, seamstresses, farmers, and much of the working class citizens would consider themselves to be within this second class. The highdruí, though excluded from the class system as religious figures, maintain a successful wine business throughout the kingdom and live relatively common lives.

Third Class: Poor

The poor of Draíocoinnigh make up a "silent" portion of the population that has been largely dismissed and ignored during the reign of King Cashel. Due to the lack of opportunity and advancement, many of the kingdom's poorest turn to black market dealings, drug (Ama) use, and theft.

Fourth Class: Foreign

One of the lowest classes in the kingdom, foreigners are seldom found within the borders of Draíocoinnigh. Visitors from the bordering nations of Dún and Iranndair are unwelcome in the Kingdom and only those from the trade partners in Oleaíncudd are ever met with friendly greetings. The largest population of foreigners can be found behind the walls of Báscogar Prison.

Fifth Class: Creature

The lowest class in Draíocoinnigh is reserved for the creatures that dwell within the borders of Draíocoinnigh and in neighboring nations. Faeries, dragons, merrow, and banshees are just some of the members of this class (though some in Draíocoinnigh would also consider the Tinmallachts to be creatures in their own right).

CREATURES

Banshees

Terrors of the forest, the wailing women that hunt along the ever-foggy borders that separate the Borderlands and Romiodóg are known for the loud cries that rip through the night when they come near. Illusive as they are, one is wise to bring the children inside when they hear the ominous call, as they are known to go missing when the air falls silent again.

Dragons

Formidable beasts of the ancient world, the dragons of

Tinemallacht are revered and dreaded in equal measure. They breathe fire so hot it is said that the Barrens dried up completely when they made their homes in the sand, and their nests reside below the surface, closer to the hidden Falacht and out of reach from the sun's endless rays. Known to be short in temper and easily offended, their only interest lies in protecting their home from the terrors of man.

Faeries

Faeries are the second most common creature found on the Thoirmór continent. Easily recognizable by their tall stature, razor-sharp triangular teeth, and long fingers and hair, faeries have long since been feared among humans and were banished to the northern kingdom of Dún during the Great Conquest of the Continent. It was not until King Fergal's reign, however, that faeries found over the border in the colder regions risked imprisonment. Faeries are said to live approximately 2000 years, enjoy a mixture of faerie ale and can tolerate a human diet, though human meat has often been said to be their favorite. One may find small, breakaway faerie camps near Báscogar Prison in the Romiodóg mountains, and within the unincorporated Borderlands territory.

Merrow

The people of the Murcean Sea are half-fish, half-humans who live beneath the surface and frolic in the crystal waves for three hundred years. This shy creature is often at odds with the fishermen and merchant sailors of Tonnfórsca for their hand in sinking ships in the bay. The King of the Merrow, however, insists it is humans that are the true threat to the seas.

Shadow Lurkers

Prone to seek shelter in the darkest shadows of the kingdom, the shadow lurkers fear sunlight most of all. Subsisting on a diet of the blood of man and beast, shadow lurkers have skin as black as night and veins protruding from beneath the taut, inky abyss. With a lifespan of 150 years, they collect secrets as currency in exchange for bargains of less than noble deeds.

TERMS AND OBJECTS

Ama

A liquid potion made from the marrow of an Aos Sí—a type of nymph found in the magic woods of the Borderland. Ama is commonly taken as a powerful drug and pain reliever that can make one hallucinate and is widely sold on black market.

Bornus Tree

Infamous for it's terrible beauty, a bornus tree can be found in the Borderlands and emits a toxin that confuses the mind and makes travelers lose their way.

Crown of King Fergal

Made in the third year of King Fergal's reign, the first of the Moran line, the crown boasts a solid gold frame, eighty sapphires, and nearly three thousand diamonds.

Faebond

A substance found in the poison trees of Dún, Faebond is commonly mixed with metal to be made into cuffs or chains, though on its own is a pliable gum-like object as clear as glass and able to be melted down into liquid form. Faebond is classified as an illicit weapon within the kingdom of Draíocoinnigh and makes magic unwieldable if it comes in contact with the person trying to wield. It is illegal to use on another person unless they have been found guilty of the four high crimes.

Four High Crimes

Though there are a number of acts punishable by lashings, incarceration, or death, none are more serious than the Four High Crimes. Murder, treason, siphoning another's powers, and possession of Faebond all carry the same, horrible punishment: a lifelong sentence at Báscogar Prison.

Iaslium Gum

Iaslium Gum is a healing ointment made from the fat of a fish pulled from the River Fìrinn.

The White Night

A time during the summer months in the central territories of Draíocoinnigh when the sun refuses to set below the horizon at night, darkening to only twilight at the latest points of the evening.

ABOUT THE AUTHOR

Whitney Welsh Gibbs is a storyteller at heart, with a love for history and a curiosity for discovering new worlds—both real and imagined. She grew up on California's Central Coast, where the fog-draped mornings and salty sea air helped spark the imagination that fuels her writing today.

She holds a Master's in Intelligence and Security Studies from the University of Leicester and honed her craft through a blend of academic work and years of creative writing. Whitney has self-published three novels—Lucas Taite and the Mysterious Armor of God, Broken Anchors, and Lucas Taite and the Mountain of Örlög—each one earning praise and a growing base of loyal readers.

Her latest series, The Steel Citadel, brings together her love of layered plots, complex characters, and rich, magical worlds.

When she's not writing, Whitney can usually be found reading, exploring new places, or catching up with friends—often gathering sparks of inspiration along the way. She currently lives in Burbank, California.